THE KNIGHT
& THE SERPENT

A Legend of Medieval Normandy

John R. Gabourel

Illustrations by Baird Hoffmire
Mounted knight engraving by Hayes and Co., London, 1879

For Kimberlee and Allison
You are my rock and my light

ISBN-13: 978-0984134427
ISBN-10: 0984134425
LCCN: 2011907364
John\Gabourel, Aloha, OR

Summary: Embittered Norman squire, Gaspard Malfort, plots to steal his lord's wife and lands in medieval Normandy.

FICTION / Fantasy / Historical FIC009030
FICTION / Christian / Fantasy FIC042080

[1. Medieval history – Fiction. 2. Norman history – Fiction.
3. Jersey history – Fiction.] I. Title

CONTENTS

FORWARD

I first learned of the legend of La Hougue Bie when I was a young man. My grandfather was ailing, and the generational transfer of family heirlooms had begun. Every time we visited San Francisco, we would return with a box or two of historical curiosities and books. Among the collection was a book written by my great-great-grand aunt, Harriet Gabourel, titled *The Knight and the Dragon*. Harriet was a minor Victorian author whose only other work, *True to Her Faith*, is still in print today.

The Knight and the Dragon, while not forgotten, was certainly out of my thoughts for many years. It was not until my own father passed and the book came into my care that it again piqued my interest. I was in the midst of researching and writing my first manuscript, *The House of Gabourel*, when I finally sat down and read Harriet's tale of adventure. More than a simple fiction, I learned it was the recounting of a true legend. Suddenly, I wanted to bring that legend to life once again.

While *The Knight and the Serpent* is its own story, I did my best to remain true to accounts of the legend and pay tribute to its core characters. Had not my great-great-grand aunt made her accounting of the legend in 1879, the tale would surely be lost forever. I am grateful to have the opportunity to walk in her footsteps.

JRG

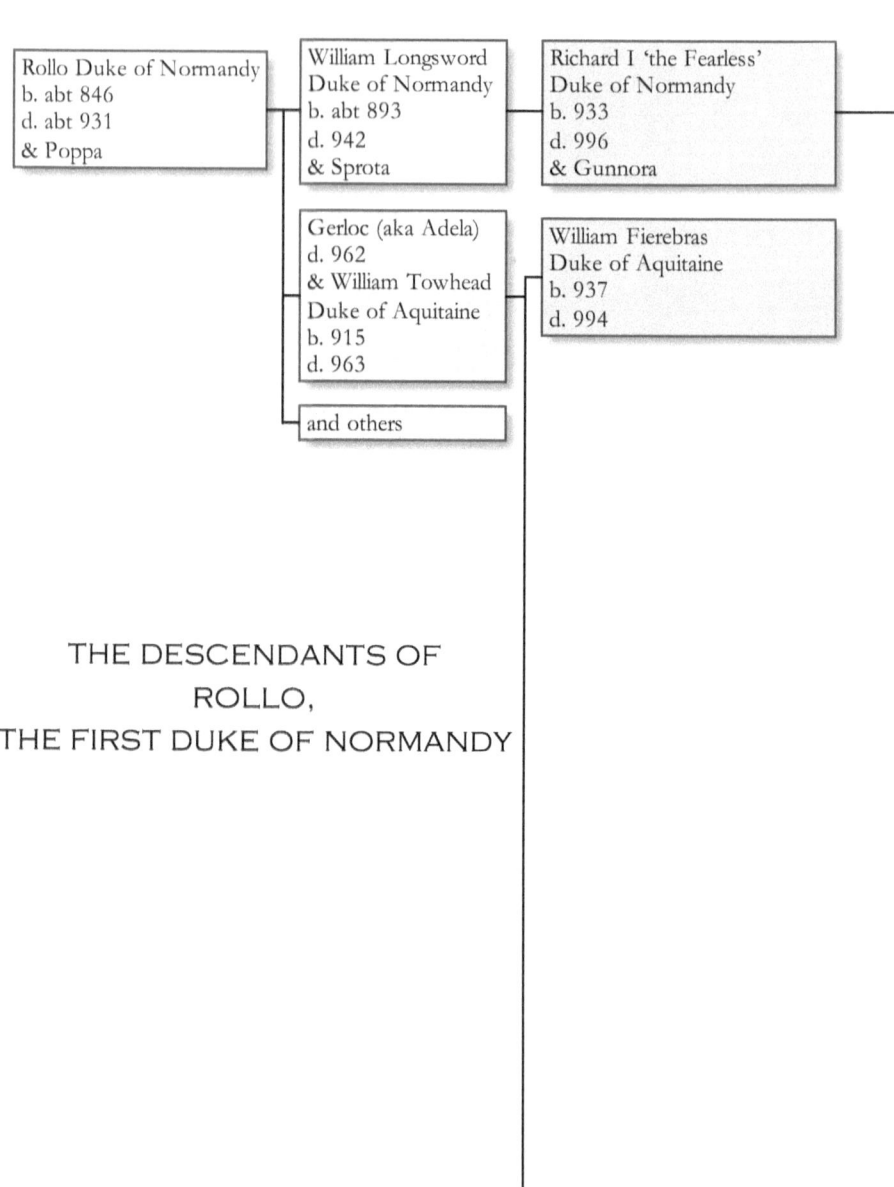

Rollo Duke of Normandy b. abt 846 d. abt 931 & Poppa	William Longsword Duke of Normandy b. abt 893 d. 942 & Sprota	Richard I 'the Fearless' Duke of Normandy b. 933 d. 996 & Gunnora
	Gerloc (aka Adela) d. 962 & William Towhead Duke of Aquitaine b. 915 d. 963	William Fierebras Duke of Aquitaine b. 937 d. 994
	and others	

THE DESCENDANTS OF
ROLLO,
THE FIRST DUKE OF NORMANDY

Adelaide of Aquitaine
d. 1004
& Hugh Capet King of France
b. 939
d. 996

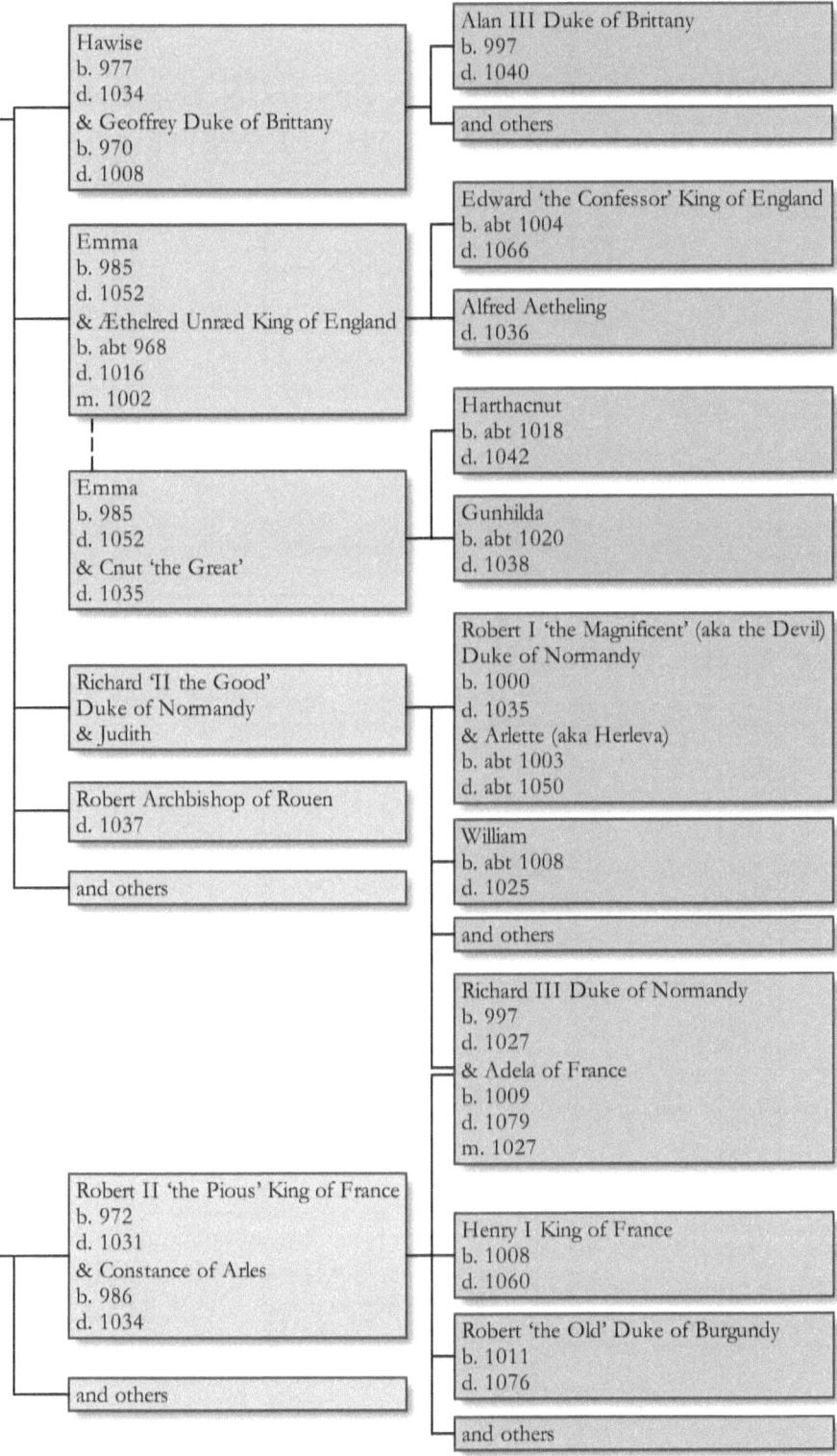

Hawise
b. 977
d. 1034
& Geoffrey Duke of Brittany
b. 970
d. 1008

Alan III Duke of Brittany
b. 997
d. 1040

and others

Emma
b. 985
d. 1052
& Æthelred Unræd King of England
b. abt 968
d. 1016
m. 1002

Edward 'the Confessor' King of England
b. abt 1004
d. 1066

Alfred Aetheling
d. 1036

Emma
b. 985
d. 1052
& Cnut 'the Great'
d. 1035

Harthacnut
b. abt 1018
d. 1042

Gunhilda
b. abt 1020
d. 1038

Richard 'II the Good'
Duke of Normandy
& Judith

Robert I 'the Magnificent' (aka the Devil)
Duke of Normandy
b. 1000
d. 1035
& Arlette (aka Herleva)
b. abt 1003
d. abt 1050

Robert Archbishop of Rouen
d. 1037

William
b. abt 1008
d. 1025

and others

and others

Richard III Duke of Normandy
b. 997
d. 1027
& Adela of France
b. 1009
d. 1079
m. 1027

Robert II 'the Pious' King of France
b. 972
d. 1031
& Constance of Arles
b. 986
d. 1034

Henry I King of France
b. 1008
d. 1060

Robert 'the Old' Duke of Burgundy
b. 1011
d. 1076

and others

and others

THE DANISH AND ENGLISH KINGS IN THE ERA
OF THE KNIGHT AND THE SERPENT

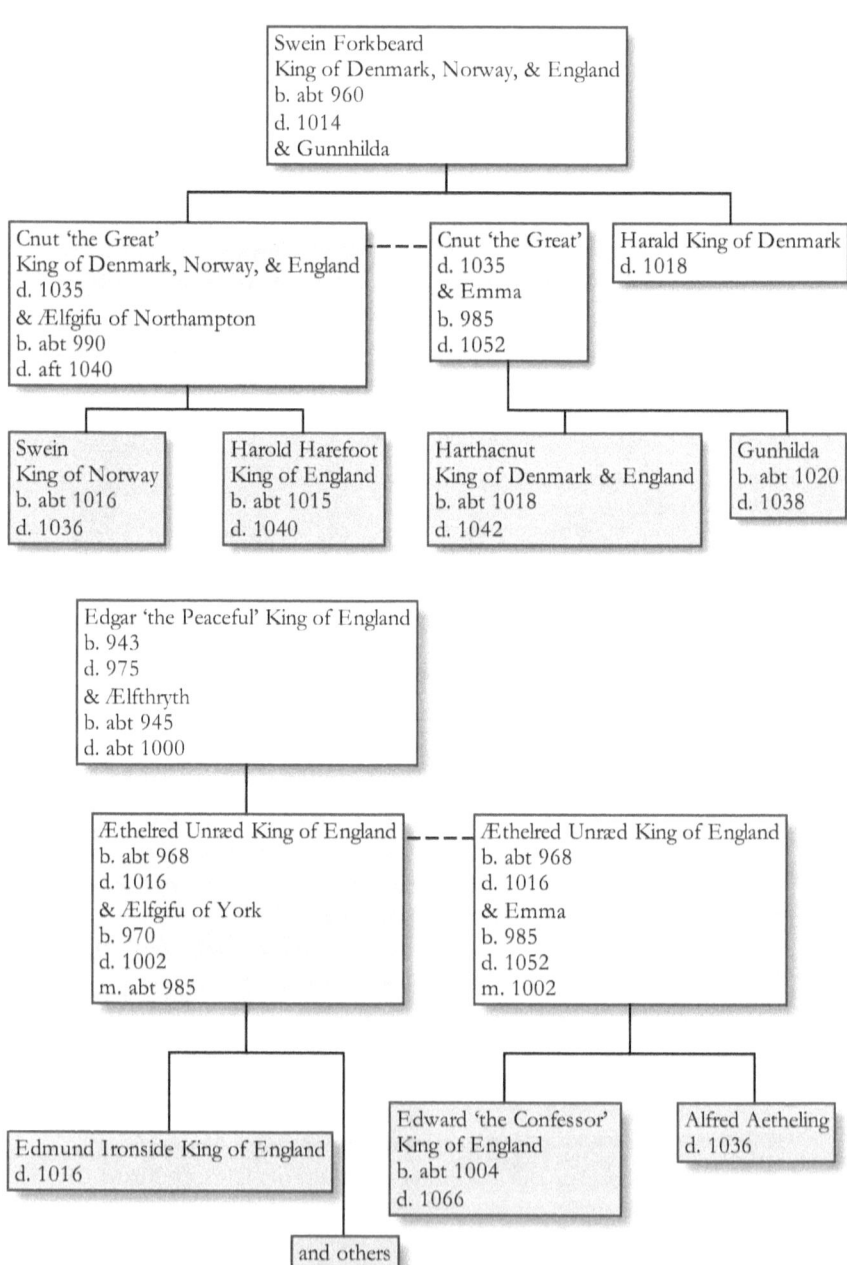

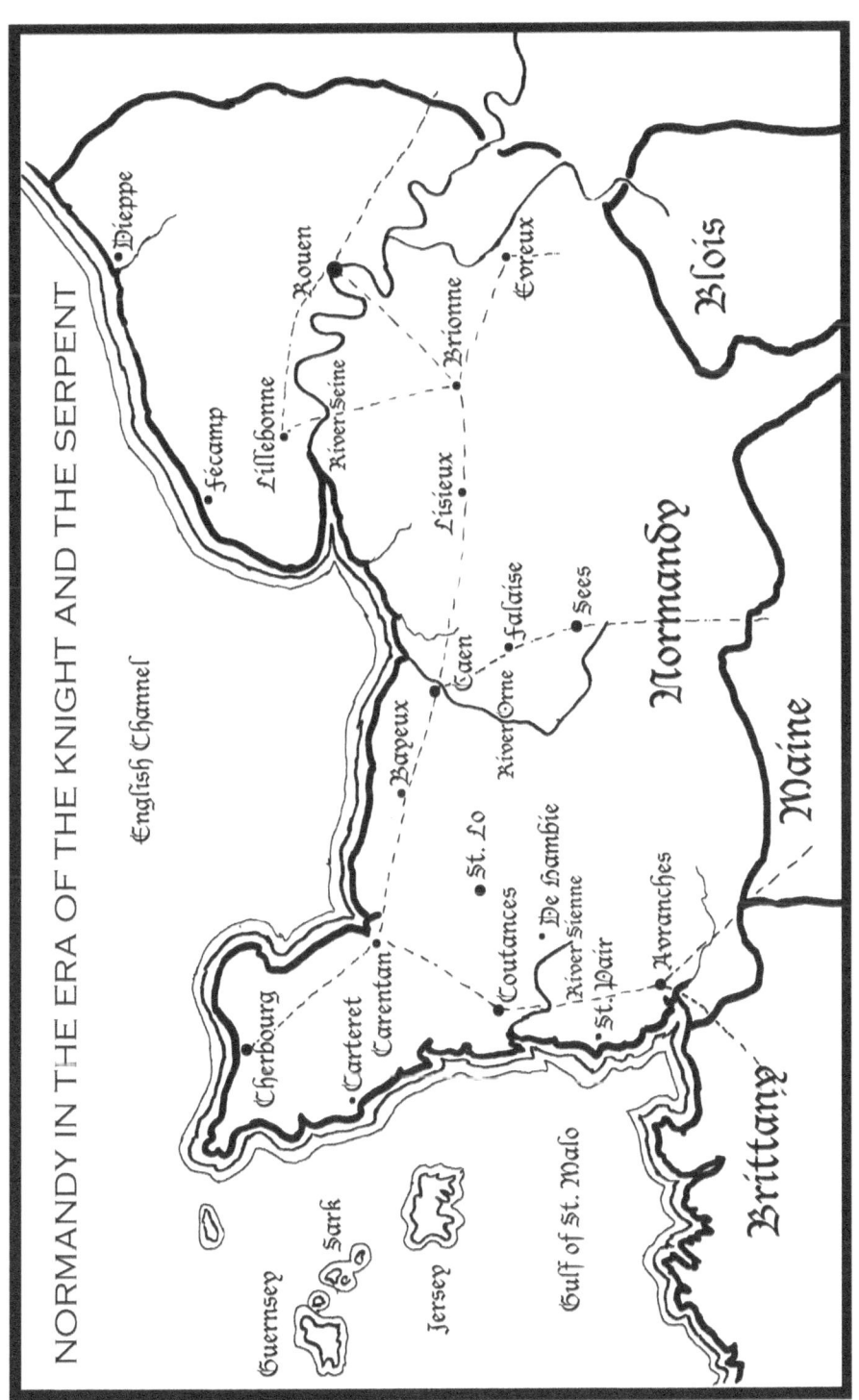

NORMANDY IN THE ERA OF THE KNIGHT AND THE SERPENT

English Channel

Dieppe
Rouen
Évreux
Blois
Brionne
River Seine
Fécamp
Lilleborne
Lisieux
Falaise
Sees
Caen
River Orne
Normandy
Bayeux
Maine
St. Lo
De Hambie
Coutances
River Sienne
Avranches
St. Pair
Carentan
Carteret
Cherbourg
Guernsey
Sark
Jersey
Gulf of St. Malo
Brittany

CHAPTER 1

The Buck and the Bull

The gray chill of autumn's morning had crept up and supplanted that small warmth Gaspard's brazier provided his little chamber during the night. The young boy, dark and strong, lay curled snugly beneath his thick woolen blankets, a nose just peeking from beneath the rough covers in search of the damp, cold October air. The room, little more than an alcove with an abused tapestry door, sported little luxury. A plain wooden chest sat against the wall, securing all his worldly possessions—a meager wealth well beyond his station. His chamber pot was near a simple table that supported a small basin and a tallow candle. To Gaspard, the dark, windowless room reflected Heaven above. It was not his lot to take shelter in a crack in the ground beneath a great mound of leaf mold as the wild man of the forest, or to sleep in servitude on the cold clay floor of some cooper, smith, or miller. No, he would wake to warm timber beneath his feet and the smell of cakes baking in his lord's kitchen. Only, not quite yet. Not until the night sentry trumpeted the first rays of dawn. Not until nature called him from the warmth of his nest demanding relief. Not yet…

"Gaspard!" came the impatient whisper from outside the alcove. "Wake up lazy bones! Have you forgotten?"

The fabric of his door was thrown aside and an older, fair-haired boy ducked, lamp in hand, through the opening and into the room. In defense, the smaller boy fiercely grasped the edges of his covers with his hands and feet, tucking tightly in a ball like a hedgehog. The older boy, setting the lamp aside on the table, was quickly upon him, his own grip vigorously wrestling for control over the warm, protective blankets.

"Get off me, Fulk!" cried the young boy. "'Tis cold and dark! Get off!"

The elder boy, being much stronger, stripped Gaspard in a great heave, pulling the boy cleanly off of the bed, spilling him onto the floor. Gaspard immediately grasped Fulk's ankles, driving his strong, wiry shoulders into the elder boy's shins, sending him windmilling to the floor, and finally pounced upon his chest clutching for the blankets. Fulk quickly reversed Gaspard's temporary advantage, using his long, lithe limbs to encase Gaspard's squirming form, pinning his arms to his sides and entangling his legs.

"Well done, little squire!" panted Fulk, laughter playing about his lips. "Well done, my little man. You took me down!" He held Gaspard firmly until the struggling and grunting ceased and the sulking began.

"Come now!" jested Fulk as he saw the color rise in Gaspard's face. "No need to blubber! You and I are going hunting today. I declare myself a man, and you about to become one. Secure your belt and ready yourself."

The flame of Gaspard's hurt vanished as a candle in the wind. Today was the day—his first hunt with his lord! The dangerous daring of their plan quickened the child's heart and swept the bleary sleep from his eyes. Fulk righted himself, touched his flame to the candle on the table, and then ducked out of the chamber. Gaspard quickly pulled his breeches over his stockings. He replaced his nightshirt with a heavy tunic and then slipped on a pair of old, worn boots Fulk had given him the past summer. Opening his chest, he pulled out a knife and tucked it in his belt. He also pulled out a cloak, another of the older boy's outgrown garments. From the chamber's corner, leaning against the wall, Gaspard fetched his small bow and quiver filled with arrows that Hambie's fletcher had made especially to fit his youthful stature.

Outside Gaspard's small chamber was a short hallway with heavy doors on either end. Three tall, narrow windows opened out through the thick castle wall to the dark and damp courtyard below. The low, flickering light of Fulk's lamp lit the way to the door of his room. Unlike young Gaspard's simple space, Fulk's chamber was that of a lord's son. It was spacious and well furnished, with lovely tapestries hung on the walls, hides on the floor, and a raised bed with a feather mattress. It revealed much about the elder boy's station in his world.

"Your father may well not be pleased," observed Gaspard as Fulk dressed.

"My father is not here," Fulk retorted grimly, then after a pause, "Not to worry, little man; if trouble comes, it comes my way, not yours. You will not be my whipping boy."

Taking up his bow, Fulk handed Gaspard a heavy wallet, and the two made their way down the short hall to the door leading to the rest of the castle. Opening the door just a crack, Fulk peered and listened intently to the hallway beyond.

"All clear," he whispered. Gaspard nodded, and the two boys quietly slipped into the hallway. With Fulk's lamp flickering in the darkness, they made their way first to the stairs and then to the kitchen.

There were few hours in a day when the kitchen of the Castle de Hambie stood silent and empty. The staff rose early and then spent their day cooking, serving, and gathering foodstuffs from the village for the larder. They had been especially busy in recent days outfitting the men-at-arms of Lord Hugh Paynel, Baron de Hambie, as Sir Richard was mustering a force to invade England. Just four days prior, in full, shining regalia and with the white and gold standard de Hambie held high, Lord Hugh, mounted high on his chestnut destrier, led his column of well-supplied men to Normandy's coast and the awaiting fleet.

Lord Hugh's son, Fulk, had begged his father, "I am a man! Have I not proven my worth with a bow? Have I no skill with the sword? I, too, wish to relieve my English cousins of the Viking devils that plague them!"

"A man you may be," replied his father sternly, "but hardened for the likes of these adventures, you are not. That usurping dog Cnut knows neither God nor conscience, and there will be no honor on this battlefield."

With that, Fulk Paynel, son of Lord Hugh Paynel, Baron de Hambie, found his lot lay with the old men, women, and children, and not by his father's side, holding their gold and white standard high. His father would accept no argument, for he allowed none. To press the matter, to question his father's decision, would have revealed a wrath no man except Sir Richard could meet, such was Hugh's passion.

The column, capped by dull steel helms, bristling with spears, sounded off with the crunch of soldiers' feet. The men were followed by wagons bearing all the paraphernalia for war as they departed Hambie's village on a cold, misting October morning. From the donjon's highest window Fulk watched them travel the road northwest along the river until they vanished into the forest. A thirst for adventure boiled in his heart and set him to thinking. The larder was heavily taxed by the needs of so many men going into battle. Turnips and eggs, that was for the peasant farmers to provide, the herders of chickens and milkers of cows. Providing meat, that was the hunter's purview, an adventurous and glorious pastime. Yes, if he were not to fight, he would take his young squire and hunt.

The boys slipped quietly into the empty, dark kitchen and quickly filled their wallet with apples, cheese, stale bread, and greasy, cold mutton left from the previous day's supper. Fulk filled two small skins with water, and they quietly moved to the delivery door.

"Have you yet told Master Josue of our leaving the castle?" asked Gaspard in a soft voice as Fulk carefully unlatched the door.

"And give him time to come up with some objection?" Fulk said, grinning, "Certainly not!"

"Will not Rupert seek to detain us at the gate?" worried Gaspard.

"Oh, I have seen to that," chortled Fulk quietly, "I gave him a flagon of strong wine to keep his old bones warm just after the bells of Compline. Surely he is now sleeping comfortably at his post. He will be between the hammer and anvil when I kick him awake!"

Gaspard pursed his lips, stifling a giggle, and nodded. Fulk snuffed out his lamp, and the boys slipped silently through the door and into the misty gray of predawn light. They carefully made their way to the castle's heavy oak and iron main gate. The world existed as only the varying shades of charcoal on a gray canvas, absent the details of day. Slowly, carefully, they picked their way until they arrived behind a low garden wall near the gate's guardhouse. It was a crude wood enclosure, closed on three sides, with enough room for a man to stand or sit out of the elements. Above the guardhouse, mere shadows against the dark sky, stood the towers of the main gate. A lone, aging foot soldier by name of Evard stood at his post, staring numbly out into the darkness beyond the barbican. He was utterly oblivious to gentle snoring coming from the guardhouse in the courtyard below.

Fulk scrubbed up a pebble from the soft, damp earth and tossed it gently at the enclosure. The soft click brought no start to the soft, regular wheezing coming from inside the door. The boys silently crept around the garden wall then down the path to the gate, pausing just before the shack, listening intently to Rupert's light, steady snoring. All that was visible was a slack, booted foot protruding from the dark doorway. Fulk then set his bow and the water skins on the path and silently stalked the guardhouse. Ever so gently, he stepped over Rupert's leg and into the shack. From outside the shack, Gaspard heard a muffled cry and a brief struggle.

"Asleep at your post? Again?" hissed Fulk angrily.

"Please, milord," croaked the wine-soaked old man, "It was just for a moment—the night was so peaceful—it was just a light doze, is all, I would have heard Evard had he called!"

"I should hate to call Master Josue from his bed to report you!" threatened Fulk grimly.

"But 'twas you who gave me the wine," complained Rupert.

Fulk picked up the empty flagon and grunted. "Enough for several men, yet it is empty. I gave you the wine, yes, but you got yourself drunk. I find no excuse for that."

Outside, Gaspard snickered into his hand.

"I will make you a bargain, old man," demurred Fulk, "My squire and I are going on a hunt today. You will call up to Evard all is well and we are coming out. Then you will secure the gate behind us. Then you will say nothing more until Master Josue arises in the morning and inquires as to my whereabouts. Only then will you inform him of my decision to hunt, and that we intend to return by dark. Do this small thing for me, and I will forget your indiscretion."

"But Master Josue made an oath to your father..." complained Rupert.'

"An oath I will not have my seneschal break!" returned Fulk seriously, "I will bear full responsibility upon my father's return. For now, I am your lord, and you will do as I command."

Rupert resigned himself and struggled gamely to his feet, "Shall I bring your horses?"

"Nay, not this time, my old friend," replied Fulk, "We make for the valley of Dalr."

Rupert nodded and sighed. Moments later, the two boys found themselves walking down the slopes of the castle's mount and through the midst of Hambie's orchard. The apple trees had been planted around an ancient stand of walnut when Hugh Paynel was but a small boy. Now they were in the prime of their life, carefully tended by the castle gardeners. Below the orchard lay a barren wheat field near the village, where now remained only the decaying remnants of chaff left from the summer harvest. Beyond that, the autumn forest and the hunt.

The crisp, autumn weather lingering over Normandy had changed the barony's forest to a kaleidoscope of brilliance. Fresh, damp leaves littered the forest's floor and thickets like a never-ending patchwork quilt.

"The does are just ready to mate," advised the elder boy in a whisper. "This drives the bucks mad, making them careless."

Gaspard nodded sternly, feeling that to be a man, he must not let on to his excitement for this new adventure. Instead, he furrowed his brow, pursed his lips, and stepped in a way he felt displayed caution. It was not long before Fulk had led Gaspard deeper into the forest than he had ever ventured at play.

After an hour of stalking in a northeasterly direction, growing hunger pangs struck Gaspard, and his gut growled and squealed, breaking the silence with a horrible noise. The wild convulsions of his innards went on for a long count, freezing Fulk's face in a look of incredulous surprise.

"I think I had best have something to eat," Gaspard observed.

"Do you think so?" laughed Fulk. "All right, breakfast it is."

The boys broke into the wallet and quietly chewed bits of bread, mutton, and cheese, followed by crisp autumn apples. In all of his life, before and after, Gaspard never had a meal its equal. No king's feast would ever match the day his lord treated the bastard son of an unknown father, a motherless orphan, as a man and a trusted equal. Standing next to Fulk, staring absently through the thickets and trees, Gaspard felt the warmth of his growing affection for the older boy. Though he was in a position of service, he was made to feel as a loved friend.

By mid-morning Fulk had led them to a rocky bluff above a small meadow. Beyond the meadow lay the valley of Dalr and its dense thickets and streams.

"To many lords, the hunt is all about the chase. Certainly a thrilling and gay pastime—akin to the excitement of the tournament. But a hunter, a true hunter, must learn patience. To really hunt, one must learn to sit and wait," began Fulk as they climbed the bluff. "I know this valley to be a place where many does bed. It is thick and protected, and not even the stealthiest of hunters can penetrate it without alerting their quarry. The mating scent of the does is thick in the air just now. As you will soon find, a good woman is hard to resist for any man. All the hunter has to do is wait for the love-struck fool to pass nearby."

Finding a protected spot among the rocks with a clear view and good angle for their bows, they settled in and waited. A peregrine circled the heavens. Legions of geese broke the flat sky as regiment after regiment flew south in formation. Three ravens screamed simply to hear the sound of their disharmony. A small hare appeared from the brush. Gaspard fingered his notched arrow. The hare found its morsel and vanished again. An iridescent black beetle clicked an angry warning then dug its way under the fragrant, damp leaf mold. The joy of flight was discovered as a young squirrel leaped from tree to tree. A distant wolf's mournful cry echoed. Out of the grass sprang a hidden fox, snapping, wrestling, and biting, then trotting away to the east, prey dangling limply from between its teeth. The day wore on, its small warmth first waxing then waning. Each boy occasionally closed his eyes while the other patiently watched the indifferent world.

As afternoon moved toward dusk, a sudden thrashing at the far edge of the meadow brought a young buck bursting out of the thickets. He shot into the open and spun round, head down and back arched. An older bull with a glistening auburn coat rent the brambles and crashed into the open. He stamped his hooves, steam blowing from his nostrils. In a flash the bull charged and struck the buck head on, pushing, heaving, twisting. His large rack ensnared the young buck's smaller antlers. With a mighty display of strength, the bull gave a wrenching twist that took the buck cleanly off his feet. The buck kicked wildly as the bull drove its head into the ground, both males grunting and filling the air with the hot vapor of battle.

With hearts leaping within their chests, each boy stood and drew back his bow with all his might. The arrows flew. Fulk's long, heavy arrow struck the bull's haunch. Gaspard's slender dart bit the nape of the bull's neck above the shoulder. The bull leapt in pain, but could not untangle his own rack from the still wildly thrashing buck. The boys drew down on the combatants once again, but only Fulk's shot flew to true to the mark. The panicked buck regained his feet and continued to push against his confused, wounded adversary.

"Stay true to the bull!" cried Fulk. "Let the young one go!"

The boys fired another volley, this time plunging into the muscle and sinew of the bull's blood-spattered side. The arrows bit deep, and both deer, who moments before fought for territory and mates, now battled to unlock their racks and flee.

The buck broke free and bolted into the thicket, vanishing, while the boys scrambled down from the perch on the bluff. The bull stumbled and crashed into the brush, leaving a bloody trail in its wake. Fulk set a quick pace ahead of Gaspard in pursuit of the valiant beast, leaping over tussocks and through the grasping branches of brush. In a matter of minutes the boys were hundreds of yards deep into the brambles of the valley, whooping and cheering so that every beast within the quiet place had been alerted to their presence. On and on they raced, tracking the bull further and further into the darkening valley, tracking broken branches and blood-streaked leaves.

The colors of day were fading to gray when they finally caught up to the noble bull in a small clearing with a stream-fed pool. He had collapsed halfway out of the muddied waters on the bank of the far side, his flecked, bloodied chest gasping. Only the broken shafts of the arrows remained. As Fulk circled the pool, he considered his prey. A beautiful beast with great, haunting, dark eyes. Well muscled from a summer generous with food. Handsome and noble in every way. Did he feel pain? Fear? Hatred? Did he understand this was his death? Or did he just understand suffering? Without hesitation the hunter drew his knife and ended the hunt.

"He is awfully big," breathed the awestruck Gaspard.

"Thirty stone if he is a pound," replied Fulk grimly. "Help me pull him from the water."

The boys wrestled the beast onto the bank, struggling to move him just a few feet. Gaspard stood staring wide eyed at the dead bull, crowned by a lordly five-point coronet. The boy was in awe that his slender arrows brought down such a creature.

"How are we going carry him back home?" he wondered aloud. "It is a long way…"

In silence they stared at the massive carcass for some minutes. Gaspard opened the wallet, and they chewed thoughtfully on their mutton and remaining crusts of bread, leaving only a bit of cheese and two apples. The light of the gray, chill day was fading quickly. A starless, ink-black night awaited them. A distant wolf's call drifted by. A flock of spotted flycatchers took wing. A second mournful howl answered the first. The wolf was no longer alone.

Fulk's cheeks flushed, and his jaw tightened. *"Back by dusk"* he had said when took his secret leave from the castle in defiance of a father away at war.

"Fulk?" hesitated Gaspard, "I am not afraid, but what of the wolves?"

Anger flooded the older boy's heart and furrowed his brow. In his father's absence, he was master of Hambie! Subject to none save Richard, Duke of Normandy, and his own father. To abandon their quarry would be ignoble. Why should he feel obliged to observe any sort of curfew set forth by any man, including himself? His household's worry for his welfare was their duty. His duty was to see his hunt through to the end. He glanced around the clearing until his eyes came to rest on a thorny bramble hedge. He looked upon the ruddy face of his squire, who was his charge and his responsibility. They would weather the night and return on the morrow. The court de Hambie would have to accept his late return, and he would not tolerate being questioned for it.

Handing Gaspard the axe, he pointed to the hedge, "Make one of your hidden fortresses in yonder thicket, little man. A small entrance. Then build a fire. We are staying the night. As for our prize," he looked down at the bull, "we will take the lion's share and leave the rest for the wolves."

With that he began the gruesome task of gutting and butchering the bull and then carrying the entrails and pieces of hindquarter to the opposite shore of the pool, heaving them into the thickets and shrubs. Gaspard, meanwhile, built their roomy cave quickly and efficiently, having had much practice among thorned blackberry canes near the castle during the leisurely days of summer. Using a bit of wool lint and fine, dry twigs, he methodically struck the back of his knife against Fulk's flint. He coaxed the sparks until tendrils of smoke rose from his bits, then breathed flame out of the smoke. At first he burned the debris from his bramble fortress, and then he went in search of windfall branches. Finally, as darkness took the valley and night closed in on the firelight, the boys pulled their prize into the cave. The howls grew nearer and more numerous.

From supple branches of aspen they cut and sharpened several crude spears. Fulk produced hearty slices of venison and carefully skewered them on two of the spears. A cold wind whipped and crackled through the fire. Gaspard shivered, and Fulk threw his cloak about them both.

"Did you know a wolf smells as well as we see?" commented Fulk while their meat sizzled and smoked. "They know all that goes on here just by breathing. They smell you, me, our fire, and the blood of our kill. I only wonder what is keeping them."

As if in answer, growls, footfalls, and panting approached from the darkness. Fulk's and Gaspard's hearts leapt into their throats. Fulk pulled in the roasting meat, thrusting the butts of the skewers into the ground and drew up his bow. Gaspard took up a spear and drew his knife.

"They fear fire, don't they?" asked Gaspard. "I have heard that."

"Yea, 'tis so…and they fear man, up to a point," replied Fulk.

Two of the great canines erupted in a fight in the blackness beyond the pool. More joined them, and the night was filled with the sounds of meat ripping and tearing, growls and the gnashing of teeth. The thickets shook violently as the predators smelt out the blood amongst the brush and bracken. How many? Four? Six? Eight? Minutes passed. The unseen beasts savaged the darkness as they fought and feasted. From their bramble fortress, the boys' hearts pounded with excitement, waiting for an attack.

Out of the tumultuous darkness, snout moist and flared and ears cocked forward, padded a lone female. She was young and slender, with ribs showing through her snowy, white coat. No blood showed on her muzzle. She had not partaken of the feast.

"Leave here, beast!" cried Fulk in cracking voice, "Ya ya…away, lest I shoot you as you stand!"

"Get away!" squeaked Gaspard, "Arghh argghh!"

She backed up indecisively, lowering her head and wrinkling her brow. Turning, and turning again, her ears lay back flat, and she lay down and whined.

"What new devilry is this?" puzzled Fulk.

"Is she so hungry she begs from her enemy?" questioned Gaspard.

The young female looked into first Fulk's, then Gaspard's eyes, before looking away. She shuffled forward a few steps and whined yet again. Behind her in the darkness the battle for the remains slacked as the remainder of the pack carried the spoils off to feast and feed pups.

Fulk considered the wolf in the flickering firelight. "Gaspard, fetch a hearty slice of venison and throw it to her."

The young boy plucked a roasted slice from the stick and tossed it beyond the wolf into the shadows. As she rose to chase the morsel, the boys noticed how she favored her right hindquarter. Some wound, unseen in the darkness, plagued the young female, explaining her plight.

In silent exhaustion, Fulk added to the fire. The boys split the remaining pieces of now cold roasted meat then wrapped tightly together in their cloaks, succumbed to exhaustion and slept.

Dawn found the boys tightly curled together, backs to the remains of the great red deer. Their fuel was exhausted and the warming fire no more than a wisp of smoke curling over banked coals. The air was calm, though a light drizzle wet the ground outside their bramble cave. The mix of cold morning light, bone-chilling damp, and stiff necks roused them from their uneasy slumber. Fulk made short work of the remains of the aspen, cutting several sturdy poles while Gaspard gathered wood and coaxed the fire back to life. The underbrush from the far side of the pool was rent, crushed, and scarred with the paw prints of the previous night's frenzy.

The boys warmed themselves by the fire, roasting chunks of venison for their breakfast. The hot, lean, rich meat sizzled and smoked, burning fingers and tongues.

"Do you know anything about my parents?" asked Gaspard, staring into the fire.

"No," replied Fulk quietly. "You have asked brother Carthusian this question, yes?"

Gaspard nodded. "He claims ignorance."

"I know that story—you were left with the brothers in St. Lo as an infant."

"Some of the men say my mother was a jaded woman. What is a jaded woman?"

Fulk took a bite of meat and stared uncomfortably to the edge of the clearing. A tuft of short reeds shook, and from behind them the white face of their she-wolf appeared, her great, golden eyes gazing upon them.

"Be still," whispered Fulk. "Look there!" He pointed his skewer toward the slender, wild lady.

The boys glanced at each other, then in unison gently tossed their remaining bits of meat into the clearing to draw the wolf out. She ducked out of sight and then reappeared. A quick panting, a great, pink tongue wetting the mottled, black nose. A hesitant step forward with lowered head.

"She is beautiful," breathed Gaspard.

"Yes…" Fulk trailed as she cautiously approached the meat, "Our White Lady…"

A quick dart, a flash of white fangs, she snapped up the nearest hunk then quickly retreated to her cover. Gnawing, chewing, gulping, and then peering from the reeds to make sure the boys remained still, she limped forward cautiously once more, took hold of the last piece of venison, and then gingerly turned and disappeared into the underbrush.

"Your mother was not a jaded woman," sighed Fulk, picking up his axe. "My father told me that much, but no more."

"Lord Hugh knows of my mother?" asked Gaspard hopefully.

"Perhaps…possibly…but how much? I know not," replied Fulk.

Gaspard's color rose, "Will you help me to ask him?"

"Yes."

But it was not meant to be.

The boys cleverly lashed together the poles with leather thongs, creating a yoke upon which they could suspend the remains of the bull, using leverage to reduce their burden. They kicked out their fire and began the long journey back to Hambie. It was early afternoon by the time they came within sight of its stone walls and high turrets rising high above the valley. The rain had fallen steadily the day through. Their feet, hands, and shoulders were painful and blistered. A horn blew, the gates opened, and two hooded riders rode down from the keep. It was Hambie's seneschal, Master Josue, along with their aging chamberlain, Thomas de Lunel.

"Lord Fulk, you have needlessly worried the residents of Hambie with your escapade!" chastised Master Josue from beneath his hood. "We have had riders out since dawn in search of you!"

Master Josue was a portly man of middle years and jolly, balding features. He owned a character loyal, patient, and politic, and he could read and write proficiently. With his days of battle now behind him, he settled into a life managing the daily routine of his lord's household.

"And I see you have brought an omen with you!" exclaimed the chamberlain as he pointed through the trees behind the boys. "For good or ill, what say you?"

The boys turned in surprise to see their white wolf had followed them all the way back to Hambie.

"She is our White Lady!" exclaimed Fulk boldly. "From this day forward she is under my personal protection. And as for you two, Josue and Thomas, in my father's absence, I am the Lord de Hambie. Best you not forget that. Question me not! Now, dismount and relieve us of our burden. My squire and I need dry clothes, hot food, and drink to restore us."

Master Josue and the elderly Thomas considered Fulk and Gaspard grimly for a moment. A change had come over the son of their lord in the past day. His chin was set, his brow knit, and his essence suddenly commanding. As he gazed unblinking on the two riders, his hand gently loosened his long knife in its scabbard.

"Yes, milord!" Master Josue replied clearly. He and Thomas dismounted, handing the reins to Fulk and Gaspard. Thomas knelt and cupped his hands providing Gaspard a step in order to climb the tall stock horse. The boys swung into their saddles, clicked their tongues, and trotted into the keep.

Thomas gave a puzzled look to Josue.

"That boy will need no regent if the Lord Hugh fails to return," considered Master Josue carefully.

"Véthe!" agreed Thomas.

The men hoisted the makeshift yoke that suspended the torso and head of the bull and carried it to the scalding house. As dusk fell upon Normandy, dark, boiling clouds rose on the shoulders of a wicked north wind. Animal and man alike sought shelter in barns, sheds, cottages, hovels, and keeps. The heavens opened, and a torrential storm unleashed upon England and France, and upon Sir Richard's fleet caught in between.

CHAPTER 2

The Wolf, the Dragon, and the Lady

It came to pass in the year 1014 with the death of Swein, the heathen King of the Danes, conqueror of England, and murderer of Ælfheah the Archbishop of Canterbury, that four men rose to lay claim to the throne of England. Two were Swein's sons, Harald and Cnut. One was Swein's sworn enemy Æthelred Unræd, the true king of England living in exile. The last was Æthelred and Ælfgifu's son, Edmund Ironside.

Æthelred acted quickly and decisively, catching Cnut unprepared. From his exile in Normandy, he invaded and regained his rightful throne, and Cnut was forced to flee with his forces from England for over a year. Withdrawing from the conflict altogether, Harald satisfied himself with the crown of Denmark, leaving Cnut unmolested to rally his armies and bend his will against Æthelred.

The following year when Cnut returned, he found his enemy's house fractured. Edmund had rebelled against his father, seeking the crown for himself. Cnut fiercely, mercilessly swept across England, finally setting his will to the taking of London, where he found Æthelred and Edmund had reunited in defense of the city. Whether by providence or design, just a matter of weeks before Cnut laid siege to the city, Æthelred died, and the English Witan of London then elected Edmund Ironside king.

For six months Cnut and Edmund battled to a standstill. Marches were countered, fields of battle shifted, with no clear winner emerging until October's battle of Assandun. Edmund was overwhelmed and decisively crushed. Cnut forced Edmund to sign a treaty that left him only the rule of Wessex. In a strange coincidence most believed to be assassination, Edmund mysteriously died in Oxford just a few weeks later.

Cnut then went on a murderous purge of all England, killing all his long imprisoned hostages and putting to death nobles he feared or mistrusted. His savagery brought swift and clear control of the land through fear. His soldiers then brazenly went about extorting a comfortable life from the island's helpless citizens.

News of Cnut's atrocities came to the ears of Sir Richard, Duke of Normandy, who took great offense to the ignoble king. Rather than using the church simply for political ends, Richard was a true champion of Christianity and justice. Richard's sister, Emma, was the second wife and widow of Æthelred. The sons of Æthelred and Emma, Alfred and Edward, were under the protection of the duke and were the rightful heirs to the throne of England. Richard took council with his loyal barons, including the Baron de Hambie, and decided to mount an expedition to relieve all England of the invader. With his closest advisors at his side, he drew a plan to launch a great fleet, thousands of men strong, against Cnut.

It was autumn in the year of our Lord 1017 when Richard's army arrived on the beaches of Normandy prepared for war. With great labor the flotilla of longships were outfitted and set sail, making for the English coast. The fleet was not long at sea when the demons of weather turned violently on Sir Richard, as though conjured by the Devil himself. The curling swells of the channel, driven to a frenzy by a boiling tempest from the heavens above, broke over the rails and tore the sails. Sheets of rain blinded the men as they valiantly fought to make England's southern coast. Many were swept into the frigid waters to be lost forever to the sea. As the storm worsened, entire ships vanished into the troughs of the great swells, never to be seen again.

The gale out of the north pushed the longships south until Sir Richard ordered they make for shelter in the lee of Guernsey's southern coast to ride out the storm. By the time the wind slacked and the swells calmed, much of the fleet had been lost. Sir Richard was forced to return to Normandy in defeat, having never laid eyes upon the enemy. It was nine days before news reached the household de Hambie that Sir Hugh Paynel was lost at sea.

News of the failed expedition struck fear into Cnut's heart. The valiant spirits, strong arms, and fierce nature of the Normans were renowned throughout Europe. They were descendants of the Danish Prince, Rollo, who was betrayed and sent into exile by King Olaf the Brash. Rollo and his wandering army were the scourge of the seas until France's King Charles sued for peace and gave Rollo the region then known at Neustria. While the Normans slowly became a part of France in language and culture, even converting to Christianity, they never truly lost their Viking roots and instincts.

Now aware of what lay in Richard's heart, Cnut sent an emissary to the duke of Normandy hoping to head off any further attack. Cnut proposed to declare the sons of Emma heirs to the throne of England—in exchange for the hand of Emma in marriage. Sir Richard accepted Cnut's terms, and nine years of peace ensued between Normandy and England.

It was in these years, during the reign of King Robert the Pious of France, that Fulk Paynel, Baron de Hambie, grew to be one of the most respected and admired men in all of Normandy in both mind and body. He grew tall, fair, and handsome, with great physical strength and symmetry. At his side was always his loyal squire, Gaspard Malfort, with flowing black hair and piercing blue eyes, whose youthful bud of manhood was just folding out in magnificent glory. The two fought valiantly on the battlefields of their duke, and if Duke Richard came to the aid of King Robert, the men de Hambie brought victory to the king. Fulk was an excellent tactician and always availed good council, first for Duke Richard, and then for Duke Robert when the time came.

His vavasors, freemen, and villeins also loved the Baron de Hambie, for he administered his barony with a just and Christian hand. He was said to live under the protection of a guardian angel sent by St. Peter in a form of a white she-wolf. Many a tall tale was spun in local inns from peasants who swore they witnessed the young man and his squire cavorting in the forest with such a creature. When Sir Fulk ordered the face of a white wolf with golden eyes added to his standard and shield, all of Normandy, with a knowing wink and nod, knew these tales to be undeniably true.

He could not be defeated by even the most seasoned of knights in any of the King's tournaments. His lance cracked countless shields as he thundered down the list on Hardelle, his roan charger. His great sword pricked at the throat of his opponents as they admitted their defeat before the roaring crowd. The nightly feasting and dancing at those gay events found Fulk light on his feet, considerate of tongue, and respectful even of the lowly. Only those nobles given to petty jealousies ever spoke against him, and then only carefully and quietly. Sir Fulk Paynel guarded his honor closely and would not hesitate to call out a slanderer and demand the retraction of spurious talk.

It so happened in the year 1024 Sir Richard II, Duke of Normandy, held a great festival and tournament in the town of Rouen in celebration of May Day. All the most notable knights, nobles, and distinguished warriors from all about France were invited to attend. The eligible daughters of the lords and merchants put on their finest in hopes to find the best possible arrangements for marriage. They came from Brittany, Maine, Aquitaine, Toulouse, Blois, and Burgundy. Merchants from far and near prepared their best in goods to take for trade. Wine merchants, glovers, smiths, clothiers, cobblers, potters, magicians, herbalists, charlatans, and the like put forth their best effort to part the wayfarers from their money. Traveling troubadours, musicians, and acrobats entertained the crowds in hopes generous lords and peasants alike would have a spare coin to throw their way. Sword swallowers, fire breathers, and jugglers performed side by side with knights and squires to entertain the masses.

That year Richard III thought to add a joust to the many competitions of his father's tournament as a display of the superiority of Norman knights on horseback. He even convinced his own brother, Robert, to tilt for the honor of Normandy. The midline of the list was directly in front of the duke's box so he could witness each brutal strike.

There was the scudding whistle and thunk of arrows—the finest of the fletchers. Daggers flashed, quick and dancing. Swords clashed and smashed as knights fenced. Lances crashed, pierced, and cracked. Manes were braided, standards hung, shields repaired and painted afresh. All this brought together Sir Fulk Paynel and Sir Bertrand Ducaen, two seasoned and fierce Norman barons, in the final event of the tournament—the championship joust. Fulk unseated Sir Grimoult du Plessis once and struck his shield solidly twice to advance, while Ducaen struck Sir Robert so hard on the first run, Robert was forced to retire from the match. Now the two most feared knights in Normandy would sit couched in the saddle and face each other.

A shadow briefly paused against the back of the tent then vanished. A soft footfall went unheard over the din of the fair. Gaspard glanced through the open flap to Master Josue's man, young Philippe. Philippe was sitting idly on the ground away from the tent whittling a bit of wood. He raised his left hand and rubbed his nose. The signal. Someone lurked behind the tent of Hambie. Master Josue knew Ducaen to be a man not above unchivalrous trickery such as spying to gain an advantage, so he had suggested a trap. Time would tell that truth as Josue's plan of false conversation went into effect.

"We have watched his matches," commented Gaspard loudly enough to be overheard, "as he has watched ours."

"Yes," replied Fulk, "his style is much like fencing. He wields his lance like a sword, such is his strength."

"He will parry your aim, then riposte against your shield. Quick as lightning! It is his opening tactic in each match."

"Yes, I believe I can match the move," said Fulk as Gaspard dressed him in his surcoat over his hauberk. "I have noted he leaves his shoulder open in this maneuver. It gives me an advantage."

Gaspard paused. "I think not...he is no fool. I believe he has fought each match with this defect intentionally. Ducaen is crafty—he wants you to believe he has a weakness. It is like bait on a barbed hook. Instead, make your play at his midriff. He will not leave his shoulder open against you—it might be his midriff."

"That might work, feinting then going for the midriff. Unexpected..." Fulk considered.

"Whose honor shall you ride for this bout?" asked Gaspard, a certain flatness in his voice that escaped Fulk's attention.

"Again, the Lady Gisla de Grentmesnel." Fulk furrowed his brow. "Her honor is paramount to me."

"Ducaen has fought for her all this tournament, also," warned Gaspard.

"He dishonors her by speaking her name!" spat Fulk. "But enough talk," and with that the trap was set.

Gaspard finished work on his lord's dress and armaments, and then exited the tent to tend to the accoutrements of the roan. Their shadow from behind the tent was nowhere to be seen, though a sign from Philippe confirmed the spy remained within earshot long enough. When all was prepared both knight and squire knelt at a makeshift altar in their tent and prayed to the Lord on High for victory.

Black and gold, the dragon. Gold and white, the wolf. Squires tightened and secured gear and balanced both knights and horses. Crowds gathered in excitement. Children climbed to parents' shoulders; nobles climbed to their places in the stands. Two knights faced one final contest for glory. From each end of the list the knights, helms off and tucked against their sides, cantered their mounts to the midline and acknowledged the aged duke of Normandy and his sons, the Duchess Poppa, and the other nobles. With Sir Richard sat his nephews Alfred and Edward. To his right sat Reginald, Count of Burgundy, and his wife, Adelaide. To Sir Richard's left sat the Count Albric de Grentmesnel, his son Rohais, and daughter Gisla.

"Noble barons and defenders of Normandy!" bellowed Sir Richard, "You bring honor to your houses and all Normans with your chivalrous and knightly exploits!"

The crowd erupted in cheering. They knew that between Sir Robert, Sir Grimoult, Sir Bertrand, and Sir Fulk, Normandy had defeated all the best from the rest of France.

Once the crowd settled, the duke spoke again.

"We all know you fight for the honor of Normandy in all endeavors, but perhaps you fight for something...*or someone*...more genteel?" boomed the duke, a mischievous smile on his face.

Before Fulk could open his mouth, Ducaen called out in a strong voice, "I fight for the honor of the Lady Gisla!"

A concerned murmur went through the crowd. What would Sir Fulk do? Gisla had been chosen. Would he choose another? Would he abstain? Even the whispers and sniffs of the haughty nobles floated through the air.

Fulk looked briefly at the ground and smiled. Raising his sparkling blue eyes, he gazed briefly at Sir Richard, and then found the gray, somber eyes of Lady Gisla.

"I would be remiss in my duties as a man, knight, baron, and Christian to abandon the lady I have fought for this whole tournament," his voice was clear and strong. "I therefore must join my noble opponent in defending the honor of Lady Gisla!"

The volume of the rumbling murmur swelled and washed over crowds around the list.

"So be it!" commanded the duke, nodding to the herald, who raised his horn.

A trumpet sounded. Hardelle flexed beneath him with excitement. Before trotting her back to the end of the list, he glanced in Ducaen's direction. The man's gray eyes, framed by his flowing black hair and tightly clipped beard, bored coldly through him. Neither warmth nor grimace of determination crossed his clear, unmarked face, only calm repose and a flicker of hatred. Ducaen held Fulk's gaze for a brief count, then with a light pull of the rein turned his black Moroccan stallion and cantered to his end of the list and his waiting squire. Fulk did the same.

The Baron Bertrand Ducaen, twelve years Fulk's senior, had attained his reputation as a cold, disciplined warrior during Fulk's youth. While time had tamed the violent and lusty exploits of a young Ducaen, his associates knew his cruelty, arrogance, and haughty disdain of all lawful authority, be it God or man, made him a dangerous enemy. He was a widower whose wife had left him no son, and it was common knowledge he was pressing the Count de Grentmesnel for his daughter's hand in marriage.

To title Gisla de Grentmesnel the fairest woman in all the land would be a very presumptuous declaration, as all true men know a woman's beauty lies in the eyes of the beholder. Tall and slender, she held the light and fair features of her northern ancestors. She had hair of lightly spun gold, eyes as gray as the sea's horizon just before the dawn of a clear morning. Her pale lips, neither voluptuous nor pursed, were set beneath a sculpted nose and cheeks. She had laughter taken from the babbling brook. Her long delicate fingers were cool to the touch yet warm with compassion. She had a visage as somber and joyful as an empty winter coastline.

A noble once asked brother Carthusian, "How would you describe an angel?"

"An angel of war or an angel of mercy?" inquired the brother.

"Let us say an angel of mercy," replied the noble.

Carthusian paused, and then said with a smile, "Gisla de Grentmesnel, not that I notice such things."

Fulk's roan and Ducaen's black Moroccan champed at their bits and flexed their powerful, trained bodies in anticipation of the contest. Their hooves dug in the mud as they each pulled insistently at their master's reins. Their soft black eyes locked on the herald's flag, awaiting it to drop. A hush fell over the spectators. The knights' faces were now hid beneath their helms, and their lances stood erect. The great oaken shafts were painted in each man's colors. Fulk's was tipped with a wolf's head, while Ducaen's sported a clenched fist. Sir Richard gave the signal, the herald slashed the air with his flag, and the horses surged in a mass of tangled hooves.

With his shield on the left arm and lance tucked under the right, Fulk rumbled down the list to meet the thundering charge of Ducaen. Each rider dropped his lance to take aim at the chest of the other. Fulk held his weapon low, then unexpectedly raised the lance forcefully and thrust it forward, lunging with all his might. Ducaen attempted to parry the rising lance before his own thrust, but underestimated the force and reach of the taller man and was a fraction late. Fulk struck Ducaen's shield square in the center of the chest, below the chin, like a thunderclap, throwing him backward on the Moroccan's hindquarter, though he was not unseated. Despite succumbing to Fulk's trickery, Ducaen also scored solidly. Though a fraction behind Fulk's blow, he landed a low, midline strike that Fulk barely had strength to deflect. Pain shot all through his arm, and only the instincts of Hardelle kept him seated. Gasps and cheers briefly surged through the crowd while the combatants righted themselves in their saddles, finished the run, and wielded their mounts.

With the drop of the flag, the horses surged forward a second time. This time both Fulk and Ducaen centered their lances early, leaving no obvious opening for either man. Lunge, parry, riposte, parry—both points went wide, and the shafts glanced off the shields. There was no score. Again the riders turned and faced each other. Again the flag dropped.

Hardelle surged forward for the third time. Fulk assumed the same defensive position as the second run to meet Ducaen's charge. Just before the strike he rolled his lance out and up, pulled his shield across his chest, and thrust down with all his might. There was a great crash and the snapping of wood. The great fist of Ducaen's lance struck high of the left side of Fulk's shield with such force the shield bent, cracked, and bit painfully into Fulk's arm. The fist shot by the shield and glanced off the side of Fulk's helm. His head snapped back, and all he could see was blackness and stars. His own lance had twisted and torn from his grasp, and he reeled desperately. Hardelle pulled up under him, keeping him in the saddle. He grasped for the thick hair of her mane and clung to her neck. The crowd was roaring! His helm was askew and blocking his vision. His left arm was in agony. He brought Hardelle to a halt and clumsily tore the dented helm from his head, throwing it to the ground. Confused, he glanced about, sweat stinging his eyes. All were looking his way, cheering, smiling, and pumping their fists. The nobles in the stands were on their feet. Finally he eased Hardelle around and faced what lay behind him on the list. His lance was burst asunder and lay in pieces all about the midline. The black Moroccan was walking, riderless, on the far end of the list near a very agitated Gaspard. In the mud directly in front of Sir Richard crouched Ducaen's squire, Atraso, hovering over a barely moving Ducaen, who lay sprawled on his back. The duke's surgeon pushed his way through the crowd and hurried to the fallen man's side. The joust was over, and victory belonged to Fulk Paynel.

The Baron de Hambie gathered himself as he walked his roan to the center box of the stands where Sir Richard stood waiting. He nodded to the duke, Sir Reginald, and the Count de Grentmesnel, and then allowed his eyes to gaze upon Gisla with the greatest sense of relief. Sir Richard began speaking with a loud booming voice, addressing Fulk and the crowd. Grand, celebratory words that elicited cheers from the peasants and polite applause the nobles—words that fell about Fulk unheard as he lost himself in the gray clarity of Gisla's eyes, the tears of deliverance upon her cheeks, and a gracious smile upon her lips. The pale green silk veil that once covered her face now slipped from her fingers and gently floated to the earth before Fulk's feet.

Gingerly Fulk dismounted, ignoring the shooting pains in his left arm, and retrieved the veil.

"Milady, your veil slipped your grasp," he said softly as he stretched upwards towards the rail and her waiting hand.

She leaned forward toward him and lightly touched his gauntlet in protest. "It is yours to keep if you choose to make it so, good Sir Knight," she breathed in a whisper only he could hear.

He gently withdrew his hand from her touch, retaining the fragile token. Tucking the veil away, he bowed low to Sir Richard, and then took up Hardelle's reins and gamely made his way back to Gaspard.

CHAPTER 3

A Leaf upon the Wind

The warmth of a cloudless day and the joyous aroma of glorious Normandy in springtime did little to lighten Gaspard's mood. He rode in lead with Master Josue, darkly disdaining the banter in which Josue and the men engaged. All together they numbered twelve, a lucky number Fulk believed, also a well-seasoned lot of veterans, loyal and true. Their mounts were well groomed and the men had bathed, combed their hair, and put on their finest attire. Each man carried a freshly repaired shield emblazoned with the white wolf, while Gaspard displayed his lord's standard at the end of his spear. Dispersed among them, tucked deep within their saddlebags, was hid a most generous dowry to be carried to the town of Caen and the castle of Count Albric de Grentmesnel. It was Master Josue's charge to present Fulk's marriage proposal with all eloquence and then return to Hambie with a response.

The manor of the de Grentmesnel family was no less than twenty-seven leagues to the northeast and a journey of three days. The delegation would first follow the rutted country road from Hambie along the river Sienne until it crossed the ancient Roman highway that ran north to Coutances. From Coutances, the highway would take them north to Carentan, then east through Bayeux, and finally to Caen. Were they to continue past their destination, the stone cobbled highway traveled through Lisieux and

Brionne before finally arriving at Sir Richard's city, Rouen, the capital of Normandy.

Their horses carried them through farmland, vineyards, and light, airy forests scented with cherry blossom and wild rose. Cotton-white clouds made of daydreams drifted lazily across the azure sky. Snakes, warming themselves on the worn stones of the highway, slithered away in panic, alerted by the rhythmic clip-clop of the approaching horses. Butterflies scattered themselves among the fresh blooms of the wildflowers. Among the delegation, only Gaspard resisted the serene landscape, keeping his thoughts and mood dark, confused, and unspoken. With a wry sense of the ironic, he thanked God the men de Hambie attributed his morose demeanor to a cause only near the truth.

Sir Richard's feast the final night of the festival and tournament had been a legendary event. Every noble who held Richard's opinion of importance was in attendance, at least by proxy. It was a vast atmosphere of delicious fare with roasts of all sorts, pheasant, goose, fish, eel, bread puddings, legumes, and sweet cakes, where the wine and ale flowed freely. They dined and they danced, but most importantly, they cajoled, commiserated, and parlayed. After all, chivalry dictated they behave honorably and leave petty grievances and feuds at the door. Except, men being men, behaving true to the ethic of chivalry proved so beastly difficult!

"He is as a brother to me!" laughed Fulk testily when the porter raised his eyebrows about Gaspard's presence at his side, being a mere squire, as they entered the castle's great hall.

Fulk, with his baron's coronet upon his brow and decked in his finest suit of white and gold, kept his injured left arm restrained with a sling beneath his cloak. Gaspard, sporting a tailored black and green tunic, cape, and hose, a gift from his lord and beyond the station of an ordinary squire, matched his lord's step as they entered the wondrous din of the great hall. Long tables end to end were set near the walls, leaving a large open floor for mingling and dancing. A goodly band of musicians were on a raised stage near the entrance, with fiddles, flutes, mandolins, tambourines, horns, and drum. They played music so magical; Gaspard imagined them as those who played in eternal homage to God himself.

"As champion, I will be seated at Sir Richard's table," Fulk had said as they dressed. "I have made an arrangement for you to sit at the table of Count de Grentmesnel. This affords him a way to inquire about me in depth and for you to get a sense of how receptive he will be in regards to my marriage proposal."

"I will represent you honorably, milord," was all Gaspard could manage. He felt his heart race and his hands grow cold—to be seated near the fair Gisla—to converse with the fair Gisla. Would that God on high save him from his desires! He both coveted and despised his ordered task.

"Then you shall go lightly with the wine, I am guessing," laughed Fulk.

"Only enough as is mannerly," returned Gaspard with a forced smile.

Upon their entry, a congratulatory crowd of important men and hangers-on immediately surrounded Fulk. There were many quips and much laughter along with firm handshakes and claps to the shoulders. Sir Richard and his sons, Robert and Richard, mixed among the people, dressed in kingly attire. The duke's jester, Configlio, was dressed in a gaudy, laughable suit of rainbow colored patches. He capered about the room, joking, juggling, performing tricks, and roasting the occasional unsuspecting lord. All the while servants appeared and disappeared from behind beautiful tapestries, laying a rich meal upon the table and replenishing drink as the nobles drained their cups.

Sir Richard clapped his hands, and one of the musicians announced the beginning of the feast with his trumpet. Fulk and the other tournament champions joined the duke's closest family and friends at the head table, raised on a dais above all others. Gaspard was invited to sit to the left of Albric, between the count and his son, Robert, and directly across from the Lady Gisla and her brother, Rohais. The subsequent table next to the count's held the Baron Bertrand Ducaen and many of his friends.

"The Baron de Hambie looks upon you with great favor, as an equal, it seems," commented Albric.

"Both Sir Fulk and his father before him have treated me with great kindness," replied Gaspard respectfully. "He is a Christian man of conscience with a good heart. Were I able to choose a father or brother, I could find no better than he. I serve him with a glad heart."

"Not to be brash in the asking, but how does a man such as yourself come to Hambie and into the service of the Paynel family?" asked Robert with a droll smirk.

Gaspard met Robert's gaze briefly and replied in an even tone, "Of course, my past is of no consequence, especially in the telling. I lived with the brothers in Saint Lo as a child. They are very learned men, and I am grateful for the attention they gave me. One of the brothers, Carthusian, who is very close with the Paynel family, was also my teacher and mentor."

The colored question, meant to shame Gaspard, left him unruffled. It was Gisla whose cheeks flushed as she looked at the table, her lap, and the floor as though to distance herself from her brother's haughty ridicule. Albric's quick and deathly eyes upon Rohais and Robert cut off further mockery of Gaspard's station. He quickly moved to more polite questions, allowing Gaspard to tell of the beautiful Castle de Hambie and its country setting along with many adventurous tales of Fulk's heroic deeds. All the while Gisla remained quiet, only listening with glad eyes until a brief pause as maids refilled their empty cups.

"Tell me of Sir Fulk's standard," ask Gisla, finally breaking her silence. "My father tells me it was not adorned with the white wolf in Sir Hugh's day."

"*Ah*," breathed Gaspard, "two most excellent stories...part of our early adventures together as lord and squire, as I recall."

He began with the tale of the hunt, the buck and the bull and their fight for the right to mate, the attack of the wolves, and the appearance of the white she-wolf. Having a great love of language, poetry, and literature, Gaspard was in his element when telling a story. As the words fell from his lips, he garnered more than polite interest. His audience was firmly in his grip. After recounting the fell day when it was learned Lord Hugh was lost he paused a moment, allowing the melancholy memory its due respect.

"It is said your wolf is an enchanted creature," said Gisla, whose rapt attention brought both a sense of pleasure and discomfort to Gaspard. She looked on him with an admiration he knew belonged to his lord. Though he was the center of his audience's attention, and certainly he had the right to meet her eyes without shame, he averted his gaze lest his affections for her be discovered.

"Our wolf? No, milady, she is not our wolf. The white wolf de Hambie belongs to no man," replied Gaspard carefully. "As for enchantment, I shall tell you a story and you shall judge her nature for yourself.

"It was nearly four years after the death of Sir Hugh. Lord Fulk had come fully into manhood, and I had left childhood behind. A great silver boar had haunted the forests of the Sienne Valley for several years. We had seen it at a distance twice the previous summer and knew it to be a stout male with great yellow tusks. It was powerful, dangerous, and very clever. It had maimed a number of men and even killed one, and Fulk set his mind to slaying the beast by his own hand.

"To know Fulk Paynel is to know he is a man of singular mind. Once he is set to a task, there is no denying him...much like his father. You would think that, just as ordinary hunters, Fulk would organize a party of men to pursue the beast with dogs, drums, crossbows, and spears. No such thoughts crossed my lord's mind. Instead, in the early spring when he knew it to be at its hungriest, he decided he alone would hunt and kill the boar.

"Of course our seneschal, Master Josue, was against Fulk going out alone. 'But I shall have Gaspard!' was Fulk's incredulous reply. It would be untruthful of me to say the two did not argue...heatedly...and this time Josue lost."

At this comment, Lord Albric and his sons chuckled. Master Josue was a man they all respected. His honesty, wisdom, and loyalty had done much to lead Lord Fulk on a true path in the years since Hugh's untimely demise. With the love of a father he tempered and strengthened Hambie's young baron.

"We hunted the boar deep into the depths of the forest for many days, searching dense valleys and rocky edifices. We followed spoor and tracks across streams and through marshes yet failed to lay eyes on the beast. Until one morning we awoke, cold and stiff—Fulk would allow no fire—to the sounds of snorting and snuffing near our camp. We were among some rocks for shelter and must have been down wind, for the boar appeared witless to our presence.

"We took up our spears and begin to creep silently from our hiding place among the damp, mossy boulders. Our adversary was rooting among the bracken and leaf mold just out of our view. The snorting sounds of the boar snuffling the forest floor grew nearer and nearer. Its search for a meal had brought it just opposite us with only a large, damp rock in between.

"I had only hunted boar once before, and then only beat the drum to scare and corner the beast. Still, I had heard tales of how fierce they became when cornered, and my heart was racing with the thrill of being so near our unsuspecting quarry. With such great care we crept, hardly breathing, making not the slightest sound," Gaspard paused and looked down, laughing softly to himself.

"Did I say the beast was clever? Just as we made to leap forth and run it through with our spears, we were caught off guard by a great clattering coming over the rock. Even as we were stalking the boar, it was actually stalking us! With a great jump it charged over the rock and leapt down upon our heads. Even at winter's end, it was at least sixteen stone of bristling, angry monster. I was immediately bowled over, striking my head on a rock, and Fulk was unable to bring his spear round in time to mount a defense. The snarling boar rammed Fulk and gored his leg even as he dodged away. Fulk went down under the beast's weight and was barely able to hold back its great, gnashing jaws.

"Death was upon us, and we were lost. I was stunned and could not rise, while Fulk was buried beneath the thrashing fury of the boar. It had *led* us deep into the forest, away from the haunts of man. Just as we had tracked it, the beast had hunted us. In our game of cat and mouse, we were the mice, and we were done for."

Gaspard paused and looked away to Fulk sitting at the duke's table. Gisla, who could not contain her excitement, followed his eyes until she, too, took in Fulk's handsome visage.

"It was the white wolf, wasn't it?" she asked, wide eyed.

"Véthe, milady!" he replied gravely, "Just as we and the boar had played out our dangerous game, our White Lady had hunted us both, never giving away her presence until the moment she was utterly needed. From nowhere she leapt upon the silver boar's back, sinking her gleaming fangs into the beast's thick neck. It squealed in surprise and pain, falling off of Fulk in favor of its new adversary.

"The boar was easily three times her size, far stronger and just as agile. Even as Fulk and I scrambled to retrieve our spears, the fight was going ill for the White Lady. All was flying fur, snorting, growling, and sprays of blood as she was driven back by the boar's snapping jaws and thrashing tusks. Even as we stabbed at the boar's haunches, we could see the blood flowing from her shoulder.

"Fortunately, the boar, bleeding heavily from the wounds we three had inflicted and seeing his advantage was gone, broke off from the lady and fled for the thickets and undergrowth of the forest. To Fulk's dismay, our own wounds prevented us from mounting a pursuit. My skull had a nasty gash, Fulk's breeches were soaked with blood, and the flesh of the White Lady's shoulder was torn. We built a fire and tended our wounds. We kept to that camp several days as we recovered, and every night the White Lady would bed down between us for warmth. She was protecting us in our time of injury just as we had once done for her. Despite my physical hurts, I was never happier than those days..."

Gaspard momentarily trailed off before continuing, as though remembering the most pleasant dream. Seeing the others looking at him expectantly, he cleared his throat and continued.

"Then one morning we awoke and she was gone. We knew she likely remained nearby, but was telling us it was time to return home. We kicked out our fire, slung our packs across our backs, and gamely made the journey back to the castle."

"And what of the silver boar?" asked Rohais. "Did Lord Fulk ever slay the beast?"

"Nay," replied Gaspard, "Though there were rumors here and there, we never came across the boar again. I believe it left the Sienne Valley for safer haunts. A very clever beast, indeed."

"And the White Lady?" asked Gisla, leaning forward, "Was that how she came to be on Fulk's standard?"

"Véthe, milady. Once we returned Fulk had her face stitched and painted on all that is de Hambie. She remains wild and free, and a holy creature by my estimation. She is seen when she chooses, just as she is unseen by her own will."

"A guardian angel, indeed," stated Albric.

"Indeed," agreed Gisla.

As Gaspard told his adventurous tales, Ducaen's table became increasingly noisome and bawdy. He sat with Breton, Lesbirel, Pipon, and Remon, and the wine had flowed a bit too freely for the five men. They began trading stories about village wenches and buttered boys, much to the distress of the ladies within earshot. Finally Ducaen himself, a bit louder than the rest, quaffed his goblet, turned toward Gaspard, and slapped his hand down on the table.

"Tell me, Sir Squire," his voice loud and mocking, "How exactly does a low-born, bastard son-of-a-whore orphan end up seated as a noble at the duke's table? Has someone *buttered* you recently?"

While Ducaen's friends laughed lustily at the question, the guests near the two tables grew suddenly quiet. Color rose in Gaspard's face, but his voice remained calm, quiet, and even.

"My apologies, good Sir Knight, though it is not my place, I am forced to remind you there are ladies present to whom you owe more gentlemanly conduct than your present state of drunkenness," he replied steadily.

Ducaen abruptly stood, murder in his eyes, "How dare you speak such words to me, you filthy whelp! I shall see you whipped for such insolence!"

The count laid a restraining hand upon Gaspard as the young man also stood to defy his antagonist. The musicians stopped their play to gawk at the disturbance.

"Once again, my apologies—this time for abusing the word *good*," responded Gaspard, both his voice and hands trembling with anger.

The sons of Albric, Robert and Rohais, looked upon each other, faces flinched with fear. Ducaen whipped out a long, thin dagger from within the folds of his cloak and pointed it at Gaspard, announcing to the crowd, "You are my witnesses; this fatherless bastard has insulted the honor of a baron of Normandy! He owes me satisfaction!"

While Ducaen did not quite rise to the height of Fulk, his eyes were level with the eyes of Gaspard, and he possessed the stout and powerful build of a mature warrior rather than the lithe nature of the young squire. The wiser of Ducaen's companions (or the more fearful of the duke's wrath, which was more likely the case), Breton and Pipon, rose to lay a restraining hand upon the baron's shoulders.

"Let it be!"

"The duke is watching!"

"The boy is not worth it!" came the whispered advice.

Gaspard, his own knife untouched, kept his steady, defiant gaze upon the eyes of Ducaen, "You already own two losses today, milord. Do you really wish for a third?"

Before Ducaen could scarcely respond, a loud crash startled all the guests. To clear his way to main floor, the old duke had overturned his own table with a strength that belied his age. With fire in his eyes, he motioned to the men around him and strode across the hall to table of Ducaen.

"Bertrand Ducaen, what goes on here?" he demanded, "How dare you draw a weapon against any of my guests! Explain yourself!"

"This boy has insulted me! I demand satisfaction," snarled Ducaen, lowering the blade.

"Albric, did you witness this?" the duke turned on the count, who rose and stood solidly behind Gaspard.

"Sir Bertrand began the dispute and offered the lad little choice," replied the count warmly in Gaspard's defense. He certainly admired the squire's foolhardy courage, knowing neither of his own sons would have been so quick to chastise a man such as Ducaen. "He has also taken issue with whoever allowed the boy a seat...in a rather vulgar manner, I might add. Something about butter, I believe..."

"How peculiar," a cruel smile twisted across Sir Richard's face as his old eyes bored into Ducaen, "for it was *I* who indulged the squire to sit in proxy for Lord Paynel at this very table. I must say, I also feel the sting of insult! How shall I be satisfied?"

Ducaen held the duke's piercing stare just a moment and then lowered his eyes. He returned the dagger to within the folds of his cloak and swallowed hard. Then in a slurred, whispering voice, he said, "I meant no offense, sire. I beg your forgiveness for the misunderstanding between me and the lad."

The duke leaned across the table and whispered softly into Ducaen's ear, upon which the baron noticeably stiffened. Candles flickered and smoked as the soft evening breeze carelessly moved through the hall. From behind one of the tapestries came the clatter of a dropped platter followed by a distant curse. An aging viscount found the tickle in his throat uncontrollable and burst into a fit of embarrassed coughing. The duke pulled away from Ducaen, clapped his hands, and then smiled brightly at the musicians.

"I believe we knights and nobles are remiss in our chivalrous duties!" he called out to the guests. "Please extend your hands to our ladies for the dance!"

The music began, and once again conversation rippled about the room. The ladies and the gentlemen soon lined the floor of the hall and began their ballad. The laughter and gaiety of the event returned as the lines of dancers moved in rhythm to the music. Fulk's and Gisla's eyes met. Their hands touched, and for a brief moment in time they were alone in the crowd...then separated again to continue the dance.

Though Gaspard did not note the exact moment Ducaen and his companions left the feast, they did not remain long, vanishing like ghosts. He had held his tongue once Sir Richard intervened, but could not assuage his own emotions. Anger, humiliation, jealousy—all unrequited. Ducaen's blade—not his to cross. Sir Richard's authority—not his to question. Gisla's hand—not his to touch. Gaspard was a comely man, possessing what some would name a feminine attractiveness in his young features, and he did not go unnoticed by the ladies of the dance. Yet he was as ignorant of their longing glances and soft touch as Gisla was to his presence. His cheeks flushed. The great hall of Sir Richard gradually became a poisonous atmosphere, the music and laughter evil to his ears, and a great craving for the cool dusk air overcame him. With only a cursory "beg pardon," Gaspard fled the dance and ran from the keep, pushing past laughing ladies and surprised lords, ignoring the guards and courtiers.

He stumbled out into the darkening streets of Rouen, a city of thousands, to be lost and alone. The city was alive the last night of the festival as merrymakers walked the lengthening shadows between the buildings alongside cutpurses and whores. In the distance the bells of Vespers rang. The strong smell of humanity, a fragrance unique to large towns and cities, reminded him of his childhood in Saint Lo. He wandered the muddy lanes and narrow alleyways for a time until the merry sounds of laughter and yells carried him to a well-lit alehouse filled with raucous commoners. Inside a throng of cheering people formed a ring around two men who were thoroughly engaged in beating each other senseless.

Gaspard, with a vicious smile on his face, pushed his way through the crowd and announced loudly, "I will fight any man here!"

And fight he did! With a wicked splendor that belied his youthful and innocent face, he thrashed three stout fellows before being beat down by a hulking, ham-fisted man. He drank absinthe and ale. He sang bawdy songs with his companions, songs that left the throng in fits of coarse laughter. He lightened his purse to ensure all had a full cup, and they cheered him for it. He drowned his anger and let his crude companions liven his mood.

He awoke the following morning in the hayloft behind the alehouse, his arm around a woman whose name, easily spoken the night before, now escaped him. The pain of bruises and splits to his face paled in comparison to the throbbing in his skull, the washed up leavings of last night's flood of spirits. His purse was nearly empty, and his dagger was gone. A vague, clouded memory left Gaspard with the impression he gave the lordly knife to the beefy lummox who finally sent him bloody and reeling from the ring. His generosity had made him quite popular among the crowd, as his present company attested. What was her name? Marie? Cherie? Larie? He did not care. He gently disentangled himself from her sleeping form and laid hold of his black and green cloak. He untied his purse, laid it beside the girl, and then climbed down from the loft. Staggering out into the narrow street, he covered his eyes against the bright light of day.

Fulk attributed Gaspard's ill-mannered departure from the feast to the bait placed by Ducaen. He understood a man so riled, without hope of satisfaction, would need outlet. Gaspard's bruises and explanation proved satisfactory.

"Understand, there are intrigues at play here beyond you and me," explained Fulk as they traveled the highway back to Hambie. "Sir Richard has had much trouble with Ducaen of late. When I saw Ducaen seated so close to the table of the Count de Grentmesnel, I suspected something was afoot. Did you notice how attentive the servants were to Ducaen's cup? They kept it overflowing with wine while Sir Richard kept a close eye on Ducaen. He must have hoped for such an outburst. I believe the duke is attempting to isolate him."

"The duke shamed me by not allowing me to answer that pig's filth on the field of honor!" retorted Gaspard irritably, "I looked a fool to everyone—an ill-born bastard whose honor matters naught!"

"We were both tools in his politics; that is for certain," replied Fulk. "But a fool? Nay, Gaspard, you put the count's sons to shame when you chastised Ducaen in their stead. Albric is quite taken with your character. You did Hambie a great honor by facing Ducaen."

This brought a wry smile to Gaspard's bruised, cut face.

"And how was your dinner, sitting at the right hand of the duke?" he inquired.

"Mostly thinly veiled bickering among Sir Richard and his sons," replied Fulk with a laugh. "Robert is upset his father will not give him control of the town of Falaise even though it lies within his territory. I suspect our table would have been overturned even if you and Ducaen had not exchanged words!"

Fulk and Gaspard laughed easily at this.

"So what of Ducaen now?" asked Gaspard.

"He has become a boil on the buttocks of the duke. He will either subside or be lanced," considered Fulk. "You may yet have your chance against Ducaen if Sir Richard rallies us against him."

Those easy countryside hours on horseback followed by the shelter of the local inns at night quickly lost color for Gaspard. Much to his discomfort Fulk persisted in confiding his plans to approach Count Albric with a proposal of marriage with Gisla. Though he deeply loved Fulk as his brother, all talk of the fair Gisla left Gaspard torn and despairing. He wanted to shout, "Please, my lord, do not bring that woman between us!" but could not. Instead he was forced to don a dishonest mask and feign support for his lord's plans. His unusually quiet, morose nature he simply laid at the feet of Ducaen. If the highway took them to a town or village with a saintly shrine, Gaspard would slink away from his companions as they enjoyed the inn's hospitality, and beg prayers of a saint on his behalf to relieve him of his desires. By his own hand his back felt the bite of a switch in penance for his jealous thoughts. He would be controlled! In God's name, he would be controlled!

As was his duty, he made letters for Fulk. Over the years he had not neglected his learning under the tutelage of brother Carthusian of Saint Lo. He enjoyed a quick mind for words, writing, and poetry, along with a gift for drawing. With a formal elegance Fulk had no desire to achieve of his own hand, Gaspard penned the letter that he would ultimately deliver to Albric de Grentmesnel on behalf of his lord. By the time they reached Hambie, the letter had been completed, signed, and sealed. All that remained was for Master Josue and Gaspard to lead a contingent to the count's estate near Caen and make the offer of marriage on Fulk's behalf.

All of this brought Hambie's contingent of twelve to the gates of the Castle de Grentmesnel on a glorious May afternoon. Built at the edge of the river Orne, the castle was both a beautiful and well-fortified country estate. Trumpets sounded their arrival as they proudly rode through the barbican into the castle. Albric's men-at-arms and household stood at attention, lining the courtyard on each side to greet the men de Hambie. At the head of the line stood the count, surrounded by Robert, Rohais, and Gisla. Master Josue and Gaspard reined in their mounts and brought the riders to a stop in front of Albric.

"Master Josue! Gaspard! Welcome to the Castle de Grentmesnel," exclaimed Albric.

Master Josue nodded. "Lord Fulk Paynel, Baron de Hambie, sends greetings and salutations to you and all of your household," he replied.

"We trust your journey from Hambie went well?"

"Yes, milord, 'tis a good time of year for travel."

"Come then, let us tend to your horses and provide you and your men refreshment!"

The men dismounted, each freeing his saddlebags before allowing his horse to be led off to the stables.

"My servants will tend to Gaspard and your men. Please, allow my man Nicholas to show you to your quarters where you may refresh yourself."

"You are most gracious and kind, milord," responded Master Josue. "A cool splash to the face will be welcome after the warm day's ride."

While Gaspard and the other men of Hambie were provided fare in the soldier's common room, Master Josue supped at the table of the count with his family. After the meal was completed and cleared, Albric dismissed Gisla.

"Now, the business at hand," announced the count.

Each of the men de Hambie entered the chamber one a time and laid their treasures, Fulk's offered dowry, on the count's table before him and his sons: golden goblets, jeweled necklaces, precious wrought arm-bands and rings, and silver blades with gem-encrusted scabbards. Lastly, Gaspard entered and placed alongside the other gifts a finely crafted silver box about the size of a bible. With the dowry laid upon the table, they silently exited the room. Master Josue broke the seal on the scroll and read aloud to Albric and his sons:

> *To our most noble and esteemed friend Lord Albric, Count de Grent-mesnel, whose benevolent and good character are renowned throughout Normandy and France, Fulk Paynel, Baron de Hambie, sends glad greetings, good tidings, and sincere wishes for every prosperous fortune in the coming year.*
>
> *In that I see God's covenant with the people of Israel as an everlasting bond, and Christ's fidelity to his Holy Church an unbreakable contract, I hold it my duty to extend that love and fidelity to all those of my household both within my walls and without. As I find my duties to duke and king well fulfilled, my valor on the fields of honor and battle unblemished, and the mood of my tenants joyful and content, I must now give my considerations to the natural progression of events that bring a sense of fulfillment and satisfaction to the life of man. Your friendship, courtesy, and many kindnesses granted to me and members of my household in recent days have left me hopeful you would lend your ear and consideration to this, my request.*
>
> *It has been many long years since Hambie has had a lady to oversee her household and walk her halls. She longs for a woman's soft touch and joyful laughter as the parched deserts of the holy land long for rain. She awaits the new life a union between man and woman brings much like the winter in stillness and silence longs for spring. Hambie cries out in need of a chatelaine.*
>
> *In the whole of this world created by the Lord on high, there is but one lady whom I would choose, and only if she would willingly accept my proposal, to take in marriage as my wife. I first, with all humility, ask your permission and blessing to ask for the hand of your daughter, Gisla, in marriage. If you are agreeable to my proposal, then I would have you present my offer to your daughter to accept or reject at her own choosing. This is foremost in my mind, for it is my intention this marriage be not only advantageous to both our houses,*

*but also a joyful union befitting a woman of her station and quality. Her
honor and her joy are paramount to me.*

*In hopes you will look upon my proposal with benevolence and kindness,
I have authorized the two most trusted men of my house, Master Josue le Sau-
teur and Gaspard Malfort, to act as my agents in the details of this matter.
I await your most wise and just decision.*

Signed with the mark of Sir Fulk Paynel, Baron de Hambie

"Inside the silver box is the Paynel family's most treasured possession, the blessed and holy relic, the hand of Saint Aprus of Sens," continued Master Josue. "For many years its presence has brought prosperity and
calm to the barony."

"A blessing for a blessing," the count mused. "Very well, we shall
consider your offer. In the mean time, my chamberlain will see to your
desires. You are excused."

It was a restless evening for Gaspard. Though they thought him
haughty for it, he shunned the company of his men, rather seeking the
solitude of the count's gardens. It was a spacious annex, surrounded by
high walls, attached to the southern wall of the castle. The paths wound
their way through menagerie of trellised flowers, hedges, ferns, and fruit
trees. Carp rippled the surface of a small pond while the heady scent of
the spring blossoms hung heavy in the air. He gazed back upon the keep,
numbly wondering if any of the balconies, flung wide before the scented
breeze wafting up from the garden, belonged to the lady Gisla.

All propriety aside, it was a given Albric would bless Fulk's proposal.
The gift of a holy relic, while likely an unnecessary gesture, would certainly
secure Fulk's claim against any other suitors. It carried a great symbolic value
when compared against the real value of the income Gisla's dowered prop-
erty would add to Fulk's already prosperous lands. As for Gisla, Gaspard
despaired in knowing she returned Fulk's feelings of affection. Just as he sat
on a bench, cold and empty, oblivious to the gnats aimlessly flying about the
water's surface, she was tingling and alive and embracing her father a thousand times over, completely unaware of him that sat far below her.

Minutes stretched to hours. Prayers. Darkness fell. Pleas. The moon rose in the clear night sky. Entreaty. The hour was late when the soft fall of approaching footsteps on the garden path broke Gaspard's reflection. The garden in the moonlight was like ink on washed paper, bright with contrast but lacking color. From beyond a curve in the path bent round a hedge appeared a slender, unfamiliar man wrapped in a dark cape. His clean-shaven face was a stark white reflection of the light of the night sky. Gaspard tensed at the approach of the stranger, his hand reflexively loosening the knife at his side.

"It is a fine evening to enjoy the count's garden, no?" opened the stranger in a soft voice at a safe distance.

"Yes, milord," replied Gaspard, rising cautiously to his feet. He was the taller of the two.

"You are one of the men de Hambie, yes?"

"Yes, I am Gaspard."

"Ah, I have heard of you. You are reputed to be more than a squire, but yet not a knight."

"You have me at a disadvantage, milord. You know of me, yet I am not familiar with you."

"My apologies. My name is Gregar Penscalus. May I sit with you awhile?"

Gaspard hesitated, neither comfortable nor wanting to appear discourteous.

Gregar laughed pleasantly. "I am neither armed nor mean you any harm, young squire."

Gaspard nodded, and the two sat upon the bench and gazed upon the still waters of the pool. He noted Gregar had his long black hair tied in a braid that disappeared beneath the collar of his cloak.

"Are you a member of the Lord Albric's household?" asked Gaspard.

"No, though I do provide council for some of its members from time to time."

"What sort of council?"

"Questions of a spiritual sort. You have been here...alone...for some hours. Are you troubled?

"My business is my own. Are you a priest or a brother?"

"Neither. That has not been my calling. I have…a bit broader experience than the church in Rome provides. I have been far to the north, traveled to the south, and studied in the east."

"You have been to the Holy Land?"

"Yes, and beyond. There is so much to this world, seen and unseen, that is beyond the limited vision of your church. Great mysteries. Lost secrets."

"I have often imagined what Jerusalem is like. The great city of God."

"She was ancient even when King David took her for himself. Thousands of years of men have spilt their blood storming her walls. The Muhammadans rule there now. Always at war and never destroyed. That is Jerusalem.

"I respect your solitude, Gaspard, and your desires to remain a private man, but I assure you, any confidence you entrust to me shall remain safe and secret. If I knew what your troubles were, I might be of good council."

Gaspard snorted bitterly. "Can a bird council a leaf upon the wind? Or perhaps a fish bring solace to a bit of drifting wood? I live at the discretion of others. My life is to be acted upon. I cast no shadow and vanish in the shadow of others. If you know of me, then you know from whence I came, a false bloom from a broken stem!"

"A life at the discretion of others. I understand. The miller has his stone. The smith, his forge. The lord, his manor. The squire of ignoble birth has nothing by which he may live, yet his stomach is full."

"Do not mock me!" spat Gaspard.

"It is not mockery," said Gregar quietly. "Some men do not mind the life of a dog—a collar and chain in exchange for a full belly. You are like the wolf. Freedom is worth not knowing from where comes your next meal. No matter the hand that trained you as a pup, you cannot deny your true self."

"My true self? I do not even know who I am! Even my name, Malfort, is a cruelty forced upon me."

"Yet you know who you are not! And that eats at you instead of enlightening you."

"What do you mean?"

"The duke's son, Robert, shares much in common with you. He is not duke, nor likely to become duke when his father expires. He rules his little valley at the pleasure of his brother and cannot even enforce his rightful claim to the town of Falaise."

"I see no similarity whatsoever," Gaspard retorted.

"You want what you cannot have. You want *whom* you cannot have. You survive by keeping your…"

Gaspard burst to his feet and laid hold of Gregar, pulling him up by his collar.

"You presume far too much, milord. I would gladly snap your neck if you were to repeat such slander!" he hissed viciously.

It was then Gregar placed his hands firmly upon Gaspard's wrists, displaying a large, twisting, serpentine ring on his left middle finger. His faced remained serene to the confrontation.

"Robert is also in love, you know," he said calmly.

Gaspard's eyes grew wide with the fear of consequence. If Robert were covetous of Gisla, Fulk would surely be in danger! It was so tangled… First a rival in Ducaen. Now a rival in the son of the duke of Normandy! Gisla was well admired by many nobles, but of all of them, only Robert and Ducaen had little fear of Fulk. He weakly released Gregar, his arms sagging to his sides. Gregar straightened his collar and cleared his throat.

"Fortunately for you and Sir Fulk, he is in love with a tanner's daughter in Falaise. Gisla is far too sedate and prudent for his taste. He longs for a woman a bit more devilish, I dare say," Gregar smiled wryly. "As for your secret affection, it is safe with me. That I will swear to."

"What are you, that you know such things…that you see into my mind?" rasped Gaspard.

"I am one wise with council. Will you hear my words for you?"

Gaspard hesitated and then nodded.

"Go home. Be loyal to your lord. Attend to his lady faithfully. Act as the loving brother they already take you to be…and most of all calm your desires and be patient. Your day will come."

"Easily said, milord!" retorted Gaspard.

"I find you an interesting young man, Gaspard Malfort," advised Gregar, "I will be sure to stop in at Hambie from time to time to take further council with you. If I am wrong, I will own it. For now follow my advice, and it will serve you and your desires. I will bid you farewell."

As he turned to leave, Gaspard laid a hand on his left shoulder, "Your ring, milord, 'tis stranger than I have ever seen."

"Yes, though darkness does not it justice," said Gregar with a distant smile. "I unearthed it in the lost city of Babylon many years ago. I shall show it to you more closely upon our next meeting."

"That would be kind, milord."

The men parted, and Gaspard made his way back to his quarters. He flung himself, exhausted, on to his bed and slept a dark, dreamless sleep. Upon rising, he found himself in good spirits for the first time in many weeks. His step was light and he was cordial with the men once again. He joked with them and slapped their backs. The men de Hambie, a hearty lot of manliness, thought him quite queer for the change.

CHAPTER 4

Valediction

As all marriages of nobility, that of Lord Fulk Paynel, Baron de Hambie, and Gisla de Grentmesnel, daughter of Count Albric, was a lengthy and dull procession. Held at the Castle de Grentmesnel on the morning of the autumnal equinox of the year 1024 and performed by the bishop of Caen, it left its many guests yawning and footsore. Just because the man had connections through family and friends and so had gained such a high position did not make him an inspiring priest. Longwinded and monotone was the bishop's homily. Gaspard, decked in a suit of finery, mouthed his responses correctly and on cue, while keeping at bay the temptation to roll his eyes and fidget. At least the feast was well laid. Finally it came to a glorious, boring end with Fulk and Gisla disappearing from the castle in a gilded carriage surrounded by Gaspard and his men.

They returned to Hambie with great fanfare. The villagers came out to cheer, and Fulk's house lined the bailey to greet their new mistress. She was most welcome by all and joyfully received. A woman's touch had been so long absent! Gisla soon won all their hearts with her graceful, gentle hand. Gisla believed every human, and therefore every member of her house, was of value to God, and therefore of value to Hambie, no matter his or her station. She was kind to all, and they loved her. Those were happy days for all the people of Hambie...except one.

The first snow of winter of the year 1025 blanketed Normandy in crystalline white on a mid-January night. The storm spent its wrath bringing misery to the Scottish highlands, and by the time it crossed the channel to touch the shores of France, it was gentle and loving. Every season possesses it own scented colors. In that year, the spring's high notes were vivid and sharp like fresh perfume; summer was low and rich like the nape of a good woman; autumn's dank, musty decay was a feast for the earth. The first snow of winter stood alone, above all. It brought the pleasure of clean air, new and untainted by the earth, which refreshed the palate and renewed the spirit.

The anticipation of the new winter landscape, its blinding beauty already piercing the chinks of the shutters in the bedchamber, called to Gisla from the depths of her bed where she lay surrounded by the warmth and strength of her man. Her flaxen hair spilled about her shoulders as she slipped from beneath the covers and glided across the floor to the tall, narrow window. She lifted the latch and pulled the dark, oiled shutters inward to be met by the streaming morning sun. The vapor of her breath froze upon the winter air as she stared in wonder at the purity of fresh snow, now a mantle upon the Sienne Valley. What had been a waving sea of wheat in the height of summer was now silent, white, and still.

Never before had she felt such peace and well-being, such a singular moment in time. It took her breath away, and her eyes stung with joy as well as cold. It was a time between strife and struggle. It was a time when the world around her took a needed respite from its labors and inhaled deeply.

Behind her Fulk stirred and sat up. Gisla turned, the sun behind her pouring into the chamber, and smiled softly at her husband. He was noble, strong, and good, and her heart ached with happiness.

"Have I died?" asked Fulk with a voice low and filled with awe. "I have never seen such heavenly beauty as stands before me now."

Gisla flushed and extended her hand to Fulk as he stood. They gazed out the window for some minutes, silently taking in the new landscape. She leaned into him and he drew his strong arm protectively about her.

"I should like to ride this morning," she decided. "I want to see the land. I want to remember it this way."

Fulk pressed his bearded face against her fragrant hair. "It will be so."

Within the hour, dressed in their winter mantles, Fulk and Gisla rode forth from the gates of Hambie and wound their way down the castle slope. The village was coming to life and the rich smell of wood-smoke hung in the air. After exchanging greetings with several villagers, they turned their horses south toward the headwaters of the River Sienne.

Through the skeletal groves of winter trees they passed, the fetlocks of their mounts soon coated in burs of snow. The forest was silent except for the creaking of trees and the muffled clip-clop of the horses. They passed by cottages and lofts and watched shepherds tend their flocks in the open fields. Overhead, Gisla caught sight of a wild peregrine riding the wind. She watched in wonder at the grace and beauty of the fierce creature as it methodically searched out its prey.

"Tomorrow we shall bring Gaspard and set our own to wing," commented Fulk as he looked to the sky. "It is time for you to try your hand with the falcons."

Turning to the east they rode through thinning trees until they finally broke the tree line and began to cross an open field. On the far side of the field a handful of sheep had wandered away from their flock to a winter loft and were enjoying the hay within. Fulk silently reined up and motioned to Gisla to do likewise. As he unslung his bow, he pointed to the fringe of the forest some two hundred yards distant, near the loft. A sleek gray form was creeping carefully through the bracken to the left of loft. It was a large wolf, so intent on the sheep that it failed to note the arrival of the two riders.

Fulk notched his arrow and drew slowly back against the stiff yew stave. The wood flexed and creaked as the baron methodically took his aim. Hardelle was as still as stone beneath him. The wolf came to a halt under cover of a thick, snow-covered tuft of grass. Fulk calmly held the bow steady, waiting for the great predator to again reveal itself.

As Fulk held the flexed longbow at the ready, patiently waiting for the wolf's next move, Gisla noted a tufted mound of snow to the right of the loft suddenly began to shift and change position. She blinked her eyes, thinking it to be an illusion of the morning light, but the shape continued to move toward the sheep as they mindlessly chewed the dry grass found in the loft's door.

"Husband…" she whispered, "Look to the ri…"

Before she could finish, the white form sprang forward and was on a sheep, snarling, thrashing, and pinning the bleating creature to the ground. It was a second wolf, with fur as white as the snow around it. The remaining sheep fled right into the path of the gray wolf, who only then leapt from behind the tufts of grass into their frightened midst. The two wolves easily overpowered their prey while the rest fled across the open field.

Fulk furrowed his brow, but instead of loosing his arrow, he relaxed his draw on the string.

"The White Lady…" he whispered solemnly. "It is her right."

Gisla gazed across the snow and breathed, "He must be her mate."

"Never have I seen her in another's company," replied Fulk softly.

For some moments they had watched the wolves at their work until suddenly Fulk called out across the cold, white expanse.

"Lady!" he called.

The white wolf de Hambie plucked her ears and stared uncertainly across the open field. The gray wolf looked at her, then across the fields, and then motioned as if to flee. When she did not move with him, he lingered in the tufts of grass at the side of the loft. Fulk dismounted, handing Hardelle's reins to Gisla. He walked forward fifty paces and called to her again.

"Lady!"

With shy hesitation she slowly padded toward Fulk as he walked toward her. Her head was down and wary, and her muzzle was still red with blood and flesh. As they grew near, perhaps ten paces apart, they each instinctively paused and looked back, the wolf towards her mate, and Fulk towards Gisla. Gisla knew in wordless thought that it was a time of greeting and a time of parting. She slid from her saddle and draped the reins on a branch. As one, she and the great gray wolf hesitantly walked across the snow.

He was a beautiful beast with a blue merle muzzle. She could see the anxiety and distrust on his face, and she fully knew his confusion. Never had she been close enough to such a creature as to read its eyes and sense its mind. In her and Fulk existed the gray wolf's only fear and only enemy.

The air was silent and chill, and the sun, nearing its zenith, allowed all four to see even the smallest details in brightest clarity. Though Gisla came all the way to her husband's elbow, the gray wolf remained behind a few paces with his ears flattened, sniffing the air and furtively glancing in all directions.

Fulk knelt in the snow and extended his hand.

"Remain still," he cautioned. "Do not mistake her for a tame beast."

The white wolf first sniffed and then gently licked his outstretched hand. Then she came near enough to Gisla to take in her scent. For a moment the wolf considered them both, and then stretched her muzzle up to Fulk's cheek, gently nuzzling him.

"I am happy for you," he whispered in her ear as he gently caressed her neck. "I am glad you are happy for me."

The gray wolf whined to his mate in warning, who then returned to his side. For just another moment the two couples considered each other, and then the wolves turned and loped their way into the forest beyond the loft.

Gisla reached for her husband's hand and said sadly, "I feel as though she has released you to me. I feel as though she is saying goodbye."

Fulk turned to Gisla and smiled somberly. "Though it was Gaspard and I who saved her all those years ago, nursing her through the winter and making her whole, we have always been her pups. Perhaps now that we are grown, she can bear a litter of her own. If only Gaspard could see her now, he would glad of heart."

"Yes…" said Gisla vaguely, though she possessed an uneasy suspicion that an emotion other than joy would be in the heart of her husband's squire.

CHAPTER 5

The Minstrel's Tale

The events of the following few years, while certainly worthy of a tall tale or two themselves, were all in a day's work for Fulk and Gaspard. Duke Richard, so impressed with Sir Fulk's skill on horseback, charged the mighty baron with training the best men of the Norman suzerain. The mounted force was soon called into battle. Prince Henry I and Prince Robert III of France rebelled against their father, King Robert the Wise, a matter of extreme and bloody delicacy for the nobles of France and Normandy. Fulk and Gaspard also rode with the duke's son, Richard III, against Hugues de Chalon to free the duke's kidnapped son-in-law, Reginald. Poor Chalon suffered more than a little violence as punishment for Hugues's daring disregard for the duke's authority.

To hone their skills of war, Gaspard and Fulk often fought alongside one another in tournaments. They came by a simple arrangement where archery would be their one friendly competition. In all others they never entered the same event, and therefore never had to come to blows.

Gaspard commissioned Hambie's smith to temper him a special blade, both long and slender, and with it he became a most feared competitor. While he, in jest, always fought in honor of Hambie's pantler, the matronly Agnes Marie, in his heart every victory was for his master's wife, who never strayed far from his tortured thoughts.

Thirteen months after the wedding Gisla bore Fulk a hale son whom they christened Raymond.

Around the same time Sir Bertrand Ducaen murdered a priest over a matter of taxes, was excommunicated at the behest of Sir Richard, and fled Normandy hours before the duke's army set upon his keep.

It was the following summer of 1026 that Richard II, Duke of Normandy, known as Richard the Fearless, came to his natural end. He was succeeded by his eldest son, Richard III, who had been his right-hand man for the previous seven years. The new duke's younger brother, Robert, was told to be satisfied with the lesser title of count of Hiemois.

This did not sit well with Robert, who promptly invaded and occupied Falaise, forcing Richard to surround the city and procure his surrender. Through negotiations, the brothers appeared to make peace and they ordered a large celebration…at which Duke Richard III and several other nobles mysteriously died of similar illnesses. It was widely believed the men were poisoned, but Robert moved quickly and spent freely and was made duke of Normandy without any substantive resistance. However, the suspected foul play was the means by which Normandy's duke earned the title Robert the Devil, Duke of Normandy.

Following the death of Richard the Fearless, Cnut, king of England, voided their agreement to make Richard's nephews his heirs. This piqued Robert, who was now seemingly stuck providing for his cousins forever, so he organized a fleet, much like his father's, and set about invading England. In a strange twist of fate Robert's fleet was also caught in a storm and forced to return to Normandy, landing his army on their southern coast.

As raising an army was a costly venture, Robert opted to turn his invasion force against the Bretons, coming to the aid of Norman forces engaged in battle against his cousin, Alan, Count of Brittany. Alan's thinly veiled ambitions prickled Robert, who was obliged to remind him the rule of Normandy would not be easily obtained. The plunder more than covered the cost of his failed English adventure.

Then came nearly two years of calm and peaceable living. Aside from aiding the duke in putting down the rebellious sons of Baldwin, Count of

Flanders, there was little to excite these men of action. The summers were long, the crops plentiful, winters mild, and the men de Hambie grew bored and restless.

It was a dark and stormy night in late February when at the gate of the Castle de Hambie arrived two rain-soaked wayfarers. The rain had fallen without respite for six days, leaving the river Sienne swollen and the lane along its bank an impassable bog. Fulk's dogs were restless in the kennel, his falcons lethargic in their coop, and horses dull and sleeping in the stables. Fulk himself paced about the castle like a caged beast, irritable and meddlesome. His pantler, Agnes Marie, chased him from the kitchen where he was looming over her shoulder while she and the kitchen staff worked on the evening meal.

Gisla, her ladies-in-waiting, Isabelle and Clothilde, and her tire-woman, Jacqueline, were entertaining themselves in her bower working on a tapestry. From behind the door, Fulk could hear their chatting and giggling and was far too proud to enter in hopes of being entertained. Gaspard, taken with one of his dark moods, was locked in his chambers writing what Fulk presumed to be some glum bit of poetry. Even young Raymond, now all of five years of age, was indisposed as brother Carthusian was teaching him his letters.

He snuck into the buttery, absconded a small keg of ale, and wandered through the rain to the castle's barracks near the main gate. There he found four of his men keeping boredom at bay by means of arm wrestling, throwing knives at a sturdy oak beam at the center of the room, and trading stories. Glad they were to share a few pints and elevate the spirits of their lord, who promptly bested them all in strength of arm. When the guard from the main gate burst through the door, announcing that a man naming himself Raoul de St. Pair had arrived in the company of a minstrel, Fulk leapt up and rushed to the gate, mindless of the storm.

As part of the larger structure, there was a small door with a tiny window to allow individuals entry to the keep without going to the trouble of unbarring and fully opening the main gate. Fulk peered through the window and called out to the shadowy horsemen standing in the rain outside Hambie's barbican.

"Raoul, my old friend, is it really you?" he yelled into the rain.

"Yes, milord, 'tis I! Still flesh and blood after all these years!" laughed the rider from beneath his hood.

Fulk turned and called to his men, "Open the gate at once! Come on, be quick about it."

The men laid hold of the crossbars, lifted them, and then pulled the heavy oak and iron portal inward. The two horsemen entered the bailey, rivulets of water running from their cloaks and the flanks of their mounts.

"You look worse than two drowned cats!" exclaimed Fulk through the downpour with a laugh. "My men will tend to your horses and bring your bags. Come with me, and I will see you in dry clothes and with hot, spiced wine in your hand before the next clap of thunder!"

The three men dashed along the cobbled path through the bailey to main entrance to the tower. Bursting into the entry, Fulk called out for Old Rupert, who, aged as he was, was busy refilling and lighting the lamps and candles of the great hall.

"Yes, milord. Coming, milord. As quick as these old bones can manage," he called as he approached bearing a lantern and a long brass candle lighter. "Why master Fulk has brought visitors! The young masters are drenched! Oh my, let Old Rupert get you out of those wet things and into something warm and dry. Oh my, come with me right off. Agnes!" he yelled toward the kitchen in his rough old voice. "Agnes Marie, call Naper!" he paused and smiled at the travelers with his watery eyes, "Now you young masters just come with me, and I will have you right as rain faster than a scared hare runs. Oh my!"

Fulk gave a great belly laugh and said, "We will engage proper introductions after your needs have been seen to. From the smells of my kitchen combined with welcome and unexpected company, I suspect repast will be quite lively tonight!"

Raoul withdrew his hand from his wet glove and grasped Fulk's hand with firm gratitude, "Well met, old friend, well met!"

Rupert herded the two wayfarers, like a hen tending chicks, away from the tower entry to the keep's interior. Fulk, like a hound off the leash and after the fox, ran first to Gaspard's quarters then to Gisla's bower demanding everyone dress as fit for guests coming to dine, as he had a surprise in store for the evening meal. In the time it took to turn a page, Hambie awoke from its winter slumber.

The great hall de Hambie was part of the castle's original construction. It was a grand space with a lofted ceiling supported by four heavy oak rafters hailing from the early days of the Northmen. The rafters sat atop massive supporting oak pillars, blackened by years of smoke and flame from lamps and torches. Carved into the pillars and rafters were depictions of the gods and mythical creatures once precious to Fulk's great and violent people.

The graven images of the wolves Freke and Gere, the ravens Hugin and Munin, the fates Urd, Verdani, and Skuld, and the Valkyries all lent their ancient strength to Hambie's lords. Into each beam's boss was carved a godly face common to the halls of Valhalla, eternal guests at a now Christian table. There were the handsome Baldur, Forseti, Heimdall, and the thundering Thor on the side of good. There were the murderous Fenris Ulf, Garm, Loki, and the goddess of pestilence, Hel, on the side of evil. They stared across the hall at one another, all under the watchful eye of Odin, whose face was carved into the stone above Hambie's great hearth. These graven images, so near the castle's chapel adorned with Christ crucified and his saintly parents, existed now only to mourn the loss of their power over men.

The hall's stone floor was strewn with dry reeds and straw. Down its middle was a rough-hewn, sturdy oak table with its accompanying benches, marred by decades of rough use by hearty Norman warriors. On the dais, between the end of the main table and the hearth, sat the lord's table laid with a linen cloth and Hambie's best silver. The hearth was massive and a room unto itself. It held a heavy iron grate that supported flaming logs six feet in length over a great bed of red, hissing coals. It was the central heat for the keep's main tower. Its stones were thick and heavy, and would provide warmth for hours after the fire went cold. Ornate tapestries, some ancient and some new, lined the north wall telling the stories of the lords de Hambie since the days of William Longsword. Displays of shields and swords adorned the south wall, and crossed spears leaned against the wall on either side of the hearth.

The room was lit by oil lamps attached to the walls, two chandeliers suspended from the rafters, and several candelabras on both tables. During the days of fair weather, six tall, narrow windows in the south wall, two between each oak pillar, allowed the light of day entry. Now they stood tightly shuttered against the darkness, wind, and rains of winter.

Much to his kitchen staff's distress, Fulk ordered their simple evening meal be changed to a feast for the house. Master Josue, Thomas, Rupert, brother Carthusian, Agnes Marie, and Jacqueline were invited to sit with Gaspard, Isabelle, and Clothilde at the main table while Fulk and Gisla sat with the two guests at their table. By the time Rupert returned with the travelers, bathed and well mended in fresh, dry clothing, all were gathered in the great hall awaiting their introduction. Only young Raymond was absent, already tucked into his bed and lulled to sleep by his nurse.

Rupert finally reappeared in the company of the two guests. The first, much shorter than Fulk and Gaspard, was a lean-built man perhaps in his late twenties. His twinkling blue eyes brightened his chiseled, weathered face. While his hands were strong and confident in appearance, they were also clean and well cared for. His brown locks spilled down to his shoulders, and his beard was trimmed and thick. His companion, while older and balding, had a much fairer, rounder face. Though taller, he was more slightly built than the first. His ease of smile, deep-set brown eyes, and clean-shaven face were trusting and unassuming. His hands were clean with slender, soft fingers. Over his shoulder he carried an oblong protective case made of wood, in which he stored his lute.

Rupert cleared his throat.

"To the Lady Gisla, the Lord Fulk, and all the household de Hambie, I would like to introduce our two most honored and talented guests, Sir Raoul de St. Pair and the minstrel Aymer de Cangé."

"Welcome to the house de Hambie," said Fulk with a smile as the men bowed to the group. He stepped forward and firmly extended his hand in greeting. One by one, Fulk introduced his household. The men shook hands, and the women curtsied while extending their hands to be kissed. A servant then directed Raoul and Aymer to sit at the lord's table, where they were given a bowl of warm water to dip their hands. Once Fulk, Gisla, Raoul and Aymer had been seated, the others washed their hands and sat, women first, then the men.

The servants brought out a generous repast, served on hard bread trenchers for the main table and on silver plates for the lord's. The wine, meat, and bread were generous, and the tubers with onions, sauced with meat drippings, were particularly satisfying. A fresh wheel of cheese was produced and divided among the tables, and the conversation was alive with pleasantries.

"I do believe we last met at your wedding!" laughed Raoul.

"And you promised to soon follow in my steps," replied Fulk. "And yet here you are, a bachelor as ever."

"Never the right time or the right woman," said Raoul as his eyes wandered to Isabelle sitting next to Gaspard.

Isabelle was a bright and fair woman, open and full of life and curiosity. Her fair hair and gray eyes were a contrast to her quieter, darker sister, Clothilde. Her physical beauty was set afire by her enthusiasm for life. She noted Raoul's gaze and met his eyes without fear or shame.

"Methinks milord has a greater story to tell his hosts," she stated assuredly. "I, for one, am far too excited to hear of your adventures, what exactly brought you to our door, to engage in any more small talk—even if it is of marriage!"

A wide-eyed smile crossed Raoul's face, and he laughed aloud.

"Hear, hear!" seconded Master Josue. "I smell an adventure for sure."

"In agreement," confirmed Fulk, "I do believe, now that you are warm and well fed, your stories are in order."

Raoul, still taking in the visage of Isabelle, took a deep breath.

"Our story is long, and it is mostly my companion's to tell," he began. "These past three years I have been on a most secret and sensitive mission in the name of Duke Robert. I secretly entered England on business I cannot disclose here, and was much traveled. While I was partly successful in my purpose, ultimately I was betrayed by a beggar-of-a-man, Ranoldo le Varkan. I was forced to flee once my identity was compromised, and only through good fortune found passage back to Normandy. My solace was in receiving the news Ranoldo was promptly murdered by the other side following my escape, as he was no longer of any use to them. Once his deceit and betrayal was revealed, none trusted him, and he had nowhere to turn for protection.

"The voyage from England during the winter is perilous at the best of times. It cost me some generous coin to find a captain of fishing vessel brave enough to risk his boat and his life to give me passage. It was fortunate I purchased a good and honorable man in the process. We left from a village near Brycgstow, and while the wind was wicked cold, it was southwesterly in its course. All went well, God be praised, and in several days time we found ourselves approaching the west coast of Jersey in the evening."

"Jersey?" remarked Fulk, "That is the den of the dreaded pirate known as 'the Dragon.' Local merchants and fisherman avoid the island's shore if they value their goods and their lives."

"As strange as this may sound, it was fortunate that in my years in England I missed out on such news, and my captain only fished his own waters and was unaware of our peril. As darkness was falling, we decided to run his vessel up on the beach and camp for the night and make the last push for Coutances the next day.

"The surf of the bay was mild, so we tacked against the wind and landed at the north end of the western beach. We disembarked, secured a line, and then set about building a fire to warm ourselves. It was my experience that the natives of the island kept to themselves and we should go unmolested. But to our surprise, out of the thicket burst a filthy, ragged man of a most desperate nature, eyes wild with fear. 'Put out your fire or you will be seen,' he begged miserably. Of course we were taken off our guard. I leapt to my feet. 'Calm yourself, man,' I said. Ignoring me completely, he began kicking sand on our fire. Of course I accosted him, and being the stronger man, quickly wrestled him to the ground."

"You also punched me bloody, as I recall," interjected Aymer.

"Well, yes, but you were quite mad at the moment," retorted Raoul, "and since this is my part of the tale, so do me the courtesy of waiting to make your minor corrections.

"As I was saying, I took him down and restrained him, perhaps knocking his head about to bring him to his senses. Once under control, he insisted we set sail immediately and take him with us. He said the Dragon would be upon us at any moment and we must flee. Of course talk of a dragon excited me, for I had only heard of them in legend and never truly seen one. I was about to buckle on my sword and have our new found madman show me to its lair. It was then he informed me the Dragon was instead a pirate and scourge of channel for near three years. He and his murderous lot came from the Mediterranean and created a fortress in the caves of Jersey. They stationed guards all about the island to keep a watch on the shore and to keep the natives in fear. The ragged man, who now sits before you, called himself Aymer, and he had just escaped the Dragon's clutches. His captors were combing the island in search of him at that very moment. If we did not set sail now, we would surely be captured, tortured, and killed.

"It was then I noticed the raw and bloody ring about his right ankle right above his tattered boot, the telltale mark of a fetter. My captain and I looked at each other in horror. We quickly doused the fire and flung our gear back into the boat. The tide was receding at that moment, and had we been ashore much longer we would have had a devil of a time getting the craft afloat. Aymer helped me push the boat out into the surf while the captain worked the halyard and raised sail. And none too soon! As we pulled ourselves into the boat and manned the oars, we saw a line of men carrying torches coming down from the rocks just to the north of our position. The frigid wind filled our sail and we fled the bay in the nick of time. We quickly disrobed from our wet tunics and wrapped up in the captain's rough wool blankets."

"That stank of rotted fish, mind you," added Aymer with a laugh.

Here Raoul paused, took a deep breath, and finished, "Once warmed and grateful for both the escape and the thick blanket, Aymer began his story," he nodded to his friend, who then cleared his throat.

"The good captain sat at the tiller and securely guided his vessel through the dark waters, only occasionally needing to check the night sky to gauge our direction. It was my good fortune Raoul had in his possession something stronger than wine for me to warm myself with. After a bit of food and drink, I fell to the story of how I came to be on the island," Aymer started.

"My name is Aymer de Cangé. I am a minstrel. I earn my living through my words, songs, and music. I am a master of many instruments, but prefer the lute to accompany my songs and my travels. Many of the nobles of France have enjoyed my voice, and I have found steady employment for most of my life. My last employer was a noble who owned a manor on the Mediterranean coast near Marseilles. It was a wonderful life filled with excellent wine, warm days, beautiful women, and olives. I do love olives! Then in one glorious summer night of terror it was all gone. My lord was entertaining a number of his wealthy friends, and the party had gone on to a late hour. The wine was good and plentiful, and everyone was many flagons into our host's supply. Many of the drunken partygoers fell asleep on my lord's couches, right there on the veranda overlooking the sea. The air was warm and fragrant, and I had performed well for many hours.

"Then suddenly there was screaming and yelling and the sounds of slaughter from all around us. Fierce pirates, brandishing swords and axes, came screaming in from the darkness on all sides. Some of my lord's men-at-arms put up a fight, but they were cut down by a great beast of a man with flowing black hair and cropped beard—a man I soon came to know as '*the Dragon*.' All was fear and confusion. When the pirates came upon me, their blades soaked in blood, I just stood there holding my lute and shaking. Surely I was going to die right there in the flickering light of the paper lanterns, and I was terrified.

"But then the man with the flowing black hair and cropped beard stopped, looked me up and down, and smiled quite pleasantly...though despite the curve of his lip, his gray eyes were cold and heartless. 'Play me a tune,' he asked in a quiet voice. I obliged him, though my hands shook as I plucked the strings. 'Sing a bit, please,' he asked. So I sang, though my voice was dry and cracked, and I could still hear cries of anguish coming from the shadows about the villa. 'You are quite good,' he remarked. 'I wager after a good night's sleep, you will be quite excellent.' Then he turned to one of his men and barked, 'Bring him!'

"To fully describe the scene, I believe would offend the delicate nature of the present ladies, so I shall be brief in this part of my story. The manor house and its occupants were stripped clean of valuables. Gold, jewels, books, tapestries, fine clothes, wines, foodstuffs, and many expensive delicacies. The men, save me, were all dead or fled into the night. Some of the women were violated on the spot and tossed aside. Three of the most beautiful were taken, unmolested, down to Dragon's three longships. We must have been the last in a series of raids, for the ships were already laden with treasure. We were all chained, and by dawn the crew was at the oars and their black sails unfurled. Behind us we could see the thick, billowing smoke of the burning villa rising through the morning air. We sailed along the coast, through the straights, and then north to Jersey. On occasion another pirate vessel would come near our ships, but when the Dragon's men showed their fierceness of arms, the enemy always broke off.

"The maidens and I were treated quite well once at sea, though we started our servitude immediately. I played for the Dragon and was rewarded with decent fare that the captured maidens served us. He was a well-mannered man with a noble and refined character. He enjoyed our conversations and appeared intelligent and thoughtful. He soon revealed his hardness of heart when he confronted one of the poor girls. She was crying miserably about her captivity and the murder of her family. He beat her in front of everyone as an example, then whispered into her ear, 'Your tears defy me. I have no room in my kingdom for this or any other form of rebellion.' She never cried openly again."

Aymer paused, drawing up his cup and letting his eyes wander about upon his rapt audience. His gaze settled upon Gaspard, whose ruddy cheeks now sported the dark beard of a young man. Aymer stared at the young man for a long moment upon which he furrowed his brow, causing the squire some discomfort.

"You have something to say, yes?" challenged Gaspard with a frown.

Aymer quickly looked away and laughed with embarrassment.

"'Tis nothing, milord. My apologies."

The minstrel took another drink of wine and cleared his throat to continue.

"After weeks of sailing we landed at night on an isle that I now know to be Jersey. We were blindfolded, shackled, and marched across the island to a complex of caves that was the Dragon's fortress. I have been in many a lord's keep across this land and have never seen such an immense treasure! There are chests filled with gold and precious stones in stacks next to piles of gold and silver wrought platters, goblets, cups, chalices, bowls, candelabras, scepters, swords, daggers, strings of pearls, tapestries...*and books*! He has books on shelves and in stacks in his great hall, perhaps hundreds of them. It is a library hard to imagine anywhere but in a great city such as Rome, Constantinople, or Alexandria. Certainly not in a pirate's cave.

"Walls and chambers are built within the caves, fresh straw is strewn about the floor, and flowers and herbs are everywhere to scent the air. In some areas there are holes in the ceiling allowing an amount of daylight; in others there are open courtyards built into ravines and pits. As I came to find out over time, the Dragon cultivates crops, has shepherds in the field, and behaves more like the lord of a manor than like a pirate. He even has a number of excellent falcons and hunts them frequently.

"He has lieutenants, navigators, and masters of arms, and trains his men with military efficiency. They are the foulest of men you can imagine! Criminals from England, rebels from France, slavers from Persia and Africa, mercenaries from Greece—all of them murderers and thieves lacking normal human conscience. These are who welcome the worst privations of cold, heat, starvation, and thirst in order to satisfy their own horrible lusts! Only by force of will does the Dragon control his evil lot. They both fear and love him at the same time. They accept his leash, and he ensures they have a seat at the table of the Devil's feast.

"There are also women there, all kidnapped during his murderous raids. He keeps them well fed, well dressed, and in good order, but make no mistake, they are his possessions. As for me, I was allotted a small, lightless prison cell of my own. Fortunately, I spent little time locked within except to sleep, as I was kept busy plying my trade. The Dragon encouraged my play by providing me a number of different instruments to practice with. I was given parchment and ink to compose, and then told to write ballads to celebrate the Dragon's greatness. It is strange to think that after I am dead, someone may read those songs and believe them to be something other than a complete lie."

"How many men do you estimate the Dragon to employ?" asked Fulk.

"I would guess perhaps one or two hundred, possibly more. They crowded into the caves for only the most foul of weather, so I never saw them all in one place. There are men scattered about the island in various hovels or at sea, so it is difficult to say with any accuracy," replied Aymer.

"We fell into an uneasy routine, where a docile manner and held tongue were the easiest route to a peaceable existence. The Dragon would disappear for weeks at a time on raids, always to return laden with treasure and a possibly a slave or two. He would tell about the adventure, and I would compose a song to its remembrance. The women act as maids and servants...and more, at his whim," the minstrel paused briefly, noting the distressed looks upon the rapt women upon this revelation.

"There was even a small amount of trade with a few islanders, though I suspect it was more like extortion than fair trading. On occasion there would be summary executions of pirates who displeased him. Everyone would be summoned to an ancient place they called 'The Fairy's Table,' an ancient stone circle on the eastern side of the island to watch some wretch butchered. The man's guilt was irrelevant. The Dragon killed to remind everyone he could. I was witness to one such killing. I will not call it a murder, for to the last man, all of the Dragon's men deserved death. The guilty man was bound, hand and foot, so tightly he could not move. Then he was thrown across the back of a horse and carried across the island to the Fairy's Table. We were led on a procession following the horse until we arrived at the stone circle."

Aymer paused and looked upon the women. He then cleared his throat, "It was a cruel death...one I will not describe.

"My imprisonment went on for nineteen months as the Dragon further entrenched himself as the 'King of Jersey.' Of course my mind was always on escape, but my options seemed slim. I would have to get free of one of my fetters of which I had two, one that chained me to the wall of my cell and another attached to a heavy ball of iron to slow me when I was out. I would have to elude the pirates. Finally, I would have to find a boat, all of which were well guarded. I did not like my chances.

"Then I received the strangest of deliverances! One night I entertained the Dragon and his lieutenants until they were all soundly drunk and sleeping. The guard, a bony man with bulging eyes they called Newt, retrieved me from the table and prodded me back to my cell. It was a routine I was used to, I in the lead, followed by Newt with a torch and his keys. Newt always stank and had diseased teeth, but reveled in setting things afire, a trait the Dragon enjoyed. Newt pushed me into my cell and was preparing to unlock my fetter when silently, out of the darkness, a man with a clean-shaven, lily-white face and black cape appeared in the passage behind Newt. With one swift motion he drew forth a wicked dagger, slit Newt's throat from behind, and grasped up the torch without making a sound. He raised his finger to his lips, looked gravely at me, and then handed me the torch as Newt gurgled, bubbled, and died.

"The stranger, whose black hair ran in a braid down his back, quickly moved Newt to my pallet and covered him with my blanket. He then unlocked the fetter from my ankle and set the weight and chain aside.

There was a substantial pool of blood on the floor we quickly covered up with straw.

"I was both enthralled and horrified as he calmly cleaned his dagger on the wool of my blanket! It was a strange weapon with runes engraved on the blade and a gold hilt with two wingless serpents entwined about the guard,"

At this description, Gaspard started with surprise and opened his mouth as if to speak. Aymer paused, again piercing Gaspard with his questioning, deep-set eyes.

"'Tis nothing, minstrel, pray continue your tale," Gaspard answered.

Aymer nodded, then went on, "He took the torch and silently beckoned me follow him. 'This is madness!' I thought to myself, 'There are guards everywhere! If I follow this man, I will certainly be caught and butchered at the Fairy's Table.' Yet I followed. We wound through the caverns to the entrance, where we found the guards fast asleep. The stranger simply placed the torch in a bracket in the stone and led me out onto the rocky flints of the small crevasse that led away from the caves. Having spent so much time in the darkness underground, I found it easy to follow him through the night. Once again, no one impeded us, though I am sure guards were at their posts. By what magic we slipped by the Dragon's men, I know not, but I am certain the Dragon executed the entire night watch for allowing my escape.

"Once away, he handed me a cloak and a wallet with food enough for a two days. 'Here, take these,' he said. 'Head west. You will find a boat there by which you can make your escape.' 'Who are you and why do you help me?' I asked. He just smiled thinly in the dark, 'Your release is a gift—take it,' and then he disappeared into the darkness.

"I immediately began making my way in the direction he pointed. I suppose, had I been a woodsman or a huntsman, traveling through the woods and thickets in the dark of night would have been child's play, but at it was, Jersey had great sport with me, tearing my cloak, catching my clothes, and cutting through my thin boots. By dawn I was thoroughly lost, footsore, and exhausted. I cast about for a place to hide, settling on a thicket behind a fallen tree. I burrowed under heavy pile of leaf mold and quickly fell asleep. It was the first sleep out of the cave I had had in more than a year and a half.

"I awoke in the afternoon and emerged from my burrow, blinking against the sun. Devilishly hungry, I opened the wallet and found hard bread, cheese, and two bruised apples. I made quick work of about half the contents and then stood to get my bearings. Whatever lead I had on my captors was likely gone, and they could just as well have been in front of me as behind me. With this in mind, I moved slowly, keeping in thickets and shadowy crevasses as much as possible. Occasionally I smelled the smoke of a fire, perhaps a village or hut, but managed to avoid these places and not be seen. Eventually I came to a stream that went in a southwesterly direction and I followed it until it emptied into a large shallow bay. I could see miles of open sand in either direction, but no sign of a boat anywhere. I made my way first south, keeping in the brush, searching for the boat the stranger promised I would find. By dark I was at the southwest tip of the island, but no boat presented itself. I ate a bit, and then hid for another long, cold night.

"The following day I worked my way northward along the same stretch of beach. A few times I saw or heard some of the Dragon's men but managed to avoid them. Jersey is a big place for so few men to search, even with the aid of islanders. By early afternoon I found myself at the northwest end of the bay and still no boat to be found. I was expecting something dragged up on the beach or hidden in the bushes, but there was nothing but the seaweed the islanders called vraic and driftwood. I began to despair. It was a certainty the pirates would blame me for Newt's murder. I began imagining all sorts of horrible ways the Dragon could put me to death. I thought myself a fool for following the stranger. I should have shouted an alarm and warned the pirates and saved myself. At least the Dragon kept me warm and fed. Now I was cold and hungry and facing death from every direction. Likely even a reward for my capture! I ate the rest of my food and sat hidden in the scrub and watched what I believe to be my last sunset as a free man, and perhaps my last on this earth."

Again Aymer paused to take a long drink of wine. He stared into the fire merrily roaring in Hambie's great hearth.

"As I watched the sun setting I noted a small vessel heading toward my position. I naturally assumed it was someone on pirate business, but continued to watch from my hiding place. The boat had only two men aboard. They broke through the surf and ran the craft up on the beach. Imagine my surprise when they made camp and built a fire within a stone's throw from me. They would have every pirate within a mile on us in an instant! If they did not see the boat land, they were certain to see the fire. What fools! Of course it turned out to be Raoul and his captain.

"It was then I lost my head and crashed through brush and accosted them, attempting to put out the fire. After a bit of an unneeded tussle where Raoul needlessly struck me, I was able to plead my case. Thankfully, the good fellows moved quickly and we pushed off and made for Coutances with all speed.

"I know not whether Raoul's boat appeared by simple chance, or if my liberator used some mysticism to divine their coming and then set me free in time to make my escape. While it leaves me troubled, I do thank God for my freedom."

With that he leaned back in his chair and stared into the fire.

"I agree," sustained Master Josue. "How could any man have known Raoul would have landed at that place at that hour?"

"'Tis queer, indeed," continued Fulk. "Almost too strange to be mere coincidence."

"Jersey belongs to the duke of Normandy!" interjected Gisla. "How is it a man such as the Dragon can so easily thwart his will?"

"The Dragon certainly galls Sir Robert. He sent a small expedition to oust him last summer," replied Fulk. "They were never heard from again."

"I do recall a time of great military excitement last summer," affirmed Aymer. "I believe your duke's men were defeated upon landing and executed. And in answer to the lady's question, Jersey falls within the diocese of the bishop of Coutances. The bishop is well paid to turn a blind eye and ignore the Dragon's doings. In return, the Dragon largely leaves Normandy alone."

"What is that you say?" exclaimed Fulk. "The bishop Robert is a traitor to the duke?"

"As God is my witness, milord," replied Aymer, "I overheard the Dragon discuss the tribute with his lieutenants several times."

"Such a betrayal will not go unpunished!" growled Fulk. "The dukes of Normandy have put many resources into the rebuilding of Coutances in recent years. The bishop will regret this choice for the rest of his days!"

CHAPTER 6

The Dragon Revealed

For the remainder of the evening Aymer entertained the house with his songs, stories, and legends of yore. All too soon the fire of the great hall burned low, and the party disbanded in favor of their beds. Gaspard, the last to leave the hall, fetched a hot ember from the hearth and placed it in a clay pot. He made his way back to his quarters, intent on lighting his brazier against the cold, wet winter night. Rupert was making his rounds, snuffing out the candles and lamps. Gisla and Fulk had retired to their shared bed. Gaspard found himself, lamp in one hand and pot in the other, walking the halls alone. The minstrel's tale was most fascinating, and he mulled over its meaning and ramifications.

He entered his room, closed the door, and cast his cloak aside. He put flame to his candles and set his lamp on the table. He set the burning ember in the bottom of his brazier and carefully laid several pieces of sea-coal over it. He placed the brazier under the crude flue he had constructed beneath his window to carry some of the smoke to the outside.

The soft squeal of a floorboard emanating from his shadowy bed-chamber alerted Gaspard to the presence of an uninvited guest. Without so much as a flinch, Gaspard straightened and called out softly, "Good evening, Gregar. How went your travels from Jersey?"

A shadowed form stepped into the doorway and pulled back his cowl. A slightly built man with thin bloodless lips, black eyes, ghostly white skin, and long black, braided hair stepped forward with a smile. The intruder was indeed the mystic, Gregar Penscalus.

"It was a success," he replied, mildly surprised at the question.

Gregar had not neglected Gaspard over the years, secretly visiting Hambie on a number of occasions to give council and shore up the young squire's resolve. Always arriving in the dark of night when Gaspard's despair was at its tortured heights, he would sooth and reassure the young squire that deliverance from his spiritual anguish would soon be at hand.

Here he was met with the broad smile and quick embrace of his young disciple.

"Sir Penscalus, my old friend, you are always most unexpected and most welcome!" Gaspard kept his voice low, "As always, evading all detection. Are you ready to tell me your method of coming and going?"

"That is for another day," said Gregar with his usual odd smile. "However, I am curious, myself as to how you divined my recent travels."

"Your dagger is as rare as your serpent's ring," confessed Gaspard. "It caught the minstrel's eye when you slew his jailor."

"Ah, yes."

"And divining the arrival of Raoul's boat is a trick few can perform. The real question is why? How do these threads tie together? What has this minstrel's tale to do with me that you were there and now are here?"

"You always have been one impatient for clarity," chuckled Gregar, taking a chair near the brazier and holding his hands out to its growing warmth.

"I have suffered my place for nearly six years, and you call me impatient," argued Gaspard. "I have lived in the shadow of a tree of forbidden fruit, seeing its sweetness yet unable to taste. They have a son, a testimony to their love and an heir to the barony! I have endured this solely at your behest. Yes, I want clarity. I have earned clarity!"

Gaspard pulled the stopper from the flagon of wine sitting on his table, poured two cups, and then pulled up a chair and sat across from Gregar, offering him the drink. The mystic held up a refusing hand and did not take the wine, causing Gaspard to smile slightly.

"One day you will break from your disciplines and share a cup with me," said the squire seriously.

"Perhaps," replied Gregar with a shrug. "Though it be a small thing to set your heart on."

Gregar paused and leaned back in his chair.

"What do you know of the Dragon?" asked the mystic.

"He is a murderous Mediterranean pirate who began haunting the channel about three years past. He is reputed to have a well-defended fortress on Jersey from where he launches his expeditions. Wilder tales claim he is in league with the Devil and can change into the form of a great flying serpent. By the minstrel's account, he is also fabulously wealthy and well-bred, and has declared himself the king of Jersey."

"How did the minstrel describe him?"

"Tall, powerful, with cold gray eyes and black hair and a thick beard," puzzled Gaspard. "Why?"

"A portrait of Bertrand Ducaen, no?"

The revelation left Gaspard slack-jawed and staring at Gregar.

"After fleeing Normandy, he licked his wounds and turned to piracy. He now seeks new alliances to satisfy all his old grudges," continued the mystic.

"And he despises Sir Fulk…" breathed Gaspard, "and also me, to a lesser part."

"He will attempt to rally the enemies of the duke. He wants rebellion and bloodshed, and has the gold to purchase the loyalty of many men."

"The duke must be warned against this!"

"And he will be. Do as I say, and your lord will see to it…and more, I wager!" commanded Gregar.

The storm broke overnight, and the following morning sunlight streamed into the great hall as the fire roared in the hearth. Sir Fulk, lady Gisla, and little Raymond broke their fast early with Raoul and Aymer at the table. The stories were as light as the sweet cakes the cook served fresh from the oven. The house de Hambie, glad for respite from the rain, was bustling with their many chores. The huntsman ran the dogs while Fulk and Raoul agreed it was a fine day for loosing the falcons. With little Raymond upon Raoul's shoulders, Fulk led Raoul, Aymer, and Gaspard across the bailey to the coop.

Fulk donned a heavy leather gauntlet and retrieved a hooded peregrine from the enclosure. Likewise, Gaspard soothed and took up his faithful lanner. From there they went to the stables where four fine horses were saddled and waiting. With Raymond sitting before his father, the hunting party trotted out the main gate and down through the orchard. It was a leisurely ride past rows of skeletal grape vines and along the edge of the wheat field to the meadow beyond. After so many days of rain, they were all eager to feel the sun against their faces.

As they rode, Gaspard engaged Aymer in conversation.

"As I recall, you mentioned the Dragon has black hair and a beard," he commented.

"Yes, he keeps his beard clipped, much like your own, though your locks are a bit straighter."

"And gray eyes?"

"Cruel and heartless, like the cold before a winter storm."

The men reach a rocky hillock with a good view of the surrounding fields and forest. They dismounted, and Raoul set little Raymond upon a rock while Fulk removed the peregrine's hood, launching him to the sky.

"Pray indulge me and describe the man's features," continued Gaspard.

"He is a handsome man with a clean complexion. No scars or pocks of any kind. His nose is straight and has features, once again, very like your own," replied Aymer thoughtfully.

"And what of his height?"

"He is a tall man, though not as tall as Lord Fulk. Perhaps your height with Fulk's girth. He is a physically powerful man."

"You mentioned he carries himself like a man of noble birth."

"'Tis true. He is well spoken and has refined tastes. I believe he engages in some amount of legitimate trade to obtain his luxuries when he is unable to plunder them."

The Peregrine had attained the heavens and began circling far and wide in search of prey. The conversation idled while the men considered the grace of the powerful bird.

"What of the man's character?" pursued Gaspard.

"While he can be courteous and demurred, it is all quite calculated. He has not love, only lust and cruelty. He often rages when he drinks heavily."

Fulk's bird of prey spotted movement, tucked his wings, and dropped like a rock from the sky, speeding toward the earth. The men cheered as he thrashed among the tussocks and then launched himself skyward with either a rabbit or hare in his clutches. Fulk tossed little Raymond onto his back and with Raoul sprinted across the meadows towards the forest's edge where the peregrine had come to rest. Aymer and Gaspard remained on the hillock with the lanner and awaited their return.

Then it was the lanner's turn to take flight. Gaspard removed her hood and released her to the sky. Her wings, sure and powerful, beat the crisp air as she climbed high into the heavens. He then returned to his query of Aymer.

"It is said the Dragon came to Jersey from the Mediterranean. Does his accent give any clue as to from where he hails?"

A puzzled look came across Aymer's face.

"Why, I had not thought of it till just now. He and several of his lieutenants speak with the same tongue as you! How peculiar that they are men of Normandy."

This final comment drew Fulk's full attention.

"What is this? The Dragon is a Norman lord? This cannot be!" he said sternly.

"What's more, milord," said Gaspard with a frown, "the man he describes bears all signs of being Bertrand Ducaen. I puzzled over it as I retired last night, and Aymer confirms it can be no other man."

"The Devil take him! These are ill tidings for the duke, a secret pact between Ducaen and the bishop. They will have many powerful allies. This unholy alliance makes the bishop of Coutances's treason doubly evil!" Fulk raged.

"Fulk, you must come away with me to see the duke immediately!" interjected Raoul, "He values your council and your loyalty, and I believe rebellion may be afoot. If Ducaen has even half the treasure Aymer tells of, he has amassed enough gold to hire an army. Will you make the journey with me to give the duke these ill tidings?"

"We will leave on the morrow!" stated Fulk.

The lanner folded her wings and dove into a copse of trees. Gaspard looked with satisfaction upon the scene.

CHAPTER 7

The First Dream

He left the highway and walked along the dusty lane. The cloudless sky possessed only a muted light. To his left a low stone wall separated him from a tilled field of young greens. To his right a thin row of silver birch broke the wind for the open fields. He knew what lay at the end of the lane—a cottage and a girl. The longing pained him.

The wall ended at a broken gate. A path ran to the cottage. She stood by the door in the still, dry air. The pale green fabric of her dress was so thin it revealed the white linen gown beneath. He felt ashamed, for her belly was swollen with child. He came to make it right.

He barely noticed her feet were bare, for he was lost in her somber eyes. Her glowing, flaxen locks spilled about her shoulders and down her back. She stepped toward him and he moved to take her hands. Her sad radiance washed over him. He knew he loved her. He would never hurt her. He could not confess, yet penance he offered.

From behind her, the girl's gaunt, old father appeared from within the cottage. His breeches and tunic were ill fitting and his jerkin soiled. His hair and beard were grizzled gray, and his eyes were afire.

"How *dare* you come here!" The father pointed a bent, accusing finger. "Be gone, bastard!"

He stood still, confused, and torn. She withdrew her hands and looked away. A single tear trickled down her cheek. Though powerful of arm he was powerless. A sword appeared in the father's hand to accompany the rage in his eyes.

"My daughter you shall not have, bastard!" threatened the father. "Leave here or I will kill you!"

He reached for his own sword, but found only a limp leather strap in his hand. By vain force of will, he attempted to make it stiffen and act as a weapon, but it simply dangled in his grasp. The father raised the sword and pulled the girl behind him. Two angry sons, both with swords, appeared from the fields.

"Be gone, evildoer!"

"Gisla, I am sorry for what must be," he said.

The girl turned her back and vanished into the cottage. The father, Albric de Grentmesnel, glared with damning eyes and pointed the sword menacingly. Gaspard weakly left the yard and walked the lane back to the highway. Gulls cried.

Gulls cried. Graceful and aggressive. The small fishing boat dipped and rolled as it sliced through the waves, driven before a brisk channel breeze. Gaspard awoke from his dream. It was just dawn. He lay upon the fisherman's nets under a blanket at the bottom of the foresheet.

"Now that you are awake, good sir," commented the fisherman, "perhaps I could throw in my nets to add some profit in my service to the duke?"

"Keep your course straight and true with no delays," retorted Gaspard with irritation.

The fisherman's boy sat, blue lipped, at the tiller, impatient for the rising sun to warm his shivering bones.

"Boy, come warm yourself with these blankets," ordered Gaspard, "I will take a turn at the stern there."

He wrapped the shivering lad in the rough wool, tousled his hair, and took up the rudder's lever.

"Meaning no disloyalty to Sir Robert, but this little boat is life to my family," commented the rough, leathery fisherman. "Making the run to Jersey is a fool's errand. Even if we manage to navigate the rocks and shoals and make the beach, the Dragon will likely chain us to a rock at the first low tide."

"I have faith in your skill as a seaman," replied Gaspard grimly, "and I will guarantee your safety once we make land."

"Well, I won't have it be said I refused to do my duty to my liege," sighed the fisherman, "but if God grants us a miracle and we return unharmed from your quest, I will give the one fifth of my spring catch to the convent in return." He performed the sign of the cross and looked to the heavens.

As the sun rose, the boy turned his face and welcomed its warmth. Baiting a hook, he tossed a line off the stern.

"I like to tease the birds," he said simply.

The line, baited with a bit of dry fish, dragged behind the boat, floating and skipping along the surface of the sea. The noisy gulls, whom had been following and circling the boat expectantly, soon spotted the floating morsel. They dove at the water's surface and the boy jerked the line. The bait leapt out of the bird's grasp and the boy cried with laughter. He let out the line again and another of the gulls dove for the floating bit of dried fish. Again the boy jerked the line, squealing joyously as the gull was left with only a bill full of salt water and a confused face. The simplicity of his happiness brought a smile to Gaspard, washing away the unease of his dream. The game continued until a crafty and most unfortunate bird anticipated the boy's trick and caught the baited hook as the boy jerked the line. With a good tug, the boy lodged the point of the hook through the roof of struggling gull's bill and out its nostril.

"Pull it in, boy!" ordered the fisherman. "Save my hook and let it go. Gulls are poor eating."

With a practiced hand the boy pulled the panicked and struggling gull across the water and to the boat's quarter. Quick and sure, he landed the unruly thing and removed the hook.

"Away with you, you beggar of a thief!" chortled the boy as he stood and launched the gull skyward.

"You have the practiced hand of a true falconer," observed Gaspard.

The boy beamed with the compliment as Jersey's eastern coastline loomed in the distance.

Sir Robert, Duke of Normandy, had raged upon hearing the news brought by his vassals, Fulk Paynel and Raoul de St. Pair. That some minor pirate had taken up residence on Jersey was an irritation undeserving his full attention. That the pirate was none other than an enemy long thought banished was cause for grave consideration. That the bishop of Coutances was in league with said pirate was an outrage.

The duke's first impulse was to launch a full-scale invasion of Jersey while arresting the bishop.

"But there will be no guarantee of capturing Ducaen, himself," cautioned Fulk, "and they may have allies who forewarn the bishop, allowing his escape."

"You have a plan?" inquired the duke as he paced about the chamber.

"My squire, whose counsel I value as highly as any man's, considered the matter with Raoul and I at length as we traveled here to your court. An invasion of Jersey could prove costly in both men and financial resources. Resources better served by other uses.

"As we considered, there may be one man whom Ducaen despises more than yourself. A man who robbed him of glory both on the field of honor and at the altar. A man against whom Ducaen is desperate to redeem his honor."

"You speak of yourself," Robert's eyes narrowed.

"Verily! Send my man, Gaspard, to Jersey with my challenge of single combat. Ducaen always felt he was robbed when we jousted. I will offer him the chance finish what we started those many years ago. To the death! I will cut the head off of this Dragon and bring it to you. Then as I rally my men and set sail to attack his rabble, you will confront the bishop with no less than the head of your enemy."

"And if you fail?"

"You will have lost little for the gamble."

"None besides your squire are to know of this intrigue," warned Robert.

Raoul and Fulk swore themselves to secrecy, both kissing their liege's ring. Gaspard was secretly dispatched for the west coast of Normandy to procure transport to the island. The duke, under pretext of a hunting and falconry trip to the estuary of the river Sienne, organized his most loyal retinue and departed his court in Caen. The bishop could hardly refuse his invitation to join in such noble sport! Fulk and the duke's agent would rendezvous with Gaspard in Coutances. All was in motion.

The small vessel, with the sun and the wind behind them, sped toward the crescent-shaped shore.

"Grouville Bay," called out the fisherman, "as good a place to land as we will find."

He took the tiller from Gaspard and maneuvered the boat away from the stretch of rocks and shallows off the port side of his craft.

"Land us in that open area in the middle, away from those rocks on the north end," directed Gaspard.

The beach was a stretch of sand perhaps two miles in length. Beyond the sand a forest of deciduous trees, aspen, ash, and oak, all with signs of spring's bloom, rose onto the island's highlands. Goree Rock, dominating the north end of the bay, jutted far out into the water. To the south the sandy beach turned into a treacherous, rocky shore ending at St. Clements Point. The surf, while kicked up by the wind at their back, would be easy enough to breach.

Once the small boat was within a few hundred yards of the beach a small group of heavily armed men broke the tree line and spread out along the sand. Gaspard placed his helm on the end of a spear and held it aloft.

"Get the boy down behind the thwart," he ordered. "They may fire a volley."

But they did not. Instead, as the boat cut through the surf and ran aground, three men grasped the prow and heaved the boat onto the sand. The fisherman and Gaspard both had to grab hold of the sheer strake to keep their footing. Seven more men, three with crossbows and four with longbows, drew down on Gaspard and the fisherman. The last man, and obvious leader of the group, leaned on the butt end of a heavy, cruel axe. He was the ugliest man Gaspard had ever laid eyes on. Warty nodules and pock scars misshaped his face. His teeth, what was left of them, were bent and stained. One eye was clouded white, while the other harsh and blood-shot. His beard was thin and sparse and suffered gaps from several scars. His tan scalp was clean-shaven.

"That's a nice boat," commented the ugly man with the axe in a southern French accent. "It will serve the Dragon well, I am sure."

His men all grinned.

"My name is Gaspard Malfort, and this boat, this man, and this boy are under my protection and shall come to no harm!" stated Gaspard dangerously.

The pirates one and all burst out in laughter.

"Come ashore and welcome," laughed the ugly Frenchman. "We have hot porridge, ale, and a warm bath prepared for my fine lords just beyond those trees."

He shrugged in the direction of the forest, and his comments brought forth yet more cruel laughter.

"Your jest is duly noted," responded Gaspard icily as he climbed out on to the sand, holding his sword by its scabbard, "and I find it nearly as offensive as your face!"

The ugly Frenchman snarled and raised his axe. "When my master guts you like a cod, I will rip out your heart and eat it before it stops beating."

Gaspard simply threw his sword at his antagonist's feet, "I think not, for I am under the Dragon's protection, just as this man and boy are under mine. I bring him greetings from an old friend, Lord Fulk Paynel, baron de Hambie. I am here for audience, where you best pray I have forgotten your lack of manners."

"You are not in some snobbish Frank court, boy!" sneered the Frenchman. "You…"

Gaspard cut him off, "You, my maggoty friend, are closer to death than ever in your miserable life. I *know* your master. We have shared the same table in years past. I know what he will do to you if you fail him."

The man grimaced, opened his mouth, and then thought better of it. Instead, he pushed his way through his men and headed for the tree line. A short time later he returned with another man in lead of two horses. The new man, just as rough in appearance as the other pirates, wore a sturdy suit of studded leather armor in excellent repair. His olive skin, large nose, and dark, stiffly curled hair led Gaspard to believe him a Persian. He appraised Gaspard from head to toe, judging his height, symmetry, and cleanliness.

"We will take you at your word until such time as the Dragon says otherwise," he said with his thick, eastern accent, "You will wear a blindfold as a matter of security, but I will allow your hands to be free for riding. You will not touch the blindfold, nor will you attempt to control your horse at anytime. You will remain in the saddle until allowed to dismount. In return, your companions will remain unmolested, and we will take you to the lord of this island."

Gaspard nodded, and the ugly Frenchman blinded him, none too gently, with a thick, dirty piece of rolled linen. Guided to a horse, he lightly mounted and was led into the forest. Quickly several riders fell in ahead and behind him as the scent of the sea breeze quickly faded away in dense foliage of Jersey's interior.

Without sight, Gaspard used his other senses to remember the path. He caught the warm, sweet scent of gorse. They rode first alongside, and then across a babbling brook. Laurel and thyme hung in the air. A gentle incline. The defiant call of a kestrel. Across his cheek he felt light and warmth flickering with cool and shade. The noon sun came and went. The horses wound down into a cool, still valley. He heard a new stream, crossing with a waterfall to the left. They picked their way up a rocky ravine, hooves clattering and slipping on stones. He caught the sounds of a stream to the right, splashing across and then along the opposite bank. There was a flat plateau with the smell of Jargonelle pears. Now they went down a narrow ravine with the clatter of flint and shale under hoof. There was a cry of mews on a salty breeze.

The Persian reined up his horse.

"Remove your blind and dismount!" he ordered.

A man approached from the left across the talus.

"Alright, sieur, off that pony," a Breton voice accompanied a firm hand at his elbow.

Gaspard slid easily out of the saddle. He found himself in a narrow slit in the rocks facing a short, broken slope leading to the rough entrance to a cave. He looked backwards to find the ravine bent quickly out of sight on its crooked path. His escorts led him up to the entrance where he noted the iron bracket where Gregar had left the torch as he aided in Aymer's escape.

Aymer had not lied about the state of the Dragon's cave. Between the torches, candles, lamps, and frequent galleries open to the sky, it was anything but dank. In fact, rather than being a single, subterranean hole leading to the depths of the island, is was more a series of ravines, galleries, and alcoves connected by rough, natural passages and halls. At times a timber roof covered areas open to the elements or extended passages past their natural terminus. It felt more like a keep than a cave. Once through the entry passage, his guards led him immediately into a gallery open to the sky where a small rivulet ran down the wall into a fresh pool. A young woman, beautiful and handsomely dressed, was at the pool's edge with a net, fishing old flower petals from the surface of the water. In the pool's center stood a Romanesque marble statue of some noble woman long since dead and gone. The sculpture's caretaker met Gaspard's glance with dispirited, unreadable eyes.

As they walked they passed the residents of the Dragon's fortress. The men were all a hard lot, though of varying ages and appearances. The women, just as the first he laid eyes on, were all young, well made, and desirable. Though clean and well fed, in their somber eyes Gaspard saw the sadness of human chattel. Some stood, swollen with child, while others held babes close to their breast. The women regarded Gaspard with a vacant fear.

The riches and stolen splendor of the Dragon were on display everywhere. The chests overflowed with gold. He saw piles of weapons, tapestries, fine furnishings. Altars where fragrant incense burned stood near basins filled with scented herbs. Gaspard noted several alcoves where chests were haphazardly stacked against the walls. Could even the duke rival these riches? Surely it was enough to purchase an army of Danes, Lombards, or Swedes to lead against Normandy!

The soothing sounds of a woman's voice accompanying a harp faintly drifted from the passage before them. Soon they came to a spacious grotto with a large, smoking fire pit at its center. Over the fire a young Nubian boy slowly turned a spitted pig. Drops of sizzling, hot fat fell from the roasting beast, flashing upon the glowing coals. Near fire were the stocks, now empty, that the Dragon must use to punish the disobedient. Better than a score of men lounged about the area, some sleeping, some playing games of chance with bone dice, some idly leaning on a spear or axe, staring at the stranger under guard. Among the men was a woman, black as night with a fierce and beautiful visage, sitting on a stool plucking a harp. Was the spit-boy her son? There to remind her that her life was not her own? Gaspard imagined the noble woman would have been just as comfortable with a spear in her hand as the harp. The grotto itself sat at the bottom of a rocky pit some fifty feet below the sunny isle surface. On the far side of the courtyard a large timber building was built into the receding cavern.

"I will present your request to my lord," warned the Persian. "You would be well served to pray to whatever god you worship that my lord shall look kindly upon you."

The Persian left Gaspard to the bemused and curious stares of the Dragon's men and entered the building. Despite his confidence in his mission and his plan, it was an uncomfortable moment for Gaspard to stand in the presence of men who thought nothing of committing cruel and murderous deeds. They had no fear of God, no honor or care for law, no trouble of conscience or ill dreams. They did not even rise to the nobility of animals. They were monsters, with hideous and dark lusts, merely masquerading as men. What sort of man could find such as these, bring them together, and then control them? Such was Bertrand Ducaen.

It felt as though hours had passed as Gaspard stood uneasily in the courtyard. The Persian, after announcing their arrival, joined his comrades around the fire. The afternoon light faded, and the torches were lit. The pirates ate, but when a slave-girl motioned as though to bring Gaspard food, she was quickly warned off. Having only chewed a small meal while still at sea, his stomach growled with a hunger that was only inflamed by the scent of the roasting pork. In times when the music stopped and the men's conversation waned, he could hear the distant sounds of the surf reflecting down the walls of the pit. New men joined the group as their day's duties came to an end, while other men buckled their gear and left for their appointed rounds. His ear caught a cacophony of languages. Some he recognized, such as the Normans, Franks, Saxons, and Bretons, while some tongues were as strange as the men who used them.

As darkness fell, the Persian summoned him to the timber building. It was a large, well-made structure with few chinks to let in the elements. The entry hall was decorated in a kingly fashion and highlighted by an orderly display of shelved tomes at the far end. There were more books on that one shelf than Gaspard had seen in his whole life. He was forced to calm the desire to run his hands along their spines, open them, and learn their secrets.

To his right, an ornately carved set of double doors sat closed. From beyond, he could hear conversation and laughter. The Persian struck the door twice, then pulled it open to reveal a spacious, well-lit room with a low ceiling. The entirety of the floor was covered with skins and rugs. Upon the walls hung tapestries and paintings. A long, polished table ran the length of the room and had proper chairs rather than benches. Set upon the table was a great feast featuring pheasant, fish, a variety of tubers, fine wines, olives, fresh breads, sweet meats, all heavily spiced. The platters and goblets were all of gold and silver, and each setting had not only a knife, but also a silver spoon and fork. Twelve men, six per side, sat at the table, with Bertrand Ducaen sitting on his ebony throne at its head. Four fair maidens stood back from the table awaiting the men's whim. Immediately before Gaspard at the foot of the table sat one empty chair, a silver platter, jeweled goblet, and carafe of wine.

Ducaen himself sat on his black throne in kingly attire with his great sword near at hand. A gold circlet crowned his brow and his fur-trimmed robe was richly dyed a royal purple. His black hair and beard, now sporting streaks of gray, were as neatly kept as always. To his right sat the Norman traitor, Remon. To his left was a young man, tall and comely, though with a haughty face and cruel eyes. To Gaspard this young man seemed somewhat familiar from years past. One and all, Ducaen and his council looked over Gaspard as though he were a piece of butchered meat at a Cairo market. It was Remon's gaze that immediately troubled Gaspard as he met the man's eyes. Remon knit his brow in confusion, glanced sideways at Ducaen, then back to Gaspard, then down at his plate. When again he looked up, he did so with a look of fear and puzzlement. Remon's reaction did not escape Ducaen's notice, but the pirate's eyes remained steady.

"Welcome to Jersey, lé Sieur Malfort!" said Ducaen with an easy voice, "Your place is set and your hunger wetted. I would have you join my table and satisfy yourself before any business."

From behind a tapestry on Gaspard's left came a fifth beautiful maiden. She approached his place, lifted the carafe, filled his goblet, drank from it, and then handed it to him.

"You see, Gaspard?" chuckled Ducaen warmly. "You have nothing to fear at my table. Sit!"

The warmth of his demeanor could not hide the coldness of his eyes. Ducaen's offer of hospitality was, in truth, a command. His stare burned like ice, forcing Gaspard to draw upon his own burning hatred of the man to quell the rising fear.

"As you wish," Gaspard said as he accepted the wine and took his seat at the end of the table.

Though of great thirst, he did not quaff his wine. Though of great hunger, he ate with deliberation. He examined the men of Ducaen's table, taking in their peculiarities. He noted an aged man with wispy, white hair and watery eyes. His hands were soft and his nails long and clean. Perhaps he was a mystic or physician. Remon was a broad-faced man with narrow eyes who always found enjoyment in Ducaen's cruelties. Next he noted a slender fellow with a tangle of thin scars on his face and a missing right eye. He wore falconer's bracers on his arms. The youthful man to Ducaen's left was taller than the rest with broad shoulders, though slender. His sandy, tousled curls framed clear, blue eyes and ruddy cheeks—an angelic visage of depravity. There was a stout, lean, muscular fellow with a clean-shaven face and skull. His face was scratched and bruised, and his knuckles were scarred and scabbed. He would be Ducaen's master-at-arms. There was a middling, fat man with a red, veined nose and a God-given tonsure. His thick, ink-stained hands were soft and unworked. Perhaps he was a scribe.

"It has been several years since I set foot on the soil my homeland," began Ducaen, "What news, what stories of the Sienne Valley, do you have for me?"

"I came here neither to bring good news or ill tidings," replied Gaspard blandly.

"Not even a retelling of the duke's thrashing of Count Alan and the Bretons?" cajoled Ducaen. "You were there, were you not?"

The young man to the left of Ducaen's suddenly scowled in anger. Whereas his eyes before had been locked arrogantly on Gaspard, they now focused on the remains of the meal immediately before him.

"Yes, I was there…and no, I will not grant you the tale," replied Gaspard, taking note of the young man's discomfort.

"Gaah, boy, you are as presumptuous as ever! You have come full into manhood since our last meeting," observed the ever so slightly piqued Ducaen. "How many years ago? Five? Six?"

"Six," replied Gaspard. "As I recall, you mocked my station and questioned my right to sit at the duke's table. Now here I am, an invited guest at yours! A strange turn of events."

A dark shadow flickered briefly across Ducaen's face. Then he smiled and laughed.

"Yes, as I recall, you were doing your lord's bidding then as you are now," returned Ducaen. "Only now surely you have earned your spurs! It is Sir Gaspard, is it not?"

Gaspard glowered and said nothing. Earned? Yes. Been given them? No.

"Oh, my apologies," continued Ducaen, "I am sure Sir Fulk and the duke have their reasons for withholding what is duly yours. Perhaps your lineage?"

Gaspard, quick of wit and haughty in his own right, collected himself.

"As I recall, the last time you insulted me so, Sir Richard intervened on your behalf," he retorted sharply. "As it stands, now my mission prevents me from demanding satisfaction."

"On my behalf?" snarled Ducaen, "That doddering old fool hid you behind his skirts like a mother hen guarding the runt of her brood."

"And it still pricks you," observed Gaspard mockingly, "that you failed to test your blade against the squire of the man who left you on your back in the mud."

The room grew deathly quiet as the two men faced each other. Gaspard's heart raced, and his hand trembled. Ducaen's faced twisted with darkness and rage. Then suddenly all was passed. Ducaen smiled and exhaled.

"You are everything I expected," he said easily, "Now what is this business that brings you so far from Normandy? Pray tell!"

Gaspard stood and plunged his right hand deep into his tunic and over his breast. His sudden movement brought quick reaction from Ducaen's lieutenants, and before he could bring his hand forth bearing a sealed scroll, four swords were drawn and at his throat. Ducaen barked at his men.

"Quit!" he ordered sternly. "A man of honor he is; an assassin he is not!"

His men relaxed and put their weapons away. Ducaen nodded to Gaspard to break the seal and read.

To the king of frogs and excrement, Bertrand Ducaen, who is an ignoble thief and murderer, who cowers in his hidden cave, stripped of his lands and title, Sir Fulk Paynel, Baron de Hambie, deems you found and challenged.

In the name of peace and loyalty to the duke, I left you unmolested in those years you retained your standing in Normandy. Once fled, as a cur dog with his tail between his legs, I considered you and your insult to my house to be dead and burning in the fires of the abyss. Now you have returned like a poisonous cyst begging the blade of the surgeon.

I do hereby demand satisfaction upon the field of honor for all insults past. If you refuse, you shall forever be branded a skulking coward. Far and wide, your name will become a curse, and you shall be the patron saint of cowards and thieves. Your answer and terms shall be given to my squire, Gaspard Malfort.

Signed with the mark of Sir Fulk Paynel, Baron de Hambie

Once Gaspard finished reading, he again reached into to folds of his clothing and withdrew Fulk's chain gauntlet, throwing it down on the middle of the table. None of the men at the table dared make a sound. The squire's heart pounded in his ears. On the throne, Ducaen's face blackened as though all light fled his presence. His eyes narrowed as he stared at the gauntlet and slowly stood, placing both hands flat on the table. For a moment Gaspard would have sworn before him stood not Bertrand Ducaen but a great black lion. He had no choice but to meet the Dragon's eyes unflinching. To look away, to display anxiety or fear would bring only shame.

"You will retrieve your master! Bring him here six days hence. I will guarantee safety for you and him alone for three days. Land your boat as you did this morning; my men will be pulled back. Climb Mont Orgueil. From its height you will spy your tents and the field of honor. On the morning of the second day my man and I will meet you upon that field. There, before your eyes, I will kill Fulk Paynel."

"Sire," broke in Remon, "surely we cannot pull our men off our Grouville defenses? What if this is just a trap set by the duke?"

"You do not know this man as I," growled Ducaen, staring not at Remon but at Gaspard. "For him the means is everything, and the end is just that, the end. An end ordained and written in blood. His end. He would never agree to any sort of trickery."

Gaspard's eyes widened and flinched with Ducaen's comment. Ordained in blood? What dark art was the Dragon involved with? Ducaen did not miss Gaspard's reaction, and a cruel smiled played about his lips. He then looked about the room at his lieutenants. "As for you lot, I bid you retire from my presence. On pain of death, you will not speak of this, even amongst yourselves. Be about your duties!"

The men all rose and obediently walked to the doors. In turn, they each faced Ducaen and bowed, then walked backwards from the room so as not to turn their back on their lord. The slave-girls all retreated through the door behind the tapestry. Once they all had left, the Persian, who had apparently been waiting outside, again closed the doors, leaving Gaspard alone with Ducaen.

Ducaen, his visage returned to its normal state of unreadable coldness, grasped his own decanter of wine and walked to where Gaspard stood. Eye to eye the men stood, each reflecting the other. Ducaen filled both their goblets and motioned Gaspard to sit as he sat next to him.

"This is excellent wine—a first pressing from a Spanish vineyard," commented Ducaen, "It slacks my thirst just as well as the merchant from whom I took it."

"Now dead, I assume," Gaspard raised his cup and drank. It was truly an excellent vintage, strong and well spiced. Nothing like the watered, second pressings drunk by common folk.

"It is so fine, I imagine the vintner must have used only the feet of young, fresh maids to crush the grapes." Ducaen closed his eyes and breathed, "I can see them now. The jealous, old crones looking on…"

Gaspard said nothing, only taking another draught from his goblet.

"Do you know the tale of how I came to my current fortunes?" asked Ducaen.

"You are said to have murdered a priest," replied Gaspard.

"Ah, yes, that was ill timed," mused Ducaen, "though make no mistake, that man was no saint! He was as corrupt of heart as any of us. Neither celibate nor charitable nor impoverished. He cloaked himself in ill-gotten arrogance, believing the power of the church would shield him. He thought to brow beat me, insult me, rob me of my money—then preach to me about my 'sinful' ways. So I caught him by his filthy-rat neck and did Christendom a favor. Can you imagine? He believed my vassals tithe was owed him before I collected my revenues.

"You must see, Gaspard, we are either dogs or wolves! A dog lives a long life if he has the right master and submits to his demands. He might even get a bitch now and again. That same dog, if living under an unkind hand, may suffer untold deprivations. Either way, the time and way of his death are not his to choose. Now the wolf, he chooses his own path. He lives and dies by his own discretion. His end is always glorious and bloody. I killed that man because he attempted to make me his dog! I am no man's dog.

"Alas, that was but an excuse the old duke used to turn on me and drive me from Normandy. The old man had the Archbishop of Rouen, who just happened to be his brother, excommunicate me! He drove me out, stealing my land and my chattel, out of fear! I refused to kiss his ring, let alone his foot. For what did I owe him? Nothing! And I am not alone. There are many lords who despise being vassals for no better reason than to enrich an inferior man of higher station. Our ancestor, Rollo, was such a man. Afraid of no one. That his seed has become no better than a Frank is bitter gall!

"Now take your master, Sir Fulk. He is a wolf. That is why he comes to me! Surely that wife of his will complain and protest, but she will have no effect. He and I, we know this contest is inevitable. I had hoped to choose its time and place, but will not deny it now that it has arrived. There is but one thing I would know—by what means did Fulk become aware of my presence here? Few know that Bertrand Ducaen and the Dragon of Jersey are one in the same man!"

Gaspard smiled and rubbed his eyes. "In the unlikely event you gain your preordained victory, I will reward you with that tale."

Ducaen leaned back in his chair.

"You puzzle me, boy! When I look at you, I see a wolf languishing in a cage. I understand loyalty. But I cannot fathom why you have not sought your fortunes elsewhere! I have many agents in Normandy and do receive regular news. I know you have rejected positions far better than your status in Hambie. Why?"

It was true. Gaspard's freedom to be his own man was there for the taking. Fulk would not have faulted him, either. Not only was he an imposing and skilled warrior, deadly with both bow and blade, he could also read and write. Why did he stay? There was but one shadow in which he would gladly walk. Only one voice from which he craved the kind word. Only one heart for which he would sacrifice all. Gisla. To live without her passing scent would be a greater torture than suffering the sight of her son.

"I came here only to convey my lord's message and obtain your response," replied Gaspard tightly, "not to engage in brotherly talk. Besides, I am satisfied with my lot."

"Your eyes say otherwise!"

"Cast your net elsewhere, Ducaen," retorted Gaspard.

"Even were I to offer you a ship, a crew, and all the Mediterranean as plunder? Eventually your own land and title? Wenches for your lust and a wife for your station?"

Gaspard glanced down and drew his cup to his lips. He drained the wine, set the goblet down, and met Ducaen's steady gaze.

"You, sir, possess nothing my heart desires. Except, perhaps, your life. I would gladly take that! Had not my lord sent me with his challenge, I would have come to kill you myself," replied Gaspard softly.

"And left your cage to do so, no doubt," said Ducaen as he turned and walked back to his throne. From behind the ebony chair he took up a sword hidden in the shadows—Gaspard's thin blade.

"This is a fine blade," commented Ducaen, withdrawing Gaspard's weapon from its scabbard. "A novel idea, light, balanced and quick. Completely useless against an armored man, and a poor defensive weapon. It would shatter under a heavy blow. Why do you carry such a toy?"

"Even the greatest of men, be they knights or kings, spend little time burdened by armor," replied Gaspard. "Look at yourself. Where is your armor? Elsewhere and of no use to you at the moment. With that blade I could pierce your breast three times before you drew forth your great beast…and its temper is greater than it appears."

With a sudden motion Ducaen reversed his hold on the sword and tossed the weapon to Gaspard. Reflexively, Gaspard plucked it out of the air by the grip.

"Then strike if you dare!" commanded Ducaen. "I give the advantage. Run me through the heart and satisfy your desire for revenge. I even permit you to consider it an avengement of your bastard honor."

Bewildered, Gaspard stared at his blade, then at Ducaen. Was this enemy mad?

"Perhaps you would consider it a fairer contest if I, too, was armed?" continued the self-proclaimed king of Jersey as he strode to his throne and took up his own great, heavy sword, "In *your* god's eye, I am a despot, rebel, and murderer. Send me to Hell if you dare!"

"Why do you yet again seek to test the temper of my sword," cried Gaspard in rage, "knowing now as then, I am merely my lord and lady's tool? Yea, gladly I would have at you and feast upon the carnage in victory or defeat! Alas, my purpose is beyond my vanity and your taunts!"

With that Gaspard dropped his slender blade on the table.

"I cannot slay you anymore than you can slay me," Gaspard continued darkly. "Do not think you can escape your destiny so easily."

The two men, so alike in visage and symmetry, stood quietly for some moments until Ducaen heavily took his seat. "Would that we could both escape…" he whispered.

"Would you be surprised to know I have never made redress to any man? It is easier to either kill that man or make him so afraid of death the need for contrition becomes like vapor under the sun. This one time, were I to express regret, could you reconsider your hatred?" the Dragon continued with a near melancholy tone.

"And betray the honor of Hambie's chatelaine in the same thought? It is she you must grovel before like a dog and beg forgiveness, not I! I am merely a shield to her. I could no more abandon my charge than your sword could shatter in its scabbard."

A troubled look came over Ducaen's face. He opened his mouth as though to speak, then closed it. Finally he said, "No matter. Your lord and I have unfinished business. No poison. No assassin's dagger. No intrigue. Only honor. When you arrive, climb to the small plateau above Goree Rock. Look to the west and you will see a tent on a field before a great mound. It is there we will meet."

"I will convey your terms. We shall return on the sixth day."

Ducaen clapped his hands, and the young woman who had poured Gaspard's wine reappeared from behind the tapestry.

"Find a comfortable cell and see to this man's needs, whatever they may be," he ordered, and then, with eyes softened, looked upon Gaspard. "She is beautiful, no? The night will be chill; she will keep you warm."

She was dark, like a Sicilian, and her hand was cool and smooth to Gaspard's touch as she led him from the room.

Once Gaspard had left, Ducaen summoned Remon, who joined him at the table in the hall. A clean-shaven man, Remon sported a broad face with narrow eyes and nose. He was stolid, plain spoken, and unafraid to disagree with Ducaen. Remon was not given to much humor or passion unless in a state of drunkenness, and Ducaen greatly valued his flat pragmatism.

"Your thoughts?" asked the Dragon.

"We are either betrayed here, or our escaped minstrel divined your identity...or both. We both know he could not have escaped his cell and got off the island without help. Either way, if Sir Fulk knows you are the Dragon, we must conclude the duke also knows. If apprised of Fulk's plans, Robert will likely honor the quest out of friendship. That buys you precious time. But make no mistake, Robert will soon come for you with a force we cannot repel."

"We must not be here when he arrives," agreed Ducaen. "Make preparations to move the treasure to the caves of Sark. I want you to personally sail to Gotland and speak with Osbeorn. The longships will have to be finished sooner than agreed and our allies ready to move before summer. At most, we have ten days to be on our way. Now you know why pulling our men back from Grouville is of no consequence. Except for the lookouts, bring everyone in to ready our departure."

"Osbeorn will sense our desperation. He will raise his price," said Remon, "and we will be at his mercy."

"Then remind him to betray me is to betray Cnut and Count Alan!"

"And the men who move the treasure to Sark?" asked Remon.

"Two groups," replied Ducaen, "First, impress a number of the island men. We will use their labor then kill them on Sark. Second, from our own men, select the least useful. Offer them the woman of their choice and gold if they complete the mission successfully. Upon their return give them spiced wine laced with Devil's Cherries to enjoy with their lady. Both should be dead by morning. Only you and I are to know the location of our treasure."

"Do you intend on killing all the maids?"

"They are a luxury we cannot afford once we are on the move, and I am certain some of them know enough to damage our plan if we leave them alive," replied Ducaen dispassionately, "They are replaceable. Besides, the men have long wanted to make sport of them."

"Do you truly intend to meet Sir Fulk on the field of honor?" asked Remon bluntly. "It would be more expedient to set a trap for him and that arrogant squire of his."

Ducaen glowered darkly and turned away from Remon.

"If I am to destroy Robert and regain my lands, Gaspard Malfort must return to Normandy. He must report my honorable victory over Normandy's champion. It will give heart to our allies in Brittany and cause fear in those loyal to Robert. Besides, his death is foretold. Fulk Paynel will not leave Jersey alive."

"Foretold?" asked Remon, puzzled.

"Just as it was foretold that in letting the minstrel escape, Fulk would be delivered to me."

"Letting?"

"Yes."

"So the executions…"

"Were a necessary ruse, yes."

"Such prophesies do not come without a price, milord," mused Remon.

"I chose my path long ago, my old…friend," Ducaen laughed to himself. "Agreeing to stay the course is not so difficult."

Remon nodded and paused. With hesitancy, he then asked "Milord, how much do you know of this young squire, Malfort?"

In an instant, Ducaen's passion returned and he grasped Remon by the throat with his powerful right hand. His hapless lieutenant, gasping for breath, clutched at Ducaen's tightening grip, but to no avail.

The Dragon drew Remon near and hissed through gritted teeth, "I know enough to tell you, you will say nothing because you know nothing! Now, go and tend to your duties!"

With that he flung Remon backwards and watched the man stumble hastily out of the hall and out of view.

Once alone, Ducaen sat upon his throne considered the events for some time, mulling meaning and possibility. Even after his decanter was empty and the wine had gone to his head, he sat, a mind full of agonies. So cruelly did the brothers of St. Lo name the boy! The last guardian of an evil house. Gaspard did not know his lineage, but the brothers surely did. He was not just any orphaned bastard raised in a convent. He was the only son of a once noble Norman house, now disgraced and soon to be forgotten by all of history. He was Gaspard Ducaen, only son and heir to the house of Bertrand Ducaen. In the young man's face, Ducaen saw a younger self whose only divergence were the deep blue eyes given to Gaspard by his mother. The angry, accusing eyes of a woman who rejected Bertrand Ducaen, yet was taken by his lust despite her protest. He had not seen himself in the lad all those years ago, beardless and ruddy cheeked, but he saw it now. Fulk Paynel's squire could be no other than his son.

There was no return from the evil life of the Dragon, Ducaen knew for certain. What would be the greater evil, or in turn the greater penance? To make Gaspard know who his father was and acknowledge him as his son? Or keep this secret that could destroy the young squire if the truth be told.

CHAPTER 8

A Knight's Duty

Today the Castle de Hambie exists only in memory, erased from history first through decay, then the plunder of its stone. It was built in the days of William Longsword, and for centuries was home to the lords of Sienne Valley of West Normandy. The castle's edifice was built into the summit of the rocky eminence rising above the valley floor just east of the river Sienne. Its central tower, the donjon, rose one hundred feet above the gentle mount's apex. From the castle's uppermost windows the shore of Jersey, some twelve leagues off as the gull flies, was visible on a clear day west by northwest. The ramparts surrounding the castle were thick with tightly fitted stones well guarded with battlements and turrets. Inside, the bailey was highlighted by a spring-fed well, stables for the lord's horses, barracks, a smithy, the great hall, chapel, and donjon.

Hambie's village was scattered about the lush, green lower slopes below the castle. The village was primarily wattle and daub cottages interspersed with grape vines, orchards, and tilled fields. Beyond the fields, the Sienne valley was a forested haven of rolling hillocks and babbling brooks that meandered through the woodlands and hamlets until they joined the river Sienne. The river itself, no more than a shallow trout stream during the height of summer, gaily wound its way northwest until it formed a tidal estuary just southwest of Coutances. The day that Fulk prepared for his adventure, with the winter rains nearing their end, the river Sienne was a dangerous, silt-laden torrent.

"I ask you, husband, why must you take this quest upon yourself? You could have easily obtained the men and resources needed for a sure, swift victory! Yet you come to me and propose such a risk...and beg my blessing?" though Gisla's voice did shake, her brow remained knit and her gaze steadfast.

The lord and lady de Hambie stood, alone behind the closed door of their solar high in the main tower. Once separated from Gaspard, who would make for Carteret on the coast and gain passage to Jersey, Fulk had spurred Hardelle to make all haste in their return to his domain. Though now of middle years, the mare retained her power, endurance, and yearling-like love of the chase. Fulk simply gave her the rein and called her name, "Home now, Hardelle," and she surged beneath him, taking flight.

His men must be rallied and ready to march within three days time, while he had the delicate task of presenting his plan to Gisla. He passed the gate of Hambie late in the evening, well after sundown. Hardelle was soaked with sweat and happily exhausted. After a brief repast, where he briefly gave orders to Master Josue, he joined his wife in their chambers. He had gently taken her hands in his and laid out his design to slay the Dragon. His hands she pushed away upon completion of his tale.

"We need more than a victory in battle, more than a taking of the island," replied Fulk sternly. "Ducaen must not slip through our grasp a second time. He must be killed. The security of Normandy demands it!"

"And this is your vainglorious proposal? To walk into his den and expect fair and honorable treatment? What is there to keep him from murdering you upon your arrival?"

"To win victory in a war against Normandy, he will need many lords to side with him. Who would align themselves with my murderer?"

"You too easily see men through the eyes of your own honor, husband!" criticized Gisla, "The lords of Normandy, just as all others, place power, gold, and lust above honor and God until the hour of their death... only *then* do they repent. Only when they have nothing left to gain by the sins of this life do they make their peace with God before entering the next! If the purse were rich enough…"

"Say not such things, my love!" warned Fulk, his cheeks coloring.

"And forgo the truth? Cnut is a savage heathen, yet the English lords did not fail to fall in behind him. And our own duke did away with his brother," Gisla continued fearlessly. "Fratricide! Yet he is the duke. There are rewards for those who turn the blind eye and exile for those who do not. If the Devil himself offered to kill you in exchange for Bertrand Ducaen's soul, Ducaen could throw in his five most trusted allies and still be ahead. He will need you dead more than he will need his honor if he hopes to return to Normandy!"

"That Richard was murdered is most likely, but there is not one shred of evidence against Robert," Fulk's voice rose dangerously, his eyes narrow and angry. "And I, like many, follow him because he is a great, God-fearing Norman, and rightful duke by blood! Not due to favors or gold! You will not disparage him by casting him as made of the same stuff as Cnut. Cnut betrayed and murdered all who opposed him through lies and trickery. What lords did Robert do away with? Whom did he split open while they were still breathing and pull out their lungs? Whom did he hang from the rafters of their own halls? Or burn alive locked in their own barns? You compare the archbishop's exile to torture and murder? You believe Archbishop Robert would have lived long enough under Cnut's hand to lay down an interdict? Foolishness!"

Gisla blanched at his outburst, shrinking before his anger. Never had he raised his voice in such a way with her. She had seen him rage, fume, and threaten, but never toward her. It had always been her cool touch that tamed his passions. Her soothing words to soften his anger with forgiveness. For just the briefest of moments, revealed as though by a flash of lightning in the darkest of nights, Gisla knew the fear Fulk caused upon the field of battle. Immense was he, his eyes afire with anger, his hazel locks and beard flowing like a mane spilled upon his broad and powerful shoulders. His mere presence stole the courage from the hearts of his enemies and emboldened his allies.

"As for Ducaen, do not believe for one moment he has not dined on bitter gall nightly all these years," continued Fulk angrily. "His acid rises when he thinks of me. I have already pierced his pride and left it a wounded beast. He will be loath to have the Baron de Hambie also strip from him his bravery! His need to reclaim his nobility is a weakness that preys upon him. He wants to, *needs to* kill me with his bare hands, in a fashion that no man will have grounds to rightfully avenge my death—on the field of honor! No, no, he will not cast aside my challenge, and God help the man who councils him otherwise!"

And then it was gone. Through his anger he saw his love quake before him, and he was filled with shame and self-loathing. The tear on her cheek and fear in her eyes was as a dagger in the heart of a man otherwise without fear. Before her, Fulk suddenly was small and powerless. The horror of his own wrongdoing, his unjust and prideful anger, washed over him and knocked him low as a wave of cold, salt water, driving him to his knees. His anger extinguished, he could no longer meet her tearful gaze, so cast his eyes to her slender feet and the hem of her pale, green gown. There was silence between them.

"Oh my wife, you are my love, the breath of my life, my chatelaine," choked Fulk finally. "I would deny even God's demand if you asked it of me. I will go to Robert and beg him to release me from this quest."

Gisla softly stepped forward and placed her hand lightly on his cheek.

"God is love, and neither of us shall deny him..." she bent and whispered. "If this is your destiny I will not willfully keep you from it. You are my husband, my love, and the lord of my heart. I know no man who is your equal. I speak not of war, but of your steadfast conscience. If you are to go into darkness, you shall have the light of my blessing."

She drew him into the folds of her gown and pressed his face to her breast to still his trembling, suddenly realizing that precious thing called freedom was not a gift kings and lords alone could give. She, too, could grant this or deny it to her husband this day.

"Forgive me, Gisla...forgive me my anger," he said softly. "You are wise and know me well. I do desire to face Ducaen on the field of honor.

I will not deny his insult to our house in years past still festers, but I also feel driven to free Jersey and rid the world of his evil. This duty is greater than my pride, though my pride be part of it."

"And forgive me, husband," replied Gisla as she gently drew him to his feet. "Robert has proved a just and even-handed lord. Any sin of his past is between him and God." With her arms around his waist, she leaned into his strength and lightly kissed his lips.

It was a lasting embrace, and for that moment the outside world and its unknown future left them alone, as though time had come to a stop. Passion without lust, gentle yet insistent, tender, delicate, and aware, the man and woman clung to each other as God intended. The lamps flickered and candles burned low until darkness and sleep finally took the chamber.

Brother Carthusian's gaunt stature gave the illusion of height that only dissipated when near the likes of Fulk or Gaspard. While nearing fifty years in age, his hair remained dark and belligerent, requiring regular service to maintain his tonsure. His hawkish nose, sallow cheeks, and dark, quick eyes belied his gentle, instructive nature. He loved and was loved by both Gaspard, whom he taught through his childhood, and young Raymond Paynel, his current pupil. In an age of ignorance and corruption within Christ's church, Carthusian saw God's goodness in all things as easily as breathing.

Before Gisla took command of the household, long had Hambie been without a chatelaine. Fulk's mother had been taken by a terrible fever when he was a small boy. Her death was a terrible blow to both father and son, neither of whom soon wanted a new wife to cloud her memory. The two bachelors, quite dense about those things a woman's touch brought to a household, let many things fall by the wayside. When Gisla arrived, she found the castle's little chapel in a state of disuse and disrepair.

"Husband," she asked, "Perhaps it is time to bring some brother or cleric here to maintain our chapel and keep the daily offices?"

As Carthusian had long years of friendship with the Paynel family, Fulk sent word and received permission from the father abbot to bring

Gaspard's teacher and mentor to Hambie. With a glad heart Carthusian did repair and bring life again to the chapel. A pleasantly veiled threat brought the curé of the local parish, a fat, lazy, boorish man whose position was granted due to his familial relation with the bishop of Caen, to perform mass once a week. Carthusian was on good terms with Father Sergius from the nearby convent of St. Cyprian and saw to it he came once a month.

While he could not hear confessions, leaving that duty for the priest's monthly visit, Carthusian knew God's word chapter and verse, and he proved good council for Hambie's household. With the blessed arrival of young Raymond, born healthy with strong lungs, Carthusian immediately loved the boy and strived to teach him as he did Gaspard.

This morning it was the young, tousle-haired Raymond who taught Carthusian. As soon as the child overheard his father had returned home, he ran screaming joyously through the hallways and up the stairs toward the solar. Carthusian was hard put to capture Raymond, whose agility and speed bested the aging monk. He gave chase, a comic performance, but could not manage corners or stairs with the quickness of the lively youth.

"Peire! Peire!" cried Raymond as he burst upon his parents' bedchamber. "Peire, you are home!"

The boy leapt upon the bed and grappled his waking father, leaving a mortified and blown Carthusian on the stair outside of the solar's door. Gisla, who loved her son dearly, could not in good conscience deny him his impudence. She laughed gaily as her husband ensnared her son in blankets from beneath, leapt from the bed with boy and bedding tossed across his shoulder, and raced about the room with a beastly roar. The playful cries of Raymond were muffled from inside the blankets until Fulk tossed the tangled mess onto the bed next to Gisla. Raymond fought his way from beneath the folds, crying out, "Again, Peire, again!" upon which, Fulk tossed the boy high over his shoulder and chased about with more noisome and monstrous sounds.

When the game came to an end, Fulk sat his son on the edge of the bed and took a knee.

"I have something of importance to tell you," he said with all seriousness. "I have a quest and leave on the morrow. There is a monster haunting the isle of Jersey, terrorizing the villagers and attacking ships at sea. This great beast is known as the Dragon, and Jersey knows not how to rid itself from his evil. Our lord, Duke Robert, has commissioned me with the task of sailing to Jersey and slaying the Dragon."

"Is it a real dragon, with great wings and breathes fire?" asked the wide-eyed Raymond.

"No, this dragon is a man, making him all the more dangerous and evil!" replied Fulk. "At this very moment, Gaspard is sailing to Jersey to bring the Dragon my challenge to single combat on the field of honor. He will not refuse me. He cannot, for to refuse me or betray the field of honor will brand him a coward, and that he cannot have."

"Will you cut off his head as though he were a real dragon?"

"Yes!"

"You will bring it here that I may see it?"

To this question Gisla cut her husband to the quick, "I forbid it! You will see no such violence!"

"The boy is simply curious," defended Fulk.

"You will have him in your world soon enough, husband," retorted Gisla. "For now you will leave him in mine."

Looking to escape her glare, Fulk grasped Raymond and tossed him upon his shoulders.

"The morning is fair, and the sun is shining. I shall show you Jersey's shore."

Fulk carried Raymond up the spiraling stair from their chamber to the uppermost room of the tower. Through the door and into the cold chamber they went. Fulk lifted his son from his shoulders and set him on the narrow window's sill. West by northwest he pointed, directing the boy's gaze to a distant shore across the waters of the Channel.

"Gaspard may well be landing upon the Jersey shore at this very moment," he said quietly, "Taking my letter of challenge to the very hand of the Dragon."

"I should like to see a real dragon," the boy said idly. "Carthusian says they exist. He says Father Abbott saw the bones of a dead one once... buried in the desert."

Fulk laughed lightly. "If I should find a real dragon, I promise you I shall battle it honorably and bring its head here for you to see, but you must promise not to tell your mother."

Raymond reached up and grasped his father's directing hand and gazed across the waters. "I promise, Peire."

As Fulk strengthened the bond with his own son, many leagues away on the open waters of the English Channel, Gaspard sat at the tiller of a small fishing boat. Another young boy, whom young Raymond would never chance to meet, sat at Gaspard's side. With hook and line in hand, the fisherman's son merrily teased the gulls.

Gisla dressed in silence, without aid of either Isabelle or Clothilde, whom Fulk had dismissed upon his arrival. Despite the sun's rays streaming through the windows, she felt an ill wind caress her flaxen hair. Men who ride off to war often did not return. It was a fear their loved ones, peasant or lord, lived with every moment of every day. It mattered not that Fulk always survived—always came home to her. She knew it to be an inalienable part of him that he must always again leave. She drew a ragged breath, glanced to the stair where her two most loved men had ascended, then quietly left the bedchamber for the seclusion and comfort of her bower. There, she carefully cut a length of her long, flaxen hair and began weaving it with a length of pale green ribbon to form a necklace for her love.

CHAPTER 9

The Moon over Coutances

An unfavorable wind. If he could have walked upon the water, he would have made the shore of Normandy in less than half the time. If he could walk upon the water, that would have made him a son of God with a clear destiny. What of God? Where was God? Were storms, famine and disease God's anger? It seemed God brought suffering to the good in equal portion as to the evil. Perhaps even more, for the good not only suffered God, but also the dark hand of man. The good suffered, and the evil profited in this life with only the promise those roles would be reversed in the next. Beat thy sword into a plowshare, turn thy cheek, and love thy neighbor are all well and good, except when the king must build an army of men easily offended, with sharp swords, and ready to kill that unpleasant neighbor simply to protect the sensibilities of those who refuse to fight. Men of war are the walls of Jerusalem, protecting the innocent within. Does God give salvation to those who make up the wall even if, from time to time, they go mad with their duties and become the enemy? If Judas had rejected his destiny in favor of a righteous life, and Christ crucified became Christ living to a ripe old age, would he have been more or less damned? Are men destined, their lives foretold, or are they free? Could any truly be the wolf? God!

The fisherman expertly brought his boat to a halt just before entering the gentle surf that scrubbed the beach of Normandy just west of

Coutances. Night had fallen, and only the stars and the faint lamplight leaking through the shutters of the small fishing village lit the Norman coastline.

"Best you jump now, milord," he said as he dropped the sail and thrust the oars in the water to stabilize the craft. "No use all of us gettin' wet landin' and pushin' off."

Gaspard pressed a small purse into the weathered man's hand, wished him well, and then stripped off his clothing. He wrapped his goods inside his cloak and slid naked over the strake and into the cold, chest-deep, water. The fisherman handed him the bundle, along with his sword and knife, and Gaspard turned and pushed his way through the water. Holding his goods above his head, he waded through the surf and slogged up the beach past several fishing vessels grounded by the low tide. His companions of the past three days vanished into the darkness, sailing north toward their home. The first days of March had come and gone.

Fighting the chill effect of the cold night air against his damp skin, he dressed as quickly as his numb fingers would allow. At the first hovel he found, Gaspard rapped sharply on the low, ill-fitting door. Nets hung from the sides of the shack and the place smelled strongly of boiled fish and onions. Away in the darkness a dog barked to alert the villagers a stranger was in their midst.

"In the name of the duke of Normandy, open your door," barked Gaspard.

He heard shuffling and muffled whispers from within. A stooped old fisherman with the look of dereliction about him cracked the door and held a crude lamp up to the narrow opening. Balding, with unruly brows and a gaping mouth, he sized up Gaspard in the flickering light. From head to toe, he stared fearfully at the shivering young man, face hidden partially beneath the hood of his trimmed cloak, and his expensive, sand-caked boots. At last his eyes fixed upon Gaspard's sheathed sword, hanging from his back outside his cloak.

"We wants no trouble, 'ere, milord," crackled the old man.

"Then you will afford me a bit of that pottage I smell and show me the path to Coutances," replied Gaspard through chattering teeth.

The old man knew he could not refuse, so he nodded and stepped aside as Gaspard ducked under the lintel to enter the smoky, single room cottage. A shrunken old woman, barely more than half Gaspard's height, stood opposite an open fire, stirring a small, blackened pot of fish stew suspended over the flame. It was a small portion, barely enough for two. Gaspard immediately crouched by the fire and rubbed his hands near the flames. While decrepit, barely better than a hovel, he noted the cottage was kempt and well tended on the inside. The ceiling was low and left little room for a man of Gaspard's stature. Braids of dried onions and garlic hung from the roof, and several crocks, likely containing wheat and oats, sat neatly on a shelf. Tools for a life garnered from the sea were hung in an orderly fashion on the walls. A small table with two sturdy stools was set near the fire. On the table were two simple, dark, unleavened wheat cakes, and two clay bowls with wooden spoons.

The old man nodded to the old woman, and she filled one of the bowls with stew and set it on the table, motioning to Gaspard to sit. The portion was the lion's share, leaving little in the pot. Her gnarled, arthritic hands shook, and she kept her eyes downcast. Quickly she joined the man's side, who remained near the door. Only then did she dare look at Gaspard as he took his seat. The stare of the old couple gave Gaspard a strange sense of discomfort. "So this is what it feels like to demand hospitality from a poor vassal," he thought to himself. Often had he, when accompanying Fulk, been treated well by some merchant or well to do tenant, but Fulk had never exercised his rights over the poor in such a way. Gaspard felt a sudden, awkward pity for the salty old codger and crone, and the weakness aggrieved him. They should be nothing to him.

He looked to the stew. Plainly seasoned, it was a thin broth with large chunks of hake. Before tasting it, he drew his knife and carefully sliced one cake in half. Then he deliberately stood and poured half his bowl back into the pot. He broke apart the half-cake and dipped it in the stew, slowly chewing, while ignoring his hosts. Only when his bowl was empty and the bread gone did he address them.

"'Tis meager fare, barely enough to sate my hunger," he mused, "but if I eat all of it, you will then have none. Why would a lord do such a thing?"

"Because a lord has the right," replied the old man fearfully.

"I never said I was a lord," whispered Gaspard with much melancholy, as though his hosts were no longer near him.

"*But you long to be one, so it is time to act the part,*" replied a whispered voice heard only by his ear, so faint it was almost simply a thought.

"What?" he said sharply. "How dare you speak so!" but it was plain to see, neither the old man nor old woman had uttered the words, for they shrank back in fear. They stood mute and pressed against the wall by the door, with the crackle of the small fire the only sound in the room.

Distant rasping laughter from beyond the cottage floated to his ears, mocking him, belittling him. Gaspard bolted from his stool, struck his head on the roof, and cursed. His foot caught the rod that held the pot over the fire, upsetting and spilling much of the remaining stew.

"Someone is out there! Do you hear them?" he demanded. They shook their heads, panicked. "Deaf old fools!" he muttered harshly.

Gaspard rushed to the door, threw it open, and bent his ear to catch the voice again. The wind gently rustled the dry coastal grasses and shrubs. The dog had quieted.

"*Gaspard!*" the low whisper was directionless, "*weakling...*"

He drew his sword and spun in a circle. "Show yourself!" he cried.

"*A test is coming, Gaspard...*" the voice grew faint. "*You will be tested, and your dreams are on the balance...*"

"Who are you? Show yourself! Test me now if you dare!" But his demon had faded away. The voice spoke no more, and he was alone. Inside the cottage, the old man and old woman heard only the ranting of a madman. Gaspard's angry cries fell about village, disturbing the quiet of the cold, winter night. Folk peeked from doors and windows with a mixture of fear and curiosity.

Sword still in hand, he returned to the cottage, roughly took hold of the old man, and dragged him outside. "Show me the path to Coutances!" he growled.

"Y-y-yes, milord," rasped the old man.

Gaspard pushed him in the back and followed him away from the cottage, past a number of other hovels. As they passed by, the villagers quickly secured their doors and shutters against the stranger. No one came forth to confront Gaspard or aid their neighbor. Gaspard followed his host through the village to the east until they came upon a wheel-rutted path leading inland.

"Coutances is a long league to the east," the old man pointed down the lane.

"You have a boat, no?" demanded Gaspard. The fisherman nodded. "In good repair?" Again the fisherman nodded.

Gaspard opened his purse and pulled out a silver coin. "I will be back in a few days time. It will be to your profit if you and the crone can hold your boat...and your tongues...until then." He then grabbed man's hand, placed the coin in his palm, and painfully closed his fingers over it. "It is not a matter of choice for you."

With not another word, the young squire, Gaspard Malfort, turned up the rutted, muddy lane and left the village in the darkness behind him. He returned his sword to its sheath, tightened his cloak against the cold, and walked a quick pace. A pale glow to the east slowly gathered, and soon Gaspard's way was illuminated by the rising moon.

His anxious thoughts turned to many nights of council he had taken with the mystic, Gregar Penscalus.

"If you leave Hambie for a position elsewhere, your passion for your lady will become only a greater torture," replied Gregar when Gaspard explained a position with a noble of east Normandy had been offered him.

"She will become a memory carved in white marble upon a pedestal. You will take your lust with other women with her always in your thoughts. She will not age to you, will not change to you, except in your ever-growing expectation of who you desire her to be. Then when Fulk is finally slain on some distant battlefield and petty lords and nobles vie for her hand to obtain her inheritance, you will be a long forgotten face in a crowd of onlookers as the duke gives her away to another as a favor. Is that your heart's desire?"

"No," whispered Gaspard, "but in staying, my love for my lord turns to hatred. I despise how he looks on her and she on him. I despise having to avert my eyes lest they see my desire. I draw her image with charcoal upon parchment simply so I can gaze upon her beauty without fear of discovery. I caress those perfect lines while he enjoys her bed. Whilst I remain, I wish only for his death! It is a lonely existence."

"His death is foretold in the stars, whether you remain or flee Hambie," counseled the pale mystic. "Fulk Paynel will perish on a field of battle while his wife lives to marry another. What man wins her is yet beyond my sight. Perhaps your unclear path clouds my vision. For Gisla, falling into the clutches of a man who failed to love her would be a fate worse than death. By taking the path that leads you away from her shadow, you guarantee her this destiny. To save yourself the agony of her presence, you may well damn her to share the bed of some aging, flaccid lord. Again, I ask, is that your heart's desire?"

"No," replied Gaspard flatly.

"Then sacrifice on your part remains necessary," followed Gregar plainly.

"And how would the baron's squire gain the hand of the baroness? I have no name, no wealth, and such a match is well beyond my station."

"Your worth will be noted in due time."

"And what of the child, Raymond?" asked Gaspard pensively.

"He will have to be removed to make way for the House of Malfort," answered Gregar assuredly, "just as any lord, to clear the way for his own progeny, would remove him."

"Removed?"

"Yes, removed. Perhaps sent to some convent or foreign war. It really matters not."

Gaspard refused the offered position and remained the loyal squire of the Baron de Hambie. With violence he threw himself into the training for war. While he was never truly liked by the men he first trained with, then commanded, they did respect and fear him. He bloodied them all without humor or mockery. He was aloof, dark and moody, and strangely unaware of the effect his wayward beauty had upon women. His deep blue eyes, dark locks, and clear complexion distracted many maidens even as maturity thickened his beard. He kept long hours alone away from the other warriors, either in his chambers or beneath some tree away from the castle. It was only those rare times when he was among his men in a city such a Coutances, Avranches, or St. Lo, and he opened his purse strings in some inn or public house, that they felt he was one of them. He would sing, drink, brawl, and laugh. He would encourage their wenching, laughing at their successes and failures, but then sleep alone.

Only Fulk seemed unaware of, or at least untroubled by the changes in Gaspard's demeanor, always seeing his squire through the eyes of a brother and a friend. Still they sparred, hunted, and made war side by side. They feasted in the great hall and loosed their falcons all about the Sienne Valley. Never once did Fulk suspect the dark, hateful stare that pierced his back whenever he strode ahead of his squire. Never once did he recognize Gaspard's reserved service to his wife as anything more than duty.

Gaspard crested a gentle rise just as the bells of vigils tolled. He broke from the trees and descended to the cultivated plain that lay before the city of Coutances. The city appearing in front of him, both old and new, was built on and around a large hill now brightly awash in moonlight. Laid waste by the Northmen before they settled the land, the dukes of Normandy now bent their will toward rebuilding its greatness. The duke's own grandmother, Gonnor, was benefactor of the city's new cathedral, now under construction by Bishop Robert—a bishop who would have much to answer for when Duke Robert exposed his relations with the Dragon.

No less than a sense of doom, of dark confrontation, fed upon him as he approached Coutances in the still of the night, seasoned by the unheard, mocking voice in his mind. He knew his destination—an upstairs room, secure and away from prying ears, at the home of a coppersmith loyal to Fulk and the duke. His face was his password no matter the hour. He would enter, a grim smile on his face, a serious embrace to his chest. Despite the hour, Fulk would be roused and a meal served. Their council would be dramatic and serious. Fulk would be assured, even emboldened, in his quest to slay the Dragon. Gaspard would appear the dutiful messenger, the squire. Then he would explain his fatigue and throw himself to sleep on a mat near the hearth. Fulk would be restless. He would pace about the room or perhaps draw a chair to the fire and stare into its flames. Finally he, too, would regain sleep.

On the morrow, in the company of a trusted agent of the duke, they would prepare for the contest then ride to the fishing village. They would procure, fairly, a boat from an old villager whose cottage lay at the northwest end of the village. The duke's agent would then turn south and lead their mounts to the duke's hunting camp, where Duke Robert and Bishop Robert were exercising their most esteemed falcons over the estuary of the Sienne. Fulk and Gaspard would load their craft and set sail for Jersey. With the wind, it would be a quick trip. Against the wind, it would be a tedious, long drawn affair pitting Gaspard's wits with sail and oar against the mischievous, unforgiving channel. No matter the ease of crossing, they would make Jersey's shore. There, in single combat, Bertrand Ducaen would kill Fulk Paynel, and Gaspard would then have his chance to take Gisla for his own. Gaspard smirked and laughed wryly to himself in the night as he passed through fields now awakening with the approach of spring.

The lane led him first through scattered, then closely built cottages, up the gentle slopes of Coutances. Most were simple wood structures, though the occasional wealthy merchant built his residence of stone to proof it against fire. The hour was late, and the city was quiet and dark while Gaspard, hood and cloak drawn close, moved like a ghost through the shadows. A twisted knot, more than hunger, burned in his gut as he approached the darkened doorway of the smith's house and shop. Though now hidden in shadows, Gaspard knew the board that ran across the door's lintel bore the painting of a smith at work, the house of Tormod Coppersmith. He swallowed tortured anxieties, putting them away in their proper locked box, then softly rapped the door and waited. His alternate self, the loyal squire and faithful friend, took control of his form, as though he simply slipped on a pair boots, well broken and formed to his feet. Moments later a shutter covering an upstairs window squeaked softly over his head. The upper story of the house overhung the doorway and Gaspard was forced to step backward into the moonlit lane.

"Pull back your hood, stranger, that I may see you!" a voice whispered in the darkness beyond the window.

Gaspard revealed his face, and moments later the door was quietly unbarred and opened enough to allow him to slip into the ground floor shop of the coppersmith. Once the door was again secured, Gaspard's invisible host removed the hood from his lantern and lit the room. It was Tormod. He was a short, stout man with calloused, muscular hands, thick neck, and a shaved head. A scarred and soiled leather apron protected his rough clothes.

"Welcome, Gaspard. We have been expecting you," began Tormod. "Your lord arrived at noontide today and has been anxious for your arrival."

"But for an uncooperative wind, I should have arrived much sooner," commented Gaspard cordially. "As it is, I am late, footsore, and most famished."

Tormod's shop had more than simple copperware in its inventory. He worked well with silver, brass, and bronze as well, and he crafted everything from pots, buckles, and jewelry to small weapons, candlesticks, and buttons. He either had or could make whatever his customers called for. Beyond the shop and up the stair Tormod lived with his family in the upper floor of the house. Behind the building, under a sturdy canopy, sat his forge.

A quick and heavy step punished the stairs, who in turn loudly betrayed the man descending before he made the landing. The approaching glow of a quick moving light suddenly vanished, and Gaspard caught a soft curse from the dark hallway. In his haste Fulk blew out his own candle. The distress lasted only a moment, and then Fulk was in the shop and embracing Gaspard.

"What news of our enemy?" he asked excitedly. "Is our challenge accepted? Will he fight?"

"The mission went better than we could have hoped, milord," replied Gaspard sternly. "You judged him quite rightly. He still believes himself the superior man and greatly desires your defeat to mark his return to glory. His vanity, just as Narcissus's, knows no bounds."

"You have much to talk about," said Tormod as he touched flame to Fulk's candle. "You should retire upstairs and my wife will prepare a meal for you and bring you drink."

Gaspard gladly thanked Tormod, begged a tankard, and then followed Fulk up the staircase. In the back of the upper floor was a large room warmed by a large clay fireplace that vented its smoke through a set of louvers in the ceiling. As though prepared by an innkeeper, the room had comfortable pallets, sturdy chairs, and a table that could accommodate eight men if need be. For now it was simply Fulk, Gaspard, and the duke's man, Gwylliam.

"He has sworn to leave his Grouville defenses unmanned for three days that we may come and go unmolested," continued Gaspard.

"How strange," replied Gwylliam. "Understanding Ducaen, would he not suspect a surprise invasion?"

"He believes Lord Fulk too honorable a man to engage in such deceit," replied Gaspard, "as do I."

Fulk nodded, "Véthe! Though it seems he is tempting me. I do believe he would gain some satisfaction if I betrayed my word and arrived on his shore with two hundred swords. Then he could say we were men cut from the same cloth."

"The duke would find no fault with you should you take that tactic," returned Gwylliam. "Ducaen is a traitor and an outlaw and should not be afforded such a privilege."

"Should not?" retorted Fulk testily.

"I mean no disrespect, milord," replied Gwylliam uneasily, "but with this new intelligence, you could mount a serious attack with little cost."

"Suppose he is lying…and instead waits in ambush?" countered Fulk, "He could easily place all his resources on the beach of Grouville and bury us under a hail of arrows before we touch land. The duke's men were killed to the last man this past summer. If I were to think like Ducaen, I would fortify Grouville until the last moment. I would not pull my men until it was a certainty my enemy was alone. Even then, I would leave lookouts posted about the island to warn me if a fleet threatened from any direction. Jersey is a small island and only vulnerable to surprise under cover of night. Even then, the rocks and shoals of her coast limit the number of beachheads safe for a large-scale night landing. Even with a relatively small number of men, I could defend any one of her beaches quite vigorously. With Ducaen alive and in command, Robert would have to likely attack with forces from the east, south, and west at the same time to spread the pirates thin. Those men would have to be fed and paid. With Ducaen dead, well, I believe chaos would then reign. There is no honor among thieves! They may be loyal to the Dragon, but likely hate each other. Men in chaos are easily defeated."

The conversation was interrupted by a knock on the door. Tormod's wife, Annora, entered bearing a large tray laden with bread, meat, and cheese and a large pitcher of fresh ale. Gaspard gladly and heartily ate while his companions shared in the ale. He was comfortable and warm, and allowed the pleasure of the simple food and drink to wash over and fill him. They continued to talk and plan as he ate.

"Remon is his right-hand man," offered Gaspard between bites. "There was only one other who was familiar to me, though I cannot recall his name or from where I know him. A young fellow. Younger than I. The rest were a motley assortment of vile men from many lands."

Gaspard paused to take a long draught of ale, and then recounted his tale omitting only his strange conversation when alone with Ducaen and the details of a night's warmth taken from a slave. At the end of the tale, Fulk sat silently for a moment, and then spoke.

"Gwylliam, I would ask you to leave us for a moment," he ordered the duke's man out of the chamber. Gwylliam nodded, gained his feet and left, closing the door softly behind him. Fulk added wood to the fire, drew a chair close to the flames, and motioned Gaspard to join him. Anxiety surged through the young man as he pulled his chair near and sat next to his lord. What did he know? What did he suspect?

"You are loyal to me, yes?" asked Fulk after a long pause.

"Yes," lied Gaspard, "to whatever end."

"You are as a brother to me," continued Fulk. "I trust in you better than even my closest cousins. Is it trust well placed?"

"Have I ever betrayed you? Or failed you? How many times have we deflected those otherwise mortal blows away from the other in battle? Your trust is well placed, milord, and I pray you will always see it as so," replied Gaspard without hesitation, his answer long prepared.

After another long pause, Fulk continued, "My mind is in anguish these past few days. More so than any time past. Gisla is against this undertaking. I believe she senses a greater ill than I can comprehend. Her foreboding has forced me to consider my own death through her eyes. What if I should die? What becomes of my wife and my son?"

"She will become chattel tied to your estate, as all widows are. Tremendous pressure will be brought to bear from all sides for her to remarry. You know those politics," replied Gaspard grimly.

"Yes…" breathed Fulk. "That is why I ask you, as my friend and brother, to intervene on her behalf as best you can. The duke respects you as a warrior, and Albric de Grentmesnel has always been taken by your boldness. Sway their thoughts. Vet her suitors. Act as my ghost corporeal. Be her shield against any lord not worthy of her in spirit. Swear to it before God!"

With those words, Gaspard's heart began to race and the sweet sensation of his hearty meal turned to painful knots in his gut. He firmly grasped the arms of his chair, lest Fulk see the trembling that coursed through his limbs. In his innocence and naivety, Fulk was bringing to bear the full weight of his curse. Gaspard could do nothing but take the oath, for to refuse would reveal his own betrayal of the man who gave to him everything good in his life.

"Though I am but a common man, without land, title, or authority, I do swear before God, to protect Gisla as you wish," replied Gaspard hoarsely.

Fulk sighed in relief, drew Gaspard to his feet, and embraced him.

"Thank you, my friend. You have eased my mind."

Unseen in the hallway, the duke's man, Gwylliam, fulfilled his own oath with an ear pressed to the door. A duke's key to power lay in more than knowing the secrets of his enemies. It was also in knowing the secrets of his friends.

CHAPTER 10

The Dragon's Welcome

Upon the rising tide, with wind and wave driving the small fishing vessel forward, Gaspard found himself in the company of his lord and again nearing Jersey's shore. The wind he fought against just days before now sped the craft easily toward Grouville Bay. Fulk gave the old fisherman more than his boat was worth, much to the aged couple's joy.

"We hope to bring your fine vessel home within a few days," said Fulk cheerfully, "Half of the purse is yours at that time. If your boat is lost, then the whole purse will cover its replacement with a bit extra for your troubles."

While the peculiar story of two lords sailing a small fishing boat "to a tournament in England" might reach the ears of Bishop Robert's agents, it was unlikely the truth of the matter would unravel in time to warn the bishop himself. The duke would keep the bishop attached to his hip with their falconry until Fulk and Gaspard returned from Jersey. It was Duke Robert who would then have the honor of confronting the bishop if all went according to plan.

They landed at the north end of Grouville Bay, in the lee of Goree Rock. Waves washed over shoals teeming with dogfish and mackerel, only to gently die upon the empty beach. Mews floated upon the channel's breeze, crying mournfully and expectantly, the only trumpeters to mark the approach of the men de Hambie. No man greeted them, and the only signs of human life were the fading footprints in the sand above high tide. Even the sense they were being watched was dim and distant. After they pulled the boat up onto the sand, anchoring its rope to a tree so the tide might not steal it, they unloaded their gear and packs. Upon the lonely beach both men felt a sense of isolation and abandonment.

Fulk's hauberk was freshly repaired, and his shield clean with fresh paint. His lance was no tournament piece blunted for friendly competition, but was instead capped by an iron spike, able to pierce both shield and armor. He expected no less from Ducaen.

"If Ducaen has truly left us alone to our devices, we could look about and find his fortifications," commented Gaspard as he unfurled his lord's standard and hung it from his spear. "It would aid in landing when we return with our men."

Fulk did not immediately answer, instead shouldering his packs and taking up his lance. His mood, light with excitement while still on the shores of Normandy, had grown grim as they crossed the water. He gazed beyond the beach and up the modest, bracken-covered slope that eventually disappeared into a forest now waking from winter's slumber. Her arms, sparse and skeletal just weeks before, were now alive with an eruption of flowers and green buds that in due time would replace those dead, moldering leaves now blanketing her roots.

Finally he grunted, distracted. "After," he said and then began to heavily ascend through the brush.

Gaspard strapped his sword to his waist, hefted his packs, raised the standard, and followed his lord up the slope. As they climbed they began to hear a noisome din of carrion birds ahead through the trees. Moments later the line of trees came to an abrupt end and they found themselves standing on the edge of a grassy plateau. There they were met by a squalling flock of ravens, black as night, fighting, feasting, flying, and landing about a peculiar arrangement of stones at the plateau's center. Above the ravens, cowardly gulls circled and cried, but rarely touched land. The stones themselves were elongated, arranged on end and buried in the turf. Not so high that Fulk and Gaspard could not see over them, they were arranged in a circle of sorts, with an east-west alignment. A short, narrow alleyway entered from the east, and a large stone table, set upon rock pillars, dominated the western edge of the circle. The circle itself was lined with stones of approximately equal height to those of the alleyway.

Both men instinctively let their packs slide from their shoulders and unsheathed their swords. With the wind at their back they caught no scent of whatever death that the ravens feasted upon. Together, they slowly advanced upon the stone circle and its ominous keepers. Known as dolmens, this was not the first time Fulk and Gaspard had come across such a place. The careworn, lichen-covered nature of the stones hinted at the circle's ancient origins, built by men whose legend had long passed from memory. Perhaps ancient druids practiced their arcane arts within the circle. Perhaps here barbarous men sacrificed goats or sheep, or even one another, to their pagan gods. Perhaps a king, great in his own day, slumbered long forgotten in the earth beneath. All that was certain was that living man had found a new use for a place they cared little to understand. As the feasting ravens continually tore flesh from within the circle and took flight, they also brought along bits of colored cloth. They dined on the corpses of men. The place could be none other than the Fairy's Table that the bard, Aymer, had described as the place the Dragon chose for his executions.

Though the ravens expressed indignation at the men's presence, they gave way as Fulk and Gaspard reached the stones and looked to the circle's center. The remains of three, perhaps four, men were strewn about the circle's interior. The savagery with which they were dismembered was beyond what the small beasts or carrion fowl of Jersey could accomplish. These poor souls were rent by the hand of man and left for the stoat, fox, mew, and raven to then carry off.

"It appears as though the Dragon welcomes us to dine at his table," commented Fulk absently.

"Or perhaps he draws us here to be certain we do not lose our way," replied Gaspard as he walked to the west end of the circle where the thick, stone table sat heavily on a circle of stone legs. With ease, he hefted himself up on to the table's top and gained his feet. Looking westward from his perch, he spied beyond the valley and its trees, a half league in the distance, the top of a striped tent.

"Our host has pitched our camp just a short walk to the west," called Gaspard from atop the table. "I suspect he means us to accept his hospitality."

"And show us my fate should I be killed, no doubt!" said Fulk darkly, staring at the human remains within the circle.

"I would never allow such a thing, milord," said Gaspard in a firm voice.

"Yet his alliance with harbingers of evil, such as these carrion birds, leaves me ill at ease," replied Fulk.

"Do not allow Ducaen into your mind in such a way, milord," assured Gaspard. "These ravens surely do not care who or what they feed on."

"So you say, yet I like not the evil eye they cast my way," retorted Fulk. "Foul birds!"

Gaspard said nothing, but mused to himself how arbitrarily the pigments of black and white were seen as dark and light, evil and good. Were the crow of white feather, would that make him a dove? Was the black sheep truly a prodigal son? What did that matter if the black sheep saved the dyer effort? He was what he was, created at the hand of God to be what he would be. Truly, the black sheep as well as the black-feathered bird were blameless tools of their creator! Gaspard lightly leapt from top of the table and joined his grim master as they walked back to their packs. On a whim, Gaspard strung his bow and drew down on a raven.

"See, milord," Gaspard with almost a mocking tone. "They are no less prey than we are."

He loosed his arrow, and it flew straight and true. With a soft thwack, it struck a raven sitting atop a stone of the circle's edge, impaling the bird and knocking it to the ground beyond view.

Fulk said nothing, but gazed darkly upon his squire. Gaspard, noting the disapproving stare, laughed lightly and shouldered his packs.

"Fulk, my friend," he chided gently. "Were I Ducaen, and I noticed these hapless birds gathered every place I left a dead body, I would certainly place fresh bait upon this very spot in hopes of disturbing your mind. 'Tis nothing more than that. What I see before me makes you all the more righteous in your quest. Jersey must be freed from the beast."

Fulk pursed his lips and sighed. "You are right, Gaspard. I am letting my mind be distracted from my task."

He lightly clapped his squire's shoulder and then bent to take up his packs and lance. The two men then walked westward, leaving the ancient stone circle behind them and descended into the thickets of the valley that separated them from the looming field of honor. By the time they made their way across to the arranged camp it was late afternoon and the clear skies of the previous week had turned overcast. The wind at first swirled, then turned, bringing with it a chill mist out of the north.

The tent was pitched on the edge of a large, open, treeless meadow. The spoor of sheep was scattered about the short-cropped turf, yet not one of the creatures was to be seen. In a makeshift corral of freshly stripped branches stood six worthy horses, three stallions and three mares. Set beyond the corral was a simple list, consisting of two long wickets, one white and one black, about fifty paces apart. In line, centered between the two wickets, a length of rope was stretched between two posts. Beyond the meadow, to the west, rose a strange, symmetrical mound resembling a tumulus. It was covered with grass and shrubs, and was perhaps forty feet in height.

The tent, spacious and round, was made of heavy panels of indigo and white hemp canvas, stitched together to form vertical stripes. Inside, found on a table heartily laden with choice food and wine, was a scroll sealed with thick, red wax impressed by a dragon signet. Gaspard broke the seal and read aloud as Fulk considered the furnishings of the tent.

To our acclaimed enemy, vassal and champion of Duke Robert of Normandy, Sir Fulk Paynel, Baron de Hambie and lord of the Sienne Valley, Sir Bertrand Ducaen, the Dragon King of Jersey and Norman baron, whose lands and possessions were unjustly stolen, bids you welcome to his king-dom on Jersey.

Your lonely presence confirms your honorable intent. In that spirit, we provide you a good tent, soft bed, delicacies untainted, and the promise of safe passage to and from our land for your esteemed squire, Gaspard Malfort.

In acceptance of your challenge, we exercise our right to dictate the nature of the duel. In our previous meeting, upon the list of Rouen, two great warriors tilted thrice and you gained the narrowest of victories by virtue of remaining in the saddle. We demand a rematch. You will put away any lance on your person in favor those provided, for they are blunted to ensure neither combatant is slain during the joust. You may divide the lances as you see fit, each combatant receiving three. Of the six noble steeds, all excellent beasts, you will choose not only yours, but ours as well. We will suffer you no disad-vantage. Again, two great warriors will tilt three times to finally determine the greater man in the saddle. After the third tilt, we shall test our steel against one another to the death.

The Dragon and his second shall join you at dawn.

Signed by the Dragon, Sir Bertrand Ducaen

Two comfortable pallets covered with fine linens and furs were raised from the floor, set on low timbers. The table bore roast pheasant, sweetmeats, fine cheeses, and fresh bread. A pairing of silver platters and jewel encrusted goblets were set near two carafes of wine. Six tour-nament lances, all tipped by Ducaen's clenched fist, stood in a stand at the center of the tent. An oil lamp was located atop a basket filled with sea-coal next to a large brazier. The brazier was quite warm, and Fulk found live coals banked within. Two beautifully tooled saddles straddled a wood stand. In all, a most hospitable welcome! A wry smile crossed Fulk's face.

"Truly, Ducaen's arrogant expectation of victory knows no con-straint," he observed.

"Do not be fooled, milord," warned Gaspard. "While he has no fear of you, his mind is ill at ease. He is a calculating man and would not be drawn into such a contest by choice. Now here, he must appear fearless. Were you in his place, could you display anything but arrogant confidence?"

"No," replied Fulk, thinking of Raymond. "No, I also would reject any outward notion of worry."

"*As does he*," said Gaspard, "but his inward self will be as hard as stone, accepting and giving no quarter."

There was a moment's pause between the men as Fulk hefted one of Ducaen's lances. Gaspard took Fulk's standard, the gold trimmed white wolf, and planted it deep within the earth next to the white wicket. When Fulk stepped out of the tent to examine the horses in the corral, Gaspard, as was his duty, laid out his lord's helm, shield, and armor. Quietly and carefully, he unpacked and built a small altar—a miniature olivewood table from the holy land covered by gold-spun cloth and adorned with a blessed crucifix, a small bronze bowl, and prayer candles—and set it against the eastern wall of the tent. Into the bronze bowl he carefully placed several pieces of myrrh resin on top of a handful of cedar incense. He then pulled forth the banked coals and added fuel to the brazier, breathing life into their dormant fire. Finally, Gaspard left the tent to join Fulk who stood inside the corral among the horses.

"All but one are excellent beasts," commented Fulk when he noticed his squire standing outside the corral. He was stroking the neck of an aging chestnut mare past her prime. "My enemy tempts me, allowing me to choose him a weak steed. 'Tis a mocking gesture, no doubt. Should I spite this gesture and allot him the inferior mount? Or should I take this old mare out of pity and pride?"

Gaspard began to climb over the rail. "I would argue that Ducaen knows each of the beasts well enough. He will not fear—" but he found himself cut short when out of the group charged a black mare. She was the finest of the lot and Fulk's clear choice. She reared, snorted, and stamped her feet, blocking his entry. Her eyes were wild, nostrils flared, and her neighing was a shrewish scream. Gaspard was forced to leap clear, tumbling on his back as her sharp hooves crashed against the rail, leaving a deep gash in the green limb.

Fulk rushed to the mare as she snorted and scuffed the ground angrily. Speaking soft words and caressing her neck, he first settled her then led her to the opposite side of the pen. When he finally turned and made his way among the horses, he spied Gaspard regaining his feet with an angry grimace on his face. A curious sense of familiarity suddenly dawned upon Fulk. Why would a horse, completely unknown to them and very welcoming with Fulk, react with such hatred toward Gaspard? The answer slowly emerged before Fulk, and he shuddered. In his mind, he had always seen Gaspard as a reflection of his childhood companion. Never aging. Never growing. Now he saw before him Gaspard the man, and that man possessed the visage of his greatest enemy, Bertrand Ducaen. Was this the mysterious secret his father, Hugh Paynel, had taken with him to the depths of the sea? Was Gaspard the bastard son of Bertrand Ducaen, secreted away within the walls of a convent then placed under the protection of Hugh Paynel? For what purpose and to what end?

"That mare is mad!" complained Gaspard angrily. "What demon occupies her mind to make her attack me so?"

"I know not," worried Fulk. "But I believe Ducaen selected these horses for traits beyond their ability in battle. We must take greater care in selecting what beast I ride, and what we allow him. Here now, remove that loose rail so I can lead the black from the corral. Once we are away, I would have you walk among the others and judge them as you can."

Gaspard removed the rail, and then stepped away while Fulk led the fiery black mare away from the corral. Once they were clear, he stepped inside and reset the rail. Walking among them, he found all but the aged mare to be excellent. Three stallions, one a dapple white, one a chestnut, and one black with a white square between the eyes milled alongside one muscular tan and white mare. The chestnut stallion was particularly attentive to Gaspard, allowing easy access to his mouth and hooves, and nuzzling the squire's hands attentively.

Fulk studied the horses' reactions as Gaspard approached and addressed each one in turn. He was good with horses and nearly Fulk's equal in the saddle. Of them, only the dapple white stallion feigned indifference with Gaspard.

"I would choose this chestnut male if I were to ride into battle," said Gaspard. "He is responsive and compliant."

"Why not the dapple white?" asked Fulk.

"He feels unfamiliar," replied Gaspard. "Perhaps with time, but we do not have time."

"None the less, I would have you saddle him for me," commanded Fulk.

Gaspard glanced questioningly at Fulk but saw his lord was decided. He climbed out of the corral and returned to the tent. Some moments passed while he gathered the tack needed to saddle the horse, when suddenly he heard Fulk burst out yelling.

"Yah yah!" he cried. "Away with you!"

Gaspard ran out of the tent, saddle and bridle dropping to the ground, to find Fulk slapping the hindquarter of the chestnut stallion, chasing him from the pen. He followed by dismissing the black stallion and the tan and white mare. He chased all three away from the field, and they galloped into forest and disappeared. All that remained in the corral when he was finished was the white dapple, the angry black mare, and the elderly chestnut.

"Milord! What have you done?" exclaimed Gaspard as he watched what he thought to be the three best horses vanish into the trees.

"Narrowed the field!" said Fulk. "I will ride the white dapple. Ducaen can have his choice of the black or the nag. By my wager, he will choose the nag."

"As would I," countered Gaspard. "The black is mad!"

"But I would not," retorted Fulk. "I would choose the black."

"I do not understand, milord."

"Neither do I, but on the morrow I may, and then I will offer you what explanation I can. For now, we will not touch the repast provided by our host. Eat only of that food we brought with us."

Though bewildered by Fulk's demonstration, Gaspard gathered up the tack and carried it to the corral.

"You should take hold of her lest she charge me a second time," warned Gaspard as he readied to climb into the pen and saddle up the white dapple.

Fulk nodded, entered, and lent a restraining hand upon the incensed mare's neck. She responded by rubbing her great black forehead against his rough jerkin. This allowed Gaspard to approach the white dapple and secure the saddle, bit, and bridle. When he was finished, he climbed the rail and left the corral. Fulk approached and soothed the white dapple, and then mounted in one, smooth motion. Gaspard then opened the corral and Fulk walked his mount out.

After running the sturdy stallion through a series of healthy exercises, Fulk finally dismounted as darkness fell about the camp. He relieved the horse of the saddle, bit, and bridle and joined Gaspard in the dimly lit tent. The warmth of the brazier was most welcome as the chill mist thickened about the camp. The men made a meal out of their own stale rations, forgoing the sumptuous fare before them on the table. Once finished, Gaspard used the flame of the lamp to light the candles and incense resting on the altar.

"Come, milord, let us pray to God for strength and victory," invited Gaspard, just as he had before each of their many tournaments and battles.

Fulk joined Gaspard and they knelt, facing both the altar and the east beyond. Then as one, they broke into a lilting cadence and began reciting a prayer long remembered.

> *Blessed be Yahweh, my rock,*
> *who trains my hand for war*
> *and my fingers for battle,*
> *my love, my bastion,*
> *my citadel, my savior,*
> *I shelter behind him, my shield,*
> *he makes the nations submit to me.*

Yahweh, what is man, that you should notice him?
A human being, that you should think about him?
Man's life, a mere puff of wind,
his days, as fugitive as shadows.

Yahweh, lower your heavens, come down to us!
Touch the mountains, make them smoke,
flash your lightning—scatter them,
shoot your arrows—rout them.

Reach down your hand from above,
save me, rescue me from deep waters,
from power of aliens
who tell nothing but lies,
who are prepared to swear falsehood!

The sweet scent of myrrh and cedar filled the tent as the two men knelt, deep in their own thoughts, with their own secrets unknown to one another.

CHAPTER 11

Victory and Betrayal

Morning came and Gaspard, dressed in his finest with sword and knife belted to his waist, waited outside their tent for the arrival of Ducaen and his second. He drew up his hood and pulled his heavy cloak tight to fend off the damp, swirling coastal mist. Both knight and squire suffered fitful sleep and rose with the first break of light. Before a battle there exists such anxious energy that deep, restful sleep is hardly needed. They ate with little conversation.

"Today is the nones of March," observed Fulk absently.

"Eight days to the ides," replied Gaspard. Eight days remained until the betrayal and murder of Caesar.

In the still atmosphere Gaspard helped Fulk don and secure his heavy chain hauberk. First Fulk slipped into a heavily padded shirt, and then the long, supple, steel armor. Lastly, Gaspard placed the white surcoat emblazoned with the white wolf over Fulk's shoulders and tied it into place. Fulk's gauntlets, great sword, and helm remained on the pallet. Not once did Gaspard betray his own dark emotions, his confidence in Fulk's prophesied defeat and death. Instead, it was Fulk who betrayed his own worries. From Gisla's sense of ill, to the dawning suspicion of Gaspard's lineage, to the knowledge that Ducaen saw Gaspard in that same light, Fulk's mind was called away from the task at hand.

"Perhaps he, too, senses his own doom," thought Gaspard to himself, ignorant of Fulk's suspicions.

Once Fulk was dressed to his squire's satisfaction, the two Normans then gathered the tack and exited the tent. They found the three steeds huddled close together in the corral. Fulk distracted the black mare while Gaspard quietly approached the white dapple and led him from the corral. With a confident hand he dressed the stallion and climbed into the saddle while Fulk returned to the solitude of the tent. Much like Fulk the night before, he guided the horse through exercises to loosen and warm him. Once done, he took his position next to the standard and awaited the arrival of Ducaen.

It was not long before two riders emerged from the tree line at the northwest edge of the field. Ducaen arrived, not with Remon, as Gaspard would have expected, but with the tall, lanky youth Gaspard had seen seated at the Dragon's left hand just days before. While of imposing height and broad of shoulder, the lad lacked the bulk or manly appearance of a warrior. Instead, he sported sandy curls and rosy cheeks with only a wisp of a beard, and a look of entitled cruelty in his eyes. His clothing was the finery of a princeling, gold and blue, not the dress of a pirate or squire. Still his arrogant face was familiar to Gaspard, and still his name eluded him.

Gaspard ducked into the tent to find Fulk, back to the door, facing the altar with his hand idly rubbing Gisla's lock tied about his neck. The sight of the braided lock froze Gaspard mid-step. His eyes narrowed, lips pursed, and he felt a renewed resentment against his lord. The lock and the love it represented should be his. Would be his!

"They have arrived, milord," he said coldly, breaking Fulk's reverie.

Fulk turned and smiled vaguely at Gaspard. Seeing his lord absent the fire for battle always found in his eyes, Gaspard stepped forward and angrily grasped Fulk's shoulders.

"Milord, your enemy is here! Find your anger, your righteous hatred of him! You must burn inside!" he demanded, then thinking to himself, "So you can meet your end as a man."

Fulk stared long and hard into the clear blue eyes of his squire.

"No matter the end, my friend, know that I love you!" whispered Fulk, as though reading his thoughts. His face then hardened, and his brow furrowed. He returned Gaspard's rough embrace, then made for the door of the tent. "Bring three lances for Ducaen!"

He threw open the flaps and strode out into the open. He spied Ducaen and his second walking their light horses to the corral.

"Bertrand Ducaen!" shouted Fulk across the field at the approaching riders, "I would speak with you!"

Gaspard emerged from the tent to see Ducaen rein up at midfield and dismount. Jersey's "king" wore armor similar to Fulk's, though his surcoat was black cloth emblazoned with a gold dragon. He spoke and motioned to his young second, handing off his horse. The young prince-ling proceeded to the corral while Ducaen waited for Fulk to approach, well out of earshot of either of their seconds. From high on his horse, the princeling looked down upon Fulk briefly as he passed. His face bore an insolent sneer, and his eyes, the left of which was painfully bruised and swollen, were filled with hatred. It was a face Fulk recognized, and in it Fulk found the key to Ducaen's plan.

"I now understand why Robert values your council in the field," said Ducaen cordially once he was face to face with Fulk.

"Pray tell, what have I done to earn your praise?" asked Fulk coldly.

Ducaen nodded in the direction of the horses. "You divined I would pass on the black mare in favor of the old chestnut despite the black being a superior beast. Very insightful."

"A queer way to send a message," replied Fulk, "and dangerous. I could have left you only the black."

Ducaen laughed lightly. "Could you have? I think not! It is your great failing, Sir Fulk, this honor bound code of right and wrong you relent-lessly live by. Make no mistake, it is admirable that you possess enough strength of arm to free yourself from the deceptive intrigues of court life. However, eventually you would find yourself facing the Devil's choice. It cannot be avoided. Truly, it will be best for you if you die here this day, at my hand, than in some disillusioned future betrayed by some friend, ally, or servant. No, you had no choice but to leave me a dependable mount. All Normandy knows this, and eventually someone would use this knowledge against you. To my good fortune, that old mare still has a few good fights left in her."

"On this day of your death, I will allow you some small clarity," replied Fulk. "The end is simply the end. The means by which we find our end is everything. God will not judge me by the actions of any of my future betrayers, only by those wrongs I have done, and those rights I have failed to do. You will be judged in the same fashion."

At this Ducaen gave a single chuckle and faintly shook his head. God was no longer interested in judging him.

"But you distract me from what I would offer you. It is beyond Gaspard to suspect that you, of all men, might be his father. He still remembers your drunken insult and has not softened his view of you. Should you choose to confess yourself to him, and beg his forgiveness this day, I would not intervene. It is your right."

The cordial arrogance left Ducaen's face, replaced by a dark glower. "If I were dead, would you tell him?"

"No. No good can come of it. So if your game is to reveal yourself, for whatever end, now is your time," said Fulk sternly. "I will surely take this knowledge to the grave."

"Should I gain victory this day, I will, in time, turn his face to me. Should you gain victory, you will have killed your squire's father," returned Ducaen slowly. "Either way, I take something from you."

It was Fulk's turn to laugh. "I will not chase such fairy-fire in the mist! I am here…no, *we* are here to finish a fight started long ago, not to fight over the destiny of Gaspard. Did you believe you could return to Normandy and not pay your debt to me? I was upon your door the hour you fled. You have never been far from my mind. That you may be Gaspard's father changes nothing. If you desire him to know his lineage, as shameful as it is, tell him now. In death you will be silenced."

"As will you!" shot back Ducaen. "Have you made your peace with him? Has he not earned his spurs three times over? Have you not deliberately kept him without title? A mere squire, yet most lordly men fear him in battle? He is little better than a companion dog to you, there to lick your hand, sit at your feet, and read your letters aloud! Only now we find his blood is equal to your own. He is no longer a boy, Fulk, and has greater purpose than to idolize you. He is a man, and were he not kept from me by those accursed brothers, he would be at my side, not yours, and he would have his title and his lands."

"You speak a twisted truth. He is as a brother to me!" denied Fulk through gritted teeth, even as Ducaen's words, an inalienable truth, wrenched terribly at his heart. He now saw he could have, and should have, advanced Gaspard. His squire deserved a squire of his own, yet he continued to carry Fulk's water just as he had when he was a spindly boy. In truth, Fulk dearly loved his friend, but that love was selfish and childish. He ought to have set him free.

"Noble men do not have brothers, you young fool, only rivals," Ducaen countered, "You think him a loyal dog, but I wager he is a wolf in wait."

"His position is secure, and his title will come. I have done no ill to him," defended Fulk. "But had the duke not intervened all those years ago, you would have, in ignorance, slain your only heir! It is you who sinned against him. One last time, will you choose to make your peace while you still can?"

Ducaen glanced at Gaspard in the distance, and then returned his gaze to Fulk. His face softened ever so slightly.

"I would have him know only if I am able to give him his due," he said finally.

Fulk nodded. In death, Ducaen could give Gaspard nothing but a cursed name. Only in life, with a successful campaign to restore his noble standing, could Ducaen offer any recompense to his heir. Ducaen was silent as Fulk walked away, neither man with an easy heart. With equal clarity, the two warriors did know the other's mind.

Fulk strode to Gaspard's side and the waiting white dapple stallion. The princeling finished dressing the old chestnut and walked her to the black wicket where he unfurled and planted Ducaen's standard.

"You are right in recognizing Ducaen's young second," warned Fulk softly to Gaspard. "We came across him when the duke landed us at Mont St. Michel to battle the Bretons. He is a wealthy Breton noble by name of Drogo. His father, an ally of Count Alan, was slain when we fell upon their left flank. That he is here speaks of an unholy alliance between Brittany and Ducaen. Robert must be warned!"

Young Lord Drogo of Brittany stood with the standard of the Dragon to his left and the securely mounted Bertrand Ducaen to his right. He held Ducaen's two remaining lances and great sword, each to be used in turn. His gold-trimmed, blue cape covered his own heavy sword belted firmly about his waist. He, too, remembered the battle where his father fell, pierced by an arrow of an accursed Northman. The alliance with Bertrand Ducaen, while distasteful, would give Count Alan the advantage he needed to break Robert and Normandy.

Ducaen was obviously mad and not to be trusted except in his hatred of the line of men ruling the duchy. When Drogo pointed out that regaining his lands and title would be far less costly if he simply paid homage to Robert with both word and gold, he was confronted with angry spittle and fearsome abuse. Ducaen's rage at the suggestion of such a compromise left the young Breton lord shaken and wishing another had been sent in his stead to confirm the alliance. Surely Bertrand Ducaen, in time, would pose the same problems to Count Alan as he posed to Duke Robert. He was an unmanageable man. Alan would simply have to do away with him with more efficiency than Duke Richard had. For now, his gold and his mercenary army were as important to Brittany as his hatred for Duke Robert and his court. All of which could be lost with today's foolish duel! Drogo glared hatefully at Ducaen, helm on and high in the saddle.

If anything, the chill, penetrating mist enveloping the field thickened as Fulk and Ducaen, fully armored, met on the list. Their faces were hid beneath their dull, steel helms. Their long, tear-shaped shields bore their proud standards. Jets of steam shot from the horses' nostrils as they nervously dug at the turf by the wickets a mere fifty paces apart. A simple, thin line of rope was all that separated their lanes.

"Ready!" cried Ducaen.

"Ready!" boomed Fulk.

"Eyah!" cried Ducaen, and both knights dug their spurs into the flanks of their mounts.

The chestnut mare flexed and surged beneath Ducaen. Mud and grass flew as the white dapple leapt forward. One, two, three strides, and each man lowered and aimed his fist-tipped lance. Four, five, six, seven strides for their play. Eight! It was just a matter of seconds and a final split second's decision for a win, loss, or draw. From nose to foot every muscle was taut, preparing to strike like a coiled viper. A blow too high, too low, or too late could easily end the contest. It was the thundering clap of the lance against the shield, the crunch of wood against the jangling steel rings of the hauberk, and the crackle of the splintering shafts. Simultaneously, two mighty blows thrust fearlessly and recklessly found their marks. As the horses galloped forward, Fulk and Ducaen were both hammered backwards, out of their saddles, and slammed to the waterlogged earth.

No crowd was present to gasp and cheer, and there was no wealthy lord, duke, or king to take note or give accolades. Nor were the blows those of a friendly competition between gentlemen. Had Fulk used the lance he carried with him from Hambic, and Ducaen a like spear, their contest would have been mortally concluded. As it was, both men lay sprawled, unable to move as they gasped to find their breath. Both Gaspard and Drogo raced to their knights, straining to right them before retrieving their mounts. It was some moments before Fulk and Ducaen again swung heavily into the saddle armed with a fresh lance.

"Ready!" cried Fulk.

"Ready!" shouted Ducaen.

"Yah yah!" cried Fulk, and again the spurs bit deeply. Again the chargers dug their hooves into the soft turf and leapt forward. So seasoned was each man, so reflexive, that instinct and reason were one in battle. They had no need to take time to consider what change would be made. The changes were fluid. One, two, three strides, and again the lances came down and across their bodies. Four, five, six, seven strides for their play. Eight! Bodies twisting, shields adjusting, then a strike too high and a strike too low amounting to a pair of painful glancing blows, neither with the force to unseat a rider.

As they cantered their horses back to their standards, Ducaen paused and made to speak.

"We are still a match, enemy mine! I have killed hundreds, and rare is the man who is able to contest his death," laughed Ducaen roughly from inside his helm.

"Old men and young boys, no doubt!" retorted Fulk.

"Where are your manners, Sir Fulk?" chided Ducaen. "I compliment you, and you insult me?"

"You boast of your sins. Do not beg praise for it," returned Fulk harshly.

Ducaen scowled, reined the old mare round even with his standard, and then took up his third lance from Drogo.

"Ready!" roared the Dragon.

Fulk balanced and secured his last lance.

"Ready!" growled the lord de Hambie.

"Ayah!"

The horses thundered and the ground rumbled. Fulk roared, brought his lance low and across his body, driving the great fist with all his strength at Ducaen's midline. But Ducaen vanished! He was not where he ought to be, but instead was a half stride behind! The old chestnut mare had performed a peculiar stutter step and got off stride. Fulk did not have time to sense the light parry that sent his blow wide and the following strong repost before it exploded on the center of his shield, hurling him from the saddle. His wind was gone, and he saw only darkness with small explosions of light as his great, armored frame hit the ground.

Ducaen tossed his lance to one side, slowed his horse, and pulled off his helmet. Rather than turn back to inspect his fallen enemy, he stared at Gaspard in puzzlement. Instead of rushing to his lord's side, helping him rise, and then handing off his great sword, Gaspard simply leaned on the heavy, leather wrapped pommel and looked darkly down upon Fulk's motionless form. The angst Ducaen expected was utterly absent in Gaspard's face.

"You had best check on your lord," he said in a soft, stern, even fatherly voice.

Gaspard slowly turned toward Ducaen with cold irritation. The younger man stared at the elder, his deep blue eyes piercing yet distant, almost vacant. With a careless motion, he shouldered Fulk's blade and walked to his still body. Only when Fulk stirred did Gaspard speak, and then without turning his head back to Ducaen.

"Allow him a moment to recover so your contest can continue honorably," Gaspard said plainly, as though anything else would be considered.

Gaspard stooped, the feigned look of concern returning to his face, and helped Fulk remove his helmet. He spoke reassuring words and lent a strong hand to steady his lord. The shield was cracked, and its straps and grip no longer offered service. Fulk sat, removing the shield from his tender arm, and then he stood. At first he leaned on Gaspard, but once steady Fulk drew a deep breath.

"I am a fool, my friend," he whispered to Gaspard. "Ducaen is one step ahead of me."

Gaspard looked questioningly at Fulk, but Fulk merely shook his head.

"I will recover momentarily. Lend me your flask."

Fulk swished, spat, and then drank.

"My sword."

Gaspard withdrew the long, heavy sword de Hambie from its sheath. Fulk took it up, gripping it with firm, sure hands. Meanwhile,

Ducaen had trotted back to Drogo, dismounted, and was standing with his arms folded on his chest, waiting. The time of vengeance had arrived, and the stains of history were about to be scrubbed clean. Without hesitation, Bertrand Ducaen replaced his helm, took up his sword, and sprang upon his enemy.

Fulk met the raging onslaught with equal vim, slicing, clashing, crashing, and spinning. Knights parried blow after blow. They twisted and danced away from counter attacks. The sounds of steel rang out as the vicious slashes were deflected, followed by riposting lunges knocked away, followed by yet more counter attacks. Fulk beat Ducaen's blade back, searching for an opening, only to have Ducaen sidestep while gliding down Fulk's blade with his own, then shoving Fulk sideways. As Fulk reeled, Ducaen slashed at his legs. Fulk swung low, deflecting the blow and jumped away.

Ducaen again pressed hard, only to have Fulk deflect his blade with a smooth, powerful sweep, coming back across his chest, sheering through his armor as he drove through and past. Ignoring the painful gash, Ducaen swung around with a vicious slash upon Fulk's left shoulder before he had a chance to turn and reface his opponent. Blood was suddenly flowing freely from both men, but it failed to stem the onslaught. Instead, the sight of it appeared to enrage them both, and their efforts were suddenly redoubled!

Feints, attacks, parries, and counter attacks scored and notched each of the great swords. Fulk stamped the ground, and Ducaen barked in hopes of creating a hesitation or stutter. Fulk had the greater reach, and his sudden lunge pricked Ducaen's stomach, while Ducaen's counter met only thin air. Ducaen beat down Fulk's blade, closed, and struck Fulk full in the helm with his gauntleted fist. Fulk's mouth filled with taste of his own blood. Though his helm was askew, limiting his vision, he managed to drive his guard into Ducaen's stomach, knocking his wind from him. He thrust Ducaen away, righted his helm, and again pressed the attack.

The cold drizzle that began to fall through the heavy, morning mist was match to the salty sweat that ran down their necks and stung their eyes. The grass turned to stinking, sulfurous mud beneath their iron-shod feet. Again, Ducaen closed under Fulk's blade, only this time, once inside the sword's reach, he dropped his own weapon and grappled Fulk under the arms. Even as Fulk brought the pommel of his sword down upon his helm, Ducaen cleanly lifted him from his feet and tripped him backwards. The full weight of his shoulder driving into Fulk's chest would have knocked the wind from a lesser man, leaving him helpless, but not Fulk. The great Norman warrior had spent a boyhood wrestling his squire every day. As the years went on Gaspard grew in size and strength, and not all matches went in Fulk's favor. Now, with Ducaen atop him, he let go of his sword and reflexively locked his arms tightly about Ducaen's neck and his legs Ducaen's waist.

For a long moment the furious battle paused while Fulk's powerful lock about Ducaen's head began to crush first his helm and then his life. The Dragon's breath and blood were being relentlessly constricted. Ducaen rained a thunder of blows to Fulk's sides with no effect. He brought his knees up hoping to find Fulk's groin, but Fulk's legs were locked so tightly about his waist, he could land no blow. He could not even pull his knife from his belt. He reached for Fulk's eyes, but could not dislodge his helm. He pried at Fulk's fingers, but could not break his grip. He dug in his feet, but only succeeded in driving Fulk's back harmlessly through the turf and mud.

Ducaen, as powerful and hard as he was, found himself failing. Spittle shot from his mouth as the edges of his helm bit painfully into his neck. His lips swelled, his eyes bulged as their blood vessels burst, and his vision was turning dark. Blood, oozing from the gash in his chest, soaked through Fulk's surcoat. Frantically, he flailed about while Fulk arched his back to put further pressure on his desperate lungs. Only then did Ducaen find it…on the belt around Fulk's waist…what felt like a small pommel though his heavy gauntlet. Yes! A pommel and a hilt…Fulk's fine-pointed dagger! Ducaen fumbled for the dagger, grasped it, yanked from its scabbard, and plunged it through chain, flesh, and sinew with a mighty blow. He twisted the blade with all his strength, digging deeper and deeper into the gut as Fulk cried out in pain and blood poured from his side.

Fulk released his lock on Ducaen's head as Ducaen withdrew the narrow blade and prepared for another blow. Just as Ducaen again plunged the dagger deep into Fulk's side, sneaking through the rings of steel, Fulk grasped the front and back of Ducaen's helm and gave it a violent twist. With a soft pop and crackle, Fulk wrenched the Dragon's head cleanly about, breaking his neck. Bertrand Ducaen went instantly limp, and whatever life left in him fled seconds later as he stared at the soft, gray mists swirling in the sky above. Fulk, his strength now failing, could only just manage to pull his dagger from his side before darkness took him.

Lord Drogo, the young Breton noble, full of arrogance and vengeance, stood frozen near Ducaen's dragon standard, aghast at the sight before him. He had arrived on Jersey eleven days before, an emissary of Count Alan of Brittany, with strategic details of the alliance with Jersey's pirate king, Bertrand Ducaen. Drogo had been impressed, not only by Ducaen's wealthy war chest, but more importantly, his singular hatred for Duke Richard's stem, Robert, and his bastard brat, William. Ducaen was neither stupid nor foolish, unless plied with too much wine. He would not be outwitted easily, and certainly not by a man as young as Drogo, a truth of which Drogo had been thoroughly warned. Yet planning was a necessary part of any rebellion, and Drogo had a role to play.

The importance of his role became all too clear with the arrival of the insolent squire of Normandy's champion. While a year or two older than Drogo, Gaspard was obviously an ill-bred man who fancied a cloak paid for by the Baron de Hambie shielded him from any reprisal. And the effect he had on Ducaen was most disturbing—as though by entering the Dragon's hall and throwing down a gauntlet, he stripped away a layer of sanity, revealing Ducaen's primal core. Suddenly his fortress on Jersey, usually an orderly and disciplined place, especially for pirate rabble, became a flurry of activity. Ducaen held private meetings with his lieutenants, the wealth of his caves was packed into crates, sacks and barrels. Remon vanished the next day on some secret mission, and Drogo found himself restricted to the point of feeling imprisoned.

Drogo felt it his obligation to protest such a risky duel, offering the idea of imprisonment, ransom, or even murder, in order to protect Ducaen's necessary role for the invasion of Normandy. With little other opportunity, he finally accosted Ducaen in the grotto two days before the scheduled arrival of his opponent to air his grievances on Count Alan's behalf. Without word or warning, Ducaen struck him hard across the face, knocking him to the floor.

"You insolent whelp! I have killed men for less," yelled Ducaen angrily. "I certainly am going to meet the Baron de Hambie on the field of honor. Not only that, you will join me, so you can report my exploits to all of Brittany."

All this left Drogo standing, on the chill, damp nones of March, one of only two witnesses to the most valiant duel between the greatest warriors of their day. He had never seen as hotly a contested battle between two such Goliaths. He was deeply torn between the nobility and grandeur of their efforts, which almost brought a tear to his eye, and his disgust with Ducaen's mad self-destruction. The victory over Normandy, once as easily plucked as low-hanging fruit, now lay smashed and dead on the ground with his head unnaturally twisted halfway round.

Across from him, near the standard de Hambie, stood the contemptuous squire, Gaspard, staring blandly at the motionless bodies, utterly devoid of any dismay. What a strangely disturbing reaction to the death of his lord! Gaspard removed his cloak, slung it across his arm, and then slowly walked over to the bodies. With a casual foot, he kicked Ducaen's form off of Fulk and whistled a low note.

"That was unexpected," he said with a bemused voice as he crouched to examine the fallen men. "I call it...a draw."

He then stood and casually closed the short distance remaining between Drogo and himself. He smiled conspiratorially. "I think I may know you," he said slyly. "You are a Breton, no? And I see you are not wearing your armor."

With a sudden realization of his danger, Drogo grasped for his great sword. It was a long, heavy weapon, meant to cut down both man and horse with a single blow, and clumsy to draw forth. With one smooth motion, Gaspard dropped his cloak and drew his own thin, light blade that whispered a steely snicker as it leapt into his hand.

"Drogo…" he spoke the name as he lunged, running the young Breton lord through the heart. His face still sporting a panicked expression, Drogo crumpled to the ground, his sword still partly within its scabbard. If he was surprised Gaspard knew him, it was impossible to say.

Gaspard pulled his bloodied blade from Drogo's breast and carefully searched the forest's edge surrounding the meadow with his eyes, expecting some hidden pirate attack to burst forth and confront him. All was still and silent except for the whisper of the wind and light rain. He closed his eyes for a moment and listened for sounds far away, but caught only the faint cry of gulls. Satisfied as to his immediate safety, he wiped his sword on Drogo's cloak and put it away.

"Hmff," he thought to himself as he stood over the lanky Breton's dead form. "Foolish to choose a sword to match one's pride, rather than skill or ability. At least I can make use of it."

With that he took hold of Drogo's sword, laid the man flat, and chopped off his head. After donning his cloak, he grasped up his handiwork by its sandy curls, and walked through the morning Jersey drizzle to the tent. Once inside, his eye caught the handsome meal placed on the table by Ducaen. His stomach growled at the sight of the roast fowl, so he carelessly dropped Drogo's head and sword on the ground with a thump, wiped his hands on the bed linens, pulled up a stool, and satisfied his hunger.

First he unstoppered the wine, filled a jeweled goblet, and quenched his thirst, and then he pulled the knife from his belt and sliced into the wheel of cheese. He tore into the pheasant, broke the bread, and refilled his goblet, all the time laughing softly, with almost childish glee, at his situation. Fulk dead. Ducaen dead. A Breton lord dead. And his hands were clean. The story of how Ducaen betrayed the field of honor. How the injured Ducaen, after killing Fulk, ordered his men to attack and slay Gaspard. How Gaspard slew three of Ducaen's men, and then turned on

Ducaen and cut him down.   The story swirled and formed in his mind as he enjoyed delicious sweet meats, olives, and more wine. Robert would rage; Gisla would swoon and fall into his arms, thankful for his protection. As for Gaspard, well, he was one step closer to raising his station. Oh yes, he would spin the most heroic tale and amaze them all with his quality!

Eventually, once his belly was full and his step a little unsteady with drink, he broke his reverie and returned to practical matters. He left the tent and stared out at the field. The white dapple had wandered away, but the old chestnut mare stood near the bodies, quietly chewing grass. Ducaen and Fulk remained side by side, their blood and filth now smeared with the rain that soaked their surcoats.

Gaspard retrieved Ducaen's sword then squatting at his head, twisted his top back into place and tried to pry off the crushed helmet. He found the steel bent so tight against Ducaen's skull, that he could not remove the helm without skinning Ducaen's neck and ears. He was forced to retrieve the sweet oil from the tent and pour it through the helm's face to lubricate the inside. He then sat Ducaen up and applied his not inconsiderable strength to reshape and then remove the helm without doing too much damage to his face. Grasping Ducaen by the hair, Gaspard looked in the dead man's face and sneered.

"It is truly a shame I will never test my metal against you, Bertrand Ducaen, and that you shall never know the greatness of the gift I receive this day by your hand," he chuckled. "You are my unwitting assassin, my emancipator. You blackened your own soul with the sin of my longing, leaving me clean. My wings, clipped for so many years, are now healed, and I am ready to fly. I will take everything my lord held dear as my own. I shall drink his wine, collect his rent, command his men, and bed his wife. In return, I believe I will forgive you your insult. A fair exchange, no?"

Gaspard laughed, let go of Ducaen's locks, and the body fell limply to the ground. Picking up Ducaen's great sword, he gave one mighty swing and severed Ducaen's head from his body. Tossing the sword aside, he turned his attention to Fulk, who was sprawled face up next to Ducaen. He had waited near six years for this moment and all thought of remorse was lost to the wine he had consumed. Rather than recall his years of good life in Hambie, he stared down upon his fallen lord and benefactor with contempt, glad in his death.

"You fought valiantly, milord! Such a spectacle deserved a cheering throng, though alas, I am now your only witness. I will spin a valorous tale for you. I am confident you will not mind a few embellishments! You see, the battle was so intense, our mission would have been compromised had I attempted to retrieve your body," he feigned discouragement, then laughed again. "The pirates, they gave chase once they found Ducaen had fallen. After giving them battle, it was all I could do to escape with only your sword, and the heads of Drogo and Ducaen, of course. Before Robert's eyes I will be greatly grieved."

Gaspard then knelt and reached for Fulk's helm, pulling it from his head. His lord's lips were pallid, bloodless lines, slightly slack, and his faced was bruised and wet. He leaned close and carefully reached inside of Fulk's hauberk, feeling for Gisla's lock he knew was about Fulk's neck.

"Oh, yes, milord," he whispered spitefully in the fallen man's ear, "I covet your wife, now your widow. I always have. I will surely vet her suitors, for I intend to take her for myself."

With a sure hand, Gaspard drew forth the woven lock and made to untie its knotted ribbon and release it from Fulk's neck. Suddenly Fulk's eyes flew open, and he grasped Gaspard's wrist with his left hand and wrenched it away from the lock.

"Not while I still have breath, you Judas goat!" Fulk growled.

He was not dead! With his right hand Fulk picked up his own dagger that still lay by his side and slashed into Gaspard's ribs. Gaspard screamed in fear and pain, leaping backwards, while Fulk groaned and attempted to rise.

"This cannot be! Ducaen killed you…you are dead; it was foretold!" cried Gaspard in panic as blood ran from the wound, staining his shirt.

"What madness has taken you? Have you taken council with the Devil himself?" gasped Fulk shakily, as he struggled to his hands and knees. "My curse is upon you, brother!"

Gaspard angrily stepped forward and kicked Fulk mightily in the face, sending him sprawling onto his back. Fulk groaned as a trickle of red ran from his gashed lips. Gaspard then brought his boot harshly down on Fulk's right arm, forcing him to release the dagger, which he quickly kicked aside. Stepping back a half-pace, Gaspard twice kicked Fulk in the side where Ducaen had earlier pierced his armor.

Fulk cried out and coughed in agony, blood filling his mouth and again flowing from the clotted wounds in his side.

"Madness? Madness?" screamed Gaspard, "What do you know of madness? You, who are not beholden to any man! You, who steals the light and the glory of his squire's accolades, leaving him only as a part of your shadow! You, who married the woman I love! If I suffer madness, I lay its cause at your feet. Now I will take all that you have withheld from me and more. I will cast *my* shadow upon Hambie!"

His heart raced and his body trembled as he ran to where Fulk's great sword lay in the grass. "Yes, each man by his own sword!" was his thought. The euphoric sense of elation, with him just moments before, was suddenly crushed by fear and panic as he took his lord's sword by the grip. The damp, soiled blade was mottled and dull. Gaspard turned on Fulk, raised the sword with shaking hands, and looked down upon his lord. Was this the test the voice in his head foretold? Would it be cowardice to stay his hand at this moment? Or was it that most base quality of man pressing him to deliver the blow? He wholly believed Ducaen would kill Fulk for him, leaving him free of this stain, yet here he was with murder his only means of escape. To flinch now would shatter his desires and leave him a damned outcast. To find the scent that soothed him, darkness he must embrace.

"You shall not cheat death again!" Gaspard spat through gritted teeth, and he plunged the blade with all his strength through Fulk's chest.

Fulk groaned, his breath a shallow panting. Without expression, he gazed into Gaspard's eyes and whispered softly, "You are so like your father..."

The words struck like a bludgeon, stunning Gaspard for a good count of his pounding heart.

"What? What?" he finally cried, eyes wide with confusion.

He fell to his knees and grabbed Fulk by the collar, shaking him, "What do you know? What do you know? You gave me your oath! You did, you did! How could you know his name and not tell me? You swore!" he cried like a small boy, but Fulk's eyes grew vacant, and his breath failed. He would not see his twenty-eighth year through. On the nones of March, in the year of our Lord 1031, Sir Fulk Paynel, son of Hugh Paynel, Baron de Hambie, lord of the Sienne Valley and champion of Normandy was no more.

A sudden wave of nausea washed over Gaspard, forcing him to his hands and knees. He crawled away from his lord's dead body and vomited. The rich meal he had enjoyed just moments before was now a foul, vitriolic stew, choking and burning his throat. He had killed many men in just a few years of manhood, but this was his first taste of murder, and it was bitter, evil, and damning.

CHAPTER 12

Hail the Knight

"*I would never allow such a thing, milord,*" were his words. The minutes were as hours as he sat cold and shivering near the three dead men, his long fantasized death of Fulk all gone wrong. Mews gathered mournfully overhead and a handful of newly arrived ravens cawed accusingly from the trees. "*I would never allow such a thing, milord,*" echoed in his mind. How could a prophesied death suddenly become murder by his own hand? Was he a mere tool of the mystic, Gregar Penscalus? To what end? The pain of his wound was lost in the folds of his tortured soul. What should he do now? What could he do?

In the end it was the cold that pierced his torpor, forcing consideration upon him. How much time would he have before Ducaen's men arrived? The lack of an immediate attack did not prove some creeping spy had not lurked hidden in the brush. If Ducaen were to be believed, his men would stay clear for at least another day. Yet, even without a spy to report his and Drogo's defeat, surely they would search for him before nightfall. After all, what did Ducaen's oath matter to his filthy pirate rabble once he was dead? They would expect word soon, and when it did not come, they would surely seek Ducaen's whereabouts. "I would never allow such a thing, milord," Gaspard whispered softly as his gaze wandered to the carrion birds. He determined to hide Fulk's body, bury it, so neither foul pirate nor carrion beast could violate him in death. At least that one token of respect, as petty as it was, he could give his lord.

Gaspard rose with purpose, grasped Ducaen's severed head and Fulk's sword, and then strode to the tent. The warmth of the brazier was most welcome, and there he removed his shirt and staunched his gashed side with strips of linen he tore from the bedding. He stuffed both Drogo's and Ducaen's head into a sack and hid it, along with Fulk's sword, deep in the forest east of the tent. As he looked about for a place he could dig a grave, his eyes fell upon the tumulus mound rising from the western edge of the meadow. Covered with a patchwork of brush and small trees, its symmetrical sides rose gently to a broad, flat peak. It was the highest point he could see and would be a good place to lay Fulk to rest.

He then, and only with great effort and pain, hefted Fulk's weighty corpse upon his shoulders, picked up the helm and broken shield de Hambie, and carried his lord up the side of the mound to its top. Though weak from loss of blood and wracked with pain in his side, Gaspard made the peak with neither a fall nor a stumble. There, using Fulk's shield, he dug a shallow grave beneath a young oak and laid his lord in the earth.

First he replaced Fulk's helm that he might be protected in death, then upon his breast Gaspard gently placed his shield, after which he rose and gazed down at the man once his friend and master. He stared at the shield and its painted wolf, now as rent as the threads that once tied an orphaned squire to his knight. Gaspard knelt near Fulk's head as though to pray.

"I am sorry that it must be so," he said gravely, "but you and I, we could no longer exist together in this life…and I want to live."

He again reached inside Fulk's hauberk and pulled forth Gisla's lock of hair. His fingers, stiff with cold, could not manage the knotted ribbon, so he carefully cut it from Fulk's neck and placed it in a pocket against his breast. Gaspard then numbly covered Fulk with earth and sod until he was buried well beneath the soil of Jersey.

As he made to stand and make his way down the mound, he heard a twig crack in the bushes behind him. Drawing his sword, he quickly turned about and found himself confronted by a stranger whose face and hands were hidden deep within the folds of a black cloak.

"*Shush*," hissed the stranger, "stay hidden, the Dragon's men approach!"

It was a strange, rasping voice, like a snake among dry leaves.

"Name yourself or I shall run you through!" ordered Gaspard as he quickly closed on his uninvited guest, who was yet another witness to be killed. "Quickly, now!"

Gaspard moved so swiftly that even as the stranger made to pull back his hood, he did so with Gaspard's sword at his throat.

"Do not cry out!" whispered the stranger as he pulled back his hood to reveal his face.

"What in God's name? How…?" Gaspard choked off his cry, for the face beneath the hood belonged to none other than Gregar Penscalus.

Since their first meeting, the mystic Gregar Penscalus had appeared and vanished like smoke on the wind, and never once while Gaspard was in the company of others. Whether in his chambers or riding alone or napping in the shade of some tree, the pale Sir Penscalus would quietly arrive, often catching Gaspard off his guard. While this ability possessed a certain darkness about it, he accepted and very much enjoyed their hours of council together. However, this time his appearance possessed a foul odor even Gaspard could not ignore.

Gregar lightly brushed aside Gaspard's blade and quietly beckoned him to the thicket on the far side of the mound.

"You know I do not come in the name of your God, so why do you invoke him?" remonstrated Gregar once they were under cover.

"Should I invoke the Devil instead?" shot back Gaspard, not entirely lowering his sword. "Explain how you happen to be here? Or did you just happen by this place by coincidence?"

"Your journey here is not as secret as you suppose!" replied Gregar, a flicker of anger narrowing his eyes. "Necessary news travels quickly when need be. I am only glad I arrived in time, as you do not seem yourself at the moment."

"Due to your lies! Fulk defeated Ducaen, breaking his neck."

"Who then lies buried in that grave, if not Fulk?"

Gaspard raised his sword against Gregar once more, shouting, "By my hand! His death was supposed to be an act of *fate*, not murder! A murderer cannot call his willful acts 'Prophesy'!"

"I have murdered no one," replied Gregar calmly, "and the only lie here is the one you have told yourself. You were a fool to believe you could gain Sir Paynel's station at no personal cost—no sacrifice whatsoever! Never did I say he would die by Bertrand Ducaen's hand, only that he would die on Jersey, and I spoke truthfully. There is no other path to fulfilling your dreams than this path. No other way to satisfy your hungers. That is why you followed this fork in the road of your own free will.

"My hand did not force yours, and your shock is only in discovering you are a man capable of betrayal and killing for gain. Not unlike any great man, such as your duke. Regret is of little use, as that cannot bring life to the dead. You have no choice but to continue in your plan, else Gisla will wither away in a loveless union with some grasping noble. Though you have done it time and time again, saving Fulk has always been second to saving Gisla. Had you left his side years ago, he would still have perished, and Gisla would have been forced into a life of complete tragedy. You pay but a small price today. Now take care and heed my words. To win the mother, you must win the son."

Gregar's speech was interrupted by the ripping sound of a crossbow bolt shot through the thicket. Gaspard's outburst had not gone unheard and through the bushes he spied the warty, pockmarked Frenchman standing near Fulk's grave, holding an empty crossbow. Gaspard shouted a battle cry and rushed the foul pirate who had mocked him upon his first landing on Jersey. A second bolt tore through his cloak and he caught sight of the Persian from the corner of his eye.

He leapt upon the Frenchman like a wolf, dodging the wild, arcing swing of his great battleaxe while laying a razor's slash across his stomach. The Persian drew his short, heavy blade and ran to the aid of his compatriot barely in time to prevent Gaspard from running him through. Gaspard quickly flanked the Persian and buried a lunging riposte in his bicep. A third pirate charged into the clearing, drawing down with his crossbow. Gaspard, right between the Persian and third pirate, dropped and rolled just as the pirate loosed his shot. The Persian cried out and fell as the bolt buried itself deep in his chest.

Gaspard finished his roll and was on his feet again in an instant as his adversaries moved in. The newest arrival was a lean, swarthy fellow armed with a scimitar. He was neither quick nor handy with the sword, and Gaspard, using a practiced attack of his own design, slashed his throat before the Frenchman could draw him off. Gaspard then backed away from the warty, pockmarked Frenchman and smiled.

"Well, well," Gaspard laughed cruelly. "Your pet dragon is not here to hide behind, you filthy Frank! Throw down your axe, and I swear to make your death merciful. Come at me, and I will make you suffer as you deserve."

For the briefest of moments the Frenchman glared at Gaspard with his one good eye, then flung his axe at him and turned and fled. In a single, smoothly trained motion, Gaspard drew his knife and threw it at the retreating pirate. It buried deep in his back and the man stumbled, fell, and was still. Gaspard quickly turned back to the other fallen men. The swarthy fellow with the scimitar had quickly bled out and had the vacant look of death. The Persian stared up at him, his breathing labored.

"You're not long for this world. I would advise you to pray to whatever god *you* worship," said Gaspard grimly.

He then stood and looked about for Gregar, but the mystic was not to be seen.

"Gregar!" he called, but there was no answer. "Damn him," he muttered. Again Gregar had managed a mysterious retreat as though the earth had swallowed him whole. Whatever did he mean? To win the mother, win the son? Alas, such cryptic council was ordinary talk from the mystic. Again, damn him!

Though cold, wet, injured, and thoroughly exhausted, Gaspard found what energy he needed to drag the three dead pirates away from Fulk's grave and down to the meadow. He threw down their bodies haphazardly near Ducaen and Drogo. What was once an embellishment to his epic tale just hours before now stood as a partial truth! He had indeed slain three pirates, just as he had imagined.

Even then he could little afford to rest. He retrieved what supplies he needed from the tent and picked up Fulk's sword and the sack containing Ducaen and Drogo's heads on his way back to the boat. It was well past high tide and there were not enough hours left in the day, even with the favorable wind, to gain Normandy's shore by nightfall. Gaspard knew he could not remain on the open beach and hope to be left unmolested, so after a considerable effort to drag the boat to the receded surf, he set sail and made his way to the southeastern point of the Jersey. There among the rocky shoals just off of St. Clements Point was a tiny rock island with only a small beach when the tide was high. He landed his boat and pulled it as high on the sand as possible. Once secured, he pulled his heavy woolen cloak tightly about him, buried himself beneath the blankets in the boat, and slept fitfully until the channel waters again rose and lapped against the hull.

While the rain had slacked the previous evening, the gray sky and chill north wind continued as Duke Robert, decked in his royal hunting garb, walked side-by-side along the beach with Bishop Robert. Their days of falconry had proven enjoyable, as had their evening games and music. Bonfires kept the chill air at bay, and the duke's chefs kept their bellies full with the daily prey. The duke's entourage saw to all of their needs, and his closest friends, Amschetel D'Harcourt, Walter Gifford, and Grimoult du Plessis along with their ladies were most excellent company. Also among the nobles were brothers Robert and Rohais de Grentmesnel along with their companion Geraline de Courson.

Aside from the duke and his man, Gwylliam, not a single member of the gay ensemble suspected that hidden just east of their camp, Master Josue and the men de Hambie were bivouacked and awaiting the return of Fulk and Gaspard. Neither did they know the duke had ordered two long-ships to make their way from the port at Cherbourg to the estuary where they now exercised their noble birds of prey. No, they all were simply enjoying the break in the weather and their liege's generous celebration at the end of a long, wet winter.

When the duke suddenly invited everyone to walk along the beach with the receding tide, both servant and noble, they all went with light hearts. They chattered among themselves while the duke and bishop walked ahead engaged in a most serious discussion about the relationship of God and man and the road to salvation. Imagine their surprise and excitement when from out at sea appeared a speck of a craft making way in their direction.

As two courtiers first saw it, a murmur ran through the crowd, and everyone stopped to watch the approaching craft.

"Your Grace," called Sir Gifford, "look, a boat headed this way!"

Feigning incredulity, the duke caught the bishop by the elbow.

"What, pray tell, to you make of that, Your Excellence?" he asked.

Bishop Robert sniffed, "Just some poor fisherman, no doubt."

The duke stopped and watched the small boat continue its approach for a few moments.

"It makes for us with all speed," he puzzled, "Surely no fisherman's maneuvering! Grimoult, what do your archer eyes see?"

"A lone figure, Your Grace, darkly cloaked," Grimoult replied, his hand to his brow.

"Only one?" asked the duke sharply. "Are you sure there are not two?"

Grimoult blinked and peered again at the quickly closing craft. "No, Your Grace, just one working both sail and rudder."

"That cannot be right," snapped the duke, who grew visibly disturbed, "There must another!"

"I do not understand, Your Grace," pleaded Grimoult, continuing to stare at the craft.

"He must be laying down, wounded perhaps," worried the duke.

"Whatever are you talking about, Robert?" asked the bishop. "Even I can see now, there is but one!"

"Mind your place, bishop!" snarled the duke angrily.

The rebuke caught the nobles short and left the bishop aghast and silent.

"You err in making yourself my familiar or equal! Do not forget your place and how you are to address me!"

Bishop Robert made quickly to apologize, but the duke shrugged him off and stalked into the surf. He waded in up to his waist, heedless of his cloak and gown, and waited silently for the nearing boat to arrive. The servants, courtiers, and nobles were suddenly silent, for none wanted to earn the duke's ill will by whispering behind his back.

In those final moments of the small boat's approach only the wind and the waves dared disturb the silence. All the duke's subjects gathered quietly behind as he stood alone, the waves breaking gently around him. He said nothing as the small vessel sped toward him as though to run him down. Instead, as its bow broke into the surf, Robert stepped forward, grabbed the strake, and pulled it through the breaking waves and onto the sand.

He quickly lent a steadying hand as the cloaked figure struggled to climb out onto the beach. The figure gathered himself, put up his hand, and threw back his hood. It was Gaspard Malfort, though not all recognized his pale, disheveled face. He whispered in his lord's ear and then turned to the expectant crowd.

"We are betrayed!" he cried in pain. "Good Normans, Sir Fulk has fallen, and we are betrayed!"

Robert's face tightened while an uncontrolled whisper swept through the entire hunting party, lords and ladies alike. Gaspard gingerly retrieved the sack containing Ducaen and Drogo's severed heads. He reached in and pulled out Ducaen's head and held it out to the duke.

"Your Grace, I bring you the head of Normandy's greatest traitor, Bertrand Ducaen. He and the dread pirate of Jersey, the Dragon, are one in the same!"

The duke grabbed Ducaen's head by the hair, turned to his retinue, and held it high. "Behold, the face of my enemy! The enemy of my father! The enemy of my son! Behold the enemy…of all Normandy!" he laid his steely eyes on Bishop Robert, "Any who are his ally are my sworn enemy. What say you, bishop? What do you know of 'the Dragon'?"

Bishop Robert blanched at the sight of Ducaen's bedraggled, severed head.

"W-w-what dark news. I-I-I di-did not know the Dragon and Bertrand Ducaen were one in the same man…" came his stuttered reply.

"You are in the Dragon's pay, are you not?" shot back the duke. "Do not deny it."

"Jersey…falls in my purview…he paid his tithes due the church…" confessed the bishop in a whisper.

"His tithes? An outlaw and a criminal who pays the church a tithe? A murderous pirate who also worships at Christ's altar? Pray tell, bishop, when were you going to tell me of my new vassal? When was I to receive *my* due tribute?" yelled the duke.

"Your Grace, those moneys only helped build…"

"Oh, now you find it in yourself to address me correctly? At best you can call Ducaen's payments a bribe! At worst treason!" he continued to rage while motioning to two guards. "Take Bishop Robert and confine him to his tent."

In deference, the duke's guards laid not a hand on Bishop Robert, allowing him to precede them back to his quarters, a haughty man quite terrified.

"There is more, Your Grace," interrupted Gaspard, reaching again into the sack and pulling forth the head of Lord Drogo. "This man was in his company. Fulk recognized him as a Breton Lord by name of Drogo."

To this discovery the duke showed true surprise.

"I know this face," he puzzled. "His father was a staunch ally of my cousin, Alan…"

Duke Robert paused and looked Gaspard in the face. It was not a passing glance or necessary notice. Rather, it was a deep, searching stare, as though he no longer saw simply Fulk's common squire, but instead the man, Gaspard Malfort.

"How did this man meet his end?"

"With his sword in his hand and mine in his heart, milord," reported Gaspard.

The duke considered Gaspard quietly for a moment before speaking.

"On your knees, squire!" he commanded as everyone looked on.

Bewildered, Gaspard knelt before Duke Robert, staring at his wet, sand-caked boots. The duke raised his hand and struck Gaspard full across the face, sending him sprawling in the sand. The salty, iron taste of his own blood filled his mouth as he recovered from the blow and regained his knees, still staring at the duke's feet.

"Squire, let that be your last unanswered blow!" announced the duke. "I now strip you of that title and dub thee Sir Gaspard Malfort. Arise now, knight of Normandy, and bear no insult in silence again!"

He extended his hand to Gaspard, who despite his surprise, pressed the duke's ring to his lips and then accepted his help to rise.

"Hail the knight!" shouted the duke. "Hail the knight!"

"Hail the knight!" responded all the retinue. "Hail the knight!"

Rohais stepped forward and clasped Gaspard by the shoulders, "My father has always admired your spirit, young sir knight! Now we all know his opinion well placed! Hail the knight!"

Gaspard collected his wits and nodded in thanks.

"My sword and my loyalty are yours, Your Grace. I shall defend Normandy to the death."

Again Robert pierced Gaspard with his gaze. While stalwart in demeanor, Gaspard was damp, bloody, disheveled, and pale.

"My apologies, Sir Malfort, I can see you are in need of sustenance and the care of my physician," he said pragmatically, "after which you shall come to my tent and tell your tale."

The duke motioned for Gaspard and all the nobles to follow him back to the camp. The duke's physician tended the gash in Gaspard's side, after which the young man washed his face and hands. Fresh clothes were brought from the duke's own wardrobe along with steaming, spiced wine and rabbit stew.

In the meantime, the duke gathered his loyal nobles into his tent and briefed them on the events leading up to this moment—the discovery that Ducaen and the Dragon were likely the same man, that the Dragon had paid Bishop Robert tribute, and Fulk's plan to end the Dragon's reign of terror.

"At this very moment, the men de Hambie are marching to our position while Raoul de St. Pair is sailing south from Cherbourg with two of my finest longships and a detachment of archers. They will sail for Jersey at the turn of the tide tomorrow and root out these pirates and slay them."

"The loss of Fulk is grievous!" remarked Sir Walter.

"Certainly," replied the duke darkly, "so we shall not have his sacrifice be in vain! Amschetel, what are your thoughts?"

"I suspect Count Alan of some plot! Why else would he send young Drogo to take council with Ducaen?"

"Agreed!" the duke said with a nod. "Rohais?"

"By my honor, Your Grace, my first thought is worry for my sister. Gisla is now a widow. Her suffering for loss of Fulk will exceed our sorrow a thousand fold," he said softly.

His truth struck a momentary silence in the Norman lords. One and all, they admired the lithe and noble nature of Hambie's chatelaine. Rohais and his brother exchanged a grim glance, and Robert de Grentmesnel spoke.

"By your leave, Your Grace, Rohais and I should be the ones to break this terrible news to our sister."

The duke nodded. "Send my condolences and inform her I will visit Hambie as soon as I am able."

Once refreshed, Gaspard was conducted to the duke's tent and the awaiting lords, where he spun his great tale, weaving together truth and falsehood. All had gone as planned, their journey, their arrival, and even the great joust between the two great warriors. It was only when they crossed blades that Ducaen began to reveal his evil design. Fulk was clearly the superior swordsman, keeping Ducaen pressed for much of the combat, cutting him several times. It was only after Ducaen scored a slashing blow that Fulk began to fail. He grew weak and began stumbling about, though it was merely a flesh wound. Fulk was suddenly stricken by a terrible lethargy, and Gaspard believed Ducaen must have poisoned his blade. Even as Ducaen, bleeding heavily from his many wounds, delivered Fulk's deathblow, three pirates who lay in wait in the brush rushed Gaspard. The savage, desperate pirates were no match for Gaspard's blade, and he quickly cut them down while Drogo attempted to staunch Ducaen's wounds.

Gaspard, crazed with grief for his lord, then charged Ducaen and Drogo. Knowing Ducaen's blade was poisoned, he flanked him and focused his attack there. Unfortunately, this left him open to Drogo's attack, and even as he cut down the failing Ducaen, Drogo pierced his side. With Ducaen fallen, he madly turned on the Breton and killed him, running him through.

"I have never fought with such rage! It was as though the strength of ten men coursed in my veins," said Gaspard. "Knowing time was against me, I quickly cut off their heads and stole a piece of linen from the tent to bind my wounds. Even in that amount of time another group of pirate rabble was upon me. I took up Fulk's sword, the sack with the heads, and ran for the beach. Even wounded, I was the faster man, and made the boat with time to push off before they broke the tree line. I used the thwart as a shield, lying low against it as they fired their arrow and bolts. Once out of range I made for the safety of a small rock not far off the island and awaited today's tide."

"We must learn what Alan's plans were for Ducaen," posed the duke, "How can we divine this?"

"Begging Your Grace's permission," answered Gaspard, "let me lead Fulk's men, my comrades of many years, to Jersey. I have been in his secret caves and am confident I can find them again. We men de Hambie are bred for such a quest. We will rout his horde and learn his plan."

"And what of your wound?"

"'Tis a scratch, and your physician is an excellent surgeon. By morning I will be fit enough."

Duke Robert looked about the table judging the faces of his friends and found them stern and supportive.

"Sir Gaspard Malfort," he stated most seriously, "as your first commission, in the name of the duchy, I order you to take command of the men de Hambie, sail to Jersey, and cleanse the island of Ducaen's ilk. Do what you must to gain any intelligence of Ducaen's intent."

"It will be done, Your Grace!" replied Gaspard.

As the council finished a great commotion took the camp. In lead of a column of warriors more than one hundred strong, Master Josue arrived with the men de Hambie. By dusk the longships arrived bringing Raoul and a score of archers. The excitement for war swept through the camp as the men carried the light, speedy ships from the water onto the sand and loaded their gear.

CHAPTER 13

The Second Dream

As night fell, Gaspard gathered his men around him on the beach. He mounted his horse that they might see his face as he spoke in the flickering torchlight.

"Men of Hambie! My brothers in duty...my brothers in arms. My news is grievous. It is grim! Lay to rest the rumors, the whispers. Our leader...our lord, he is dead! Sir Paynel, whom we have known, whom we have loved, is taken from us, and we are right to mourn him...to rend our cloths and grind our teeth. It was a betrayal of the field of honor. It was murder! You all have heard rumors of a pirate called the Dragon. I tell you now, the Dragon was no less than Bertrand Ducaen, disgraced baron and exile. At his evil hand, our beloved baron was murdered by poison. At his evil hand, our beloved duke was betrayed to the filth and feces that is Brittany!

"Now is a new hour. Now is our time! Though Ducaen is dead, we yet have an unfinished task. Our duke, Sir Robert has given me a commission—no, we, the men of Hambie, have been given a commission! This one time I am to take up my lord's sword—the sword of a man I served and loved like a brother—I take his sword into mine own hand to avenge his death! To avenge the honor of our duke! To bring to task those who would plot against him.

"I am known to you. We have trained together…fought side by side. Have we ever tasted defeat? No! Today I do not order you. Instead I ask you, as my brothers in arms, to follow me. To trust in my leadership. Today, in the name of the fallen, the betrayed and the loved, will you follow me? For tomorrow I intend to return to Jersey's shore for the last time! I will either destroy what remains of the pirate filth that plotted against Normandy or I will die in the effort! Who is with me? I say who is with me?"

Gaspard drew the sword de Hambie from its sheath and held it high. The men de Hambie roared. On the morrow before dawn, with the tide, they would defy the wind, row for the shores of Jersey, and erase all memory of its Dragon. Around a great bonfire, Gaspard and his men took council. With relish, Gaspard told them of his adventures and what he knew of Ducaen's secret caves. A sense of self-importance surged through him, energizing his body and mind. The men looked to him, empowered him, and it left him feeling alive as never before.

"In those caves is treasure beyond the imagination of the most grasping men!" said Gaspard, "If any of it remains, the prize taken for Duke Robert will be great."

"With Ducaen dead, surely his men will plunder and make off with his riches," spoke Master Josue.

"Likely," finished Gaspard, "We must move swiftly and be prepared for anything."

The stiff north wind broke and drove south those clouded skies that had sullied Normandy for near three days. The gruff, hearty soldiers quickly transformed the camp, no longer a lighthearted hunting party of nobles and courtiers. They built fires, ate coarse food, and laughed boisterously at ribald jokes and stories. Eventually they bedded down around their fires, under tents and tarpaulins. The stars twinkled brightly and the moon, in its third quarter, rose so late that only those men on watch witnessed its cold arrival.

With the excitement of council finished, Gaspard retired alone to the tent intended for Fulk. To raise Fulk's sword and lead his men into battle was indeed a heady circumstance, but to quarter in Fulk's tent, to take his bed, left Gaspard queerly uneasy, as though entering a tomb. He hesitated at its door, the flap pulled aside, for a long moment before finally ducking inside. Lit only by the flickering light of the crackling fire outside the door, twisted shadows danced about in the gloom. He laughed sheepishly to himself.

"He never stepped foot here or even laid eyes on this bed. Why should this affect me?" he thought to himself. "I must take this place just as I must take Hambie."

He carefully folded the duke's cloak and removed his boots before falling into the warm comforts of what was now his bed.

"He would not have lived out the day, regardless," were his last comforting thoughts before drifting off to sleep. "I did him a mercy."

He loved the warm summer days of the Sienne valley with its scented breezes, lazy streams, and shady trees. Deep he would walk on the trails that wound past ponds and up gentle slopes. It was warm now, and he was lightly clad because of it. With an easy pace he followed the scant deer path deeper and deeper into the forest. Even as the trail steepened, his step remained effortless. As he entered the grove, with its clear, sparkling spring, it felt as though he was standing still and the place, instead, enveloped him.

From a thicket opposite the spring a movement, a pair of gold eyes set in a white face, caught his attention. It was a face he knew well.

"My White Lady! It has been so long," he said joyously.

With a hesitant step, a sleek white wolf emerged from the brush and gazed upon him. He knelt and clicked his tongue, inviting her to his side. It seemed as though such a great number of years had passed since he had enjoyed her company, and his heart leapt with joy at her sight.

"Come to see me, milady," he cajoled, extending his open hand to the wolf. "I have missed you so."

Slowly, haltingly, she came round the spring, sniffing the air and looking about furtively. Her fur was thick and shining, and the scars of her battles were gone. Again he reassured her as she approached, head down and tail tucked.

"Have no fear, White Lady! 'Tis only I, Gaspard. I mean you no harm."

He carefully moved in her direction, wanting nothing else than to run his hands through her fur and feel her warm breath against his face. Carefully she approached, as wolves do, unsure of her safety. Finally Gaspard was close enough to reach out and gently caress her flank. He sighed with happiness, for he had missed her for many years, thinking her long dead and gone.

Then like a snake uncoiling and striking, she was on him, snarling, lunging, and snapping at his throat. He was bowled over onto his back as the wolf wildly bore down upon him, tearing his flesh…

Gaspard awoke with a start, a gurgled scream dying on his lips. He sat bolt upright, heart pounding, with the image of the white wolf de Hambie savaging his throat so stark it was as though it were real and not a dream. An ill omen? Perhaps. As his mind cleared, he knew the wolf of his childhood must be long dead. She had left him alone, sending only Fulk to deliver her farewell. Though he rode out in search of her, he never knew her to return to the Sienne Valley. Even as he told himself that she was a wild beast, beholden to none, it stung him that she nuzzled Fulk last. The intent of her apparition, whether as an avenging angel or a manifestation of his own guilt, was clearly not meant to comfort him.

He sat on the edge of the bed, anxiety knotting his insides for fear of facing Gisla that first time. To look in her eyes and recount her husband's end with a grand falsehood would be no easy task. Glad was he to return to Jersey and put the meeting off yet more days. He needed to gather himself, harden himself, and reach for this forbidden fruit with a sure hand. He must put on his false self for the remainder of his days and deeply lock away his sin. His lie must become truth, and the truth become a forgotten relic.

Even had Gaspard still felt the need for sleep, he found no desire to return to the grove of the sparkling spring. He reached for his boots and cloak and quietly exited the tent to escape its burdensome accusation. The three-quarter moon was waxing in the eastern sky, and he knew the tide was now rising. He found the watch and ordered the men roused.

He felt better among the men, with their grim smiles and reassuring claps to the shoulder. They all ate a quick, cold portion, gathered what remained of their gear, and made for the longships. Catching the rising tide would speed them towards Jersey, and if they bent their backs well, they would land by sunrise.

The simple beauty and elegance of the longship's lightweight design allowed such craft to navigate shallow waters and to be carried by their compliment on to beachheads and over blockages. Powered by both sail and oar, they could defy all but the worst of gales. With Gaspard commanding one ship and Raoul the other, the men hefted the longships through the surf and leapt aboard. In just a matter of moments they manned the oars and began pulling through the moonlight.

The longships rose and fell with the rhythmic swells of the sea while their sides were slapped and battered by the white caps whipped up by the north wind. The oars slashed to the beat of the drum and the stars led the way as reflections of the moon danced like cold flame on the waters of the Gulf of Saint Malo. Even as the skies to the east gradually welcomed the muted predawn light, the island of Jersey remained an empty, black stillness looming to the northwest. The cresting tide easily carried their sleek hulls over shoals and silently onto the beach ahead of the sun's first rays.

The archers notched their arrows, and every second man raised his shield protectively against the emerging, skeletal tree line as they broke the surf. The longships ground to a halt on the sand just yards from where the fisherman landed Gaspard. The oars came in and the men slid over the strake, expecting immediate resistance, but were met only by a beach empty in all directions. Neither rock, nor bolt, nor arrow flew from the foliage. Gaspard, bow in hand, silently motioned to several men to follow him along the path he had first traveled only after being blindfolded.

Through the foliage they slipped and into small clearing. A fire pit gone cold and washed with rain, several dented copper pots, a wood bench, and an overturned table all sat near an oft-repaired, tar-soaked canvas thrown over a weathered ballista. The camp was long dead.

"Not a soul here for a lot of days," whispered Henri, a short, sturdy tracker as he stuck his hand in the dead fire pit. "These tracks be six days, maybe seven old."

"Ducaen knew we'd come. He surrendered Jersey without so much as a flinch…" breathed Gaspard. "Secure the boats and bring the men up. The caves are on the north side of the island."

With the archers interspersed in the line, the men, swords at the ready, moved quietly inland. As the morning sun cut through the trees, Gaspard closed his eyes and listened to the sounds of Jersey. He pointed a direction to Henri, who examined the ground and picked up the pirate's trail.

"Well trod, this path," commented Henri, "Old but simple to see."

With Henri in the lead and Gaspard recalling the sounds and scents of his blindfolded journey, they carefully led the men through the forest, up the vales and across the brooks. After an hour, Gaspard caught the familiar scent of pear blossoms, but the smell of death overpowered their subtle fragrance. He held up his hand and motioned his men to spread out, then moved forward, entering the fragrant copse of trees. It was not long before they found the body of the Nubian woman, still fiercely beautiful in death, lying ill used beneath the boughs.

Raoul knelt by her side, noting her knuckles scraped and bruised.

"She put up a fight," Gaspard said softly as several men gather around her body. "She played the harp…and had a son."

At the edge of the grove a sudden scuffle broke out. The quiet of the forest was broken by cries of "Ow! You little bugger, come back 'ere!" and "Got you now!" accompanied by the frantic cries of a struggling child. Raoul rose and made his way with Gaspard to the source of the excitement to find one of the men wrestling to control a wet, ragged boy of perhaps ten years with skin as black as night. Finally, caught by the scruff of the neck and surrounded, the young Nubian ended his struggles, though his eyes were wide with fear.

"I found the lad skulking about in the thicket," explained the soldier when Gaspard and Raoul arrived.

"Escaped, but couldn't leave his mother, no doubt," surmised Gaspard, undoing his cloak and smiling at the boy. "I remember you, little mousset. Fear not, we will not harm you."

He wrapped the shivering boy in his cloak, "Do you understand me?"

The boy nodded.

"We are soldiers of the duke of Normandy. Are you hungry, little mousset?"

Again the boy nodded. Gaspard, taking a knee, looked up and called for some bread.

"I am sorry they killed your mother," said Gaspard seriously. "I understand. I am also an orphan. My mother is dead, and I never knew my father. That makes you and I kin, in a way. Do you understand that?"

Tears filled the boys eyes, and he looked away. One of Gaspard's warriors brought a bit of soft bread and a lump of cheese, which he handed to the boy.

"'Tis meager fare, I know, but we are not here to feast. Rather, we are here to slay the Dragon's men, the men who killed your mother. Can you help us? Can you tell us what went on here?"

The boy ravenously devoured the bread before speaking and Gaspard handed a flask of clean water. Finally, with a halting voice, the boy spoke.

"A-all the mothers are d-dead, I think, and the b-bad men are mostly g-gone." He took a bite of cheese and a drink. "Once the master was k-killed, they fought over what was left."

"Do you remember the day I visited? You were turning a spitted pig over a fire? Do you remember that?"

"Yes."

"Tell me everything that happened after that until now."

So the boy began his story. His name was Bousa. He and his mother had been with the Dragon almost since the beginning. They had first belonged to a Mohammedan trader from the city of Tanja. The Dragon murdered the trader and took his ship. That was many years ago. More than three summers ago, the Dragon came to Jersey and began hiding all his riches there. The Dragon was mean, and his men were very bad. They hit him a lot, but he had enough to eat. The mothers were all scared... scared to talk and scared to cry.

The day after Gaspard dined with the Dragon, the pirates started taking the treasure away. They made him carry many loads of gold and silver down to a longship and whipped him if he dropped anything. The day after the ship was loaded, they brought slaves—island men—and sailed away. The ship returned the next day, empty. Again they loaded the ship, sailed away, and returned, only the second time they returned the slaves were missing.

"They could not have gone farther than Guernsey or Sark, by my reckoning," Raoul said to Gaspard. "Still, there exists dozens of rocks and hundreds of caves where a treasure could be hidden. A man could spend a lifetime searching and never find it."

"When my mother saw those slave-men did not return, she said they had been killed by the pirates to keep them quiet. She said the bad men were going to kill us, too, and we had to run away. She stole some food and we sneaked to the cave's entrance. She had a knife, killed the guard at the entrance to the caves, and we ran. They caught us here, but my mother fought them and made me keep running!"

The boy burst into tears and began to shake violently. Gaspard put his arm about his shoulders and exchanged a grim look with Raoul.

"I-I-I should have s-saved her!" he sobbed miserably.

"Then they would have killed you, too, little mousset," said Gaspard sternly, "She gave you the gift of life, that her spirit would live on in you. Be proud of her!"

For some moments Bousa could not speak, hiding his face in the folds of the cloak that the men could not see his childish tears. Eventually he gathered himself and continued his story. He hid in the thickets near the orchard, not knowing where to go. The pirates wasted little time searching for him as the hour was late and it was cold. The night was terribly long, and he thought he would die, wanted to die, but awoke the next morning cold and stiff as the Dragon and his tall friend rode through the orchard.

"What do you know about the Dragon's tall friend?" asked Raoul.

"The Dragon was going to raise an army for him, I think," replied Bousa. "He arrived fourteen days ago. I overheard them talk about attacking from the north and south at the same time. I don't know who they wanted to fight, though."

Bousa then continued his story. It was wet and raining, and he did not know where to go, so when he saw smelled smoke coming from the rocks above the caves, he snuck through the woods and thickets looking for the fire.

"I climbed up the rocks that way," he pointed north, "right above the caves. There is a lookout up there. You can see the ocean from it. It is above the Dragon's grotto. Right above where I cook the meat. The guards were gone, but their fire was still burning, so I added wood and warmed myself. That's when it started..." he trailed off.

"What started?" pressed Gaspard gently, but the boy pulled away and turned his back.

"They killed all the mothers," he whispered. "I still hear their screams. They echo forever in my head."

"Can you show us the entrance to the caves?" asked Gaspard gently.

"I am afraid," his reply was barely audible.

"We are many men and all great warriors, you need not fear," said Gaspard reassuringly, "and we shall need a sturdy guide."

The boy considered the Normans, with their heavy cloaks, thick beards, swords, and bows.

"I know the way, but I won't go in!" the boy decided.

"Agreed," replied Gaspard.

What Gaspard, Raoul, and the men de Hambie discovered within the Dragon's caves was an untold horror. Even though they were men accustomed to walking among the corpses of war, breathing the scent of blood and earth, and hearing the mewling cries of fallen warriors yet clinging to life, they were aghast at the savagery unleashed in the gloomy passages and chambers. Though few were later willing to bear witness to what they found with any great detail, it haunted their dreams till their dying day.

Yes, those finest daughters, pillaged during the Dragon's murderous raids and enslaved to serve the needs of Ducaen and his men, had met a horrific end. Justice failed and no hero came to their aid, no holy avenger to destroy evil and rescue the good and the innocent. There was no solace to be taken. How could there be? The men de Hambie, burning with a desire to avenge the horrors, found not a single living soul to save nor enemy to punish. If a pirate remained, he had long faded into Jersey's forest and thickets. Even Gaspard, who had gained so much by traveling the road of events ending in this moment, felt a sickening regret that the duke had not followed his first instinct and invaded Jersey immediately.

They made their way through the tunnels, ravines, and galleries. While little gold or silver remained, much of the luxury that Ducaen surrounded himself was yet intact. Statues and tapestries and the like, mostly in good repair, remained within, in a disturbing contrast to the broken bodies the Norman warriors stepped over as they picked their way through the passages. It was silent as a tomb, with only the whispering wind and dripping water to greet the visitors. No sound beyond their own footfalls disturbed them until they finally emerged in the Dragon's deserted grotto where sat Ducaen's hall.

In the center of the grotto, near the fire pit and surrounded by the corpses of pirates and maids, a doughy man of middle years hung, strangled, in the stocks. The stocks were a chest high apparatus, and his neck and wrists were locked tightly inside its narrow holes. The limp body was beaten, bruised, and bloody, and the once fine clothes were wet, torn, and soiled with feces. Gaspard barely recognized him due to his situation, but the man's ink stained fingers and red-veined nose gave him away. He was none other than Bertrand Ducaen's scribe.

Henri moved forward and touched the man's flank beneath his clothes. "He is still warm. Strangled by his own weight when his legs gave out, no doubt. Had he lasted a bit longer, we could have saved him for the duke's noose instead."

"I wonder what secrets he took with him," pondered Raoul.

"Or what secrets he gave away," replied Gaspard, knitting his brow. "They surely wanted something from him. They took their time torturing him before they fled."

Gaspard grimaced and glanced about the grotto as the men filed in. Pages from a book lay strewn about the sand, damp with mist, and the book itself was askew, partially burned, in the now cold fire pit. He gingerly lifted the charred tome from the ashes and ordered his men to search the hall. A strange tingling lit his fingers as he brushed away the soot and soil, and then gently lifted the stiff leather cover. Perhaps the last third of the pages had been torn from the binding, and those that remained were quite damaged by smoke and flame. It appeared to be a journal of sorts, as it lacked a title and the script was plain, uneven and artless. Strangely, its pages were made of costly vellum, rather than the linen one would expect in a personal journal.

"Look sharp!" warned Gaspard as he looked at his men milling about. "Do not trample any of those loose pages!"

He set aside the binding and began carefully picking up its scattered pages, lifting them and stacking them gently in his hand. A strange tension built in him as he glanced at the soiled words, for they seemed to describe the happenings of the very place he stood. For a brief moment they cast a spell upon him, calling to him, daring him to read their secrets. Henri calling excitedly from the door of Ducaen's hall suddenly disturbed his reverie.

"Milord, there's some things here!" he exclaimed excitedly. "The books you talked about!"

For everything they plundered, the pirates had left the Dragon's most prized treasure! Tucking the loose pages and damaged binding into his bag, Gaspard strode with Raoul to Ducaen's hall and pushed past the men to enter. Once inside the foyer, in the flickering torchlight, they saw the floor was covered with Ducaen's books. Some were broken and torn, with pages scattered about like fall leaves, but the lion's share were intact and only slightly abused. They had heavy tooled-leather bindings, some strapped in silver or inlaid with gold. Scores of them! Judging by the empty sockets, a few even once sported gems and jewels that were pried loose and carried away. Each page was a work of art, lovingly drawn in a rainbow of pigments and plethora of languages.

"Oh no…" sighed Gaspard heavily as the sight of the torn pages and broken spines, "Could they leave nothing undefiled?"

"Yet a kingly gift to bring back to our duke, no matter!" assured Raoul.

"Véthe, my friend! Gold is wealth, but books are prestige. He will be pleased," Gaspard agreed reluctantly.

They left the foyer and entered the main chamber of Ducaen's hall. In the darkness sat the Dragon's great table, the lordly chairs and ebony throne. The two men put flames to the lamps to illuminate the room and found it had been rummaged only briefly and remained largely as Gaspard remembered it.

"Ever the Norman lord," said Gaspard absently, "Henri, Robert will expect a prize. Have the men scour this place for things of value, such as these books. We will take what we can before the islanders scavenge the timbers…and Henri, organize some men to give the innocent a proper burial."

"Yes, milord, it is a shame we have no priest. They have a need," replied the tracker grimly.

Raoul and Gaspard exchanged a joyless glance. Yes, they were in need of a priest—all of Jersey was in need of a priest!

"Sir?" asked Henri, "What of the other bodies? The pirates, I mean."

"Throw them into the sea!" ordered Gaspard coldly. The mystery of the burned and torn journal would have to be set aside for the time being in favor of the task at hand. Unknown to Gaspard, it would be weeks before he would have the privacy to learn its secrets uninterrupted.

All the men took great pity on the young Nubian, Bousa, and debated what should be done with the boy. He could not be left to his own devices on Jersey, nor could he easily be sent back to the land of his birth. Certainly he could be sold into servitude at home or abroad, or handed over to Robert as part of the prize, though to treat him as a mongrel dog hardly seemed just. Finally, after much discussion, Raoul determined it was high time he took a squire. Being only a vavasor, and often abroad on the duke's business, he had never seen the need for such a vanity. Now that the opportunity for a more settled future lay in front of him, taking on a squire held a bit more appeal than in years past. Gaspard agreed, and Bousa was duly informed of his fate. From then on he would be Bousa, squire de St. Pair.

CHAPTER 14

The Castle of the Rock

It was not with a sense of malice that Gisla considered her husband's squire, Gaspard, but rather with a feeling of disquiet. He was both a cragged mountain peak, hard, handsome, and daunting, as well as a shadowy defile, morose, lonely, and forlorn. Though her husband could not fathom it, from the day of their wedding forward, she knew in some way she came between them, a wedge between brothers. While he never neglected her bidding, Gaspard did not readily meet her eyes nor join her with daily pleasantries. In her presence, subtle as it was, he was continually on his guard. Still, she was glad of him, for in battle he was lockstep with Fulk and always ready to deflect that errant blow.

That security, that luxury, was now stripped away. The field of honor was ever so different from field of battle. Either Ducaen would be killed or Fulk would be killed. For Gaspard to intervene, in either event, would brand Fulk a dishonorable man and shame his house. The lord de Hambic would not forgive such an act easily. No, Gaspard would stay his hand if Fulk fell, she was sure of it, and it left her ill with foreboding.

However, she remained composed as her husband scooped up young Raymond, roaring like a bear in his farewell.

"Peire, I want to come!" complained the boy petulantly.

Setting the boy down, Fulk took a knee and stared solemnly into his eyes. "While that day will come, Raymond, it is not today. You have much growing and much learning to do before you become a man. You will tend to your studies and give me a full report when I return."

"Yes, Peire," replied the boy sullenly.

"As for you, wife," said Fulk brusquely as he stood and faced Gisla. "Worry not. I shall be home before the first day of spring."

He embraced her gently, and she, against her own desires, clung not to his neck when he withdrew. Instead, into his hand she pressed the chain woven of her flaxen hair and pale green ribbon. To hold back the tears, she said not a word as he swung into the saddle and rode through the barbican. While Raymond raced to the castle's highest window to watch his father wend his way down the hill and take the road to Coutances, Gisla retired to her bower with her ladies-in-waiting, Isabelle and Clothilde. It was there she finally let go of her reserve and wept. Long she took solace in Clothilde's lap, while the young woman stroked her hair and whispered comforts in her ear.

Those late days of February and early days of March, both with flashes of brilliance and chilling rain, had enough warmth to begin calling Normandy back from winter's slumber six weeks before Easter. Gisla took no comfort in the sun on her face as it streamed through the open windows, nor the scent of life renewed on the breeze. Morning and night her silent supplications wafted from the castle's little chapel to Heaven above, begging the safe return of her husband.

Though the entire household, from Agnes Marie to Thomas to boys who kept the stables, put on faces of good cheer for their chatelaine, only young Raymond could bring light to her eyes. He lived in a world entirely his own, racing through the castle fighting dragons, saving damsels from brigands, and stealing treasure right from beneath the noses of pirates. Armed with a sword he fashioned from a stick and a leather strap, he would burst into the bower and declare, "Alas, the walls are breached, fair maidens! Though death is certain, I will cost the enemy dearly before I fall to their blades!" Then he would slash the air with his sword, lunging, feinting, parrying, and slaying the invisible invaders, all the while crying out, "Take that, you heathen pig! And that you godless dog! And that! And that!"

Clothilde and Isabel would gaily squeal in fear, "Save us, oh handsome knight. Save the castle! Save the queen!"

Once the enemy was slain, Raymond would bow to the ladies. "You are safe for now, but keep the door barred whilst I seek what remains of the rabble." He would then silently slip out of the bower and sneak off to the kitchen to save Agnes Marie in similar fashion, leaving the treasure of a smile upon his mother's face.

It was the dark of night that haunted her most, the chill of an empty bed in a shuttered room, and nothing but her own worried thoughts dancing with the shadows cast upon the walls by the flickering lamp for company. Though the land began to break free of winter's grip, Gisla's heart remained cold with an ill premonition. In place of the warmth and steady breath of a husband, absent from his rightful bed, were whispered forlorn thoughts she could not help but let take shape in the vapor. Her hope was but a small glimmer. Perhaps if God would hear her prayers and see, in advance, what suffering her husband's death would bring her, he would stay his hand and deliver Fulk safely away from Jersey. Perhaps if she prepared herself for the worst, a waking nightmare, he would return and all would be well. Such a small hope.

So when that dread moment arrived, with Old Rupert softly knocking at her door, his flaccid eyes moister than usual, announcing the arrival of Master Josue in company with her brothers, Gisla knew God had decided against her.

"They bring Hardelle, milady, and her saddle is empty," said Rupert in a wavering voice.

She quietly put on a black gown, hiding her reddened eyes behind a thin veil, and walked alone to the great hall de Hambie. By the lines creased upon their brow and the grim curve of their lips, she knew what message they bore. In their faces she saw her widow's lament. Fulk would return no more.

Gisla walked slowly to her chair near the great stone hearth and quietly sat with a straight back and hands folded in her lap. "Gather the house, that the tale be told but once," she said softly. "And Rupert, please ring his death knell from the chapel that the village may know." Thrice Rupert pulled a slow cadence, the count of two and eight, and sadly announced to the castle and surrounding village the passing of their brave lord.

It had been seventeen days since Aymer de Cangé brought his strange tale to the hall de Hambie and piqued its lord. Again the house gathered in the hall, with Master Josue, Old Rupert, Thomas, Jacqueline, Isabelle, Clothilde, Agnes Marie, Naper, the maids, stable hands, and gardeners, all filing quietly in to be with their chatelaine. Only brother Carthusian and young Raymond were absent. By Gisla's command, the monk kept Raymond occupied, as it was her duty to break the terrible news to her son in private.

Once gathered, Robert and Rohais de Grentmesnel embarked on their brief tale. They told of the return of Gaspard and his story of betrayal and murder, and how, for his valor and for uncovering Count Alan's plot, the duke had granted him knighthood. That very morning, despite his wounds, Gaspard had returned to Jersey with the men de Hambie to destroy what remained of the pirates.

"At this very hour, your husband is being avenged!" finished Rohais sternly.

"And his body?" asked Gisla quietly, "I should like him returned for a proper Christian burial."

"We do not know, sister," said Robert. "We can only hope…"

The days that followed were dark indeed for the house de Hambie. Word spread throughout the fief that Sir Fulk had perished, and wild rumor grew regarding the manner of his death. There were those who believed Jersey was home to a fell dragon whose poisonous breath overcame their brave lord. Others claimed Jersey's pirate king had made a pact with the Devil and was transformed into a fire-breathing serpent that turned Fulk to ash and then flew away to the deserts of the east. Some heard tell that the pirate of Jersey was indeed Bertrand Ducaen, who, seeking revenge against Fulk, brought back some foul beast from darkest Africa to set on his enemy. Many a tankard was poured as the men gossiped. Certainly the dark, handsome Gaspard deserved knighthood after taking up his master's sword and striking down the foul beast and its master! Though he be a strange, haughty young man, he had proved his mettle on more than one occasion. They were indeed glad one of their own had risen above the muck and chaff.

Gisla retreated to the loneliness of her chambers and would take little comfort from her friends. She ate only at the gentle insistence of the matronly Jacqueline, and she stared out the window in silence while Isabelle and Clothilde attended to their needlework. Her fair eyes were hollow, her lips pallid, and her step listless. The brightness and warmth that was Gisla was fading like weathered pigments. Her joyful life did not exist in the present. Her happiness was memory of the before. Her fears lay in the thoughts of the after. Though she checked her accusations, her question of God was plaintive enough, "Why?" Did this have to happen?

All those in the house had grave worries of their own future, as Hambie was a rich fief and there were many lords who would vie to enfold her into their own holdings. Would a new lord look kindly upon them or would they be ill-used? Or worse yet, would they lose their positions and be turned out in favor of others?

In all this, young Raymond was lost. His rudimentary understanding of death was enough to know it could not be undone. If the falcon killed the rabbit, that was that. Once he had found a dead badger in a thicket near the castle. With great solemnity, he had buried the small beast with all the religious ceremony he could muster. Some months later that great morbid curiosity existing in all little boys brought him back to unearth the creature to check its condition. The rotting carcass was writhing with maggots, worms, and an awful stench! That was death to Raymond, and he was angry and hurt his father would do such a thing to him.

Brother Carthusian, himself greatly troubled by Rohais and Robert's tale of Fulk's fall and Gaspard's rise, vainly tried to console Raymond, but only managed to further enrage the child.

"God did this on purpose! I hate him!" cried the boy as he eluded Carthusian's grasp and fled the study.

Carthusian knew it was not that Raymond truly hated God; it was simply that he wanted to hurt God's feelings so God would understand what he felt. A tear came to the monk's eye as he softly whispered after the boy, "God knows your pain, my dear child, and he knows mine as well."

The city of Caen sits on the banks of the Orne River about seven leagues north of Falaise, the city of Duke Robert. It was here, after several days under oar and sail, Sir Raoul de St. Pair and Sir Gaspard Malfort finally landed the duke's longships laden with the prize brought away from Jersey. Its value was assessed and the men were paid their due accordingly. From there they slung their gear upon their backs and walked home to their cottages and farms where the spring crops awaited planting. In their lead were Gaspard, Raoul, and Duke Robert, riding at an easy pace and enjoying the spring-like weather. Each man had his own private mission and cause to make the journey to the Sienne Valley. The squire Bousa, having never ridden a horse in all his life, sat behind Raoul, clinging tightly to his knight's waist, in awe of the powerful beast that so easily bore both their weights.

"I shall not rest easy while Remon and the remains of Ducaen's pirates wander freely," stated the duke darkly. "I like not this tale of horrors."

"Nor I, milord," replied Raoul. "Bousa knows their names and their faces. I shall send word abroad to my agents. Whether they make for England, France or Spain, sooner or later they will begin to surface and be seen."

"The islanders could also be your eyes and ears, milord," added Gaspard. "If Ducaen's treasure is hid on some rock between Jersey and Guernsey, Remon will know its location and will not let it sit idle long."

"Agreed," said the duke. "Raoul, advise your agents that I guarantee the bounty. Have them spread the word. It looks as though I will have you out fishing again soon."

The three men laughed grimly, then Raoul turned to the duke with another concern.

"Have you given thought to how you shall handle your cousin, Count Alan?" he asked seriously. "You have him as a great disadvantage."

"I should like to march against him and raze his castles and burn his lands!" replied Robert bitterly. "Then I would put his head on a spit in the middle of his own court...for all to see."

"That would be bloody and difficult," warned Gaspard.

"Véthe," agreed Raoul.

"Though it remains in my mind," replied the duke.

The men rode quietly for some minutes before Robert looked side-long at Gaspard.

"What counsel would you offer your liege, good sir knight?" he asked.

"Wars in the name of revenge often reap ill-rewards," replied Gaspard carefully. "The Greeks fell into disarray after sacking Troy. Appeasement can be equally damning. The Franks appeased Rollo, and now their king leans heavily on you. Æthelred appeased the Danes and lost all of England. Alan ought to be shown his place, and then be grateful for your eleventh-hour mercy. Make him afraid, then broker a peace from a position of strength."

"And who would you suggest to mediate his contrition should I get my cousin to the table?" asked Robert seriously.

Gaspard thought silently for some moments but could think of no lord trusted by both men. Instead, it was Raoul who spoke.

"Your uncle, the archbishop, longs to return from exile," he said after clearing his throat. "You could lance two boils with one needle."

The duke stared at Raoul incredulously. "What?" he exclaimed. "He accused me of murdering my brother...and laid and interdict against me. I would see him grovel before I allowed him to don the mitre of Normandy again."

"Archbishop Robert's power is not one of arms; rather it is one of opinions. Right now he is against you," replied Raoul, "If you extended the olive branch and give him a chance to broker a peace between his nephews, I wager he will retract his interdict and conveniently forget his accusations...if you can."

Robert frowned. "I would rather go to war."

"And that is the position of strength from which you deal," returned Raoul. "Archbishop Robert will be pleased he averted a war, Alan will be glad his contrition does not involve his utter destruction, and you win without paying a single soldier his wage."

Robert furrowed his brow for several minutes and then a slight smile crossed his face. "I am glad you are my spy, Raoul, and not someone else's."

The men rode in silence for some time and then began a more casual conversation.

"Now that you are returned to Normandy, do you intend to finally take a wife?" Robert asked Raoul.

"It has crossed my mind as of late, Your Grace," he replied lightly, "It would be a great comfort to have someone warm my bed after so long abroad."

"Isabelle is quite pleasing to your eye, no?" commented Gaspard.

"Verily, yes!" laughed Raoul.

"And she is not without holdings, being the eldest," offered Robert.

"And well tempered," added Gaspard, "though spirited enough for the likes of you."

"I would fear to take the girl from Gisla at the moment." Raoul shook his head. "They are close, as I understand."

"She and her sister, Clothilde, have been inseparable from Gisla since Fulk was given their guardianship," agreed Gaspard. "'Tis true; she relies on them."

"A time of courtship is all that's needed. Arlette has given me some notion as to Gisla's delicate state of mind. She will need time to grieve," the duke was speaking of his consort and mother of his young son, Arlette of

Falaise. "Her pain is fresh, yet William de Moulines has already expressed interest in her hand."

"Arlette's nephew? Walter's son?" asked Raoul in surprise.

"He is younger than I, Your Grace," said Gaspard critically.

"And vain beyond his station," replied Robert irritably, "I would have him earn his spurs before blessing such a union. No, rest assured, he is not the man for Gisla. The crux of the matter is that there will be no lack of suitors pressing both Gisla and myself. That is why I would speak with her."

The duke gazed upon Gaspard with a furrowed brow and considered the young man for some moments as they rode along the highway. The attention caused Gaspard to look away in some discomfort.

"Yes, Your Grace?" he finally asked.

"Would you consider leaving Hambie and taking a position in my court when all this is settled?" the duke asked plainly.

"Your grace honors and humbles me with such an offer," replied Gaspard, "but I am bound to Hambie's chatelaine until such time as she would dismiss me."

"Yes, I have heard that about you," reflected Robert. "You have turned down offers of advancement to remain in Hambie. Why?"

Gaspard raised an eyebrow and considered the duke's friendly but serious expression. Surely the duke would consider him unnatural if he failed to consider Gisla's sedate beauty. All men, both low and high, could gaze upon her with nothing less than admiration. Why should Robert think otherwise of Gaspard, a man who knew all of her enduring qualities? Robert would be a fool to believe Gaspard had no affection at all for his mistress, and he was no fool!

"Forever I will owe the Paynel family for taking me into their house," Gaspard said seriously. "What lot would I have been cast otherwise? A pauper's life, or at best strong arm in battle and a life behind a plow? My ambitions are tempered by my existing good fortune."

"But should I need your support on some matter?" pressed the duke.

"Is Your Grace speaking of potential suitors?" asked Gaspard wryly.

"Yes, I am. Should Gisla and I disagree…"

"I would be bound to accept and defend milady's position without subterfuge."

Robert smiled quizzically and said no more on the matter. Gwylliam's report of Gaspard's oath to his lord appeared to be an oath kept, and it pleased the duke.

In their final leg of the journey the ranks of the men de Hambie gradually thinned as each man bid his comrades farewell and made his own way home among the hamlets and vales. By the time Hambie's horns sounded from the battlements announcing the duke's arrival, his own retinue outnumbered Gaspard's men-at-arms.

As was protocol, a rider was previously dispatched to alert the house of the impromptu visit by their duke. The house was cleaned, fresh reeds strewn upon the floor of the great hall, and fresh quarters and a great feast prepared. All the members of the house lined the bailey, and Master Josue stood with the brothers de Grentmesnel before the great oaken doors of the donjon. As the duke rode in lead through the barbican and gate, every man, woman and child made their obeisance to their feudal lord. Raoul was most pleased to capture the appreciative eye of Isabelle as she stood next to Clothilde.

The duke drew his steed to a halt as Master Josue stepped forward and said, "Welcome to Hambie. Your grace honors this humble house with your presence in such sad times. It would be a great honor to us if you would take your rest and break bread in our hall, as humble as it is."

"Véthe, Josue, my heart grieves for Hambie's loss, as it is all Normandy's loss," replied Robert. "I would express my condolences to your chatelaine, but I see not her face."

"She is ill of heart, Your Grace, and does not leave her chambers," explained Master Josue.

To this Robert nodded, and then motioned to his men to dismount. The stable boys quickly took the horses by the reins, leading them away to be fed and rubbed down. The men were shown their quarters where they were able to refresh themselves, and Rupert, carrying himself with as much dignity as possible, showed the duke to his chambers and left him in the company of two boys to see to his needs. With the house set in motion to attend to the guests, Gaspard took Master Josue aside.

"How fares Gisla?" he asked sincerely.

"Not well. It is as though she has not the will to live on," Josue shook his head.

"And Raymond? Where is he keeping himself?"

"He is angry and hides much of the time," sighed Josue.

"I would speak with him. Do you know his haunts?"

"Not I, Gaspard, I am sorry."

"Perhaps brother Carthusian?"

"Perhaps…he is close with the boy…but," Josue paused and placed his hand on Gaspard's shoulder. "Carthusian is leaving Hambie. He says he desires to return to the cloister. He has been most aggrieved since the news of Fulk's death."

"What?" exclaimed Gaspard in surprise. "Where can he be found?"

Master Josue directed Gaspard to the castle's chapel where Carthusian, in his brown habit, was in the midst of reciting the psalms of Nones. Gaspard quietly waited at the chapel's entrance until the gaunt, hawkish monk broke his reverie and retreated to the stone hallway. Upon seeing Gaspard, Carthusian froze, a look of fear contorting his face.

"Brother Carthusian, you look at me as though I am a ghost!" started Gaspard.

"I am sorry, milord," responded the monk, averting his eyes.

"Milord? 'Tis I, Gaspard! Such formality is not between us," chided Gaspard, "And what is this I hear about you returning to St. Lo?"

"I am sorry, Gaspard, perhaps we can speak later. I have matters to attend to," Carthusian pushed past Gaspard and walked quickly away.

Taken aback, Gaspard called after him, stopping him, "I am simply looking for Raymond!"

The monk looked back only half way, not meeting Gaspard's eyes. "Look for him outside the castle," he answered in a stilted voice, then disappeared around the corner and was gone.

The prejudice Gaspard saw in Carthusian's eyes left him quite perplexed and in need of explanation. He determined an encounter with his beloved mentor would be his first act upon the morrow. For now, he strode to the kitchen. It was a hot, savory place, and filled with staff bustling about preparing a feast fit for the duke. Outside its door, the prize lamb was skewered and roasting over an open pit. He half hoped to see Raymond amidst the maids, pestering them as they worked, but he was not to be found.

"Emma, do me a kindness and spare me one of those loaves," he asked a young girl whose bloom of womanhood was just beginning to fold out.

She set down her board with several loaves on it, and shyly settled an out-of-place lock. Her cheeks were flushed with the heat of the kitchen, livening her dark eyes, and though Gaspard had not the faintest suspicion, she was one of the girls about Hambie who secretly pined for the young man. She looked about, tucked a loaf under her apron, and then beckoned him outside, away from the ears of others.

"'Tis good ta see you've returned," she whispered. "The mistress is in an awful way. We all wants to know…what happn'd."

"There will be a time for the telling, but now I must find the lord's son," replied Gaspard, staring solemnly down into her eyes.

"Poor lit'l Raymond," she grieved as she pulled the loaf from under the apron and handed it to Gaspard. "The lit'l boy is in such a sadness. I pray you can bring 'im some cheer."

He thanked the young maid for the loaf and smiled. "And Emma, by my order, tell Agnes Maria to seat Isabelle next to Sir Raoul." He then bid her farewell and made for the castle gate.

Gaspard, still dressed in his heavy cloak and traveling clothes, turned south and walked along the hill to a bramble covered, cottage-sized rock jutting out of the earth. He knew every tree, rock, and contour of the hill on which the castle stood. There were many places a boy could hide his tears, but only one whose natural design lent itself to being a secret fortress of solitude. It was a place all too familiar to Gaspard as he made his way round to the rock's far side, out of view of the castle walls. He himself had spent many sun-filled days cutting tunnels throughout the thick blackberry canes and hollowing out caves inside the thickets encasing the outcropping. He knew every inch of the rock, and the one place its overhang keep the ground dry in even the worst of storms. Even in late summer, when the villagers would come to pick the wild, sweet berries, hanging heavy with juice from the thorned tendrils, no grownup ever discovered the massive stone's secret places. It was as though God made the fortress invisible to all but a child's eye.

Carefully, with the patience of a hunter, he carefully searched the edges of the thicket's thorny walls, looking for its secret entrance. His old hidden doors, tunnels, and rooms would have been long overgrown and lost, but the signs of any new excavation would not be lost to his trained eye. He walked with a heavy foot that any occupant would know his presence. Soon he found it, several leafy canes stretched over a boulder whose backside disappeared into the thicket. By gingerly moving the long, stiff canes aside, Gaspard discovered a low, narrow tunnel neatly tucked against the boulder's side. It ran behind the boulder, and then vanished into the thicket's interior.

"Will the lord of the Castle of the Rock come to his gate and give shelter to a lowly traveling knight?" he called toward the outcropping's overhang. He was met with silence.

Despite living in a world rife with real brutality, Gaspard was not so old that he had forgotten the tongue spoke by young boys. The world of fantastic imaginations, where everything that was more than it seemed and there were monsters more fearsome than man, could still be understood if not rejoined.

"I have traveled far and wide, and seen many things, and could tell you a tale or two in exchange for your hospitality. I even know the legends and secrets of your own fortress, if you care to hear that story."

From within the barbed thicket he detected the soft rustle and crinkle of movement in his direction. Momentarily Raymond appeared from behind the boulder and looked up at Gaspard. His face was grubby, as though he had been crying, and his hair mussed.

"What story?" he sniffed and wiped his nose upon his sleeve.

"Why, the legend of the Castle of the Rock and the location of its treasure!" replied Gaspard knowingly, "And I have brought a feast, that we can eat whilst I amaze your ears. What say you, oh lord of the castle?"

Raymond squinted at Gaspard and frowned, a battle between his desire to sulk and his curiosity struggling in his young head. Gaspard produced the fresh loaf and passed it under his nose, making an appreciative "mmm" sound. Soon the boy's hunger joined the fray and aided curiosity's battle against the sulking as he licked his lips.

"This is a secret place. You may enter, but you must first swear by your father's name, on the grave of your mother, to Michael the Archangel, the holy knight of God, not to tell!" the boy finally decided.

"I do solemnly swear by my father, on my mother's grave, and before Michael, leader of God's armies, I will not breath a word of this place to anyone," replied Gaspard gravely.

Raymond nodded seriously and retreated inside while Gaspard took off his sword, gently wrapping it in his cloak and setting it just inside the tunnel entrance. He reduced himself to hands and knees and cautiously made his way into the child-size tunnel, taking care not to catch himself on its thorny walls and ceiling. Bent low, Raymond led him into the heart of the thicket and ultimately to a small room hollowed out under the overhang of the rock.

While its ceiling had ample room to accommodate the boy's slight stature, Gaspard had to bend low in order not to catch his head on the brambles or knock it against the rock. Within, the boy had his toy sword, a real knife, a heavy blanket, a small spade, a log used as a bench, and a flat stone for a table. Reeds and straw were strewn about the floor. A second tunnel ran from the room further into the depths of the brambles.

"Your hall is well-made, milord," commented Gaspard, setting the loaf on the table, "and much as I remember it from days of old. I am glad of heart it has been rediscovered."

"You have been here?" asked Raymond.

"When I was very young I found this place much as you have," replied Gaspard, sitting on the ground. "At first I simply was after those fat berries always out of reach, but as I delved deeper into the canes, I discovered the berries and green leaves were simply a disguise. Beneath was hidden a vast fortress. I secretly began cutting tunnels until I discovered this very overhang and the stone table. That's when I began to realize its ancient origins."

He tore the loaf and handed half to Raymond, who bit into the soft, fresh bread. Gaspard also paused to chew a mouthful.

"Go on!" encouraged Raymond, now thoroughly interested.

"Well, I set about clearing several antechambers, a spy tunnel by which I could monitor the road entering the pass to the Dark Mountains of Haggadah, and a ladder to the lunar observatory,"

"Dark Mountains? Observatory?" Raymond's eyes grew wide.

"Oh yes!" whispered Gaspard, "The pass to the mountains lies just north of here. Many strange creatures come and go throughout the day and night, especially giants! And from the observatory all sorts of heavenly events can be seen. Constellations, shooting stars, even eclipses. One day, when I was a bit careless, your grandfather, Sir Hugh, caught sight of me near my secret entrance. He took me aside and told me fairies built the stone table and now guarded this place against intruders. Then he winked at me."

"And the treasure?" asked Raymond expectantly.

"Well..." replied Gaspard slowly, "I always intended the treasure to be used to mount an expedition into the Dark Mountains. I would hate to reveal its location for anything but that purpose."

"I could go with you on such an expedition!" exclaimed Raymond.

"Hmm..." confided Gaspard, "It would be dangerous, for a fair maiden is trapped within and needs rescuing. Such an adventure is not for the faint of heart, nor little boys. Do you think yourself a brave enough man to leave your fortress and venture forth?"

At this Raymond hesitated. Being alone in the Castle of the Rock was so much better than being shooed away by the grownups, ignored by his mother, and abandoned by brother Carthusian. In his great hall under the overhanging rock, he felt self-sufficient and in need of no one. Indeed, only hunger and the cold of night drove him within the castle walls, and then unhappily.

"You will stay with me, won't you, Gaspard?" Raymond asked quietly, "I could be your squire..."

It is important to understand Gaspard's mind up to this very moment. He had thought long and hard about Gregar's last words of council. He came to believe Gisla's affections could be earned not directly through any action of courtship on his part. It would be best if she came to appreciate, even rely upon his presence during the time of her mourning, so he determined to give attention and demonstrate kindness to her son. Truly he cared little for the boy, or any children, for that matter, and only feigned tolerance or affection when it suited his needs. He sought out the boy simply to make use of him. However, young Raymond's quiet offer and pleading eyes pierced his heart quite unexpectedly and painfully.

"Nay, milord!" he choked, "It is I who would serve you, the lord of this keep!"

Raymond smiled, and Gaspard, his mind awash with unfamiliar emotions that reached beyond pity and shame, took a knee and bowed his head in fealty to the boy. Raymond's birth had caused Gaspard great bitterness. The boy was an affirmation of all that Gaspard was denied. Now, he looked on the boy, so sad and lonely, and suddenly was suffering with him. He could no longer muster ill will where none was merited.

After a moment's pause, Gaspard continued brusquely, "Now, about that treasure—it is buried in this very room! Hand me your spade."

Raymond gave Gaspard the small shovel and Gaspard moved to the back of the room and began digging near the stone wall. In a matter of minutes he unearthed a rotting leather sack that he gently pulled from the ground. Within was a small rusted knife, a bit of flint, a silver coin, several small agates, pieces of jasper, and a smooth bit of amber.

"This should be enough to free the princess, no?" asked Gaspard.

"Most definitely!" said Raymond seriously. "But how shall we get past the guards?"

"We shall need a disguise…"

"We could be a giant!" said the boy brightly, "I could climb on your shoulders and hide beneath your cloak. The guards would think we were just another giant going into the Dark Mountains."

"An excellent plan, though you should have your sword at the ready if there is trouble," agreed Gaspard.

They finished their bread and shared a drink from Raymond's flask while discussing their plans for searching the mountains for the damsel in distress. Once prepared, they quietly exited the bramble fortress. Gaspard strapped his sword to his waist and hoisted Raymond up onto his shoulders. Raymond quickly clasped the long cloak about his neck and took up his sword. Once settled in their giant disguise, with Raymond their eyes and Gaspard their feet, they walked from behind the great bramble covered rock and made their way to the heavily guarded pass that entered the Dark Mountains of Haggadah.

CHAPTER 15

The Widow's Lament

Master Josue made his way to Gisla's chambers, where he gently knocked on the entry. After a moment's pause, Jacqueline opened the door, her careworn face set in a frown.

"What is it, Josue?" she sounded cross.

"Er, my dear madam," Josue halted, "Duke Robert is arrived…"

"Is that the case?" Jacqueline rolled her eyes and pursed her lips.

"He, ah, desires to confer with the mistress," Josue explained uncomfortably.

"Does he, now?" retorted Jacqueline, "Well the mistress would like to bury her husband, yet we noted no casket in his merry entourage."

"Yes, but the duke…"

Jacqueline drew close to Josue and hissed in his ear, "We both know what is on Robert's mind. Can he not let her mourn in peace a single day?"

"He is not as hard a man as you make! Do not convince our mistress to offend him!" he shot back in a whisper. "She has not been out in days. She must gather herself and listen to what he has to say."

Jacqueline bit her lip and glared at Josue. "Give us a moment," she said after a pause.

Closing the door, she retreated into the chamber, leaving Josue standing in the hall. Moments later she returned.

"She will meet with the duke in her bower in one hour. Now off with you!"

Josue walked away, chagrined, hearing Jacqueline mutter something about "Men!" as she closed the door.

While lacking the height and girth of Fulk Paynel, Duke Robert possessed all of the potency of his bloodline, a most formidable and imposing cast. His affable, freehanded nature often turned the face of an enemy toward him, and his intolerance of belligerents swiftly quelled notions of rebellion. As Jacqueline helped repair her chatelaine, combing and braiding Gisla's flaxen locks, tying the laces of her black gown, and affixing her veil, she knew the duke would confer with Gisla with an open ear and a made mind.

The bower was a woman's haven in castles such as the Castle de Hambie, affording the chatelaine a place for music, needlework, reading, and the absence of men. When Josue admitted the duke, both Jacqueline and Gisla made their obeisance and offered him the best chair near Gisla's couch. Jacqueline retreated to the hallway, closing the door until such time as she was called.

"Your Grace honors our house by your presence," said Gisla softly.

Robert furrowed his brow, opened his mouth, and then closed it again with a grimace. Finally, he said, "The death of your husband cuts my heart deeply, milady. He was my friend and trusted counselor. 'Twas I who sent him and I who am responsible."

"Though it is a liberty, I would counter Your Grace's notion. From the moment the Dragon's true name was suspected, my husband desired this confrontation above all else. He was never a man destined for the infirmities of old age. Men of action fear only the death that comes like a thief in the night, stealing life away without warning. This you know. Had not Fulk perished this season, it would have been the next or the next, and always in the name of God and Normandy."

Robert smiled sadly, "Your forgiving words ease my pain, Gisla, and I would repay that gift with one of my own. Noble widows such as you are a rare bloom indeed. True love existed here in Hambie, a man and woman clinging together in marriage as God intended. That is not something easily put away. Such a loss is not quickly healed. My gift to you is one of time. Time to grieve and time to heal. You know many will seek your hand for the prestige of your holdings. These men will not only seek to solicit you directly; they will also attempt to sway your father, your brothers, and your duke. Flattering words, rich gifts, promises of profitable alliances. I will turn a deaf ear to any such entreaties until after mid-summer's day."

Gisla closed her eyes as the coming tears choked her into silence. Her hands trembled as she reflexively clenched the loose folds of her kerchief while she wiped her eyes and nose.

"I have offered Gaspard a position," continued the duke after a moment. "He refused me as I knew he would. He is loyal to this house. He is loyal to you. Now that I have granted him a title, he could be of greater service to you than a mere squire. If you so choose, I will give him the authority to vet any suitors who make appeal to you. His opinion will be my opinion."

"Your Grace is kind," replied Gisla hesitantly. "Would that I knew his mind, I might consider such authority, but Gaspard is a shadow to me. I cannot trust what I do not know. I beg of you, do not bring such a notion to his mind."

"As you wish, Gisla," said Robert gently. "Gaspard's authority is yours to determine. My offer remains should you choose it. Lord Fulk was as true a friend as I have had the honor to possess. In deference to him, I will abide by your choice of husband, assuming that choice is timely."

"Thank you, Your Grace," Gisla was barely audible from beneath her veil.

Robert awkwardly stood, "Very well. It is settled then! Do not let this trouble your mind this moment, for tonight we shall feast and raise our goblets in memory of the greatest warrior I have known!"

From the village at the foot of the hill a girl in a simple, homespun dress and a worn kerchief tying back her hair hurried up the road to the castle gate. A young, pretty maid, she was laden with a basket of eggs ordered by Agnes Marie, Hambie's pantler, for the custard to be served for the evening's feast. As she walked up the switchbacks, she noted a man of great height making his way along the slope south of the gate. Though a giant in height, the woman puzzled at the peculiarly small head and short arms that emerged from the closely drawn cloak. The man made the gate well before the girl, where he made a curious exchange with the guard before entering the barbican.

"What a queer looking fellow!" she commented moments later when it came her turn to enter the keep.

"Just a giant passing through," the guard laughed and winked.

"A giant? I never!" exclaimed the girl with a puzzled look.

"They come round, from time to time," replied the guard carelessly. "They pay their toll and go about their business."

"A giant paying a toll in Hambie?" said the woman defensively. "You jest! I do not believe you."

"By the Pope's nose, he gave me this," laughed the guard, holding out a small, polished piece of jasper.

The woman frowned and stared skeptically at the shiny, green stone.

"You shall get no toll from me!" she stated emphatically, pushing past. "I am on castle business!"

"Not even a kiss?" laughed the guard after her as she hurried through the gate and into the bailey, where the giant was no longer to be seen.

"This valley is very exposed!" whispered Raymond from Gaspard's shoulders as they walked across a small plain surrounded by steep, mountainous slopes. "Many strange creatures are staring our way."

"We best make for the catacombs then," replied Gaspard from beneath the folds of the cloak in an equally hushed voice, "There is a little used entrance to the left of that small crag."

They quickly crossed the valley and found a small hole through which they could escape the curious eyes that followed their progress. Raymond clung tightly to Gaspard's chin as they ducked low and squeezed into the narrow passage. Once inside, the boy climbed down and brandished his sword. His eyes were no longer swollen, though by his dirty, tear stained cheeks, he looked quite the vagabond.

"This maid-so-fair you speak of, is she high or low?" whispered Raymond.

"High, I suspect," whispered Gaspard.

Low voices and the sounds of footsteps approaching deeper in the passage, gave start to the lord of the Castle of the Rock and his squire.

"Quickly, in here," Raymond commanded, ducking into a dark chamber with stalactites hanging from the ceiling and stalagmites growing from the floor. The two took cover in the shadows until the voices passed and receded into silence. On the move again, Raymond led Gaspard through the narrow passages and up a steep, rocky incline. The passage split, one way quiet, the other with deep, muffled voices.

"I fear our maiden must be guarded," cautioned Raymond.

"By the giant-king himself, if my ear hears true," replied Gaspard.

"Stay here; I shall spy out their positions!" commanded Raymond, who then crept up to the corner around which the voices drifted.

The boy flattened himself against the floor, inching forward until he could just poke his head about corner and look down the shadowy passage. Three strange, misshapen creatures, standing outside the entrance to a prison cell were busy commiserating. Two were obviously guards, and the third, by his dress, must have been the king. After a moment the guards bowed low as the king turned and walked away in the opposite direction.

Raymond slithered back to Gaspard's position, "The king has left, but how do we defeat the guards without raising an alarm?"

"A distraction!" replied Gaspard, "Go hide in that alcove. I will make a sound, and when they come, you will attack from behind, and I the front."

Raymond nodded and quickly hid behind a rock on the far side of the passage. Gaspard then put his shoulder to a loose boulder and toppled it with a loud crash. The sound was not without its desired effect, and quickly they heard the steps running in their direction. From around the corner burst an aging giant guard with a rotund midsection, grizzled beard, and balding scalp. The look of surprise upon his face was without price.

"Hello, Josue!" smiled Gaspard knowingly.

"*What in…*" the aging seneschal started, but was cut off by the roaring charge of Raymond who appeared from behind an alcove statue and leapt upon the old man's back, staggering him.

"Surrender or die!" cried Raymond as he dragged Josue to the ground.

"We have you at a disadvantage, Josue. I would do as your lord says," laughed Gaspard.

"Josue? What on earth has happened?" cried Jacqueline as she rushed around the corner of the passage.

"Surrender or die, madam," said Gaspard with a smile. "My lord and I have business with the fair maiden you have imprisoned in yonder cell. Do not interfere!"

"You awful ruffians!" cried Jacqueline, then stooping to Josue's side. "My dear, are you injured? Are you hurt?" Then she shot back at Gaspard, "Do not believe you are too old to yet have your ears boxed, young man!"

"I will take that as your unconditional surrender, wench," laughed Gaspard, and then he cried to Raymond, "To the damsel, milord!"

At the same time, Master Josue was fighting off Jacqueline's attentions with very gruff, "I am whole, woman! Let me be!" and "I can stand without any help!" and "Arggh! My shoulder, madam, I am not a gander whose joint needs breaking!" all as Raymond and Gaspard raced down the now empty passage to the door of Gisla's bower.

"Who shall enter first?" Raymond asked nervously.

Gaspard took a knee and looked steadily in Raymond's eyes, "You must enter alone, milord. Only you can free this fair princess! She is a prisoner in both body and spirit. While I can aid in the freeing of her body, only a prince such as yourself can free her mind."

"I do not know what to do," said Raymond pensively, tears welling in his eyes. "The spell she is under makes me invisible to her."

"Then you must kiss each eye that it be opened."

"She is deaf to my words," Raymond's little voice shook.

"Then you must kiss each ear and whisper, 'I love you,' that she may hear."

"I am afraid," he wept.

"You are the lord of the Castle of the Rock. Your bravery is greater than your fear."

Never once did Gaspard's eyes waver. Never once did his true purpose flicker across his face. He was solemn as a stone, calm and serious.

"I will wait here until you break the spell. I will stay until you release me."

With that Gaspard nodded toward the door and stepped back. Raymond nervously grasped the latch with his small hand, pushed iron-bound oak inward, and then disappeared inside. Gaspard had to wait little more than a quarter of an hour before Raymond again opened the door and happily released him from the adventure.

So great was that eve's feast that the Castle de Hambie's hall overflowed with men, women, children, and ale. Their voice was their music, their toasts were to their fallen lord, and their laughter first defied, and then chased away the evil spirits that swirled about the castle. The bailey was filled with torchlight and villagers, and lanterns were hung from all the battlements. The fattened lamb, well roasted and seasoned with choice herbs, was joined by skewers of roast fowl—capons, hens, and geese—two sides of beef brought from the village, oysters, generous loaves, sauces and jellies, wheels of cheese, custards, cakes, casks of wine, and what fruits were left from fall harvest.

Once darkness fell and the ale well consumed, the song and dance grew lively and boisterous. Gaspard, cleanly repaired in his customary black and green gown, hoisted a bathed and combed Raymond onto his shoulders and sang epic tales of yore with a voice deep and true. Two young boys suddenly leapt onto the long table began a capricious dance while singing a bawdy tune that brought peals of laughter and clapping from the drunken crowd.

At the lord's table, Gisla, the brothers de Grentmesnel, Raoul, Isabelle, and Clothilde surrounded Duke Robert. Raoul enjoyed a lively conversation with Isabelle, who raptly listened to the weathered knight's tales of adventure. The duke was free with stories of Fulk's great deeds and military exploits, expounding not only his fierceness, but also his unequaled stratagems.

All this Gisla observed most sedately, with only a rare smile crossing her lips. While Raymond had banished the worst possessing spirit, and the boisterous feasting, singing, and tales drove off nearly all the rest, there was yet one wraith that clung to Gisla's soul. It grasped her with the chill fingers, not fooled by her black, veiled disguise. Though she could not name it, its fell presence was like a creeping rigor not even the warmth of the fire at her back could thaw.

She was there, sitting next to the duke, yet not there, not a part of that which happened around her, as though she merely observed without the power to affect. Gaspard and her son; Raoul and Isabelle; mouse-like Clothilde, happy yet sad; Raoul's strange, shy, and quiet squire, black as night and perhaps twice Raymond's age; Josue and Jacqueline; Carthusian there then gone; maids and men—she saw it laid out before her like the sections of a complex tapestry capturing a single moment for all time, and only her visage was not stitched among its many faces. Isolated she remained.

Gisla was not alone in feeling the chill hand of evil upon her shoulder, and had its other victim known she shared this sixth sense, he might well have stayed instead of slipping away. Perhaps it was more than mere coincidence by which Gisla numbly noted his quiet, unobtrusive departure. Alas, poor Carthusian could see little beyond his own anxieties and the dark sense of expulsion they brought upon him. Perhaps a man with a lion's heart would have fixed his will against such a driving force and remained, but Carthusian had no such quality. He succumbed and found himself driven to seek the safety found within the protective walls of his convent.

It was his intent to take his leave with proper decorum, announced and filled with fond farewells, but the sight of Gaspard shattered his resolve. Truly he loved the young man, and had tried to guide him as well he could in the days before Sir Hugh took him away, yet he could not face the man he had become. Even his vows before God could not prevent his cowardice, so he made the decision to flee.

Vows of poverty make for a very portable life, and what few possessions he had, if one could call a spare habit, a cloak, a pair of boots, a traveler's wallet, a crucifix, a quill, and bottle of ink "worldly possessions," were quick to gather and light to carry. With the feast at its height of merriment and Hambie's gates wide open and filled with people, it was a simple thing for him to slip into the darkness without so much as a curious glance.

He quickly made his way down the slope, away from the castle and to the east. The road to St. Lo was little more than a rutted walking path, wending its way through the forested hills and fields of Normandy. At seven leagues, it was a long day's walk best split in two. He knew of a few shelters, haylofts built to store winter fodder, placed along the route where he could rest if need be. For the time being, despite the darkness of night, he desired distance above all else—distance from Hambie and distance from Gaspard Malfort.

The hours slipped by accompanied by melodic hoots of owls, the rustle of the forest's nocturnal residences, and the whisper of wind among the trees. The monk's exertions kept the chill of that last night of winter at bay while the peace of the forest and growing separation between himself and his home of recent years calmed his spirits. It was not until the last quarter of the moon rose in the east, a very late hour, that lassitude brought on by the miles compelled him to seek out shelter for the remains of the night.

CHAPTER 16

Carthusian's Confession

The hour was late when Gaspard finally latched the door of his chamber sealing out the world in favor of quiet and solitude. Though his head was filled with wine and his step unsteady, he was taken with a restless energy that disdained the comforts of his bed. He threw open his shutters, breathed in the cool night air, and then sat at his table, filled a goblet with wine, and carefully considered its fragrance and spice. On the floor he spied his packs, containing all that he carried back from Jersey and Falaise. Eleven full days had passed since he exhorted the men de Hambie to follow him and avenge Fulk's death. In that time he had not a moment's solitude, no door to close, no lock to turn away unwanted company. All that time the torn, half-burned tome he had spirited away from the island remained nothing more than a forgotten bulge laying at the bottom of his purse, beneath a worn pair of breeches. Now it called to him.

With care he lit all the candles in his room and set them about the table. He opened the pack and gently lifted out the bundle of loose pages and damaged binding. As he sorted the pages, attempting to return them to their original order, he saw their tongue was his own, and the script was written with little flourish by a strong hand. It was those first pages, the ones that remained secure within the binding that suffered most from the fire. Flame had crept around all their edges, oft times charring the pages beyond reading, and leaving none unspoiled. Those loose pages suffered an entirely different sort of abuse. Some were trampled, torn, and muddied, some were damaged by what mist and drizzle touched them in the time before their rescue, and some suffered both such insults.

Again, just as the first time he touched the strange tome, his fingers tingled as they touched velvety vellum pages. Once Gaspard felt he had some semblance of order, he opened the charred leather cover and began leafing through the damaged pages. He read those words and lines he could, agonizing with an unnatural concentration on those destroyed by flame. The faint ringing of bells carried through the quiet night air marking the passing hours of vigils while the waning moon rose after their third toll. Page after page he read with increasing fascination and dread. Any notion of sleep was lost as the journal unfolded it macabre story up until its ending pages, torn and stained, cursed Gaspard with their final truth. He leapt up and backed away from the table, his face twisted in horror.

"*It...cannot...be!*" he seethed from between clenched teeth.

Taking up a candle, he stood before his silver mirror and stared at his garish reflection. The lines of his face, knit of his brow, the cut of his jaw, and angle of his nose were no longer his, but rather belonged to a twisted monster. With violence he threw the candle at his own reflection and cried out in agony. His breath was desperate as he stalked about the room in indecision. Finally he grasped the binding and pages of the journal, thrust them back angrily into his sack, and fled the room. The castle was deathly still as he silently made his way through the dark passages, down the stairs and past the chapel. He only stopped when he stood outside the door of Carthusian's Spartan chamber. Without hesitation, he rapped upon the portal. Not a sound stirred from within, so Gaspard plied the latch and pushed the door inward. Only the narrowest beam of moonlight coming through a tiny window high on the wall broke the inky gloom of the little chamber. It revealed all the intelligence needed by the frantic knight. Carthusian and his few belongings were gone.

"He must have slipped away during the feasting!" Gaspard thought darkly to himself. "I will be pressed..."

Gaspard quickly returned to his own chambers and donned his traveling clothes and sword. He quietly left the donjon and made his way through the shadows to the stables and kicked its boy awake.

"I need my horse saddled and ready to go in five minutes," he ordered the lad. "Bring him to the gate."

From the stable Gaspard strode to gatehouse and accosted the guard, "Open the gate, man, I have business and must leave immediately."

"Milord?" asked the guard.

"And mind your questions and your tongue!" retorted Gaspard.

The man jumped to attention and he and Gaspard made quick work of the bar at the gate and pulled one side open. The stable boy arrived and handed the reins to Gaspard, who stepped up into the saddle.

"I shall return in a few days' time. If the lady asks, tell her I am fulfilling a promise. Otherwise breathe not a word to anyone or it will be the worse for you! Do you understand?" he commanded sternly, then urged his horse through the gate and disappeared into the darkness.

Though he knew the guard and stable boy could do nothing but spy, he turned his horse immediately in the direction of St. Lo. In daylight, it was a simple four-hour ride, but at night greater care was needed to avoid injury to the stallion by some invisible hole or root. Still, he would be at least double the pace of a man on foot.

The quarter moon rose high in the sky as he trotted along under the budding forest canopy. Though not a main route, it was familiar to him and marked by only a few farms, cottages, and lonely lofts. The first few of these he passed without further inspection, for they were far too early in the journey to be sheltering Carthusian. It was not until the moon began its descent into the west and the sky readied for its cold transition to dawn that he left the road to explore an isolated barn in search of the monk once his mentor.

The three brothers Lunce, Batchi, and Orfi were some of the swarthiest and most desperate forest brigands a traveler could have the misfortune of crossing paths. Their clothes were pungent, soiled furs cobbled together from game they had poached, and their nails were black with forest filth. Everything on their person was taken by robbery along the small roads and paths of western Normandy or stolen by dark of night while their victims slumbered. They took their repose in a small, damp cave hidden in the hills, but tonight they were on the prowl, driven forth by hunger and boredom since the long winter rains broke.

While Lunce was the eldest and strongest of the brothers, his wits were dull and slack. Though Orfi was the youngest and smallest, he was a very clever thinker and their obvious leader. In between was the slender Batchi, who had never been willing to suffer a fair fight.

On this particular day, ever keeping an open mind for robbery, they were about the wood checking their snares. As darkness fell they found their pickings to be quite slim, being just three squirrels and not a single hare. They made their way to their last snare, hid near a decrepit hayloft next to a field culled for fodder, in hopes of at least a rat, if not a marten. Alas, it also was empty.

"Dat's it, boys," stated Orfi. "Weez gotta grab a sheep ifs weez gonna get a belly full!"

"Tricksy," followed Batchi. "Gots ta wait till late."

"Whats about da shepherd?" asked Lunce in a thick voice.

"If he's about, then you cracks 'is nob wid yurz stick!" explained Orfi logically. "You puts 'im ta sleep…forzever!"

"Good…I likes ta do de crackin!" replied Lunce with an oafish laugh.

"If'n our peire was 'ere, 'e'd be prowd o' you, boy," followed Batchi.

"Nary a doubt, Lunce, nary a doubt. Youz be a terror when it be crackin time," agreed Orfi, "de best nob-cracker I ever did know! Fer now, weez best burrow in dis 'ere barn till moonsup. Den weez goes an' finds us a sheeps for youz to carry off."

"Weez gots ta sleep before grabbin' de sheep," agreed Batchi.

Lunce scratched his head with his burly fingers and looked affectionately at his brothers, who then both flashed their rotted teeth with their most reassuring smiles. In the dimness of his mind, he knew he had to take care of them as best he could. That meant killing what they told him to kill and carrying what they told him to carry. He followed his brothers into the shadows of the barn, burrowed his way into a mound of grass, and listened to his growling stomach as he fell asleep.

Creatures of the forest, such as the wolf, hare, deer, and the brigand brothers slept lightly as a matter of simple survival, so it was not unexpected they all roused when a stranger entered the darkness of the barn in the late hours of the night. There was a quiet, careless shuffle of feet and the whisper of a cloak against gown, accompanied by the light sighs and grunts of a man fumbling in the dark shadows. As one, the brothers silently awoke and waited with the patience of a fox outside a rabbit hole. They lay hidden beneath their blankets of hay knowing the slightest twitch could alert the intruder and betray the advantage found in their concealment.

Several minutes passed, and it became apparent the intruder was intent on bedding in the dry grass much as they were, seeking shelter from what remained of the chill night. Soon, without the faintest notion of the danger he was in, the traveler drifted off to sleep, his breathing regular and light. The brothers remained still. Beams of moonlight entered the loft from the west, slowly dragging the shadow of a skewed shutter across the floor. First one hour, then two passed as the three brigands patiently waited for their prey to sink deeply into that part of sleep that deafened the ears and confused the mind. Only then, with a stealth that belied their crude appearance, did they ever so slowly emerge from hiding, making barely more than a whisper in the straw. Silently they nodded to one another in the gloom as Lunce took hold of his heavy, gnarled oak stick. Slowly they surrounded the corner where the man slept with such peace while Lunce raised his stick and prepared to crack the man's nob.

Gaspard lightly tugged the reins to the left and directed his mount to leave the road. A narrow path through beaten grass led to the silvery outline of an aging barn used by local shepherds to store fodder for their animals in the lean times of winter. The night had proven quiet, with little more than the reassuring sounds of nocturnal beasts to interrupt the steady clip-clop of his stallion and soft sound of his shifting saddle. Despite his angst, his lids grew heavy, and his dry eyes stung with need of sleep.

Suddenly the natural quiet of the night was broken by a cry of surprise and pain, and several low, rough voices coming from the barn. In an instant his fatigue vanished. A fight was at hand, and a surge of energy quickly spread throughout Gaspard's body, speeding his heart and sharpening his vision. He slid from the saddle and drew out his fine blade with only the softest of snickers. The rough voices were cruel and taunting, while the victim's was fraught with fear.

"He taint but got dese 'ere robes!" complained one ruffian, who was, in fact, Batchi.

"Takes it!" ordered another, Orfi. "He won'ts be needin' such once weez is finished 'ere!"

The third man, Lunce, sounding as though his mouth was full, said, "Dis 'ere be beef in 'is sack…an' an apple."

"Gives it 'ere!" ordered Orfi. "Stop stuffin' yourz face!"

Quickly Gaspard snuck to the low opening on the east wall of the building. From inside he heard the low, punching sound of a man being kicked, followed by the whack of a heavy staff. The victim cried out in pain and pleading. It was Carthusian!

"Please, in the name of God, have mercy!" cried Carthusian, "You can have everything. I give it to you freely that you do not have to steal. I beg of you, do not damn your souls by an act of murder!"

From under the darkness of the eaves of the barn, Gaspard stole a look inside. Outlined in the faint moonlight stood three shadows, one short, one tall and thin, and one thick and heavy who sported a heavy staff. They stood in the far corner, to the left, all gawking over a form huddled in the straw at their feet.

The ruffians laughed heartily at his plea, and Orfi spat on him. "God taint gonna saves de likes of you, brudder!"

"An' you taint gonna tell no tales," growled Batchi as he abruptly drew up his arm and lunged downward upon Carthusian.

Gaspard charged into the barn, roaring like a great bear, just as Carthusian screamed out in pain. Gaspard went for the largest brigand first, running him through the chest. Incredulous, all Lunce managed to say was, "Wot?" before he collapsed in a twisted heap, wrenching Gaspard's sword out of his hand.

The other two, knives drawn, were on the invader in an instant, slashing into the folds of his cloak. Gaspard caught hold of Lunce's staff and cut a vicious swath through the air, knocking Batchi cleanly off his feet. It was dark and all was confusion. He lost sight of Orfi while both Carthusian and Batchi moaned in pain. He whirled about with the staff, until he saw the short brigand dart through the door and out of the building. In an instant he gave chase and quickly closed the distance on the much slower man. He raised the staff and swung with all of his considerable strength, landing the savage blow across Orfi's shoulder and neck. The filthy brigand crumpled beneath the blow, forcing Gaspard to pull up and jump over the body. To ensure the man stayed down, Gaspard again swung the heavy staff, this time crushing Orfi's skull.

Without a second thought, Gaspard ran back to the barn with the great oak stick at the ready. Batchi stumbled out holding his shoulder and stared, wild-eyed, at Gaspard.

"Mercy, milor…" was all he got out before Gaspard struck three times in quick succession, dropping him to his knees, where upon he kicked the lanky brigand full in the face, spraying teeth and blood into the darkness.

Gaspard was in a panic and had no time to parlay. He had heard Carthusian's cry, and knew him to be grievously wounded. Into the gloom of the building he rushed in search of the monk.

"Carthusian!" he cried as he rushed to the monk's side, "stay with me, man!"

In the darkness Gaspard felt for Carthusian's hands. They were pressed against his stomach and covered in warm, oozing blood.

"G-G-Gaspard…" the monk gasped painfully, "I do not… understand."

"That I have found you out?" retorted Gaspard, "Or that I happened along at all to save such a wretch as you! What do you fail to understand?"

Carthusian groaned painfully, and Gaspard grasped some straw and pressed it into the wound to slow the flow of blood.

"Too...late to save...my son...my...mortal self...I am..." whispered the monk.

"Your son? Curse you, brother, damn you to Hell! You know I am not your son. You know the name of my father! All these years you feigned ignorance and kept the truth from me!"

"Not...by choice...by oath...I have...only loved..." The monk broke in to a fit of painful coughing. "Is it true? Did you...slay him?"

Only the darkness of the barn kept the horrid contortion of Gaspard's face from the dimming eyes of Carthusian.

"Confession for confession, then!" bargained the young knight. "First tell me the truth of my mother; then I will tell you the truth of Jersey."

"I swore...an oath...before God," hesitated Carthusian.

"Bertrand Ducaen has released you from your damned oath!"

Carthusian sighed with pain and a resigned sadness. He took as deep a breath as he could manage and began his tale. There were many fits and starts and painful pauses. He was forced to stop, cough, and spit the blood filling his mouth, but managed the story to its end.

"I argued against the name given you by the father abbot, God rest his soul. It was an uncalled for cruelty. Your mother came to us, desperate. Her father had turned her out when he discovered she was with child and she refused to name the father. He was a wealthy dyer in Bayeux. He passed on eleven years ago. I do not wish to speak ill of the dead, but he was neither kind nor charitable in this life. Your mother's name was Angelica de L'Aunay. She was such a beauty...that is what caught your father's fancy. Hair black as night, skin of alabaster, and eyes of purest sapphire...he pursued her relentlessly. He was but a lad, barely a man, and so arrogant, rash and cruel, just as his father raised him to be, just as his father had been raised by his own father.

"Had Bertrand's intentions been matrimonial, I am sure your grandfather would have given Angelica away without any trouble of conscience, no matter the misery brought upon his daughter. Alas, it was a different curse Bertrand intended. She refused his advances, knowing her fruit would be cast aside once consumed, yet he was relentless. Finally, he simply took her by force and without consequence. He, being the son of a wealthy lord, was immune to any sort of prosecution, and was far too dangerous for even a trained warrior to call out, let alone an aging dyer.

"She kept her rape secret, beneath the folds of robes and gowns, until very late. She came to us swollen with child, and only a desperate, pale reflection of her former self. Your birth was difficult. Angelica was ill and consumed with fever. No matter the gentle hand, once your story was told, she passed. She made me swear an oath to protect you and keep you hidden that your life could be lived without such evil influence that was the house of Ducaen. Only the abbot, Sir Hugh and myself knew your lineage…after this night, your accursed secret will be yours alone…Hugh took you to give you what protection he could. How Bertrand divined your existence is beyond my understanding.

"I have always held in my heart that God cursed your father that day he forced his violent lusts on your mother. No matter the woman, wife or maid or whore, Bertrand never again fathered any known child by any woman."

By the story's end, Carthusian's voice had turned to the soft mumble of a man being called away to darkness, "I ever saw her face when I gazed upon you, my boy…her bravery…only when…when…I heard tell of Jersey…did I see your father…I am so very sorry…I should have warned you…in keeping my oath, I sinned against you…*forgive*…"

Bitter tears of anger, frustration, and loss filled Gaspard's eyes in the gloom. So many years of false witness born against him in the name of the better path came to naught. The wizened face of Carthusian emerged, wraithlike, from the darkness with the dawn's slow and subtle approach. Blood matted his hair above his unblinking eyes. Ignorant of the younger man's greater sins, it was a face begging forgiveness and absolution. Would that a priest were in Gaspard's stead to offer such peace before passing; however, it was not within the young man's will or ability to relieve the monk of his burden.

"Go to your rest knowing you shared no hand in patricide, my old friend," was all he could choke through the tears. "'Twas Fulk who slew the Dragon..."

A bright, white dawn greeted the first day of spring in Normandy, its light and warmth quickly undoing the delicate frost laid upon the land just hours before. Behind him, Gaspard had left the bodies of the three brigands. In the lowland before him, its ramparts built on the Vire River, lay the city of St. Lo. Reins in hand, he walked ahead of his mount, which bore poor Carthusian's corpse tied across the saddle. He was only dimly aware of the gash on his right arm and dried blood on his hands that, along with a body tied across his saddle, drew curious stares from the guards at the city's gate.

This brings to some light the peculiar circumstances of the times in which this story takes place. There were no police or any sort of organized law. Certainly the church could rail against those who broke God's commandments to the point of excommunications and the laying of interdicts, and feudal lords could exact what justice, or injustice for that matter, that they saw fit. However, it remained that the rule of law was very limited in scope and virtually nonexistent away from towns and castles. There were no sheriffs, constables, or bailiffs. Pirates, brigands, and ruffians ruled the wild places and murderers usually had to await judgment until the day they stood before God. The scrutiny brought to bear on a lordly man carrying a corpse through a city gate was little more than, "What has happened, milord?" Followed by, "A brother murdered by ruffians. I came upon them, but was too late to affect a rescue. Their bodies are a few miles back. You ought send a cart that they can be buried." As simple as that.

Gaspard entered the convent whereupon his story, only a slightly twisted truth, was wholly believed. His wound was graciously dressed and his clothes graciously laundered while he slept comfortably in a cell set aside for guests of import. There was great sadness amongst the brothers as they cleansed Carthusian's body and prayed continuously to ease the passing of his soul. Stolid and stone faced, Gaspard remained as they lowered Carthusian's body into the hallowed ground of the churchyard. As for the brothers Lunce, Batchi, and Orfi, a pit was dug and their remains cast in without so much as a second thought as to the repose of their souls.

CHAPTER 17

The Third Dream

"Exactly what were Sir Malfort's words?" asked Gisla sedately. She sat on the dais of the hall in the great chair. Before her stood the night watch and the stable boy. The shutters were thrown open and sun and freshness of spring streamed through the high, narrow windows. She had awoke that morning as though from a nightmare, her mind clear...clear to accept the flat, cold pain that her was existence...clear in the understanding she did not suffer alone. The evil shade that enshrouded her in previous days was gone and again her son could bring a smile to her lips.

He had entered her chamber early in the morning demanding to know Gaspard's whereabouts, as he wanted the knight's company for play. He was not to be found, so Raymond's obvious solution was to barge into his mother's chamber with the full expectation she could name his location. She was, after all, Gaspard's keeper in the boy's mind. "Find him!" he demanded petulantly once she pleaded ignorance. Thus a brief investigation took place, ending with the guard and the stable boy bearing witness against Sir Malfort.

"Sumthin' bout a promise, milady," said the guard, stiffly at attention. The stable boy examined the holes in his well-worn shoes.

"He said to tell you he was 'fulfilling a promise and would be back in a few days,'" mumbled the boy without looking up. The guard cuffed the lad's head. "Look at your mistress when you speak," he ordered, whereupon the boy raised his eyes and shyly gazed upon Gisla's melancholy beauty.

"And what time was this?" prodded Gisla.

"After the last bells o' nightly vigils, milady," responded the guard. "He was in a terrible hurry and very short tempered. He rode east."

Gisla considered the two for a moment. "Thank you. You may go. Find Josue and send him to me."

Besides the retreating guard and boy, the hall was empty except for Gisla's lithe form upon the dais. She remained lost in thought until Master Josue entered and made his obeisance. He suddenly looked old to her, with gray wisps of hair askew around a balding head, and a round belly that defied his gown to lie well upon it. She beckoned him to a small chamber at the back of the great hall and closed the door.

"Carthusian left our company last night without taking his leave," she stated once they were alone. "Not long after nightfall."

Josue possessed the confused look of a man who took too much drink the night before, "I was not aware he was gone, milady."

"I saw him leave the hall. He had the look of a hunted man,"

Josue looked at Gisla in puzzlement.

"I assure you, you will find his chambers empty," she continued. "'Twas by no great sin you were distracted last night. She loves you, in her own way."

Hambie's seneschal became quite flushed at this remark. Jacqueline had been a part of the household staff nearly as long as he and their tenure had at times been contentious. Yet there were moments, a passing touch, a tender glance, a caring word, which belied their oft quarrelsome relations. In their twilight years, the aging bachelor and spinster, both too set in their ways to marry, did take comfort from each other's company.

"It seems Gaspard discovered his departure and went after him. Not at dawn, as you might have, but in the dead of night," her words were careful. "A dangerous ride, alone in the dark. What would drive a man, either man, to such recklessness?"

Josue pondered the question a moment, "Carthusian has been a haunted man since…since Sir Fulk's death, milady. It may be that holy men, such as he, are attuned to those dark spirits surround death and passing. Perhaps it was fear that drove him. Perhaps love steeled him to remain. Perhaps he held on these past few days for Raymond's sake."

The mention of Raymond caused Gisla to avert her eyes in shame. She had abandoned her son to dwell in her own private misery. The painful sting of a tear rose and she closed her eyes, taking a deep breath. Josue gently reached for her hand with a father's love.

"I did not mean…" he said quietly, but she raised her hand to silence him.

"Speak to me of Gaspard," she continued. "Why would he chase a fleeing man?"

Josue sighed heavily, "I do not fathom the boy, milady. I cast my line, but it never strikes, though I suspect the shoals are rocky and treacherous. However, if there ever were a man he loved, it would be Carthusian. He was quite taken aback with the news of Carthusian's impending departure. Perhaps he sought to confront him…"

"Hours after midnight?"

Josue raised his brow, "'Tis Gaspard we are talking about, milady."

Gisla relaxed and smiled, "Yes…it is."

A moment's silence passed between the two, as they thought quietly to themselves.

"He seems quite concerned with the well-being of my son," mused Gisla.

"Raymond's suffering is one Gaspard understands. He was not much older when Sir Hugh was lost. Gaspard and Fulk clung to each other in that time of grieving. I am glad he seeks to offer such companionship to Lord Raymond, milady."

"So you think Gaspard a good man?" asked Gisla in earnest.

At this Josue withdrew his hands and cast his gaze away from Gisla. After a regretful pause he said, "I cannot say he is not, milady. Yet I cannot assure you of his quality, either."

"Has he given you cause to question his loyalty?" she asked sternly.

"Most sincerely, never once," replied Josue.

"Yet you will not vouch for him?"

"I do not know his mind, milady. Only Sir Fulk seemed to understand him. The answer is no, I will not, cannot vouch for him, but Fulk most certainly would, and I can produce no evidence to the contrary."

"Neither can I…" replied Gisla distantly.

The unadorned stone hallways of the convent, more narrow and dark than in his childhood memories, felt close and stifling. Oily smoke blackened the walls and ceilings above and behind the flickering torches as he made his way along the shadowed corridor. Not sure whether he was wandering or seeking, he entered into a small courtyard where he was confronted with a stone Christ crucified. Torturously bent, bronze nails were driven through the image's outstretched hands and dangling feet. The head, slumped forward in that moment of strength failed, was crowned with thorns of copper, green with age and weather. Though he could not see them in the flickering torchlight, his memory recalled those pleading eyes of the savior. They begged not for personal mercy—no, they asked that mercy be granted to the persecutors.

It was with a morbid fascination—nearing horror—that Gaspard the child spied upon the statue. He swore, at times, the man cast in stone to suffer eternally for all mankind shifted his head or moved a finger. Now he approached with a reluctant and confused mind. It was not rational that he sought out this place, and he could not even recall a conscious decision on the matter. The courtyard was empty of life, and Gaspard had a vague notion the brothers must all be gathered for Compline. Yet there was movement among the shadows beyond the stone effigy, something darker than darkness gliding along the concourse.

"You, man!" called Gaspard to the dark form. "What are you doing here?"

The form, no more than absence of all light, stopped short and turned toward Gaspard but did not approach. It remained motionless, and

Gaspard found himself paralyzed, unable to close the distance himself. Off to the right, a monk exited the building and came along the concourse, unaware of what hid in the shadows ahead of him. Gaspard tried to call out but had no voice. With desperate force of will he fought to move his feet forward against the repelling entity. It pressed its cloaked form against the wall and lay in wait for the innocent brother to leave the flickering, red torchlight.

There was a cry of surprise and a brief struggle. The dark form stepped forward and seemingly enveloped the passing gaunt, tonsured man. Step after agonizing step, Gaspard pushed against the devil's wind that resisted his forward motion. The monk's sandals scraped and kicked against the stones of the path and his hands fought against the grip of white, skeletal fingers grasping his throat. The creature tore deep into the folds of the plain, brown habit, and Gaspard could see they struggled for control of the simple wood crucifix strung about the monk's neck. For a moment the struggle hung in the balance—the monk and creature clutching for both throat and cross. Gaspard was nearing and could see the thin, scaled arms of the attacker flexing tightly with unholy strength.

The creature was gaining the upper hand and managed to wrench the crucifix away and tear it from the brother's neck. As the simple bit of wood flew into the darkness, the brother clawed away the creature's hood to reveal the white, scaled face of a serpent. The eyes were a hideous, luminous pink, and the teeth of the gaping mouth were translucent needles. Gaspard worked all the harder to urge his leaden legs forward and was nearly to the concourse when the serpent finally laid both sinuous hands upon the weakening man's throat. The desperation of the monk's feet began to wane as his breath was strangled at the hand of the fell beast.

At the very moment the man gave up the battle, Gaspard finally was able to reach out and grasp the creature from behind, wrapping his powerful arms around its neck and pulling it off the failing monk. The serpent jerked away from his victim and turned on Gaspard with surprising strength and agility. Its forked tongue whipped the narrow space between their faces and it struck as though to sink its fangs into his face. He thrust the creature away, but not before it struck him with the back of it smooth, scaled hand. A black, serpentine ring upon the creature's finger bit deeply into the flesh of his cheek, and before he could counter, the creature made its escape into the darkness.

He quickly knelt and rolled the fallen monk onto his back, only to recoil in horror. The man's tonsure was matted with blood and his habit was saturated from a wound in his stomach. The man's eyes flew open, and he grasped Gaspard's collar.

"There is still time, my boy," gasped the man desperately, "Repent!"

Gaspard's scream echoed through the night, for the face of the monk that lay dying in his arms was none other than that of his beloved mentor, Carthusian.

The cry died upon Gaspard's lips as he sat bolt upright from his mat. His room was dark, and for a moment he was at a loss as to where he was. Outside in the hall he heard the shuffle of feet, panicked voices, and then pounding on his door.

"Messire? Messire? Are you in need of assistance?" called a man through the door.

Gaspard rose and staggered to the door. He felt drunk, and as he fumbled for the latch in the darkness, he realized, indeed, he was. Finally he pulled open the door and squinted at the light of the lamp held by an aging innkeeper in company with his wife.

"My apologies. I frightened you good people. 'Twas nothing more than a bad dream," said Gaspard thickly.

The old couple backed away, fear still in their eyes. The man, in no more than a nightshirt, lifted his finger and pointed at Gaspard's face.

"Messire, what sort of dream cuts a man's face so?" he asked in a fearful voice.

Gaspard touched his left cheek, the one struck by the serpent's ring in his dream, and felt the sticky warmth of his own blood. He stared in wonder at his red moist fingertips, and mumbled as though alone, "I am a cursed man…"

The old couple blanched at his muttering and began slowly backing away down the hallway, the old woman clutching her husband's shirt. Gaspard, unmoved by their fear, closed the door, barred the latch, and flung himself down upon the mat to be taken by a dark, dreamless sleep.

The following day, conscious of the scabbing, serpentine wound branding his cheek, he walked through the narrow, stinking streets of St. Lo to the stables where he boarded his stallion. He purchased a denier's worth of pottage and bread along with a tankard of weak ale from a street vender, too ill at ease to eat at the table of the innkeeper. The old couple remained anxious in his presence and he was none too pleased by their suspicious stares. Once his hunger was slacked, he continued his walk to the stables where he paid his bill with little conversation. It was not till he noted a small, black pony tethered near his own horse that he spoke even a bit of pleasantry to his mount's host.

"You man…is that pony for sale?" he asked.

"Might be, milord," said the man, who was covered in manure.

"Who is the owner?" asked Gaspard.

"A burgher, here in town," replied the stable hand.

Gaspard pressed a silver coin into the man's hand, "Bring him here, man, be quick about it! Tell him that little horse would be a gift for Hambie's lord."

The man ran off, leaving Gaspard alone with the small, child-sized mount. It was just the gift to amaze and bring light to the eyes of young Raymond and warm the heart of his mother. Soon the burgher arrived and the two haggled over the price. He bargained well for the animal, finally settling on what coin he had left in his purse though it was less than the animal's value. By noon he was ascending the rutted path into the hills above St. Lo and on his way back to Hambie.

The local curé, to Gaspard's good fortune, spread the tale of his knightly prowess in bringing to justice Carthusian's murderers. He heard the story direct from a contact in the convent that ventured to look on the bodies of Lunce, Batchi, and Orfi before they were covered over. Gaspard's original account was then embellished in the retelling, growing by each mouth that spread the story. The curé was more than happy to take on the needs of the castle chapel until the position could be filled, for it gave him a most rapt audience. When added to the tale of Gaspard's valor in the time of Sir Fulk's death, the deed greatly fortified his growing reputation.

In the days and weeks that followed Gaspard fulfilled his duties tirelessly. Gisla, still wary of his person, invested him with the authority to collect Hambie's due rentes, which he exercised with a just if not forgiving hand. The soldiers also fell in under his authority, and he also spent many free hours with Raymond, teaching him to ride and shoot a bow, as well as practicing letters and reading. He and Raymond rebuilt the observatory of the Castle of the Rock, clearing away the brush and debris on the rock's apex so one could lay, eyes to the heavens, and observe the mysteries of the night sky. Raymond named his pony Potithon, or Black Beetle, and often rode alongside Gaspard among the vales and hamlets to meet his tenants.

It was that first suitor who came to Hambie in mid April that caused Gisla to finally take counsel with her husband's squire. An emissary of Ernest Fitz-Ernest, on behalf of his young son, Robert, arrived bearing two sleek Arabians, a paired mare and stallion, and a proposal of marriage. The lad was eleven years her junior and would be incapable of acting as a man for some years.

"Fitz-Ernest is a reputable man loyal to the duke," offered Josue.

"His son needs a mother, not a wife!" complained Gisla in exasperation.

Isabelle and Clothilde exchanged a furtive glance as they worked needle and thread through their tapestry.

"It is customary for you to at least allow the emissary audience, milady," sighed Josue.

Gisla paced about the bower, wringing her hands, "I do not wish another husband, Josue!"

"*Milady…*" exhaled the seneschal.

Gisla went to her window and looked out upon the domain that belonged to her, yet was not hers to own, "Am I prisoner? A slave? The prize mare? What am I, Josue, what am I?"

"You are this house's chatelaine and mother to its future lord, milady," replied Josue earnestly.

Gisla was silent some moments, her back to the seneschal, leaving him neither dismissed nor engaged. A spring squall brewed in the distance and she watched sheets of rain falling from the belly of a dark, low hanging cloud.

Reluctantly she spoke without turning back to Josue, "Is Gaspard about today?"

"Yes, milady," replied Josue.

"I would speak with him," her voice cracked.

"Yes, milady," said Josue, glad she did not turn to see the concern in his eyes. He bowed and left the bower.

She turned back into the room to find both her maids-in-waiting staring at her. She looked away and smiled nervously.

"Milady, have you yet spoken to Gaspard since his return?" asked Clothilde meekly.

Gisla shook her head, and paced to and fro nervously. She had watched him, listened to Raymond's stories of their play, and had Josue dispense his new duties, but had not found the courage to hear his tale directly. Isabelle and Clothilde again exchanged glances.

"Shall we remain with you when he comes?" asked Isabelle gently.

Again Gisla shook her head, returning to the window, and then back to the couch. "I am a baroness, and must have the strength to confront any in my house!" her voice was almost shrill.

When there finally came a knock upon the bower door, Gisla, taking a seat on her couch, nodded to Isabelle who then opened up to find Gaspard, dark and stoic, in the hall. He was dressed in simple forest garb and carried the scent of being recently out of doors.

"The mistress summoned me?" he inquired, emotionless.

Isabelle looked into his deep blue eyes and hard face, but saw none of the openness and mirth that drew her to Raoul. He barely saw her, and his slight bow was perfunctory at best. The scar upon his cheek, though healing, remained red and angry. She stepped back into the room ahead of Gaspard. Once he caught sight of Gisla, he stepped forward and took a knee in front of her, bowing his head.

"I am at milady's command," he said softly, staring at her feet, and then closing his eyes against the desire to caress them.

Gisla caught Isabelle and Clothilde's eye and dismissed them with a look. "Please, sit," she indicated a lesser chair, farther from her person than that which the duke had used.

"I...I wish to thank you for the attention you give my son," she started.

"He is a fine boy, milady. 'Tis no burden," replied Gaspard, straight-backed in the chair.

"Josue reports you are fulfilling your duties to his satisfaction," she added.

"I would not sully milady's reputation with less," said he.

An awkward silence ensued with both parties failing to look on the other. Finally Gisla spoke.

"An emissary from Ernest Fitz-Ernest arrived today."

"Yes, milady."

"With a proposal marriage," confessed Gisla.

At this Gaspard snapped his head and looked into the widow's eyes with a furrowed brow.

"A union with his son, a mere child. I cannot...cannot..." she nearly sobbed and felt tears again rising.

Gaspard, longing to go to his knees and take her hand, remained silent and motionless, as though of stone.

"This proposal is preposterous!" she cried, rising to her feet in frustration, "I want you to send them away. All of them! I do not care what lavish gifts they bring, or what their reputation is, or their age or appearance. I will not willingly have another husband."

"But the duke..." replied Gaspard in surprise.

"Robert said I may choose and you may speak for him to all who cross my threshold. No offer will ever be acceptable, therefore…therefore you can reject all suitors!"

"Milady wishes me to…?"

"To act as my voice and my shield. I ask you to hear and reject all offers. Josue is too old and pliable. He may be willing to hear a voice of reason…to council me against my wishes. My bed is to remain empty to the end of my days, and if you be a knight de Hambie, you will see it is so!" cried Gisla.

So that was her wish, and who was he to defy the desires of the woman he loved to the point of murder. He could gain her confidence, even, perhaps, her friendship, but forever she would be as one encased in clearest ice, near but untouchable. Forever in her servitude, never having to share her, yet never able to have her. What private hell had he wrought out of the iron of his sins, shackles and bars of his own design? This was a place of inescapable torment he both coveted and feared.

Gaspard stood and then dropped to his knee before Gisla, "I give you my oath. Your wish will be observed," his voice was low and resolute.

CHAPTER 18

Chorchiéthe

As spring waxed and waned, bringing such lush life back to Normandy with her warm days and quenching showers, a seemingly endless parade of suitors sent emissaries to Gisla's door. The Viscount of Heismer, on behalf of his son, Robert Bigod of Avranches, sent a pair ornately carved elephant tusks. Roger de Moulines, a wealthy noble of Caen, led his own retinue to Hambie's gates. Emissaries of Gautier Montacute and Jean de Lacy had the misfortune of arriving on the same day. Robert de Mortimer's men arrived with two coffers filled with gold and an attorney at the ready.

Gaspard greeted them all in the Castle de Hambie's great hall, and stoically listened to their proposals. He extended only meager hospitality to these men, as he saw it was not his duty to fill the bellies of his unwelcome guests. They flattered and they bribed. They offered him lavish positions and valuable trinkets simply to gain access of Gisla's ear. True to his nature, he neither gave any a hint of good humor nor cordiality, and true to his oath and dark desires, he sent them all away. Only William d'Aubigny's man dared argue with Gaspard, demanding to make his presentation to Hambie's chatelaine, which finally did bring forth the dark knight's mirth.

"There is not a man among you!" he laughed at the delegation, standing up so as to bring his hand to rest on the grip of his sword. "You are but little boys who still suckle their wet nurse. You have no standing here.

You cannot make demands. Are you such idiots that you would draw your lord into a conflict with me and mine? Tell William to find another wife!"

William d'Aubigny's delegates, stung by the derision and hot under the collar, stormed out of the keep, chased by Gaspard's laughter. Neither they nor any other emissaries caught sight of the mistress of the castle.

Still, their presence was not without its effects. Despite Gaspard's efforts, Gisla's angst gathered as the solstice grew near. She took ill nearly every day, still keeping in her chambers much of the time and spending little time out of doors. Her wits had returned, though she remained melancholy with an occupied mind. Each rejected proposal brought her nearer to a second confrontation with the duke, and she feared to think on what pressures Robert could bring to bear against her in the matter of marriage. Little did she know the fulcrum would be her father's own hand.

It was the evening of the last day of June when a messenger arrived announcing Gisla's father was on the road with a retinue of fifteen men and would be to Hambie in two days time. Among Albric's company were Gisla's brother, Rohais, a middle-aged count, Gislebert de Tracy, and his son Turgis de Tracy.

"What cause does this messenger give for my father's visit and the company he keeps?" asked Gisla pensively.

"None," replied Gaspard, "I pressed him, but gained naught. I know of Turgis de Tracy, however. They are a wealthy family with many holdings and he has yet to take a wife."

"You think he comes to persuade me?"

"It would be a powerful union, milady," replied Gaspard.

Gisla was quiet some moments, then grimaced and rose, pressing her hand suddenly to her stomach. She gasped from some discomfort and swayed unsteadily on her feet. Gaspard, seeing her sudden pang, rushed to her elbow to steady her, worry rising in his eyes.

"Is milady ill?" he anxiously asked. "Shall I call Jacqueline?"

"'Tis nothing but a cramp, Gaspard," she replied with a short breath, "I shall be fine in a moment. Answer me this, would this union be powerful enough to disturb the duke's peace of mind?"

"Perhaps, milady."

Thinking better of remaining on her feet, she returned to the couch.

"I should not refuse my father," she mused, "neither is it your place to defy him for your mistress or your duke."

Gaspard remained silent.

"However, Robert's person could certainly forbid such a union... without bloodshed...but at what price? As you know, such favors are not free."

"That is true, milady. We know not yet which lords have whispered in his ear. Both Eudes and Herbert have sons, and Geoffrey Martel has yet to take a wife. An alliance with any of these troublesome lords could strengthen Robert's position."

Gisla sighed in resignation, "I have thought on little else these past months. I would find only misery in marriage to any such as these."

Slowly she stood, steadying herself against Gaspard, and walked to a chest against the wall. Gisla hesitated, and then opened it. Inside, she retrieved a leather scroll case bearing her wax seal. Taking a shallow, painful breath, she turned to Gaspard and handed him the hard, leather tube.

"I have prepared a letter to the duke. On the morrow take the fastest horse from the stable and make haste to his court in Falaise," she commanded. "If he is not there, pursue him and deliver this. Explain to him at this moment my own father presses me to enter into an unhappy arrangement."

"As you wish, milady," answered Gaspard, "Now shall I fetch Jacqueline?"

"Yes, perhaps a bit of broth would be soothing," she smiled appreciatively.

Gaspard left Gisla's presence and hurried to find her tire-woman. Though greatly concerned over her apparent illness, he gave no hint to the matronly servant of his anxieties. Instead, he left her to her duties and carried on with his preparations for the journey to Falaise. It was quite late when he finally retired to his chambers to take a few hours sleep before departing in search of Robert the following dawn.

It seemed his eyes had been closed only a few minutes when a frantic pounding on his door awoke him from his slumber. The night was warm, and he was only scantily clad in a linen nightshirt when he leapt up and stumbled through the darkness in answer to Jacqueline's hysterical cries from the hallway.

"Gaspard! Open the door. Quickly! The mistress has turned gravely ill."

The young man flung open his door to find a terribly distraught Jacqueline in the hallway, a candle in her shaking hand and her face white with terror.

"The nearest medicine lies with the monks of St. Cyprian," replied Gaspard. "I shall make for their convent immediately."

"No, no, no! Gaspard, she bleeds! I think she may be with child!" countered the terrified Jacqueline. "She needs someone who knows of these things. Fetch Chorchiéthe!"

"The old witch?" Gaspard shrunk back in horror.

"You tell her I beg of her to come!" ordered Jacqueline. "Tell her my name!"

"She is an evil woman who practices dark arts! I would not have such a creature lay a finger on my mistress!" argued Gaspard.

"Shut up, boy!" ordered Jacqueline angrily, "You know nothing of Chorchiéthe. You tell her my name and what I have told you. Unless you want the mistress to die this night, you will bring her here!"

Without further comment, Jacqueline hurried away as quickly her candle would let her, returning to Gisla's chambers. Chagrined, Gaspard quickly dressed and ran to the stables. Already his stallion and a smaller sumpter were saddled and the gate flung open by the guards. Even as he leapt into the saddle he could hear Gisla's muffled cries coming from the donjon. The waxing moon had yet to rise and thin, whispering clouds dulled what little light the stars provided the land. One of his men handed him a shielded, oil lantern, and with only a gentle spurring to his mount's flanks, the trusty and loyal steed trotted quickly through the barbican into the dark of night.

The witch, Chorchiéthe, had terrified Gaspard as a boy. She was a vision of utter ugliness, with a large hook nose, skin erupting in hard nodules, bristling gray hair that defied control, and a back so bent and twisted that her head was but a protrusion from between her sagging breasts. The old witch's face lacked any sort of symmetry, with her eyes of different size and placement, offset mouth, and bent nose. Had her back been straight and true, she would have been a woman of perhaps five feet in height. However, with her disfigurement she rose not even four feet from the ground.

She lived alone in a small mud and stick hut built against the remains of a crumbling stone wall in the forest a few miles southeast of the castle. Outside her abode were three small cauldrons that were constantly filled with various reeking, boiling stews, and within the ceiling and walls were strung with flowers, herbs, and various dried creatures, both fragrant and foul. From these she produced many potions, salves, powders and tokens, some efficacious and some noxious, for which desperate and superstitious peasants bartered to cure their troubles.

Aside the pranks and dares of young boys, she led a relatively unmolested, though shunned and isolated existence under the auspices of lords of the Sienne Valley. She returned human cruelty with hatred and would often exact high prices for her cures and wards—more than merely keeping the thatch of her hut in good repair or her woodshed well stocked. A child's cure might be worth the prized calf, a salve for piles may cost two chickens. A handsome woman's price would be more than the idiot, and lepers were refused. The high and mighty she cursed, so a wise lord would don peasant garb and place a pebble in his boot before his approach.

A Breton lord had once journeyed to Hambie seeking a cure for his young son's madness. Rather than approaching with humility and deference, he took a high hand with the evil hag. With a smile, Chorchiéthe granted the haughty man the cure he demanded, and free of charge. It was a candle of rendered bat tallow she instructed him to light at midnight in the presence of his son. He was to hold small taper in his hands and both inhale the fetid smoke until it had burned itself away. True to her word, the possessing madness left the boy and he was cured, but in exchange that very same insanity entered the lord's mind and he leapt to his death from his castle's highest tower before the sun rose. At least that was the story traded across every farmer's fence and every innkeeper's table from Avranches to Coutances.

Gaspard rode through the inky darkness of the midnight forest, his heart pounding with fear and anxiety. His natural abhorrence to seek council with the likes of Chorchiéthe was well overcome by his desperate worry for his mistress. The footpath was narrow and ill kept, with wind-fall branches and trees frequently blocking Gaspard's stallion, diverting the horse and rider through the trees and thickets. Had the wafting scent of Chorchiéthe's cauldrons not crossed Gaspard's path, he would have missed her hut entirely, finding himself some hundreds of yards east and following the wrong stream. He wrinkled his nose and sneered as he pulled the reins in the direction of the stench. Soon he broke from the trees and entered the clearing of the witch. His lantern cast evil shadows through-out, as though devils danced about the witch's grounds. The fires under her cauldrons were mere embers as he dismounted and called out to the hut.

"Chorchiéthe! Old woman! Wake up!" he commanded in a strong voice. He waited a moment, then called again, "You, witch, come out. You are to come with me; my mistress needs your skill!"

The hut remained a silent tomb of blackness, so Gaspard walked up and banged on the slats of the door. When there was still no response, he popped the latch and shone his light inside. The floor was covered in vials, flasks and jars surrounding a small fire and an empty straw filled pallet covered by several blankets. The air was heavy with the scent of all sorts of herbs and plants—deadly nightshade, hemlock, buckthorn, licorice, devil's cherries, anise, and foxglove were just a few of the species hung to dry from the walls and ceiling. A table cluttered with a variety of metal bowls, utensils, green beetles, and dried newts. The only thing missing was the old witch.

"Damn that hag. Where is she?" he growled.

"Behind you, Jewel of the Dark House," cackled a rough, unnatural voice from behind him.

Gaspard started with fright and spun around to find the shrunken Chorchiéthe staring at him with her tiny, black orbs.

"Why do you trespass here?" she demanded.

"Trespass?" asked Gaspard incredulously. "You lived here first by Sir Hugh's goodwill, and then Sir Fulk's. You forget whose land you squat on, hag!"

The witch scowled angrily at Gaspard.

"Jacqueline sent me to retrieve you. Fulk's widow, Lady Gisla, is deathly ill," continued Gaspard darkly.

"Jacqueline?" laughed Chorchiéthe. "Hers is the wrong name to throw about if you wish my service! What did she say ails the most fair Gisla?"

"She bleeds…in a woman's way," replied Gaspard.

"I've a potion for such distress," cackled the witch. "My price should not be unbearable for the likes of the lady."

"Jacqueline thinks she may be with child." Gaspard's voice broke. "She is…"

To this Chorchiéthe cocked her misshapen head and smiled a most evil grimace.

"Ahhh, what be the price of a life so precious as your chatelaine's? More valuable than gold or jewels, I think," she mused, "I must think about this carefully…"

Anger flashed through Gaspard, though his emotion gave away his fears. Catching the witch by her boney wrist, he pulled her near and drew her face to within inches of his.

"Look into my eyes, witch. Do you see a man afraid of your curses and spells? Do you?" he seethed.

Looking not into his eyes but upon his cheek, she gasped and drew back from his shadowy face, twisting her arm vainly to get free of his powerful grasp.

"Arghh! You bear the mark of the evil one!" she cried in horror when she saw the serpentine scar across his cheek. "Let go of me! Let me be!"

Gaspard set down the lantern and drew his knife menacingly, but instead of holding it against her throat, he forced its grip into her hand.

"If you wish to be free of me, if you value your life so little, cut your own damned throat! Otherwise, you are coming with me and you are going to save Gisla. Your survival depends on it!" Gaspard released his grip and left her holding his knife.

Her fetid mouth gaped in terror as she clutched the blade.

"Strike, if you dare," hissed Gaspard. "Do away with yourself! No? Then stab at my heart if you desire. You will fail, and I will carry your filthy, wretched, stinking self over my shoulder if need be. However, I would prefer you to ride, to keep you down wind and less offensive."

Chorchiéthe let the blade fall from her hand, looked away, and hissed, "Did you sign his contract, boy?"

"Contract? What contract? Whose contract? What gibberish are you spewing?" asked Gaspard in confusion.

The bent and twisted witch again brought her penetrating, black gaze upon him, searching his face with her eyes. She grimaced and pushed past him. "Nothing. Bring your lantern. I have things to gather if I am to save your love."

Gaspard scowled and drew back from the witch's comment. "You presume too much!"

"Do I now?" she cackled mysteriously.

Chorchiéthe said not a word during their return ride to the castle, though Gaspard attempted to ask what evil she meant with her strange comments.

"'Twas a wound given me by forest brigands, no more," he lied about the serpentine scar upon his cheek.

Nor would she explain her question about a contract. She rode behind him in utter darkness and silence. Not a word did she speak until they passed through the gate, and then only to a manservant awaiting their arrival.

"I need a large kettle of boiled water and a basket of washed linen!" she ordered the man, who shrank back when she cast her little, black eyes on him.

Gaspard dismounted and approached Chorchiéthe's sumpter to lift her down, only to be screamed at by the witch and sent away.

"Touch me not, fiend!" she cried and pointed her bent, arthritic finger at him, then to the unfortunate guard standing near, "You there, lift me down!"

The guard, just as repulsed and fearful as the manservant, looked desperately at Gaspard for protection. Gaspard smiled cruelly at Chorchiéthe and again extended his hand.

"Mine is the only hand of friendship you will find here, old hag," he said grimly. "Take it or take your chances."

She opened her mouth to curse him, thought better of it, and then accepted his help climbing out of the saddle.

"Get my bags," demanded the witch, "and take me to the girl's room."

Despite her bent spine and uneven legs, she moved with surprising speed, tottering along behind Gaspard as he led her into the donjon and up to Gisla's bedchamber. Outside the chamber they found Josue pacing up and down the corridor, his eyes sunken with fatigue and worry.

"You've convinced her to come!" he said to Gaspard, his face a mixture of repugnance and relief. He soon wrinkled his nose at her scent, but held his tongue.

Gaspard rapped on the door, which was quickly opened by a distraught Clothilde.

"She grows worse, milord, much worse," she sobbed.

The witch stepped forward, yanking her bags from Gaspard's grasp. "Get out of my way, girl!" she snapped, "Is my ever-loyal sister in there?"

Clothilde looked down in disgust and fear at the ugly, foul hag and took a step backwards. "Oh!" was all she managed to squeak.

Chorchiéthe looked about at Josue, Gaspard, and Clothilde and laughed wickedly, "Did you not know? Do you not see the family resemblance? Jacqueline is my loving sister. My *only* family in such dark times! Ha ha ha ha!"

She pushed past Clothilde, "Get out, girl, this is not for the likes of one as innocent as you." From inside Gaspard and Josue heard Isabelle scream, the witch laugh and send her away also.

"You stay, sister!" she ordered Jacqueline; then, glaring at everyone gathered out in the corridor, she slammed the door.

The details of Gisla's ordeal in the last hours of that night and the following dawn remained behind closed doors. Gaspard sent everyone away from that part of the castle, staying only himself to do the witch's bidding. The boiled water and linens were brought, along with whatever else she requested. Each time the haggard Jacqueline opened the door to speak with Gaspard, the corridor filled with the acrid scents of those medicines Chorchiéthe burned, bathed and administered to Gisla. He suffered with every anguished cry coming from within. With an ear pressed to the door, he listened to the witch chanting in some dark tongue he did not understand.

It was not until the cocks from the village below finally stopped their noisome cacophony that Gisla's chamber became quiet. Gaspard, sitting against the stone wall, eventually succumbed to exhaustion and nodded off to sleep. Only when the door opened and the witch stepped into the hall, did he rouse.

"Fetch me a large sack, boy! One large enough to hold a bushel," she croaked. Then she whispered so only he could hear, "Your love will live, for all the evil it will bring you. She rests easy now. I gave her a potion containing poppy juice. It will relieve her pain for a few hours."

Gaspard rose silently and stared at the bent, misshapen crone. From deep inside a sense of peculiar gratitude rose up inside him, and for a moment he regretted his hatred for the woman. Without a word, he nodded, turned and walked away in search of a sack.

In a short time he returned from the kitchen with a heavy canvas sack and knocked on the door. The witch opened and admitted the man to the room. Gisla was asleep on her bed beneath a light blanket and Jacqueline asleep on the couch. In the middle of the floor, on top of a blood-soaked sheet, was a large bundle of bloody rags. The witch directed Gaspard to wrap the rags in the sheet, and then stuff the lot of it into the sack. From there, she took up her bags and beckoned him out of the room.

"Take me home now, boy," she ordered.

Gaspard escorted her down to the stables where their mounts waited. With distaste he lifted her onto the sumpter, then stepped high into his own saddle. Out of the gate and down the slope they went, through the village and its gawking residents, and then south into the forest. In daylight it was not a long ride and again the witch said nothing to Gaspard, who gained no comfort from her silence. It was only when they arrived in her clearing that she addressed him.

"Fetch that spade, boy!" she cackled, "Dig a hole so the sack can be buried."

He looked at her irritably, "Why not burn the rags and save the effort?"

"I did not guess you to be such an idiot," she said critically. "You have a head of wood. I will not suffer your foolish questions. Do as I say."

It was a strange compunction that stayed his hand from striking her, and instead he did as ordered. He took her spade, dug a sizable hole in the forest floor, and then buried the sack. Once he covered the hole over, he returned to her hut where Chorchiéthe was busy tending her cauldrons.

"Your interruption has cost me days worth of work," she complained.

Ignoring her comment, Gaspard spoke, "Jacqueline is the reason you are allowed to live in the barony, eh? Without so much as a denier paid to your lord."

"Véthe, I am the guilt on her conscience. Till now, only Fulk knew. Now that he is dead, I could not let myself be forgotten."

"You shall not be. As payment, your life here will remain secure," offered Gaspard.

She stared up at Gaspard with her beady, black eyes and frowned, "A kindly offer, boy, and I will hold you to it. Know this, though. Your mistress has already paid her price. Your love will never again bear a child."

It was a blow to Gaspard to hear such words. He recoiled from the witch and caught his stallion by the reins. He felt a sudden desire to rush to the castle and be at Gisla's side. His legs became weak and clumsy as he hefted himself into the saddle and turned to ride away. The witch called out to him with a cackling laugh as he fled back to the castle.

"It is for the best, boy. You shall see!"

Against blearing eyes and a body with somnolent desires, his anxious mind fought as he made his way back to the castle. He kept his chin up and drew on his worry to keep his stallion trotting as a good clip through the warm summer afternoon. Once through the gate he slid heavily from the saddle and made his way past the worried and distraught faces of the household to Gisla's chambers where in the corridor Master Josue met him.

The old seneschal reported there was no change and the lady was still asleep, nursed by Jacqueline. The witch had left Jacqueline with several bitter concoctions to administer to Gisla along with instructions regarding her care. Josue has sent Isabelle and Clothilde away to take some rest, and he advised Gaspard to do the same, as he was of no use to the mistress in his present state. So it was that Gaspard returned to his chambers and fell upon his bed to sleep long and deep. Never far from his mind was his mission to seek out Duke Robert and deliver Gisla's plea for assistance.

"I risk presumption, but would clear the air and make you aware of milady's will regarding any proposals of marriage," said Gaspard evenly to the newly arrived entourage.

In Hambie's great hall Gaspard, with Master Josue and four of his best men at his back, addressed Albric de Grentmesnel, his son, Rohais, along with Gislebert de Tracy, his son Turgis, and their men. They had arrived to a warm welcome in the late morning, were well fed and offered every hospitality. Gisla's father and brother were much distressed by the news of her illness and were immediately granted a short interview where upon they were greatly shaken by her pale, hollow countenance. In that somber mood, the men then gathered in the hall to discuss the underlying motivation for their visit.

Gaspard found himself in a dangerous, intolerant mood, despite the greatness of his company. Turgis de Tracy was in no way a specimen of manhood. While the cut of his cloth and edge of his blade were finely made, he was soft and fatty behind their protection. His florid jowls distracted Gaspard from his quick, acute eyes. How a father could entertain a proposal from such a chubby little man was beyond Gaspard's comprehension.

"Your daughter has no desire to have you or any other arrange her future," he said firmly, addressing Albric. "She is a baroness, and would be in command of her destiny."

Albric, lean and viral for his age, considered Gaspard silently, knowing well the young man's disposition and reputation. Instead, it was Gislebert who interjected haughtily.

"Yet you do presume!" said he. "It is her duty before God to obey her father! It certainly is not your place to…" whereupon he was silenced by Albric's raised hand.

"Sir Gaspard, in the name of friendship, please walk with me," the elder count rose to his feet.

Gaspard, eyeing Gislebert darkly, stood and followed Albric out of the great hall. The two walked in silence until they were well away from the keep and descending through the orchard and its scent of ripening apples.

"I know you to have little patience for politics," opened Albric. "It is the way of young men, so I shall be direct. Rohais has proposed marriage with Gislebert's daughter, Edith. It would be a powerful alliance and good for all the involved, including my daughter's household. Including you. Sir Fulk was indeed a great man, with influence far greater than his title. He was as a stone cast on still water, whose sway was felt over great distances. These past years of peace and prosperity for our houses, amid a world of chaos and violence, they belonged to him. Fulk Paynel was both the thundering storm that kept our enemies beneath their own roofs, as well as the just hand, keeping our vassals peaceful and content."

Little did Albric know how his words of praise, meant to soften Gaspard's recalcitrance, pricked the young knight, again renewing his hatred of Fulk. Unwittingly he poured vinegar over Gaspard's still open wounds of resentment. Though the master was dead, the servant had yet to escape his shadow.

"Now that he is gone, many lords will seek Gisla's hand in hopes of fattening their own purses," continued the old count, "She cannot deny them all. Eventually Robert will force her hand, and then only to his benefit. You know this. In Turgis de Tracy, at least she will have the protection of an alliance with her own house. There will not come a better offer. It is the best path. I beg of you, present this to her when she is well enough."

Gaspard was silent some moments as they walked down the slope and among the rows of grapevines. The afternoon sun beat down upon their brow and the air was rich and sultry.

"Milord, it may be forward of me to ask, but I am curious to know if Lord Gislebert has already blessed the proposal of Rohais to wed Edith?" he asked coldly.

Albric sighed and said, "I shall not lie to my daughter. Gislebert's blessing is contingent on Gisla accepting his son. He knows my alliance with Hambie will be weakened by any other match."

"And this man, Turgis?" asked Gaspard pointedly.

Albric looked away and paused before finally saying, "No man is Fulk Paynel."

The two men, one old, lean and gray, the other young, dark and fierce, walked through the village then turned back to the road ascending the hill to the keep.

"I will council Gisla…" assented Gaspard slowly, "but only when she is well enough in body and spirit to consider these matters. For now it is to be put away, though you and your guests are welcome to stay and enjoy what comforts and diversions Hambie has to offer. As you know, our falcons are in excellent form these days. I will instruct Master Josue to see to your needs."

It was more Gaspard's physical presence than his words that cautioned Albric against further debate. Even as a solitary figure, a lone wolf, the young knight would be dangerous to cross. With the men de Hambie at his back and a strengthening friendship with the duke, surely any insult or subterfuge would end with the spilling of blood.

On returning to the castle, Gaspard took his leave from the guests, explaining he had matters to attend to away from the castle for some days. His civility only thinly veiled his contempt for the Turgis de Tracy and his father, and his grip on the young suitor's hand was none too gentle in parting. After taking Master Josue aside with brief instructions, he gathered his gear, along with Gisla's letter to Robert, and rode for Falaise and the throne of the duke. Having the advantage of long summer days, he made St. Lo by dusk and crossed the Orne River the following afternoon. By noon of the third day he was striding quickly through the courtyard of the duke's castle, bent on delivering his mistress's letter to the duke.

CHAPTER 19

Gisla's Choice

"Have you any idea what your mistress wrote in her letter?" asked the duke, sporting a most quizzical look upon his face. Robert was regally dressed in light, airy fabrics and adorned with jeweled rings and a golden amulet about his neck. The two sat comfortably in the duke's library, a richly furnished room, showcasing many of the texts Gaspard had retrieved from Jersey. Gaspard's warm welcome in the court of Falaise had turned most serious when he disclosed both Gisla's illness and Count Albric's present company. Having turned over Gisla's sealed scroll upon his arrival, Gaspard had been afforded comfortable quarters and every courtesy. Once bathed and in a fresh gown, he was quickly summoned to a private meeting with the duke. With the door closed, Robert sat in his great chair and sized up Gaspard, all the while stroking his beard.

"She did not discuss it, Your Grace," replied Gaspard hesitantly. "I cannot hazard its contents."

"No? It involves you…" said Robert mysteriously.

"How so, Your Grace?" asked Gaspard, nonplused.

"Your mistress, were she not so…ingenuous…no, that's not it, rather so…pure of heart…so Christian…what I mean to say is, she would be a most challenging adversary were she not so damned decent!" Robert sounded as a man unexpectedly outfoxed.

"Milord?"

"You, as much as any man, know what is at stake. Rumor has come my way you have stroked more than a few cats backward! Ruffled some feathers, you have, sending away those suitors with such gruff manner. Tell me, how did you receive young Turgis?" asked Robert with a laugh.

"With equal frankness. I would become the lowest mongrel were I to serve such as he," replied Gaspard with distaste.

"Agreed! His father is powerful, and I am unsure as to his loyalties," agreed Robert with equal wryness. "I could not bless such a union. It would produce too many intrigues."

"Lord Albric has always been your ally!" countered Gaspard.

The duke harrumphed, "Only by proxy! Fulk was my ally, and Albric his. His allegiance is now negotiable."

"Mine is not!" said Gaspard darkly.

"Yes…I believe so…and so does your mistress," responded Robert carefully. "She believes you would fight to the death to defend her honor if she commanded. Yet she loathes the thought of defying her father… or me…knowing that in the bitter end, you would die, and she would be forced to wed."

Gaspard glowered at Robert, "I pray you do not make me choose, Your Grace, for there is no man I would rather serve than yourself. I would be loath to rally against you. It would be an evil moment. I care not to be in the good graces of any man but you. To ride against any other would be only that joyous, glorious thing that is war. But to ride against you would be as full of anguish as a widow's lament."

"Yet you see no way out," affirmed the duke. "Unless Gisla assents to taking a husband."

"Need she take a man?" replied Gaspard with a plaintive cry. "Cannot she remain as she is? You have the power to grant her that freedom!"

"Could I? Véthe, I could! Will I? Nay, Gaspard, I will not. Gisla's greatest strength is also her greatest weakness. She does not possess the hardness of heart to survive the intrigues of nobility. I need Hambie to have not just loyalty. I need Hambie to have strength."

Gaspard took a deep breath and rose to his feet. Turning away from the duke, he closed his eyes and clenched his fists. He desperately wanted to turn to Robert and beg him to stay his hand. He wanted to offer himself as regent for the boy, Raymond, until he was of age. He could shield them both, allowing Gisla her loneliness until the boy could stand for her. In exchange he could look upon her, smell her sweet scent, perhaps touching her hand in passing. Only he could give Gisla what she coveted. Only he could survive on what little she had to give a man not Fulk Paynel.

"When last we spoke," the duke continued, "I promised Gisla she could take a man of her choosing, and I would accent no matter. She has made that choice and attached but one mysterious, unexplained condition."

"She has made a choice?" interjected Gaspard in surprise. "She has not spoken with a single suitor since Fulk's death. She renounced Turgis most explicitly! What choice could she have made?"

"This man is not a suitor, but is the only compromise she will endure. He will likely keep Albric allied to Hambie and most certainly will keep Hambie allied with me. I deem him a worthy man, and will bless the union if he agrees to the lady's terms."

"Who is this man, that I may judge his worthiness for myself?" demanded Gaspard heatedly.

"You, Gaspard. Gisla would wed you," replied Robert most seriously.

The words of the duke froze Gaspard where he stood. He could neither turn nor flinch nor gasp for breath. Fully did he know what condition she would impose upon him should he become her husband. The putting away of a thousand nights of fantasy, the realization that his longings would never be realized, it was all there before him like a contract written in the blood of the man he murdered. He could take Gisla as his wife, but would never win her love…could never, in truth, earn her love.

The path Gregar Penscalus has set the young man on, full of twists, turns and pitfalls, had finally come to its triumphant end. He had but to reach out and pluck the fruit of glorious victory. He would have the woman he had craved since manhood swept aside his innocent youth.

In all ways…the freedom to gaze upon her without fear of suspicion or reprisal, her hand upon his arm, his seat next to hers…all ways except one. Alone at night he would be, without even the freedom to take a maid to satisfy those dark needs that a woman may understand but never feel. Unlike Eve, he knew full well the consequence of taking the fruit his serpent dangled before him. Even as he reached to take it and satisfy his hunger, it would shrivel and die in his hand. Even as he stooped to slack his thirst, the waters would recede and become dry sand. He would be a shadow of Tantalus.

"Gaspard?" queried Robert gently.

"Yes, Your Grace?" whispered the young knight, his back still to the duke.

"What say you?"

"I am not worthy, Your Grace," he rasped lowly.

The duke rose from his chair, stepped to Gaspard and placed his strong hand on the younger man's shoulder.

"In my eyes there lives no man more worthy than thee," the duke proclaimed soberly, turning his young vassal to him and embracing him. "Go, make Hambie your house!"

It took all Gaspard's will to meet the unwavering eyes of the duke. He returned Robert's grip, grimaced, and nodded his head.

"Yes, Your Grace," he said softly, "Under those conditions she sets forth, I will take her as my wife."

Thus began a strange, uneasy time in the lives of those who called Hambie home. Gaspard returned to the keep with Robert's agent, Gwylliam, and several other trusted knights. Lord Albric, under a true pretense of seeing his daughter recover, still resided at the castle, though the lords de Tracy, sensing the icy rejection of its staff, left for home. It was Gwylliam's task, one he fulfilled most eloquently, to present Robert's decision and position to Albric in the most beneficial light. Gislebert de Tracy, though wealthy and powerful, was a lesser man with a lesser son and could not match the virile bloodline of Rollo. "View Gaspard as a son of Normandy and brother of the duchy, not as an orphan," said Gwylliam. Though the idea of his daughter pledging herself to a man with no pedigree was much to overcome for the old count, he was forced to admit, at least to himself, the design was strategically sound.

If any in the house were found to be recalcitrant it was the aging staff, Rupert, Thomas, Josue, and Jacqueline. Their official obeisance gave way to very quiet, private misgivings regarding Gaspard's often morose, volatile disposition. The senior members of the staff had experienced the whole of Gaspard since he was just a young lad, and while his exploits in recent months were widely renowned, they were but a part of the sum. While most of Hambie experienced such simple relief knowing their positions were secure and life would continue on with its accustomed cadence, the four aging servants cast a critical eye upon the union. "Yet what man would not wither beneath our gaze?" mused Josue as he and Jacqueline returned to the castle after an errand in the village. "Véthe, my dear," sighed Jacqueline as she lightly brushed against the old seneschal. "At least it be by her choice."

Under Jacqueline's watchful eye, Gisla did gradually recover her strength with no relapse. Gaspard and Raymond doted on her day and night, bringing fresh flowers, reading aloud from Hambie's bible, and reciting poetry. By July's end the chatelaine was strong enough to ride alongside her son and betrothed through the shimmering fields of wheat and under rich, green canopy of the forest of the Sienne valley. After nearly five months of mourning her husband and then suffering the loss of the child growing within her belly, Gisla once again allowed herself the pleasure of a smile. A strong bond was growing between Gaspard and Raymond, and its tendrils wove around her heart and brought her a small touch of happiness. Though she would not love Fulk's squire, she could not deny her son that freedom.

Gaspard had suffered no council from Gregar Penscalus since Jersey and was glad in his absence. Thought of the mystic only reminded Gaspard of the dark path of desire, jealously, and betrayal that led to this moment of hollow triumph. When he looked into Gisla's innocent, suffering eyes all his childish visions of romance withered. She would never be that lover that melted into his arms, nor would he ever be able to take from her what she could not freely give. Any thought of confession was quickly wrestled into submission, for to admit his sins would sever that last thread Gisla clung to in this life. That she may live, he swore himself to keep his secrets and bring to her what peace of mind he could…even if it was an utter lie.

It was early August, when the moon had waxed into fullness that Raoul de St. Pair and his squire, Bousa, rode through the stifling heat of a still day to find their way to the Castle de Hambie. He had been absent from the lithesome and vivacious presence of Isabelle for better than a month, and sorely missed her gay laughter and sly speech. Rumor had reached the duke that King Robert of France was ailing, so he dispatched Raoul to Paris to learn what news and intrigues went on in the French court as the nobles prepared for a transfer of power. King Robert, to thwart the designs of his estranged queen, Constance, had elevated his favorite son, Henry, to the title of junior king some five years previous. With Henry thoroughly entrenched, King Robert hoped for a smooth and peaceful transition upon his death. It was late July when King Robert passed, and Raoul, a man excellent at gaining the confidences of courtiers and servants, learned that Henry fully believed his indolent mother and traitorous brother would attempt to wrest the throne away from him.

With this intelligence in hand, he had returned to Falaise to bend Robert's ear with the Parisian intrigues. Robert had his own tale to tell of news in Hambie, whereupon, after recovering from the brief shock, Raoul confessed his affection for Isabelle and his desire to return to Hambie at once to ask for her hand. He begged of Robert to allow him to visit Hambie in order to bring news to Gaspard of the impending struggles in France, lend the support of friendship to Gisla, and most of all, seek the chatelaine's blessing of his proposal of marriage with her ward.

"Go and secure her hand!" replied the duke, "We shall have a grand wedding celebration here in Falaise and marry both couples on the same day!"

The days of travel were hot and the grapevines heavy with fruit that promised an excellent season for the vintners. Peasants toiled in the fields much like the bees in the orchards, though they did stop their work to stare at the passing knight and his Nubian squire. Bousa had taken to the art of horsemanship quickly and befriended a young mare from Raoul's stable. Now he sat high upon her back, easy with the rhythm of her hooves. With the light of dawn they had left St. Lo and followed the very same wooded path over the hills and through the dells that Gaspard had used to chase Carthusian the night of his murder. By noontide they had passed through Hambie's village, ascended the mount to the castle, and rode through the barbican into the castle's bailey.

Since that stormy, fateful day in February when Isabelle had first caught Raoul's eye, happenstance had kept him frequently beneath the roof of the castle and afforded the two a brief courtship. It came as no surprise to any that after a hearty repast and serious council with Hambie's future lord, Sir Gaspard, that Raoul sought audience with Gisla. Though the color of summer had returned to her pale cheek, she remained gaunt and fragile. Raoul, normally a man quick of wit and word, found himself stumbling in his speech. Never before had he had cause to utter any such words, and his awkward manner brought a faint smile to Gisla's pale lips.

"Véthe, Raoul, I would be loath to lose Isabelle's companionship," she replied slowly once he had finished, "nor will it be a light consideration to separate Clothilde from her only family. They have clung to each other these many years and none could ask for better companions."

"I, too, have had this concern," replied Raoul seriously. "Though my station and my house are humble when compared to their current situation, I do have ample means to provide a comfortable and secure life for Clothilde and would have her come with Isabelle. I would be as a brother to her, and see to it she had every social opportunity."

"I will think on your proposal," replied Gisla knowingly, "and present it to Isabelle for consideration."

"Then consider this," said Raoul passionately, "Isabelle has this opportunity to know what Arlette knows, and what you have known! True love! Never before and never again will I love a woman as I love Isabelle. Unlike our duke, I can swear it before God and the world and take her as my wife!"

Unbeknownst to Raoul, both Isabelle and Clothilde were in the room adjoining the bower and listening at the door. Upon his passionate declaration, Isabelle could not contain her joy and threw open the door and rushed into his surprised arms.

"You great fool!" she sobbed in gladness, "of course I am yours!"

He crushed her to him and kissed her passionately, uncaring that it may seem improper to do so before her mistress and sister. Joyful tears came to the eyes of all three women and there was an awkward silence among the four as Isabelle slid her hand into her man's. It was the mouse-like Clothilde who broke that clumsy, magical moment when she sat on the couch next to Gisla, placing her light fingers upon her mistress's hand, and looked up at her radiant elder sister.

"I love you sister, and am glad your day is here…" she said haltingly, "And I am grateful for your betrothed's generous offer…but after much consideration—yes, I knew this day would come before either of you—I know my place is by milady's side. I wish to remain here. Hambie is my home, and I shall not leave."

Isabelle rushed to Gisla and Clothilde, who rose to meet her, and the three embraced, crying many sad and joyous tears. Poor Raoul, rugged, battled hardened, and accustomed to great privations from his many journeys, suddenly found himself at a loss for action. A queer sensation overcame him, rising up from some unknown depth and stinging his eyes. He furrowed his brow and pursed his lips as the women's overflowing emotions swept over him, battering him, daring him to shed a tear. He folded his arms against his chest, recognizing the danger he was in. Like a great oak, staunchly resisting the greatest storm, he maintained his manhood and looked upon the scene without outward emotion. It was only many months later, in the dark warmth of the marriage bed, that he confessed to Isabelle he thought it a beautiful moment.

The wedding was a grand ceremony filled with pomp and beauty. By Duke Robert's design, the day of the autumnal equinox was the chosen time and his own court the chosen place. His uncle Robert, the archbishop of Rouen, presided over the ceremony, and many nobles of note in their day, now long forgotten, attended the gay event. Gaspard and Raoul were most dashing in their finery as they awaited their brides upon the altar. The cathedral smelt of fresh flowers, and its bells tolled joyously in celebration of Christian marriage.

Duke Robert, a man known for his showmanship and generosity, put on a splendid feast for his two friends and most loyal lords. Though Gisla remained sedate, she did force some levity upon herself to dispel those rumors that would bring shame upon her new husband. Still, she could not match the joy Isabelle found after taking the vows that bound her to Raoul. Isabelle clung to him during the feasting and was unabashed when it came time for their first night as husband and wife.

The merry entourage then said their goodbyes to Falaise's generous citizens and made the brief journey home. Raoul's estate lay some leagues southwest of Hambie, overlooking the Gulf of Saint Malo, so both couples and their retinues made several days journey together during those first days of autumn. Only when Gaspard, Gisla and theirs ascended the slopes of Hambie's mount, did Raoul and Isabelle, along with Bousa, travel alone to the adventures of their new life.

The many people of Hambie came together and presented their young lord a knightly standard upon his return. On a green cloth bordered in black was the image of a black lanner falcon pinning a gold dragon to the earth. While outwardly his enthusiasm for such a beautiful gift, one he could carry before him in battle, was great, inwardly the irony of its lie mocked him daily. Gaspard found no happiness in having attained Fulk's lands, treasury, and stables.

For Raymond and Gisla's sake, he fulfilled his duties as Hambie's lord as well as he could, and the house returned to some semblance of normalcy. Within the master's chamber he had his own lonely, closeted bed, separated from his new wife by an oak and iron door. There he dreamt his nightmares on those rare nights sleep took him at all. His taste for food and wine, once as keen as his desires, abandoned him, making every sip and bite as joyless as a mouth full of sand. Raymond became his only joy, and he not only saw to the boy's training as a future knight, but also as an educated man.

Autumn turned late and lofts, larders, and pantries were all well stocked with the generosity of the land. Soon the crisp chill of October turned to the cold rains of November and the folk of farm, village, and castle turned to tasks best suited to days indoors. Homespun gowns and stockings were knit and sewn with care while leathers tanned in the summer months were turned to useful items. Minstrels and troubadours traveled the land earning their keep by relieving the boredom of those with coin to spend. Hambie held a great feast on St. Martin's eve where all were invited to eat and drink to excess before entering into the forty days of St. Martin, a time of fasting and cleansing leading into Christmas.

Things were altogether peaceable in the coming months and seasons as Hambie and its new lord grew accustomed to one another. To escape the ghosts of the great hall, Gaspard found himself traveling among his vassals with greater frequency than Fulk had done in years past, often taking shelter in their cottages at night. Though these peasants found him less forgiving than their previous lord when it came time to pay him his due, they could not dislike him, for he fairly repaid their every hospitality.

Gaspard, much more than his famed horsemen, relished his required days of service to the duke. Once again, it was another way to escape from his ghosts, nightmares, and empty bed that always lay in wait for his return to the donjon. Every day away was a day he was not confronted by his own reflection. The rough food of a forest camp or the cheap draught of an alehouse sustained him far better than Agnes Marie's best savories. He always returned to Hambie robust after days or weeks of travel, and always began to waste away if confined within its walls for too great a time.

CHAPTER 20

A Deal with the Devil

It came to be one day in the year 1033 that a rider arrived at Hambie bearing an urgent message from the duke. The French king, Henry, had been put to flight by the combined forces of his brother and Odo, the Count of Blois. King Henry had taken refuge at Fécamp, and Duke Robert was rallying Normandy to his aid. Just as all Robert's suzerain, Lord Gaspard was to muster his men, empty his stables, and make for the eastern border of Normandy with all haste. Within a matter of days, thousands of warriors were camped outside the king's tent, awaiting his word. Soon the French king, with a great army of Normans at his back, marched on the Ile de France and waged war on the usurpers. Swift and bloody was Henry's reprisal, forcing a settlement upon his brother and his allies. Although the position of the monarchy was weakened, first by concessions to Normandy's duke and then to the king's own brother, Henry was quickly restored to the throne. With the heat of victory still coursing through their veins, Gaspard was able to turn his men for home with hardly a loss among them.

Once again it was the height of summer when the men de Hambie finally returned to the Sienne Valley with lusty tales of battle at the gates of Paris. A hero's feast was held in honor of the returning lord and his warriors that went long into the night with all sorts of roast beasts, spiced wines, and the best fruits of the land. Gaspard, glad to be bathed and in a fresh gown of green and black, sat with Gisla and Raymond at the lord's table upon the dais before the cold hearth. The strong wine had gone somewhat to his head as he considered the faces of the pagan gods carved into the great timbers that supported the roof of Hambie's great hall—his hall! He had been the lord of the castle for nearly two years, and all was well in the barony. The memory of Fulk was bleached with time, as was the memory of Gaspard's sin against him. Before him were strong men of good cheer, his men, men whose loyalty was beyond question. Around him was a household who, if not glad, were at least satisfied in their lady's choice of husband.

Amid the laughter, song, and tales, Gisla caught her husband's eye with a strange light in her own. Her gown, of sea green and spun gold, shimmered in the flickering light of the hall, and Gaspard found himself wistfully imagining the flaxen locks that lay hidden beneath her wimple. She was sedate and beautiful beyond compare, belonging more on the sculptor's pedestal than seated next to a man such as he. In fear, he quickly looked away lest the wine in his wife's cup lead her to release him from that very oath she extracted from him a lifetime ago. In fear, he looked away, lest he consider that most deeply buried wish be granted.

"We have missed you, husband," she said softly, brushing her hand across his. "I have missed you."

Gaspard met her sweet eyes, calm like the coming dawn, with an unsure smile, only to again look away.

"The moon is new this night, and Raymond and I have something to show you," she continued.

"Oh?" he said, looking into the expectant face of Raymond, who smiled through a gap in his front teeth. The boy got up from his seat and extended his small hand to Gaspard.

"But our guests!" protested Gaspard.

Gisla looked about the hall filled with noisome men and women, musicians and servants, and boys and girls, all singing and laughing, and smiled lightly at them. "They will not miss us, husband."

Gaspard took Raymond's hand and followed him out of the great hall and into the bailey. There the two waited some minutes for Gisla to join them.

When she arrived, her wimple was gone and her hair pulled back in a braid that ran down her back. In her hand she carried two cloaks, one for Gaspard and one for Raymond, while she had already donned her own. As they walked to the castle's gate, Gaspard noted that somehow Gisla had exchanged her finery for a rough maid's dress. She smiled at Gaspard's quizzical glance and simply instructed him to retrieve a small lantern that hung inside the guardhouse. The moonless night shown with countless stars as Raymond led them away from the castle and along the slope. It was a trek Gaspard knew well, and soon the three found themselves removing their cloaks and ducking quietly into the bramble entrance of the Castle of the Rock.

The tunnels among the blackberry canes were well maintained and in only a few minutes and with only a few scratches they had found their way to and ascended the ladder leading to the castle's observatory. Already there were several rough, woolen mats and sacks filled with straw that would serve as pillows. Gisla drew her cloak about her and lightly laid back on a mat, beckoning her men to lie down beside her, husband on one side and son on the other. Gaspard shielded the lantern with a tremulous hand and for the first time lay down beside his wife.

Raymond pointed to the stars of the night sky and began drawing the constellations with his finger and naming them one by one. Scorpius, Draco, and Hercules. King David's Harp, Hydra, and Cepheus. Ophiuchus, Cassiopeia, and Sagittarius. For each one he begged Gaspard tell stories.

"Do you know why we do not see Orion in the summer?" asked Gaspard, "Because he is afraid of the scorpion's sting! And Cassiopeia is chained to the heavens because her beauty drove Poseidon mad with jealously. Sagittarius once held the form of a man, but being a god, could change to whatever form he desired. His wife was a shrew, so he gave himself the body of a horse so he could run away from her!"

Raymond giggled.

The minutes turned to hours as falling stars streaked across the sky. Raymond soon fell asleep, his back pressed into his mother's side.

"Husband, come closer to me, I grow cold," whispered Gisla huskily out of the darkness. From beneath her cloak, she reached for and found his hand, gently pulling him to her. As he felt the warmth of her body against his, a tortured sense of exhilaration coursed through his veins. She was so near and so very alive. Before his control crumbled, he knew he must escape her gentle kindness.

"'Tis late, milady; we should return to the keep," replied Gaspard hoarsely, needing, yet unable to withdraw his hand from hers. "You have made me most welcome this night…I…I am grateful…but we should get Raymond into his own bed."

With that he sat up and unshielded the lantern. As the dim light flickered across her face, Gaspard shamefully saw a look of longing in her eyes that rightfully belonged to another. Almost gruff in his embarrassment, he held out his hand that she might rise. Though she said nothing and accepted his hand, he saw a flicker of rejection cross her face.

Between them they were able to rouse Raymond just enough to get clear of the Castle of the Rock and return to the donjon. With but a few exceptions, the feasting revelers were found sleeping in and around the great hall. Gaspard easily carried Raymond among the slumbering bodies and then up to his chamber, a handsomely adorned room that was once the chamber of Fulk Paynel as a boy. Once he and Gisla had laid the boy in his bed, his wife again touched his arm. Though he knew it to be wrong, he could do nothing but offer it to her for her hand to rest.

In awkward silence they made their way back to their own chambers. Gaspard touched the flame from the lantern to his own candle and began to retreat to his own, small room. In the dim light, Gisla met and held his eyes and made as though to speak.

"Goodnight, milady," he said brusquely.

"I am not a good wife," she replied simply. "I have left you in loneliness only to wake up finding myself alone."

She walked to him and took his hand. Her cool fingers trembled against his, and her breath was ragged through her flared nostrils.

"I am no fool, husband. You have upheld your oath to me, though it shamed you…made you less than a man. I have given you cause to flee the comforts of your own house for the hardships of the road, yet you defend my honor and love my son as your own. Never a complaint. Never a demand. Now I release you from that oath…so I can love again."

"Milady, please…" begged Gaspard, unable to look upon her beauty.

"No, husband, your bed is in this room, not in the next. Come and share it with me."

Gaspard looked into her eyes and knew he had not the strength to deny her. She believed she knew the truth of him, and that all his denial of self was out of loyalty to her fallen husband. Never in her darkest dreams could she have imagined his service to her was one of penance for his secret sins against her. Certainly, to accept her as she now offered herself would cut deeply into his conscience. Only his conscience, as battered and scarred as it was, lacked the strength to stand against his desires. It rose up and made itself known, only to be struck down in the blink of an eye.

As he accepted her hand he found all his thoughts of regret lost their voice. His heart pounded as though it would burst as she gently tugged and untied the draws to his gown. He stood, paralyzed, as her dress slipped from her shoulders. He could scarcely breathe until she stepped into him, placing her cool hand across his bare breast and her scent rose to him. Her touch burned him like fire as she laid her head upon his chest. Despite the warm August night, Gisla did tremble in his arms. He ran his rough, strong fingers along her soft skin, and the blood on his hands slipped away out of his mind.

"Love me, Gaspard," she whispered in his ear.

He awoke but slowly and not to glorious radiance of the early morning sun that streamed into the room through its narrow windows. Rather it was a sense of darkness that called him from the comforts of his slumber, sending a chill through his frame even though the morning wafted with the luxurious August warmth. Next to him, as though still dreaming, lay Gisla with her flaxen hair spilled about the pillows. Naked, he quietly rose to his feet and gazed back upon his wife's slumber a moment. He then softly padded to the window to look down upon what was now his.

As he neared the window the sense of ill shadow intensified, nearly stopping him in his tracks on the worn, wood floor. The sensation was familiar to him, being one that had enveloped his waking and dreaming moments since the early days of manhood. It was only just at that moment that he realized it had subsided, replaced by a penitent heart, these past two years. Now, as the invisible vapor again swirled about him, and he knew it for what it was for the first time. A physical presence.

All his force of will pushed him that last step to the window's sill and he looked down past the orchard and vineyard to the shimmering expanse of golden wheat in the valley below. There, alone, stood a distant man dressed in stifling, black robes, staring up at the donjon...staring up at Gaspard. As Gaspard looked upon him, the man drew back his cowl with delicate, white fingers to a reveal the ghostly, clean-shaven face of the mystic, Sir Penscalus!

"The Devil take him!" spat Gaspard.

As Gisla stirred in the bed, Gaspard pulled on his breeches, leapt into his boots, took up his sword, and sprinted half naked from the chamber. Hale and fleet of foot was the young knight, and in just a moment's time he burst from the donjon, crossed the bailey, and was running down the mount toward the gently rolling grass below. Through the orchard, hung heavy with fruit, past the vineyard and its sweet scent, and into the dry, warm field of wheat he ran.

"*Gregar!*" he yelled, "Show yourself!" He waded through the waist-high grass, searching this way and that, but not able to lay eyes on his former mentor.

"*Gregar Penscalus!* Why hide as though you are a fiend? If you would speak, do so here and now. Utter your words or hold your peace. *Gregar!* Shadow skulker, face me!"

His words echoed and faded on the gentle fragrance of the morning breeze. As he made his way to where he thought the mystic had stood, with thoughts of finding his tracks, he noted a rustling in the grass just a few yards off. Sword at the ready, he crouched low and stalked the shaking tufts of wheat. As he came upon the spot, there was a sudden flurry of action as a number of black, screaming ravens burst forth from the grass. Screeching and cawing, they flew at Gaspard, who quickly brought his sword about and cleaved two of them in an instant. The others, full of cowardly rage, flew off toward the forest, screaming out their foul curses as they went.

The dark omen left Gaspard shaken, but he did not fail to continue forward to where the crows had lain in wait. The scent of fresh blood wafted up from the spot, and as he carefully parted the long shafts of grass with his sword, he came upon the remains of an aged, white she-wolf. The emaciated beast, frail with extreme age, had been stabbed and slashed open, then carefully set upon the ground to bleed out upon the rich earth. The blood had not yet congealed, and though fear coursed through his veins, Gaspard touched the bitch's flank, finding it still warm with recent life.

"My White Lady, what have you suffered?" cried Gaspard in anguish. "What have I caused?"

Burning anger, a vitriolic fire, began to rise from his depths as Gaspard sat and took the dead beast's head tenderly into his lap. Tears of rage spilled onto his cheeks as he stroked her sore encrusted fur. Though he had not set eyes on her for many, many years, there was no mistaking the now ancient face of Hambie's white wolf. Only by use of some dark power could Gregar have ensnared the White Lady and kept her alive all the many years. That same dark power had entangled Gaspard with its dark promises delivered. Now his mind was filled with a desire for vengeance against that power.

He sat alone amongst the stalks of wheat, cradling the White Lady, his mind a menagerie of confused images and violent thoughts. It was only Master Josue's call that broke him away from his dark reverie. His name was on the seneschal's lips. He was needed at the castle. He was needed by his wife.

Master Josue came out to the field by his mistress's order, hoping that whatever madness had driven Gaspard, half-naked, from the castle had passed. Now the seneschal looked down upon the disturbing sight of his lord, eyes afire with distant anger, cradling a dead beast in his lap.

"Look what he has done!" whispered the young man, looking up into the lined face of the elder.

"What man do you speak of, milord?" asked Josue carefully.

Gaspard stared away from Josue, grimaced, opened his mouth as though to speak, and then hesitated. Finally he whispered dryly, "Not a man, Josue!"

Gaspard did not speak for some moments, seemingly ignoring the presence of the old seneschal. Finally, having his own cause to speak, Josue broke the uncomfortable silence.

"Young Raymond awoke with some sort of poisonous bite, milord. Perhaps a spider. He has a fever, and Clothilde is tending him, but he asks for you. Will you not return with me so you can be at his side?" asked he.

Gaspard looked upon Josue and muttered, "He was up late...we did not check his bed."

"Milord?"

Gaspard stared blankly at Josue for a moment and then extended his hand. The elder took it and helped the younger to his feet. Once standing, Gaspard looked down upon the dead wolf.

"*It is her, Josue,*" he said lowly, confidently.

"That would make the poor creature better than sixteen years." Josue shook his head. "Wolves do not have such lives, milord. Though she could be the Lady's pup."

"By Saint Peter, it is her, Josue," responded Gaspard angrily, causing Josue to shrink back a step.

"As you say, milord."

The two returned to the castle where its inhabitants knew better than to stare at the disheveled, bloody state of their lord. Gaspard, having regained some of his wits, hurriedly washed his face and hands, donned fresh clothing, and then strode to Raymond's room. Upon entering, he assumed a cheerful face, touched Gisla's hand and nodded with concern to Clothilde, who sat aside the bed. Gisla looked gravely into her husband's eyes and he saw her unspoken worry.

"What has happened?" he asked.

The boy, robust and lively just a day before, now lay feeble and pallid in his bed. As Clothilde attempted to sooth his brow with a cool cloth, he struggled to lift his hand to greet Gaspard.

"Méthe says it was just a spider," he said weakly, looking at Gisla, "but I think that Scorpius came down from the heavens and stung me while I slept."

"Scorpius?" asked Gaspard abruptly, narrowing his eyes.

"You did not tell me of such a dream," interjected Gisla with a nervous laugh.

"I did not want to frighten you, Méthe," whispered the boy, "and it was not a dream. My side, where I was stung, still hurts."

The boy tried to lift his right arm to show his wound, but only succeeded when Clothilde came to his assistance. Gaspard gently lifted up his gown to find a hot, swollen bruise with a tiny wound at its center against his ribs under his arm.

"Scorpius came to my room. He had the head of a snake, white fingers, and a long stinging tail. He fled when I awoke."

Gaspard pursed his lips and held the boy's gaze, "Raymond, it is very important you remember *everything* about this creature. First, where did the monster flee to?"

"It must have been the window, for it was away from the door, though I cannot be certain," replied the boy. "He just seemed to vanish, really."

Gisla and Clothilde exchanged a terrified glance.

"Think very hard now, you saw its hands. Tell me about Scorpius's hands," urged Gaspard.

"They were slender, but not like a lady's…more like a falcon's…and a black ring of snakes or lizards or something."

"And his face? You said a snake?"

"Maybe not a snake…but having serpent's scales…he…it…turned away so quickly," said the boy, furrowing his brow.

"Husband, do not frighten him so!" interjected Gisla, who was frightened herself. "'Tis surely no more than a spider bite!"

Gaspard pulled back from Raymond's side, with a dark shadow of new rage crossing his face. He beckoned Gisla into the corridor outside the boy's room. Standing outside the small alcove where he one slept as a child, Gaspard could not meet the angry, frightened eyes of his wife.

"This be no ordinary wound!" he said grimly. "A spider's bite would have two holes, Raymond's has but one. I must fetch the witch."

"What do you mean by these words? You cannot believe some Greek myth descended from the heavens to strike down my son?" she cried in a whisper.

"No, I do not," whispered Gaspard in return, "I...I am unsure..."

"Do not lie to me husband! You know, or believe you know what has...happened," Gisla begged angrily, clutching his arm.

Gaspard turned to face his wife and saw in her eyes the absolute fear of losing Raymond. She began to tremble, then to shake, and he so desperately wanted to take her pain into himself, but knew he could but share it.

"I need to get to Chorchiéthe's cottage with all haste, Gisla. I despise myself..." he paused, "for leaving you and the boy, but if there is medicine to save Raymond, I will give her whatever she demands!"

It was his rage that sustained him at that moment, allowing him to leave his distraught love standing alone and terrified in the short corridor. He turned away from Gisla, retrieved his sword from his room, and leapt into the first saddled horse he found at the stables. He dug his heels mercilessly into the poor beast's flanks and drove it to the witch's grove as though the hounds of Hell were nipping at its hooves. They galloped through the wood, turning and twisting along the path, leaping over snags and fallen trees, until the stink of Chorchiéthe's caldrons wafted on the air and her disheveled cottage came into view.

Gaspard quickly surveyed the scene, looking all about, but saw not a living soul.

"Chorchiéthe!" he called, swinging out of the saddle and striding quickly to the low hung door, "Old witch, 'tis I, Gaspard Malfort, and I need your help!"

A moment passed before the door opened and the witch emerged into the hot August afternoon. She blinked in the bright light, and then stared up at Gaspard's grim face.

"Name any price, old one, if it be in my power to pay it, I shall!"

Chorchiéthe glared at him silently a moment while she scratched her belly.

"What good is the oath of a man who has already sold his soul to Satan?" she asked blandly.

"The beast may walk among us, and he may have branded my face, but I still possess my own guilt. You asked me once if had signed his contract. I did not understand then, but do now. The answer is no, I have not," answered Gaspard seriously, "I may be damned, but I can still swear before God and be held to it come judgment day."

"Tell me what you need, then, and I will tell you my price," replied the witch with a twisted smile upon her face.

"He stole upon Raymond in the dark of night and pricked him with his evil poison. The boy is grievously ill, and I fear the poison will…will… overcome him," choked Gaspard.

"Of whom do you speak?" demanded the witch.

"I know him by the name Gregar Penscalus; he is the serpent of my nightmares…the beast who reached through my dreams and gave me this mark!" Gaspard growled as he turned his scarred cheek to the witch. The witch's glittering black eyes bore into him, and the humor dissolved from her face.

"This thing you have taken council with, it be a demon…Lé Dgiâbl'ye, boy!" chastised Chorchiéthe angrily. "I cannot simply snap my fingers and mutter few words to draw out this poison. Do you have any notion how *rare* are those herbs of this earth that can fight a poison distilled in the world below? Perhaps I can slow its progress, give you time…"

The witch cut herself suddenly short and cried out in true fear. She shrank back from Hambie's lord as she looked to the woods at his back. In her beetle-black eyes, he caught the reflection of a dark form rising behind him holding a slender, iron stave. His horse reared, screamed out with fear and galloped off. With a single fluid motion Gaspard drew his sword and spun to face the enemy, whom he knew to be Sir Penscalus.

"Retrieve your medicines and get you to the castle, witch!" commanded Gaspard to Chorchiéthe. "I will handle this creature!"

"Peace, brother," said Gregar easily, though his wary eyes stared past Gaspard, following the witch. "I mean neither you nor this good woman any harm."

"Another lie sent by the Prince of Lies, no doubt," replied Gaspard angrily, blocking Gregar's way as the witch scuttled to her cottage, disappearing into its fragrant darkness.

"What lie have I *ever* told you, Gaspard?" said Gregar, chagrined, his hand tightening on his blackened stave. "Not once in all our days of friendship and council did I tell you an untruth. No, no, my young pupil, *I* am not the liar!"

"You poisoned the boy!" snarled Gaspard, "And you murdered the White Lady de Hambie!"

"I told you Raymond would have to be removed to make way for the house of Malfort, or, more correctly, the house of Ducaen," soothed Gregar as he attempted to circle Gaspard and get near the cottage's door. "Or has your affection for the boy clouded your memory? As for that old bitch, you have always longed to say your farewell. Do not fault me for granting your wish."

"The boy's future was my decision to make, not yours!" retorted Gaspard, countering Gregar's steps, keeping his sword raised and himself between his enemy and the witch. "And you shall pay for the wolf's blood a thousand fold!"

"I think not," replied Gregar. "Did you believe you could simply reject me? Without consequence? The day you strayed from our path was the day I collected your bitch should I have need to teach you a lesson. This is just a taste of the suffering I can cause."

The terrified Chorchiéthe reemerged from her cottage with a pack slung over her stooped shoulders. Being one gifted, or cursed, if you will, with the ability of true-sight, she saw the demonic monster, Gregar Penscalus, that stood across from Gaspard as it truly was, a slender, scaled serpent whose venom dripped from both its fangs and the tip of its barbed tail. Two sinuous arms emerged from its robed torso, and its fingers resembled those slender, scaled toes possessed by birds of prey. Its iridescent white scales writhed and undulated before the young knight, while its forked tongue occasionally flicked across its oily, pink eyes.

Nor did she perceive her guardian, the man who interposed his body between her and the serpentine demon, as the handsome and fierce Norman warrior everyone else took him for. Instead, she saw him as a man covered in blistering scars, ugly and dark, with only the stark beauty of his deep blue eyes to redeem him.

"He is as you dream him…a serpent…not as you see him!" warned the witch in a whisper as she sidled behind Gaspard. "Always face him squarely lest you be stung!"

Gregar watched her as she backed away toward the wood and again tried to close the distance between them. Again Gaspard menaced the demon with his blade, blocking its advance.

"You should really remain here!" Gregar called to the witch, "It is such a rich tale, legendary, in fact! Besides, your herbs and petty parlor tricks will not save the young lord!" Gregar then turned its attention to Gaspard and said, "Only you can, my old friend. Only you!"

Again the creature moved, and again Gaspard blocked his way to the retreating witch, feinting and threatening with his sword. Curiously, Gregar's concern with the witch appeared conflicted with its strange need to engage Gaspard in conversation rather than battle. Perhaps the demon feared she did, indeed, possess the skill to save the boy! Or perhaps he needed Gaspard alive for some purpose! Perhaps both…

"A deal with the Devil, no doubt," replied Gaspard.

"Well, now that it comes to it…yes, a deal with the Devil," replied Gregar, "But I do swear, and my word is my bond, it will be a bargain. I will give you better terms than I gave your father…by the way, you know it will take Chorchiéthe some hours to reach the castle on foot, don't you? Do you really have that time to spare?"

"As you say, she will be of no use no matter, so let her go in peace," countered Gaspard.

"As you wish, milord," replied the demon slyly, "I will certainly have her another day."

"'Milord'?" snorted Gaspard, "You use the title freely! Am I truly your lord? I think not! Tell me, Gregar, if that be your true name, what lord do you truly serve? You are not as free as you seem. Before whose throne do you bow low?'"

The creature glowered and hissed angrily at Gaspard, but did not name his master.

"You claim you knew my father. Would it surprise you to know I knew him as well?" asked Gaspard.

"Perhaps it would," the creature was now agitated, "though it would hardly concern me."

"What bargain did you make with Bertrand Ducaen?" asked Gaspard.

"In exchange for his contractual undying gratitude, I delivered him Fulk Paynel, with your aid, of course!" Gregar responded cruelly.

The shock of Gregar's words left him breathless, confusing his mind as images of a scattered truth began to take shape. His head spun with the revelation he was little better than a pawn in the greater game of selling of his father's soul. The words Bertrand Ducaen had spoken to Gaspard years ago on Jersey, *"This one time, were I to express regret, could you reconsider your hatred?"* now had such crystal meaning. Ducaen, with a bloody stroke of his quill on the Devil's note, had snared his only son in a web of damnation, and for that, and only that, he was a truly remorseful man. The man who would be a wolf in this life, free to live and free to die, was now the lowest cur-mongrel in a kingdom where there was but one wolf.

"My father was a murderer and pillager," whispered Gaspard. "He would have disdained salvation no matter…"

"Likely, but I prefer to lock these things away on my own terms. There have been more than a few who truly found salvation and slipped our grasp when they lay in Death's bed," Gregar stepped sideways, attempting to flank Gaspard, who responded with a feinted attack designed to bring him back to square with his opponent. "On the other hand, you Gaspard, you have proven another matter. That cursed Carthusian put the fear of God into you! I will have you know, I own the signed notes of every one your forefather's going back five generations! I lost you for a while as a child, but once found, I assure you, I have given you my best attentions. I will admit, it is difficult to penetrate the fortress of a penitent man. First those ridiculous brothers of St. Lo unwittingly protected you in your infancy, and these past two years, since I took Gisla's unborn child, your self-flagellation, your daily contrition, was enough to keep me at bay.

"That is what made last night such a joyous breakthrough for me! I cannot tell you how delicious it felt…no…that's a lie…you know well that dark rapture, don't you! If Hambie's chatelaine truly knew what evils you have brought upon her, do you think she would have invited you into her bed?" Gregar shook with evil laughter. "Of course not! What you did in the name of love was not better than rape! It is you who are the liar! And now you have a very simple choice. The bitch is dead. Sign the Devil's note, or the boy dies also. The choice is yours, and as I promised, it is a better bargain than your father received. He sold his soul for revenge. You will sell yours for love."

The curve in the witch's spine left her gasping for breath, and her aged, arthritic bones could not be urged to any sort of speed. Still, these maladies, that pained her so in waking and sleeping, could not hold back her wanderings and lent much to her patient eye. In the moment, however, patience gave way to an urgency she had only little ability to act upon.

As she fled through the forest, making for the castle, she saw how man and beast continued to cautiously converse, though the beast watched her until she disappeared into the thickets. She had seen this demon but once in her all long years, but knew it to be like the ancient desert djinns who, so artful with words, twisted truths back upon themselves, betraying the ears of the listener. This demon was a dark harvester of souls for the Prince of Lies, so that he and his legion could dine on the choicest of mankind's evil.

The irony that a man she despised shielded her from such a creature was not lost on Chorchiéthe, and even as she hobbled along the path
leading to Hambie, she could not see what outcome would serve her best.
While she did see life as it is, she could not see the future of things except
for the predictable hearts of man, and that was insight rather than second-
sight. While fear of the demon was a great part of what drove her in her
haste, it was her own covetous desires to see its handiwork, to understand
the nature of its poison, and then to test her hand against it that strengthened her resolve.

The witch's sack contained her rarest and most powerful curatives,
or poisons if you will, such as Egyptian Henbane, Indian Snakeroot, Afri-
can Calabar, Chinese Poison Nut, and fresh fire salamander. Her elixirs
contained the distilled madness of Saint Martial, essence of mandrake,
Turkish Nutgall, and poppy juice. Small jars and vials contained stinking,
fatty salves, oils and jellies. She could stop a man's heart or make it burst.
She could drive a sane woman mad or steal the life of her child. If she so
chose. Or she could save that same man, woman, and child.

Thus she lived, in the company of those who despised her form
and scent, yet fawned, bargained and begged for her magic, her cures.
They brought her gifts, rare herbs and spices from traders far and wide,
and did her bidding, yet none stayed in friendship, nor extended any
kindness aside her bargained price. She despised them, and despised
their children who snuck through the woods to look on and taunt the
"witch" from behind thickets and hedges. She despised the priests who
railed against her evil ways, yet sought her help when their own meager
medicine failed. She despised all who looked on her twisted, deformed
body and called her a monster. Little did they know, she could see the
monster in them all. Their sins were as boils, cysts and scars on their
skin.

Now she fled from a creature that could not be bargained with, and
her cursed bones were slow. What was a mere pleasantry to one on horseback, a quick jaunt, was an expedition to Chorchiéthe. What chance did she

have of making the castle unmolested or in time to see the boy alive? Little, was her guess, yet she continued on, believing her fate not quite sealed.

Despite Gregar's threat, Gaspard did not flinch nor drop his guard. However, his mind churned with the seemingly hopelessness of his predicament.

"What guarantee would I have such a deal would truly be a bargain in my and the boy's favor? What trust can I place in a demon such as you, when I know every word spoken is meant to work against me?" he asked.

"What sort of guarantees do you imagine? The terms are simple and clear. I will restore the son of the man you murdered to life, and in exchange, upon your death, you leave me your soul to keep," replied the demon plainly.

"I would like you to swear that Raymond and Gisla will never be molested by you or your ilk for the remainder of their days," replied Gaspard, "and that it be a genuine oath with no subterfuge."

"Your demand pains me, Gaspard," said Gregar with feigned emotion, "yet I will make that promise. They will live to their natural end of days."

Both Gaspard and the demon silently considered one another for some minutes. Finally, Gregar broke the silence, "You truly do not have much time, Gaspard. The boy fades even as we speak. Gisla and Clothilde cling to each other and weep. Your window is closing."

Gaspard's face became a mask of defeat as he dropped his guard and looked away from the serpent.

"What must I do?" he asked softly.

"Very simple," replied Gregar, assuming the demeanor of a lawyer, and then withdrawing a rolled vellum scroll and quill from within the folds of his robes. "Review the terms of the contract…you can read Latin, I assume…then mark the bottom with your signature. I will take care of the rest. Raymond will recover, Gisla will love you, and you will be great among men. I swear it!"

Gregar unfurled the scroll before him and offered the quill to Gaspard, who looked entirely defeated.

"It really is all for the best, my boy. I would have had you anyway," smiled Gregar gently.

"Gregar, I would say but one thing more," said Gaspard in a tired voice, closing the distance between them.

"Yes, my son?"

"You've forgotten your armor!" replied the young knight savagely as he jerked up his sword, lunging at his enemy.

CHAPTER 21

The Fourth Dream

Gaspard uncoiled his anger and hatred for Sir Penscalus, leaping forward and driving his quick, resilient blade through the unfurled sheet of vellum and toward his enemy's thorax. He had placed his hand on the warm flank of the White Lady and lifted the linen away for Raymond's side. His decision to avenge them, to throw his lot in with the witch, took only a single heartbeat. Chorchiéthe needed time to gain the castle and affect a cure, so time he would give her. He would no longer walk the path of darkness the demon had set him upon those many years ago.

Gregar was truly caught off-guard but possessed the reflexes of a snake on a hot rock and managed to dodge backward while bringing around his iron stave in an attempt to parry Gaspard's attack. The blow, meant to drive through and impale the demon, only barely pierced his flesh before he managed to knock Gaspard's sword away. With that one touch, a mere prick, a fantastic transformation came over Gregar, and his true form was revealed before Gaspard's eyes. Gregar the man vanished, and Gregar the serpentine demon stood in his place. He was a horridly beautiful creature with a powerful, rippling symmetry. A serpent with poised, muscular legs, his tail was a lissome, barbed whip that glistened with an oily poison.

The young knight continued to drive forward, raining down a series of vicious, controlled attacks, all of which Gregar was hard pressed to defend without giving ground. The rich, stifling air of the August forest rang out with clash of steel against iron, and sweat quickly beaded on Gaspard's forehead while a thin trickle of copper ichor ran down Gregar's chest. The demon's strength and agility surprised Gaspard, and he soon found the advantage in his furious attack to be lacking. Feigning fatigue, he slowed his attacks and ripostes and began to circle the demon.

"You mortal fool, I cannot be killed!" hissed Gregar angrily. "I shall destroy you, and you shall still be mine."

"I have yet to be defeated, so we are a match," replied Gaspard between breaths.

Gregar pressed an attack with his stave with alarming speed and determination. Gaspard eluded the iron rod as it scythed through the air, mounting his own counterattack, but was quickly turned away without a score.

"We know what happens to me should I fail," asked Gaspard between breaths. "Yet I see fear in your eyes! Pray tell, what fate awaits you should I prevail? What awaits you should I slip through your fingers?"

"That will not happen!" hissed the demon darkly, spinning the stave through air before again launching against Gaspard's dancing blade.

"Yet you bleed," taunted Gaspard.

Gregar leapt at him with a series of lightning fast blows, both high and low, forcing the young knight to give ground to remain clear. Faster and faster they came, and harder and harder it was for Gaspard to protect himself from the stave's bone-crushing might. He gave ground, backing in circular fashion through the witch's clearing. He drew his long knife and with two blades bent his will against the demon's left side, lunging, thrusting, and slashing, only to be forced again to defend and give ground. Around they danced, spilling Chorchiéthe's caldrons, kicking ash and embers on each other. Gaspard tried every combination and slight of blade he knew, yet was unable to break Gregar's wicked defenses. While his muscles began to ache from the relentless counter-attacks the demon produced, his enemy showed no signs of fatigue.

Gaspard was both a seasoned tournament combatant as well battlefield knight, and knew well to watch for weaknesses in an enemy's technique. Slowly, as they continued their feverish duel, he noted Gregar repeatedly left his right side exposed when he mounted his attacks. The demon must have been aware of the weakness, for with each attack, he brought his poisoned tail around to keep Gaspard from taking advantage. Or perhaps he was baiting Gaspard to make such an attack. Regardless, it was the only opening where a counterattack could possibly produce a score, so Gaspard determined to take the risk.

A low attack on the demon's left side resulted in a stout parry and high, back-handed riposte against Gaspard's right. The knight ducked, swung right and deflected the stave downward with his sword, pinning it to the ground for just time enough for him to lunge left and bury his knife up to the hilt in the demon's side. Gregar cried out in rage and whipped his tail around and buried its oily barb deep in Gaspard's shoulder at the neck. Despite the shock and pain of the thick needle tearing through his skin, Gaspard let go of his knife, drove past the demon while slashing his sword across Gregar's neck.

The fine blade, now notched and chipped in its battle with the iron stave, ripped through the muscle and sinew of the demon's supple neck, partially severing the head from the body. Gregar's tail convulsed with the demon's death spasms and threw Gaspard to the ground while shimmering amber ichor spilled from the demon's throat and side. Gaspard landed on his back, the demon's poison already coursing through his veins, where he watched the serpentine creature first stagger, and then collapse next to the torn and trampled deed to his soul. Despite his exertions from the battle, he felt a cold weakness creeping along his limbs and, though starved for air, his breathing uncontrollably slowed. The sounds of the forest became distant, and its airy canopy slowly faded to darkness.

Chorchiéthe's skin was drenched with sweat while the hot August sun parched her tongue. Beyond exhaustion, she slowly hobbled up the mount to the Castle de Hambie's main gate. The tower guard caught sight of her and then vanished from sight. The sound of distant shouts quickly gave way to several armed men, led by Master Josue, rushing through the barbican and down the slope to accost her.

"Where is Lord Malfort?" demanded Josue, while the other men shrunk back from her stench.

Ignoring the agitated seneschal, Chorchiéthe sneered at the nearest man and spat, "Fetch me water, boy, I am parched!" Then turning on another of the men, she commanded, "Take my hand, you, and help your witch climb what remains of this hill!"

Master Josue nodded to the men, the first happy to leave her presence, while the second twisted his face up and assisted the witch.

"The hour is late, witch! Why are you here and not Gaspard?" again demanded Josue.

"Those truths be told, he is not here and neither is he with me, then I would surmise he is dead," replied the witch nastily, "though since I am living, perhaps he is also. I really cannot say. You best send your men as quickly as possible to my cottage to retrieve him, either way. For now, take me to the child…if he still lives."

"What do you mean, hag?" said Josue angrily, "Stop speaking in riddles and make plain your words!"

Chorchiéthe grasped hold of Josue's hand as she came to rest in the shade of the barbican and glared into his eyes, "The truth is a dangerous thing, Josue! This time it is not for you!"

Chorchiéthe took her drink while Master Josue ordered six men to ride for her cottage in the forest. He escorted her through castle to Raymond's rooms and let her inside. The scene there was dire, as Raymond lay as still and pale as death with Gisla, Clothilde and Jacqueline sitting at his bedside perfectly distraught and helpless to stay the poison slowly killing him.

"Sister!" cried Jacqueline, rising to meet the witch as she entered, "thank God you are here! Pray tell, where is Lord Gaspard?"

Josue caught Jacqueline's eye, warning her without words to be quiet and ask no questions. Chorchiéthe ignored Jacqueline's query except to snort, and then hobbled to the table near the bed and emptied the contents of her sack on its surface.

"Everyone out! Except his mother, I will use her…yes, I will…" she said ominously, "And bring me fresh water and clean bandages!"

There was a moment's pause with the women exchanging helpless glances, whereupon the witch stopped and stared at them.

"Get out!" she cried, finally causing them to flee.

Chorchiéthe then took Raymond by the hand and closed her eyes, mumbling to herself in a singsong voice. "Remove his gown, woman!" she ordered Gisla, who quickly complied. Opening her eyes, she stared down on the boy, resting her other hand gently upon his chest. Her face came close to his and she grunted. His breath was so faint she could barely sense it. Pulling away, she reached for small, yellow and black newt lying limp on the table. Carefully, she drew the dead creature across Raymond's chest, leaving a moist trail of its poison on his skin.

"To strengthen his breath…for now…" she mumbled, then reached for a flask. "Hand me that linen," she demanded of Gisla, who quickly retrieved the torn cloth. The witch soaked the cloth with the fluid in the flask, and then grasped Gisla's hand. "Hold this cloth against his wound, it will sooth it."

Chorchiéthe did not release Gisla's wrist, and instead forced the dripping cloth into her hand, pressing it against her son's side. Gisla screamed out in pain as the witch forced her to touch the wound. She saw everything Chorchiéthe saw, all the complexities of the poison coursing through her son's body, the throbbing pain of the wound, his failing heart, dying breath, and fading mind. She saw that and something more, something darker and older…something evil in his bones.

"Stop this!" cried Gisla in agony, wrenching her hand away.

"Gahh! You are a pathetic woman!" snarled the witch, "You do not like what you see? You think this is pain? Your suffering has hardly begun!" She again grasped Gisla's wrist and forced her hand back to Raymond's side, "Now hold the rag firmly while I work."

Raymond suddenly took a deep, ragged breath and moaned painfully from deep within his torpor. Chorchiéthe pulled the stopper from a small vial and poured a few drops into Raymond's mouth. "To strengthen his heart," she said in her singsong voice. She continued working, applying a salve to the soles of his feet, circles of oil to his stomach, and a sticky balm to the back of his neck. After each step she would stop and chant in her queer language with her rhythmic voice, while she held Raymond's hands and gazed thoughtfully on his body.

After a time she reached for yet another small vial and slowly placed several drops in the boy's mouth. "He need not swallow it; it will enter his blood from his tongue, yes…" she whispered.

Gisla watched the misshapen, wart-covered witch with fear and fascination as she worked. Her odor permeated the already warm room, making Hambie's chatelaine faint with nausea. Though she steadfastly held the damp rag to Raymond's side, with Chorchiéthe occasionally rewetting it for her, she could not overcome her sense of revulsion at having to trust the witch yet a second time. Finally gaining the courage to speak, Gisla cleared her throat.

"Where is my husband?" she whispered.

"Your husband?" replied Chorchiéthe offhandedly. "Your husband is dead."

With that Gisla crumpled to the floor, unconscious. The witch looked critically down at her limp form and curled her lip derisively. Such a ridiculous question! Of course Fulk was dead. With that, she turned her attention back to the boy and frowned. Though she looked deeply within him, believing she had countered all the evil complexity of the poison, something yet lingered, holding him at death's door. He remained flaccid and cold with only shallow, reflexive breathing and a struggling heart, while she had but one agent left with which to attempt his revival.

Her hand shook as she reached for that last small bottle of liquid, for she knew that the difference between life and death was little more than a drop of her medicinal poison. She touched only a corner of torn cloth to the top of the bottle and carefully watched the fluid wick into the linen.

Then she placed the moistened corner of cloth in the boy's mouth, allowing it to mix with his own unswallowed spittle.

Chorchiéthe stepped away from the bedside to await the effects of this final counteragent to the demon's poison. Noting with irritation that Gisla still swooned, she hefted the basin of water sitting on the table and poured it on her face. This produced an immediate recovery, shocking the woman back to consciousness.

"He will either live or die," said the witch flatly as Gisla gasped for air. "There is nothing more I can do."

Gaspard found himself standing in the dusty wash of an arid, narrow gully. The air about him stank of sulfur and sky was a bleached, hot light that made him squint as he took in his surroundings. No living plant, nor bird, nor insect graced the desolate ravine and all was gray ash, slag, and scree. The walls of the wash were steep and treacherous, leaving him but two directions, two choices as to his path. He could move forward, following the steep, rocky wash as it ascended into the mountains, or he could go backwards and descend into the valley below, a barren wasteland of smoking craters and suffocating vapors.

The bottom of the wash ended in a cliff where, once upon a time, water likely flowed into an ancient lake or sea. Gaspard walked to the cliff's edge and gazed out onto the endless sands and ash and saw hundreds, perhaps thousands, of ragged men shuffling about aimlessly, eternally parched and forever without sustenance. Each man seemed alone, isolated from the others, though often coming within arms reach of one another. They neither stopped to speak nor hailed their companions from afar, as though they each suffered their own endless nightmare. Somehow Gaspard knew that if he climbed down the rough cliff, he would end up just as they, living an endless death. Though it was the path of least resistance, it led only to eternal suffering. He did not want to go there.

Though his body ached and his breath already labored under the acrid atmosphere, he turned and trudged up the wash and began his ascent into the ravine. Despite his best efforts to avoid them, the glass-like shards of rock bit into and cut through his lord's boots of tender leather. As the hours passed away so did the soft, sandy soil that filled the bottom of the wash and soon he was forced to scramble over the shattered rock as he climbed. Around every bend he hoped to find a level path, but was lucky to find a simple, flat rock to take his rest while he licked the blood from his scratched and battered hands.

His mouth grew dry and his eyes full of grit, as each painful step forward was a scream of agony and weakness. He could hardly lift his arms to reach for the next hold, yet could find no place to lay in rest that was not like a bed of nails. Soon he felt as though he must either turn back or simply fall to his death, for the path was no longer a path, but rather narrow chimney with only razor-sharp shards for handholds. Behind and below him was an impassable, mountainous landscape of black and gray rock and shattered volcanic glass. Before him the narrow ravine he had followed ended at a sheer cliff-face with a vertical crack that climbed to the sky.

Gaspard managed a deep, rasping breath, and entered the chimney and began to climb, pulling himself upward, shard by shard, toward the white-hot sky above. Grit-filled sweat stung his eyes as he worked his way upward, and more than once the thought of simply letting go and falling to the sweet nothingness of death crossed his mind. Yet he continued on, inch by agonizing inch, up the chimney until the light of day grew near. It was only when that last handhold was within reach that his strength finally failed him. His hands and feet were cut badly and oozing blood that betrayed his grip, while his limbs were growing numb and flaccid. Finally, knowing what fate lay below, Gaspard bowed his head and mumbled, for the first time, "Please God, help me…"

"Salut! Is someone there?" asked a surprised voice from atop the chimney. The dark outline of a man appeared above Gaspard and stared down at him in disbelief, "Véthe, man, you need a hand!"

Gaspard squinted, nodded, and extended his bloody hand to grasp the stranger's outstretched arm. With surprising strength, the man hauled Gaspard bodily onto a wide, smooth ledge cut into the rock face of the mountainside. He saw Gaspard was near collapse, so he wrapped Gaspard's arm around his shoulder and his own arm around Gaspard's waist and helped to walk along the ledge.

In a moment they came to a small cave where the man was cooking a fish over an open fire. He carefully lowered Gaspard onto a mat of woven reeds and fetched him a flagon of water, after which he sat on a mat across from his visitor. Gaspard drank long and deep from the flagon, and it was perhaps the most quenching liquid he had ever consumed. Though he drank his fill, the container still seemed to have plenty left for later. Once his thirst was sated, he looked upon his host. The man had long, brown hair and a sparse beard streaked with gray. His face was tan and careworn, and his gown was of unbleached, homespun wool that looked to be woven as a single piece. His dusty feet were clad in simple leather sandals.

With so many questions as to where he was, and what the stranger was about in such a desolate place, Gaspard only managed to ask, "Where did you get that fish?" whereupon the stranger pointed to a basket at the back of the cave near several fagots of wood.

"What is your name?" the stranger asked gently.

"Gaspard..." he replied hesitantly. Was that his name? Was he Gaspard Malfort or Gaspard Ducaen?

"From whence did you come?"

"I am a Norman," he answered.

"That is not what I meant. The road you are traveling just now..." prompted the stranger.

"I looked out on a valley of sulfur and ash and was afraid, so I turned away hoping to find...something..." Gaspard said softly, not truly understanding what compelled him to make such a treacherous climb.

"Would you like to share this fish with me?" asked the man.

Gaspard nodded and the man stood and fetched a small basin of water, which he then sat in Gaspard's lap. Taking up the flagon, he said, "Hold out your hands that they may be cleansed." He then carefully poured the water over Gaspard's cut and bloody hands, rinsing away all that soiled them. To the young knight's amazement, under the trickle of water his wounds closed and their pain diminished until finally it was gone.

289

The stranger then reached for Gaspard's tattered boots and attempted to gently remove them. Gaspard objected, feeling ashamed to be served with such kindness, but the stranger simply said, "Let me do this for you." He then removed the boots and washed Gaspard's feet, affecting the same cure as done to his hands. The stranger then flung the remains of the lordly boots beyond the ledge where they fell to the rocks far below.

The stranger retrieved a loaf from another basket, tore it in half, and handed a piece to Gaspard in a bowl. Removing the fish from over the flame, he asked, "Where is your knife?"

Reflexively, Gaspard reached for the sheath on his belt, but found it empty. Puzzled, he said, "I have misplaced it."

"No matter," replied the stranger, who then carefully tore the fish with his fingers and handed half to Gaspard.

For some minutes the two ate in silence. Gaspard had never tasted any such fish or any such bread before, and was amazed to feel their sustaining power flow easily through his body. Once finished, he gazed at the man in wonder. "Thank you, milord, you have saved me."

The man smiled gently, though in his eyes, Gaspard was sure he saw some great sadness. "Where are you headed now?" he asked of the young knight.

"I do not know where I am, milord," confessed Gaspard. "So I do not know where to go from here. Do you know where lies a safe path?"

"There is but one path, my son, and it is neither safe nor easy. However, I will show it to you," said the stranger solemnly, holding out a pair of rough, old sandals to Gaspard. "These have served me well and are toughened from years in the desert."

Gaspard slid into the sandals, did up their straps, and then accepted the stranger's hand as he rose to his feet. The two left the cave and walked along the ledge a great distance until the path opened up onto a great plateau. The stranger pointed beyond the plateau to a range of high, barren mountains that thrust up from the earth like a great row of tight, gnashing teeth. Gaspard looked behind him, and for all his struggles to this point, he had only managed to escape the foothills leading up to this great mountain range.

"That is where you are headed," said the stranger softly.

Gaspard's spirits, elevated by the food and respite provided by the stranger, crumbled before such a daunting task.

"Is there no easier way?" he asked childishly.

The stranger looked quizzically at him and said, "Yours may well be the easiest path, for you know what awaits you should you turn back. That is a privilege unknown to most men."

"Yes," Gaspard said after a moment, knowing the man's words were true.

The two embraced and Gaspard turned toward the great mountain range and began walking across the plateau. The stranger watched him walk until he vanished into the distance, whispering softly after the young knight, "Godspeed, Gaspard, and God bless."

CHAPTER 22

The Road from Perdition

He was only aware that consciousness was slowly bringing him back to the world of the living when the pain, thirst, and nausea began to pierce his torpor. He tried to shift his body in search of a comfortable position and could not help but groan when his back, legs and arms spasmed bitterly. His head throbbed, and when he opened his eyes to confirm it was night, his lids dragged heavily against his dry orbs.

He found himself naked beneath a sheet in the master's bed, clothed only by heavy bandages around his shoulder and neck. Unclear, scattered memories...images of the white wolf and his battle with the demon came and went like shimmering portraits in his mind. The memories mixed and melded with his dream of the forsaken land as the former gained strength and the latter began to lose cohesion. Again he shifted, gritting his aching teeth against the pain.

"Welcome back, milord," sighed an old, familiar voice from the darkness. It was Master Josue.

Gaspard tried to answer, but only managed rasping gasps. He found strong hands holding a cup to his mouth and he drank, choked, coughed and drank again. He did not taste the bitterness of the drink, knowing only it slacked his thirst.

"The witch said you were to drink this upon waking; it will ease your pain," continued Josue flatly. "You have been unconscious nearly three days, but she managed to bring you back."

Gaspard's mind began to flood with memories—Raymond, the demon, the White Lady, Chorchiéthe, Gisla, his sins—all of it mixed in confusion in his thoughts.

"Raymond?" he whispered.

There was a long pause, and then from the darkness Josue said grimly, "We lost him, milord."

The sting of dry tears burned his eyes as Gaspard softly began to sob. He loved Raymond with, perhaps, the only pure love he had ever been able to offer, and had ultimately killed the boy. It was an unfathomable, visceral pain, beyond the words of man.

"We burned the creature, milord," continued Josue, hesitantly, "and the scroll, also."

"Did you read it?"

"Yes."

Gaspard said nothing for some time as the bitter poppy juice he drank slowly masked the pains in his body and mind.

"Fetch me a priest," he said finally.

"Father Sergius is already here, milord. We thought you lost also, so both you and the boy were anointed," replied Josue.

"Where is Gisla?"

"Asleep with Clothilde."

"Let them rest, then. Bring Gisla and Sergius here in the morning. You, as well. There is much to the story," mumbled Gaspard numbly.

"Yes, milord," replied Josue, holding another cup to Gaspard's lips.

The lord de Hambie drank and then let the creeping dream of the poppy take him back to sleep.

The angst of her dreams, nightmares filled with suffering that lay bare her weaknesses, was no respite from her waking hours. Her household moved around her with weak smiles, furtive whispers, and awkward condolences. While she swooned at his side, her son gasped his last breath and died. She screamed, and she cried, and as she crushed his lifeless body to her breast, she begged God that it be undone, yet death remained.

Chorchiéthe, disliking those tortured emotions following the death of a child, hobbled to the door, beckoning her sister and Clothilde enter to console their mistress. Behind the mask of her laconic demeanor, the witch suffered an inconvenient twinge of empathy that she was ill equipped to express. Such emotions were best left to whole women, not the deformed wreckage that was Chorchiéthe, so she removed herself to a shadowed corner and quietly sat.

With a clatter of hooves Gaspard's men rushed into the castle bearing their lord's body. Though he stood on the shore of the river of death, and the cowled tiller-man beckoned him to make the passage, he was unable to board. Life yet remained in his body—a body lean, tough and in the prime of its days—and it stubbornly refused to yield to the poison coursing through its veins. Even as Raymond's lament spread among the household, the men and women de Hambie rushed to save the life of their lord.

Rumors that Gaspard had dueled and slain a horrid beast, a demonic serpent, swept through the castle. His men found his fallen body near a cloaked reptilian creature heretofore existing only in the imaginations of the gargoyle's sculptor. Leaving behind one warrior to guard the slain creature, the others rushed Gaspard's unconscious form back to the castle. He was taken to his chamber and laid in the very bed he had shared with Gisla the night before. Master Josue burst into Raymond's room, calling for the witch. Gaspard yet lived and she must come away immediately.

"You said he was dead…" Gisla accused Chorchiéthe through her tears.

The witch simply sneered and made a derisive grunt as she gathered her potions and salves and left the chamber.

Josue, bent on seeing Gaspard's enemy with his own eyes, returned to the clearing only to find the warrior left behind struck dead, the demon's stave in his hand, and the most contorted look of fear masking his face. The man must have picked up the demon's stave out of curiosity and been slain by its residual evil.

"Build a pyre!" he ordered in a vengeful voice as he carefully unfurled the torn vellum scroll with his knife, "Burn the beast! Careful…touch nothing…and when it is burned, bury it, and its evil weapon, beneath a mound of stone and earth."

Chorchiéthe, practicing her rare arts, looked deeply into Gaspard's wretched body to find the same venom that struck down young Raymond slowly filtering through his organs. Just as before, she methodically administered her salves and elixirs, each as they were needed, to combat all the complexities of the toxin. All the time she sang to herself in her own strange tongue until she was finally ready to administer that last, most poisonous, antidote. The boy, so small and weak, had not survived the seizures brought on by the concoction, but the man was strong. Just a drop to his lips reached his vital fluids in a matter of minutes. Quickly she placed an oak stick between his teeth and waited. First a twitch, a flickering eyelid, and then the clenching of the fists. The arms flexed, the toes pointed and curled as the calves contracted, and the back spasmed into a spine-snapping arch. His jaw clenched so tightly that his teeth ground nearly through the oak stick, muffling involuntary screams and gasps of pain. Waves of convulsions contorted the man, tearing muscles and cracking joints. A thing that came on so quickly was slow to subside, but Chorchiéthe could see she was winning the battle and defeating the Devil. Though her patient was wracked with pain, she could not help but smile.

Only when she knew she had won, did she admit Father Sergius and two brown-frocked brothers with a sneer. Sergius was a spry little fellow with a close-cropped, graying tonsure and calloused hands unafraid of a day's labor. The priest would be coming to her soon to treat his piles, and she could sense his consternation as easily as he could smell her foul odor. With derisive curiosity she watched the Christian holy men set about performing the unction of God.

"Peace be on this house," said the priest solemnly.

"And all who live within," replied the brothers.

Father Sergius had with him a small gold box filled with blessed ointment, a medicine lacking all earthly power yet infused with the power of God, that he set on the table. He carefully poured holy water into a basin next to Chorchiéthe's worldly medicines and wet his fingers, that he could make the sign of the cross on Gaspard's forehead. Next he dipped a switch of hyssop in the basin and used it to sprinkle holy water in all directions about the room, intentionally wetting Chorchiéthe as he went.

"Purify me with hyssop, Lord, that I am cleansed of sin. Wash me, that I am whiter than snow. Have mercy upon me. Glory to the Father, the Son, and the Holy Spirit."

The witch wiped the droplets of holy water from her cheek and glared at Sergius, who calmly turned his attention back to Gaspard. Though her knowledge of Latin was limited, and she had never been one for church or prayer, she understood enough to follow the rite performed by Sergius and the brothers. With the holy ointment, the priest blessed all that is sinful to a man. He touched the eyes, for they covet; the ears, for they listen to evil counsel; the lips, for they speak not the truth; the nostrils, for they stimulate his desires; the hands and feet, for they carry him to evil acts; and lastly the loins.

With each blessing, Father Sergius beseeched God to pardon Gaspard for any sins or faults committed as he gently anointed him with the ointment. With each blessing, Chorchiéthe was horrified to find Gaspard's scarred and tortured soul, whose ugliness had perversely pleased her, slowly healed and gained some semblance of wholeness. He prayed his Latin prayers and made the sign of cross, oblivious that Chorchiéthe shrank away from the sacrament. She could see what Father Sergius could not, and she witnessed a dramatic healing of Gaspard's spiritual scars even as his physical body lay limp and damaged. Shame, confusion, and fear washed over her as she watched the priest, unconcerned with the body, bring salvation to the soul. It was a thing, for all her skills, she could never do, while this priest before her, a sinner just as any other, managed to do it through simple faith in Christ. Tears welled in her beetle-black eyes, and she fled the chamber.

Raymond's corpse could not long withstand the summer heat, so he was buried in the churchyard the following morning. Brothers prayed over his body the whole night through to bring comfort to his soul and ease his passing into God's kingdom of Heaven. The bell tolled seven times, and all the people of the Sienne Valley wept and gnashed their teeth when they heard of the young lord's passing.

The morning came, and again Josue was there when Gaspard awoke. In taut silence, he helped his lord to sit up and dress. From his small chamber, Gaspard ordered Josue to retrieve a small wooden lockbox hidden at the bottom of his childhood chest.

"You will find the key hidden in a chink above the door of my old quarters outside of Raymond's room. Fetch it for me," he asked Josue who quickly complied with the request.

The sun warmed the morning breeze as it swirled gently through the room. Once Josue returned with the key, he lent his arm to Gaspard as he rose painfully from the bed and gained the couch. Though the seneschal offered, he refused the remaining poppy juice left behind by the witch. He sat quietly with his little box in his lap, nervously fingering the tiny key. When Father Sergius and Gisla entered the room, his hollow, haunted eyes met theirs. The man Gaspard, once virile and robust, was now drawn and wasting, with dark rings beneath his eyes and a bloodless hue to his skin.

Gisla, a reflection of Gaspard's suffering countenance, rushed to her husband's side to both give and receive comfort, only to be gently rebuffed.

"Please, milady, I do not deserve such affection," he said softly with downcast eyes.

"What do you mean, husband?" begged Gisla who fell to her knees before him.

"Hear me out and you will understand," he replied sadly, nodding to Josue, who then gently pulled Gisla away.

"Wait! I do not understand!" she cried, wrestling free of Josue's half-hearted grip.

Gaspard closed his eyes and sighed, "Gisla, please sit. I…I have a terrible truth I must tell…the beginning of my penance. I have such hatred for the man that is me. Though you do not yet know it, I am accursed, and you shall despise me. Josue, God bless him, believes he knows, but no… Sit and listen…please! Once I have finished, if you can still look upon my ugliness, you shall have what remains of my story." Then turning to Sergius, he said, "Father, I would have this be my confession before God. If you are unwilling, leave my presence now, for if you stay, you will be bound by your vows to hear me out."

Gisla instinctively shrank against Josue, clutching at him in confusion, while Father Sergius nodded his assent. Hambie's chatelaine stared into her husband's drawn, haunted visage and felt an upwelling of that instinctual, primal fear that was a part of all men—the fear of what lay in the darkness beyond the sphere of light. Gaspard dropped his hollow eyes and took a deep, painful breath. He would rather face Gregar Penscalus a thousand times, using his strength and skill to confront evil, than confess his own sins to the purity and light of the woman he dared call wife.

"My name, though it only became known to me...after..." he started, "Is Gaspard Ducaen, the only son of Bertrand Ducaen. The name 'Malfort' was given me by the abbot of St. Lo, one of only three men who knew my true lineage, the others being Lord Hugh Paynel and Brother Carthusian...all dead now. Though Sir Hugh and the brothers thought to protect me from the Ducaen legacy, as it turns out, it is not one easily escaped. I tell you this because the seeds of my sin were sown long before my birth. This in no way absolves me of my crimes, my lies, for every man has free will, but when that eventual question of 'why' is asked, know that there is an answer.

"From the first time I set eyes on milady, I desired you above all else," he looked only at Gisla's feet. "I cannot call my feelings love. Rather, it was a lust that filled me and consumed me all my days and nights. There is none such as you..." Gaspard's voice cracked. "That my lord courted and married you poisoned me against him. Though I loved him as a brother, I grew to hate him as a rival. I wished him dead a thousand times. When Raoul brought the bard, Aymer, to Hambie, I saw my chance and goaded Fulk into challenging the Dragon. There was no more likely a place for Fulk to meet his end than Jersey. There was no more likely man to slay him than the violent and feared Bertrand Ducaen. We were yet unknown to each other, and I hated him..." he trailed off, wondering if life could have been different, perhaps better, had he grown up in the house of Ducaen. Or would he have been just as damned as he was now?

Gaspard paused and swallowed before continuing, "However, to my dismay, Fulk prevailed against his enemy, snapping his neck after a great battle," he glanced up at their recoiling faces. "I sense surprise. No, I did not kill Bertrand Ducaen. That was a lie, just one of a thousand…and, just as you did, Carthusian believed it," he sadly mused. "That's why he fled Hambie to return to St. Lo, for he could not face me knowing I had unwittingly committed patricide. His blood is also on my hands…" Gaspard paused a moment, lost in self-loathing.

"It was the greatest battle between two men I have ever witnessed. It seemed to rage on for eternity, like two great lions pitted against one another. For the longest time it seemed neither man could be defeated. Even in the final seconds, Ducaen nearly prevailed, yet your husband won the moment, twisting the Dragon's head all the way backwards, breaking his neck. Though Ducaen failed to defeat Fulk as I had hoped, he scored many blows and Fulk collapsed once victory was his. At first I believed Ducaen had mortally wounded him, so I killed the Breton as a matter of course before attending my knight. I was most pleased by this outcome, for I had also tasted Bertrand Ducaen's insult, and was indeed glad the world was rid of him as well as my lord. I was horrified when later I learned he was my own father.

"Then I discovered my lord yet lived! He open his eyes and stared up at me as I reached within his tunic to tear away Gisla's lock," Gaspard's hand trembled as he turned the key, opened the little wooden box, and drew forth a blood-stained length of braided hair and green ribbon, showing it to his listeners. "This token you wove…I took it for my own. I was mad, and he knew my intent and, despite his wounds, found the strength to fight me and defend your honor…" He paused, sobbed softly. "The wound I bore upon my return from Jersey…that wound was by my own knight's hand, not some lowly pirate as I had you believe.

"If I let him live, I knew I would be branded and cast out into the world. I supposed he might yet die from his wounds, but did not have the time to wait while the island still crawled with pirates. To fulfill my scheme, I would have to be the agent of Fulk's death. Rather than an honorable end, he would be murdered and by my hand…and so I…I…slew him…to have what was his…I murdered Fulk Paynel because I coveted his wife, his house, and his glory, and then brought all these evils upon Hambie.

"I carried his body to the top of a nearby hill and dug a shallow grave hidden in a thicket beneath a tree. I lay him down in unhallowed ground and covered him over and fled the island. I have not had a moment's peace since."

A paralyzing silence took hold of his audience as his shocking confession left them frozen in disbelief. Father Sergius closed his eyes against Gaspard's revelations, while Master Josue's stunned visage slowly melted into utter hatred. Gisla was rigid, neither moving nor breathing, as though she were a lifeless statue of carved alabaster. Josue was the first to move as he slowly rose from his seat and pulled forth his knife.

"Say the word, milady, and I will end this right now!" he seethed through gritted teeth.

Gisla neither blinked nor uttered a sound. Her eyes stared and Gaspard, burning him with their suffering and bewilderment.

"He could have saved your son, Gisla. Raymond need not have died! This man deserves a place in Hell! Let me send him there!" Josue grasped Gaspard by the hair, jerked his head back, and pressed the knife against his throat with such force that a trickle of blood ran beneath the blade. Gaspard neither raised a hand nor made any move in self-defense.

"Stop…" she whispered plaintively.

"'Tis not murder to slay the murderer!" argued Josue.

"Stop!" she ordered quietly, "It is not for you to decide! It is not for you…"

Neither flinching, nor meeting anyone's eyes, Gaspard spoke.

"You should have Josue put me in irons, milady," he said quietly, "Send out riders to all the lords friendly to Hambie. Bring your father, your brothers, and your allies to your side. Let the law try me. Let the law execute me. Let me be buried in unhallowed ground and let every man spit upon my grave."

Gaspard looked into Josue's burning, hate-filled eyes, "You were always right about me, Josue. In your heart you always saw the evil festering, but now you know me to be right."

"Milady?" said the seneschal through gritted teeth, not relaxing the blade, "What would you have me do?"

"Let that be his last command in this house!" choked Gisla. "Let him rot, let him hang, and then let him go to Hell!"

With that she fled the room and into the arms of Clothilde and Jacqueline who waited anxiously in the corridor. News of Gaspard's confession spread quickly through the castle, and shouts to hang him from Hambie's walls rang out from the donjon to the village. He was shackled, beaten by his own men, and then thrown bodily into a windowless cell.

In the darkness he sat alone. Though he knew the truth was better than the lie, it tore at his soul he had to hurt Gisla so in order to set things right. Though it was so late an hour in his life, he found he did truly love her. He truly desired to protect her, and this was the only path.

"Someone had to save you from me, my love," he whispered in the darkness.

First days, then weeks passed as noble men made their way to Hambie to take counsel with its chatelaine. Though Robert was away in Spain, Albric and Rohais de Grentmesnel quickly found their way to Gisla's hall, as did Vaquelin de Ferriers, Valmer Montbray, and several others. It was mid-September before the last of nobles arrived to hear the case and exact punishment.

During that time, Gaspard's only visitor was Father Sergius, who spent several hours each day listening to Gaspard's story and then praying with the fallen knight. Though the portions were meager, Gaspard touched little of the food and drink provided him, and his body continually wasted. Outside Gaspard's cell, all the living world had become Gisla's prison. She listlessly wandered the castle, neither living nor dead, little better than a ghost haunting Hambie's hallways. In her bower, she stared out her window for hours, not to look on the world outside, but rather to avoid the pained, sympathetic faces within her castle's walls.

Raoul de St. Pair and his squire, Bousa, were at sea, so Isabelle, now bearing Raoul's child in her womb, had made the journey alone to bring comfort to Gisla and the house. She and Clothilde groomed her and dressed her, sat by her side as she slept, and quietly coaxed her to eat. She spoke little to them except in the dark of night when she would recount the nightmares that consumed her sleep.

"Raymond is sick. He has a darkness in his bones. He is like a corpse beckoning to me—I cannot bear it!" she wept hysterically as Isabelle and Clothilde held her close and soothed her. Yet she could not confess to them she first saw this darkness with her waking eye as Chorchiéthe pressed her hand to her son's side while he yet lived.

Finally there came a morning when Gisla could bear her nightmares no longer and left the castle alone to walk in the woods with her own thoughts.

"It is good ta see milady out an' about," said the man at the gate. "A walk ta the village?"

"No," replied Gisla absently, "I thought a walk in the woods."

"Alone? I could call a man or two…ta keep ya safe 'n all," he advised.

Gisla gave him a dismissive snort and furrowed her brow.

"What more can be done to me?" she asked him, then walked away, alone.

Though she told herself she had no destination, her feet carried her through the forest to Chorchiéthe's cottage. The forest glowed with the flickering, green light that filtered through gently rustling leaves of the canopy above. Gisla slowly walked, allowing her hands to brush against low hanging leaves and catch tiny spiders and they floated along on their single thread. The simple nature of such life did not escape her as she contemplated her own tangled skein. The witch's clearing open before her and she stood silently for a long time, noting the fires were cold and cauldrons empty. She stared at the new tumulus mound in the middle of the clearing, fearful of the answers that were buried within. The air about the mound was rancid and stifling even though the rest of the forest hung heavy with dry, musky fragrance of late summer.

Finally she rapped on the cottage's door and called out to the witch. There was no answer, so she gently pushed the door inward, again calling Chorchiéthe's name. The rich aroma of dried flowers and herbs gently pushed away the sickly odor that held sway in the rest of the clearing. The filtered light from the door and cottage's small window was enough for Gisla to see the witch was not inside among all the clutter. Even her little fire inside was long cold.

Outside the cottage, beyond the broken stone wall, Gisla saw there was a narrow, well-worn path leading behind the cottage and deeper into the forest. Still unsure what she truly wanted from the witch, she found she was determined to find her. She left the clearing and followed the path as it took her deep into the forest, wending down gentle slopes, past meadows and finally to a babbling stream.

The path then continued along the bank of the stream until it broke into a sunlit clearing teaming with blue and green dragonflies cruising the surface of a sparkling pool. Standing naked in the pool, with her back to Gisla, was Chorchiéthe, scrubbing herself with a cake of soap. Her sparse, gray hair was wet and matted, and droplets of water shone dully on her nodule-covered skin. Gisla watched her for some moments and saw how her deformities limited her reach. The witch could not touch her own neck, nor the back of her head, nor her buttocks. The cake would slip from her hand and she was hard pressed to retrieve it from the shallow water. Gisla was suddenly overcome with pity for the woman, and all her past revulsion dissipated into nothing.

Without thinking, she waded into the water, uncaring that it wet her shoes and gown. The witch started and turned in surprise. Gisla, in turn, was surprised to find the expected sharp lines of resentment and disdain utterly absent from Chorchiéthe's face. In their place was a look of utter confusion and helplessness.

"I can't get clean," she said in a pleading voice once she recognized Gisla. "I come here every day and wash, but I can't get clean."

She held out her arms, both red with scrubbing, for Gisla to see. The young woman, so lithe and well made, suddenly understood suffering and the bitterness it brought had made the witch as she was.

"Let me help you," she said softly as she took the cake of soap from Chorchiéthe's hand.

With utmost tenderness and love, Gisla washed the old woman's back and hair, not shying away from her bent, protruding spine, nor the warty nodules that covered her skin. Chorchiéthe closed her eyes and sighed peacefully as Gisla's slender fingers lightly caressed her skin, rinsing the soap away by dipping her hands into the pool and sprinkling the water on her back. A lifetime of pain momentarily soothed as cool rivulets ran down her back.

"I was once a girl…" breathed the old woman, "I still remember my mother bathing me. Then my body began to change, and I could see inside her. Her love turned to loathing. I have been alone ever since. In this moment, I am not alone. Such a gift."

Gisla took Chorchiéthe by the hand and the two waded to the sun-drenched grass at the edge of the pool, where the witch sat on a flat rock to warm herself. Her ragged bits of clothing sat in a filthy pile on the bank, so Gisla took them and the soap and washed them on a rock. Neither spoke while she worked and soon the washed garments were laid out to dry.

"No one comes to me now," confessed the witch. "They are frightened of the demon buried at my door. The Devil is taking his revenge…"

Gisla removed her wimple and wet shoes, and then sat next to the shrunken, kyphotic woman on the rock. The two quietly watched the dragonflies skim and flit over the water and through the tall reeds. After a few moments, Chorchiéthe spoke quietly.

"Can I…help you, little moussetchette?"

"You see things…differently," started Gisla.

"It is a horrid curse—to know what ails a man in both body and spirit," she replied flatly.

"When you pressed my hand against…" Gisla stuttered and could not finish.

"You saw. I forced that on you with malice for I wanted to hurt you, but the vision was true," said the witch, shamefully.

"What did it mean?" asked Gisla.

"Your son was already ill. Lé Dgiâbl'ye may have taken him away from you, but left alone, Raymond would not have survived the coming winter. He had a sickness in his bones that was ready to spread to the rest of his body. I have seen it many times, and have always been powerless against it. Even had Gaspard sold his soul and saved Raymond in the moment, the disease would have wrested him from your grasp in just a few months. His fate was already decided. The demon knew this, and knew you would suffer no matter. Lé Dgiâbl'ye cannot be bargained with, for his rewards are always fool's gold. He must always be rejected. Though the hour was late, Gaspard finally realized this truth."

"Gaspard!" spat Gisla darkly, "You should have let him die! His eleventh hour came and went on Jersey where he threw his lot in with the destroyer! He confessed it all! He murdered Fulk and returned to Normandy full of lies. With the cunning of a fox, he laid in wait for my need so he could finally take me as his. Do you understand? Finally I gave myself to him, and my son was taken from me the very next day. He might as well have administered the poison himself. He deserves damnation!"

"He does?" asked the witch, "Was it he who forced you to marry? Was it he who forced you into the marriage bed? Untangle your thoughts, little moussetchette! Great evil? Yes, his spirit is dark and scarred, but when offered even greater rewards, including your love, merely in exchange for an already withered soul, he finally rejected Evil's counsel. I do not know how long he was under the demon's sway, but it was his love for you and your son, his need to protect the both of you, that led him to defy his master. Whether you see it or no, he saved you. Would you have had him continue the lie? Continue to enjoy you and the life of a noble? He could have, and you would have been none the wiser…and your son still would have died. Freedom has a price, and sometimes that price is the loss of the security and contentment found in ignorance."

A cloud passed over Gisla's face, and she did not answer, leaving the two in silence for a long time. Around them, the living forest continued its slow dance of a thousand years, so much greater than the sum of its parts. Its sounds, the crackle of an animal unseen in the thicket, the cricket hidden in the grass, the falcon beyond the treetops, the quiet babble of the brook were as rich as the scents of decay and life wafting in the air.

Finally Gisla broke the spell and spoke, "He could have kept me even after Raymond's death. He need not have confessed. I would have believed any lie he put forth."

"Would you rather he had done so?" asked Chorchiéthe softly. "Would you rather he had locked away his secret and accepted your love? Would you trade the truth for a future with the hope of happiness?"

Tears welled in Gisla's eyes. "I do not know," she sobbed. "Do I dare say yes? What sort of woman would I be if I made that choice? Is it wrong to want to have hope? To want to give and receive love from a man?"

The old woman ran her fingers lightly on the back of Gisla's hand and spoke with a distant voice, "No, my dear, no. Alas, you cannot undo what is any more than I can…and if the Devil came to you with the promise to fulfill your desires, you would reject him."

Gisla put her arm around Chorchiéthe's shoulder and gently pulled her near. "You do not need to stay in your cottage. You do not need to be alone."

"I have nowhere else," replied Chorchiéthe lowly.

"Come and live at the castle," offered Gisla. "Be with your sister."

The witch turned to face Gisla, "You know too little of me to make such an offer. Even were I whole, I would not choose to live among people. As I am? No, lady, here I shall remain."

The women talked quietly as the afternoon waxed and waned. Chorchiéthe idly warned Gisla she must return to the keep soon as there was likely a fuss brewing over her absence. Together they walked slowly back to the cottage, and Gisla did kiss the old woman on the cheek before turning and making her way back to the castle. It was a sad vision for Chorchiéthe. The witch saw in Gisla the beginning of a sickness from which there would be no recovery. Even had Gaspard signed the Devil's note, he would have been damned to live with Gisla and Raymond only in his memory. She raised her hand in parting, knowing it was not her place to curse such a beautiful woman with knowledge of her own death. Once Gisla vanished into the woods, Chorchiéthe filled her bag with her best salves and began the slow journey to the convent of St. Cyprian and Father Sergius. She had her own burdens and knew her time to be relieved from them had come.

Such emotions as hatred, vindictiveness, and spite came quite unnaturally to Hambie's chatelaine, and they taxed her in body and spirit. The witch had turned her face to see Gaspard as a contrite man, a penitent man, and a man whose self-loathing exceeded all the loathing in the land. Ignoring the worried faces and terse chastisements of her father and brother upon her return to the castle, she made for the chapel to kneel before God in prayer.

"Leave me!" she had commanded them, and they left her…alone.

Disregarding the bitterness of the cup, she had wanted to taste revenge. She wanted Gaspard to suffer at the hands of others as he had made her suffer. Two and a half years she had suffered, unwittingly accepting his kindness, accepting his affection, and finally giving him her love. Her peers, as well as her vassals, now saw her as a woman duped into bedding her husband's murderer, and she was mortified. She had wanted him to burn and bleed and beg for mercy. Now her lust for revenge was crumbling.

Chorchiéthe had tried to make her understand the nature of the beast that Gaspard slew. The Prince of Lies is a subtle tempter. To kill the physical manifestation of the Prince of Darkness was the act of a man who, more than seeking forgiveness, sought to balance the scales. He would reject evil in all its forms, confess his sins, and make his contrition. He neither expected nor desired mercy, for his sins were great. He sought to confront his evil and bring it to a complete and utter end. This he did. Though he would never ask it, perhaps he did merit some forgiveness.

Long into the night Gisla remained in the chapel. It was not until very early in the morning that she started awake, finding that her prayers had drifted into the confused dreams of sleep. She found her heart racing while in her ears echoed the sweet voice of her son, slowly fading away in the candle lit shadows.

"He loved me, and I him, Méthe," whispered the boy.

The castle was all darkness and silence as she rose and made haste for the gaoler's key. Her candle flickered in the stillness as she glided through the halls and down the stairs to the empty storage room that served as Gaspard's cell. A guard was posted there day and night, and he was ready to challenge the intruder until he saw it was his mistress. She dismissed the man, unlocked the door, and entered.

Gaspard, ragged and ill-kept, lay in the corner on a pile of straw. He stirred in the candlelight and lifted his face. It was cut, bruised and dirty.

"Father?" he asked.

"No, husband, it is I," replied Gisla with a shaky voice.

"Oh!" he said with surprise, casting his sunken eyes down.

Gisla stepped across the room and looked down on his broken form. The place stank of urine and feces and the odor of unwashed man.

"Gwylliam arrived early this morning," she said hesitantly. "You are to be tried at the court of Coutances in fourteen days. Duke Robert will preside."

"That is good," rasped Gaspard. "He is a just man and will not show me undue favor."

An embarrassed silence hung momentarily heavy between them until Gaspard finally raised his face to his wife. His warrior's complexion had turned sallow and gaunt.

"I see in your eyes a question," he said.

Gisla breathed deeply, though the air rank, and spoke, "I want you to take me to where Fulk lays. I want you to carry his sword back to him and place it by his side. I will pray over him and lament him, as is my right. Long have I suffered. Long have I waited. Long has he been without his Christian rite."

Gaspard, holding her eyes ever so gently with his, replied steadily, "I will do this thing for you...and for him."

With the light of dawn and the waking of the household Gaspard was taken from his cell and allowed to bathe and dress in a clean shirt and breeches. Outside the castle gate a throng of peasants lined the road all the way down the mount and through the village. They came to jeer and taunt the man who had murdered their most beloved baron. They came to gawk. They came to gossip. They came so they would have a story to tell a stranger the following week, month, or year. Their presence twisted Gisla with such anxiety she could hardly dress for the journey.

"I wish they would leave us be," she complained to Isabelle and Clothilde as she looked out the bower window at them.

The entourage of Hambie, repaired and ready for the journey, finally gathered at the castle's gate. With a crust of bread in his belly and surrounded by mounted knights once his brothers-in-arms, Gaspard watched the guards open the castle gate so he could begin the long walk to Coutances. Iron shackles bound his wrists and ankles, and he looked neither right nor left nor up, keeping his eyes low on the ground before him. No knight looked upon him. No lord said a kind word. He refused the boots offered him and made the journey with his feet bare. They strapped Fulk's great sword, the very one Gaspard used to slay his lord, upon the murderer's back, so that he could bear the weapon back to its rightful master.

The clatter of hooves echoed in the bailey as Albric de Grentmesnel spurred his horse in lead of the contingent. Down the road and through the gawking, jeering crowd they went. Fulk's faithful roan, Hardelle, bore Gisla with a sure and loving gait along the dry, rutted road, as though she knew her mistress needed a steady hand. Hardelle would not let Gisla fall.

Though Gaspard did not dare look on any of those jeering at him, their familiar voices conjured their faces in his mind. He had broken bread and shared tankards with many of them as their lord. Now their taunts scourged his spirit.

"I have not a friend left in this world," he thought to himself.

First northwest to the highway, then north to the city they went, all the while Gaspard's muscle and sinew crying out in pain. His weak stride that carried him down from the castle's mount turned first to a limp then a drunkard's stagger when finally Coutances came into view.

As they approached the city's entrance, the growing mob hoping catch a look at Gaspard dwarfed the throng left behind in Hambie. Hundreds threw refuse into the lane that Gaspard was forced to walk upon. Their foul curses made the taunts of their rural cousins seem tame and respectful. As he limped and stumbled on his bleeding feet, trying to move quickly and yet avoid the worst of the filth in his path, he suddenly longed for the solitude of a prison cell.

Once within the city's walls, Gaspard was thrown into the dungeon, a dank place with a fetid stench that wafted through the narrow passages, inextricable from the mournful cries of brigands, murderers, and thieves. After the gaoler locked him in the darkness, Gaspard painfully slumped to the damp floor and sadly listened to the misery around him, wishing for a kind word that never came.

A boat was hired to take them all away to Jersey the following day. A good wind and fair tides secured their quick journey to the sandy soil of Grouville Bay. Among their company was the bishop of Coutances, Robert, now returned to the duke's good graces. Gaspard, who loved the wind, sea, and sail, found no momentary respite in the journey. Though the sun brought laughter to the lapping water and to the gulls flying playfully about the boat, he felt not even the vestiges of happiness. Fulk waited silently for him in the dark earth.

A family of islanders, men women and children, all with loads of dried vraic on their backs, pensively watched the lordly Norman longship, with its richly dressed lady and lords sitting among their men-at-arms, run up onto the beach. In their lead as they disembarked was a shackled, disheveled prisoner. Rare was news and gossip of the outside world to the natives, and they could only speculate the nature of Gaspard's crimes. The Jerseymen stared, neither approaching nor speaking, as the prisoner led the entourage inland and out of view.

Gaspard took them on a path etched in his memory as he quietly confessed the gentler parts of the tale to Gisla, Josue, Rohais and the others. Up the slopes, past the Fairy's Table, through the vale and to the pasture. All signs of the field of honor had vanished. The corral, the tents, the list. All were gone, replaced by a flock of sheep peacefully grazing on the brown September grass.

Before them, rising like an ancient, massive burial mound covered with shrubs and trees, was the small hillock.

"I left him up there," Gaspard said quietly.

Up they climbed to the summit, where he led them to the grave of Fulk Paynel, now covered with grass, weeds, and a decaying layer of leaves fallen from the oak that swayed above.

"Daughter, must you look upon this sight?" asked Albric tenderly. "Ought you not remember him as he was in life? Turn your face. We will tend to his needs now."

The Lady de Hambie, pale and hollow, swayed weakly and reached for her father's supporting hand. With a trembling chin, she glanced about to find the faces of the men hard and resolute. They had witnessed the death of thousands, and each had killed and born the wounds of battle. Though their grizzled beards covered the scars on their faces, she could still see the scars in their eyes. They were hard men, even in their fine robes. She felt frail among them.

"No, Peire, I will not be a coward before my husband's grave. I shall see this through." Her lips were thin and bloodless as she spoke, and she clutched her father's lean arm to stop her shaking.

Gaspard was far too weak to wield the spade and unearth Fulk's corpse, so Rohais stepped forward and carefully began to dig. It took but a few moments for him to strike Fulk's shield where upon the entire group became deathly still as all eyes fell on the lady. Gisla, standing at Albric's side, became still as though in a trance, staring at the spot where her husband lay in death.

"Sister?" asked Rohais gently.

Gisla closed her eyes and nodded her assent. Rohais then finished his task of uncovering Normandy's greatest warrior. His skeletal remains were miraculously still protected by hauberk, shield, and helm, as though he might have been simply slumbering beneath the shade of the tree, ready to awaken and speak cordially with his loved ones. His gauntleted hands rested peacefully beneath his cracked shield, and his decay was entirely hidden by his armor.

Vaquelin de Ferriers, a man built like an ox with the hands of a blacksmith, none too gently unlocked and removed Gaspard's fetters.

"Do you your duty, *squire*," he growled.

Gaspard glanced shamefully into Vaquelin's eyes and untied the great sword from his back that it could rest finally in peace with its master. As he knelt and laid the sword next to the great man's body, he could make out the painted face of Hambie's White Wolf on Fulk's soiled shield. The wise and gentle eyes of the noble beast seemed to come alive to him, staring at him not with anger or hatred, but with forgiveness and compassion. He gazed into her eyes and could smell her sweet, wild breath. Finally now, at the end of his journey, she came, not to say farewell, but rather to invite him to finally come and run with her...to be free and be her pup once more.

"I would make this ground holy," Gisla said distantly as she watched Gaspard lay the sword de Hambie to rest, "and build a chapel on this spot. A holy sepulcher beneath, and bring a man of God to reinvigorate the people of this island. I shall be the patron of such a place and such a position. It shall be an endowed benefice."

"I will see it done, milady," said the bishop gravely. "We shall fly Lord Fulk's standard from its peak that you may see it wave in the wind from Hambie's towers."

Upon her words, Gaspard could do nothing but fall to his knees and weep. A strange flickering of manly pride attempted to build a wall against the coming flood of emotion, but it quickly crumbled like a castle of sand crumbles with the incoming tide. Tears ran down his cheeks, and his impassioned groan was filled with shame and contrition. He was utterly broken, and as Gisla looked on him, seeing his confession complete and his penance fulfilled, she found she felt only compassion for him.

Before her flashed all the times the young man had knelt before her in service, with pledges and at the altar. Here, at the end of him, broken by his own hand, at last he found his ability to love again. To love and honor his lord and friend. To love and honor her. Gisla found she no longer desired his suffering and no longer needed to exact payment. When she looked into her heart she could find no trace of those dark seeds of anger, hurt, or vengeance. This day he embraced her last demand of him as though it was his own thought.

She left her father's side and bent close to Gaspard's ear that no other could hear her words and lay a gentle hand on his shoulder. "Thank you, milord. Rest now. I deem your task complete," she whispered softly. "Accept my forgiveness so that neither of us may suffer again."

Gaspard turned to look on her delicate fingers resting gently on his shoulder.

"How can I possibly have earned your forgiveness?" he asked weakly.

"Forgiveness is always a gift, Gaspard, and I give it freely now to you."

He looked up into her clear, gray eyes and the shadowy burdens haunting his soul began to lift.

EPILOGUE

From the moment Gaspard laid the sword de Hambie to rest next to Fulk, Gisla did not ever leave his side. She made it her duty to bring him what succor as she could, and she refused to take counsel from any who spoke against her care of him. Though he manfully protested, she tended his wounds and remained with him in his cell while they awaited the duke's arrival and the impending trial. They were not as man and wife; rather, they were companions on a journey and were capable of understanding one another's trials and suffering in a way no other could. They spent many hours in conversation, and many hours in peaceful silence as the days of September fell away.

Only when the duke arrived did Gaspard beg audience and ask that Gisla leave him alone with his liege. He was cleaned and taken to Robert, a hard man with a hard heart, whose utter disdain for Gaspard's crime was written on his face. Alone, the two men spoke for many hours and Gaspard told Robert the entirety of this story from beginning to end, from sin to salvation. Once the fantastic tale came to its close, Gaspard assured Robert that death was a just punishment, and he was finally ready. The duke of Normandy remained alone with his own conscience long after Gaspard was returned to his cell.

Gaspard's day of trial came; he was found guilty of murder and sentenced to death. He spent his last hours peacefully with Gisla, who carefully clipped his beard, combed his hair, and helped him dress in the black and green garb he had been known by for so many years. Without so much as a protest or hesitation, he climbed the steps of the gallows and bowed his head for the executioner that the rope could be placed firmly around his neck. A crowd of onlookers held their breath, the floor dropped from beneath his feet, and his neck snapped. Though the bells did not toll for his passing, Gaspard Malfort, only son of Bertrand Ducaen, was finally at peace.

The following winter proved very difficult as Gisla found her own health was failing. Bishop Robert saw to it that the little chapel was built and a priest selected. By fall of the following year, with the remains of her energy, Gisla made one last trip to Jersey so she could at least pray one time in the chapel dedicated to the memory of her husband.

In company with the aging Master Josue, Clothilde, and their attendants, she sailed for the island and made her way to the tumulus mound on which the new chapel stood. True to his word, the bishop of Coutances flew the standard de Hambie from the chapel's peak. Above the altar, the simple windowed apex of the chapel faced the east, the rising sun, and Normandy. It was cool and shadowed within its tightly fitted stones and rough-hewn timbers, and was fully lit only with the dawn of each new day.

Her companions remained outside allowing the Lady de Hambie a measure of solitude as she entered for the first time. Gisla, whose sedate beauty had yet to be conquered by her growing frailty, gently ran her fingers along the cool stone walls as she hesitantly stepped across the threshold and into the quiet interior. It was a still, peaceful place with a single wood bench resting before a plain marble altar. Above the altar hung the crucified Christ, and to its side Mary prayed for all who entered the sanctuary. Beneath the altar, buried in the hallowed ground, lay the Baron de Hambie.

As her eyes adjusted to the gloom, she saw that beneath the altar a finished stone lay loose next to a hole of exactly the same dimensions. Intentionally left for her hand, it was the chapel's final stone and with its placement her mourning would be complete. Quietly she knelt before the altar and reached into her bosom and retrieved that same woven lock she had given Fulk on the fateful day he left her side to do battle with the Dragon. While the flaxen strands and pale green ribbon still held all the stains of their long journey, they also held the tears of atonement. Though it was a solemn moment, it was also a moment of peace as she laid the ribbon in the hole and carefully placed the chapel's finishing stone into its place.

In no hurry to leave her husband's side for the final time, she sat on the bench and closed her eyes. A cavalcade of memories passed slowly through her mind, each bidding her farewell as though they were ghosts finally able to quit this world and gain the next. Fulk, Raymond, and Gaspard were now a part of history and would soon fade into swirling mists of legend. She knew she was soon to join them and become mere memory.

Not long after her return from Jersey, Gisla's remaining strength failed and she took to her bed. The last piece of worthy news she received was that Duke Robert had suddenly declared his young son, William, to be his heir. The duke was to make a pilgrimage to the Holy Land, a most dangerous journey, and in the event of his death, he wanted to make clear who would next lead Normandy. No one truly knows why he made such a pilgrimage. Perhaps it was a fashionable thing, an outward show of piety, or perhaps he did indeed murder his own brother and went to beg God's forgiveness.

The duke entrusted his uncle and cousin, once his bitter enemies now reconciled, to look after his young son in the event of his death. Their loyalty was soon tested, for Robert did not survive the pilgrimage. He died in Nicaea during the return journey in the summer of 1035, likely a victim of foul play. William, who would be later known as William the Conqueror, was only seven years old at the time of his father's death. He went on to suffer many great and dangerous adventures through his life, ultimately becoming Normandy's most storied and celebrated duke.

The Lady Gisla passed into God's care the winter of 1035. Chorchiéthe came to the castle and did not leave her side in those last days, bringing comfort and peace to her body and her mind as she made ready for her final passage. For Hambie's chatelaine the bells tolled two and seven times. She was laid to rest next to her young son and greatly mourned by all of Normandy.

And thus our story comes to an end. Today, on the island of Jersey, Gisla's medieval chapel remains atop the island's most famous archeological site. It is a great Neolithic burial mound, called a hougue, where once a powerful island chieftain of yesteryear was laid to rest. Once known as La Hougue Bie de Hambie, today the mound's name has been shortened to La Hougue Bie. Having been reconstructed more than once over the centuries, the chapel no longer exists as it was originally built. Fortunately, Jerseymen have very long memories, and the islanders have carefully preserved the legend upon which the chapel's foundation rests. The legend of the Knight and the Serpent.

www.ingramcontent.com/pod-product-compliance
Lightning Source LLC
Chambersburg PA
CBHW030019180626
46810CB00001B/120